THE OTHER WORLD

Guardians of the Path
Book Four

NICOLE DRAGONBECK

Witching Hour Publishing, Inc.

The Other World, Guardians of the Path, is a fictional work. The characters, places, and events portrayed in this book are from the imagination of the author or are used fictitiously. The publisher does not have any control over and does not assume any responsibility for the author or any third party websites or publications or their content.

Copyright © 2017 by Nicole DragonBeck
All rights reserved.

No part of this publication may be reproduced in any form or by any means whatsoever without the prior written permission of the author or publisher except in the case of brief quotations embodied in critical articles or reviews.

Cover image: © Sanjab | Dreamstime.com - Magic Door Photo

Witching Hour Publishing, Inc.

ISBN-10: 1-943121-26-5
ISBN-13: 978-1-943121-26-7

Editor: www.CourtenayDodds.com

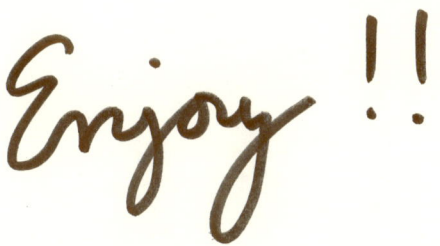

Dedicated to my siblings,
the three musketeers to my d'Artagnan:

Matthew
who looks out for me like the big brother I never had;

Danielle
who will always be my first first-reader;

and Andrew
who may or may not remember Chrystler and Bobbi and
the adventures they had.

♥ DragonBeck

CONTENTS

Acknowledgements	i
Map	iv
The Girl Who Came Back	1
Historiographer's Note	5
The Dale	8
The Maker's Friend	31
Descendants of the Seventh King	73
Death's First Call	94
Man of Tongues Part I	105
The Assassin of Spyne	117
Man of Tongues Part II	129
The Princess of Ghor	149
Man of Tongues Part III	165

CONTENTS continued

Man of Tongues Part IV	198
The Nitefolk	216
The Other World	225
Aethsiths Part I	293
A Favor	320
Aethsiths Part II	352
Aethsiths Part III	374
Epilogue	390
Pronunciations	396

ACKNOWLEDGEMENTS

Book IV is upon us, and as always, I'm truly honored there are people I have in my life that I get to thank for their contributions and support of my imaginary worlds, which could be rather lonely without some company now and then.

Thanks to Witching Hour Publishing for continuing to put up with my massive stories, and all the work, sweat, (unicorn) blood, and (phoenix) tears they entail. Lisa Barry did an amazing job with my cover (I spent *so many hours* looking at pictures of doors, and after all that I didn't think it was possible that anything could match up to my love of the first three covers. I was steeling myself for bitter yet well-concealed disappointment. Turns out that was unnecessary.) To Courtenay Dodds, who with magic fingers, makes my masterpiece perfect, and without whom there'd be far too much head-scratching on the reader end of things. Here's to many more!

To some of my favorite people on this earth: The Incredible, the Intrepid, the Indescribable Ink Slingers Guild: Lisa, for proving that gargoyles and dragons could be friends. Court, for dragon books; Erika, for making me a better person with *the list*; Desi, for being willing to tackle the garage to find me *The Princess Bride* on DVD; Jen for braving the cold with me, (and Remi for bringing hot chocolate and cheese quesadillas); Rhi, for reminding me there's more of the world to see; Alanna, for Poledark and continuing Austen education; Brandon, for the proper political classification of cream cheese icing; Alan, for my good luck Chinese dragon.

To my family, for all their love and support (Matthew's probably doing it for the heaps of money he sees in the future, but that in itself is a compliment); I have to keep finding new and exciting ways to thank you guys for your awesomeness and everything you do, which is not easy! But when in doubt, Tolkien: *guren glassui*!

And as I am particularly inspired by guitars and drums and things like that, I'd like to make a shout out to one of my favorite bands - WD HAN - who may or may not have appeared in part in this entirely fictional tale, in which any ambiguous or really obvious likenesses to people, places, events, or bands is entirely coincidental. Thank you for making awesome music! [And just so you know - if you're in my book, it means I love you dearly (because if I didn't like you, I wouldn't want you in my book) so even if things may not end well, please don't disown me!]

As always, it's important to acknowledge one's roots: Brooks, Tolkien, Gaiman, Salvatore, King, Jaques, Paolini, Rothfuss, Rowling, Lewis, Pullmen, Goodkind, Pratchet, Butcher, Lawhead, Martin, and everyone else who took me to other worlds with their words and inspired me to let mine grow - a heartfelt thank you from this writer.

And finally, to muses and music: muses can be found in the most ordinary of places, and where they are the words flow. There is magic in music and muses too. May the Path keep us all!

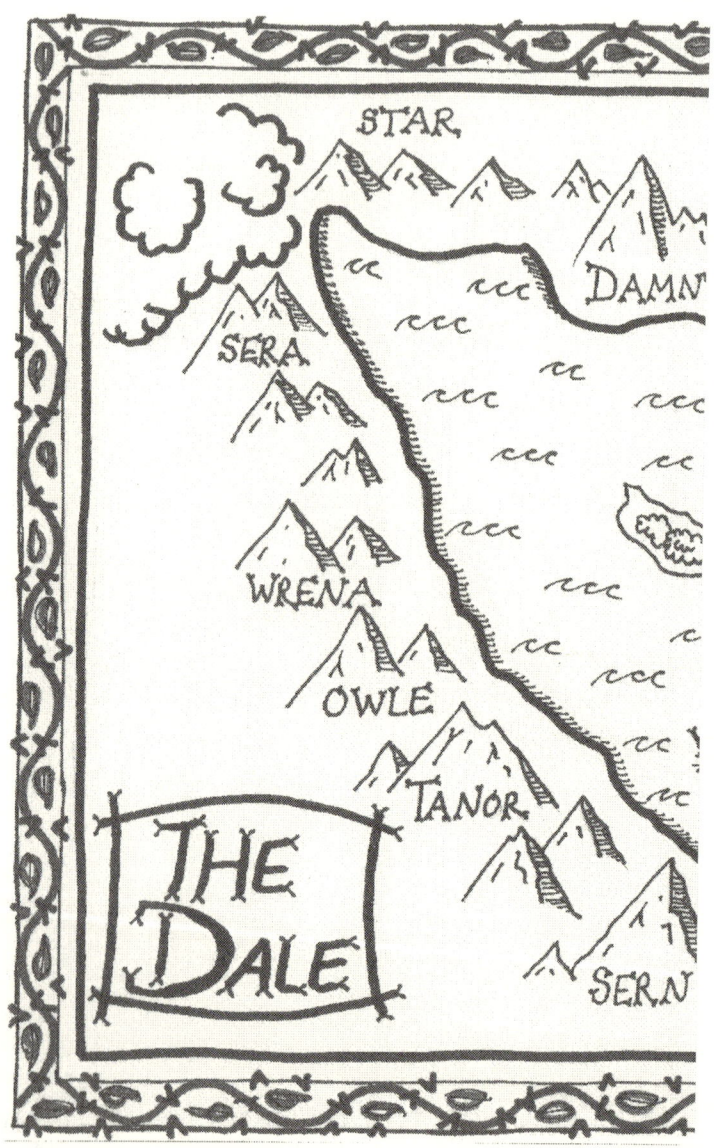

The Other World

"The Girl Who Came Back"
By Nexus
(J. Peters, A. Lake, M. Smith)

I know a girl

I'm in love with her

But she lives in a world

That she won't share

That place she goes

When she's still here

Shows in her eyes

And the way she stares

NICOLE DRAGONBECK

Her ghosts, they know
The song she needs
They haunt her smile
They're the air she breathes

She's not whole
I'm not complete
We both want
What can never be

To her, her dreams
Are more than real
They're what she sees
And what she feels

Though she says
She's here to stay
When she looks at me
She's far away

This girl came back
But her heart remains

The Other World

In another time
And a different place

She's not whole
I'm not complete
We both want
What can never be

She won't take me
When she leaves
It's not a place
That I can reach

Though she walks this world
By my side
I know it's not real
Not in heart or in mind

It won't be long
Before that girl goes home
Back to her ghosts
And the song they know

NICOLE DRAGONBECK

Historiographer's Note

 The Guardians written of herein are called to protect the force of life known to the peoples of the realms as the Path. No race, age, physical feature, or social stature define or prevent a Guardian from choosing to follow that calling. The abandoned fortress known as the Crescent Temple - the most widely accepted origin of that name being the curved shape of the structure, though some who have studied the deep wells of Etymology and Semantics theorize it comes from a phrase of a modern vulgar dialect of the ancient language spoken by the Builders, Craesinth Emplus [*translated as the (superlative)* home] *- accepts all Guardians and is said to be located squarely above a vast store of elemental magyc of eyrth, fyr, and watyr. Inside the Crescent Temple, a record of the First Guardian's Path-vision is depicted with the Prophecy of* Aethsiths *(excerpted here):*

...Chosen by the Path

Begotten by the same

Marked by the First

When Future and past Clash

She is the Songstress

Singer of the Song

To revive the Dying Light

From embers or Ashes...

These tales of the Guardians of the Path tell of the inception of the Prophecy through to its moment of fulfillment. At the close of the previous chapter, the Guardians - Cedar Jal, Luca Lorisson, Jæyd Elvenborn, and Timo of the Dale - had reached the Crescent Temple with the pieces of the Torch they had retrieved from the Sister Cities of Catmar and Balmar with the help of three women: Her majesty, Berria In'Orain, princess of Ghor; S'Aris O'Pac, Witch of Lii; and Liæna Nati, assassin of Spyne.

The girl from the Other World, Ria, was sent home by a Darkrobe, a senior Witch of Lii. The Guardians' failure to relight the Amber Torch called into question yet again the girl's identity and whether her part to play in the tale was truly over.

The party broke: Liæna Nati took the letter the Maker of Marks, Llaem Bli, had written for her, and left to complete her mission to find those who had murdered her father, the Men in White.

Berria In'Orain chose to make for the City of Elba, to find what had become of her brothers and sisters, whom she left in the City of Trees when she went to the Sister Cities of Catmar and Balmar to render what aid she could to the Guardians.

S'Aris of Lii remained with the Guardians, traveling with them to D'Ohera to seek the advice of the wise woman and innkeeper of the Tales Mane, Victoria Meech.

All of them promised to continue the search for the thirteenth piece of the Torch they now suspected existed, but on their way to D'Ohera, the Guardians witnessed a terrible Omen. A Demon Rift opened and unleashed the Nine (now Eight after the Guardians succeeded in killing the God of Bones in the first installment of this tale).

Now the Guardians must figure out a way to get the girl Ria back before the Demons get to her, but they do not know where or when the Darkrobe M'Rella of Lii sent Ria back to. Luca tries to control the power of the Demonhärt, Timo tries to come to terms with returning to the home he forsook, all the Guardians continue to set the world right as best as they can before it is overrun with sorcerers and Demons, and the story of Ria and the Guardians of the Path continues in Book IV: The Other World.

THE DALE

In all his many years as a Guardian of the Path, Cedar Jal had never felt as bewildered and adrift as he did now. He stood on the plains of Demona, his arms at his side, golden eyes staring at the blades of grass as if they were the cause of his troubles. They did not care, waving in the wind, oblivious that anything of note had just transpired. Such as the return of all the Nine in a body to this land since they had been banished thousands of years ago.

Eight, Cedar reminded himself, still trying to break the old habit.

The Guardian wore the same clothes he had changed into what seemed like lifetimes ago at the Tale's Mane in D'Ohera. The black trousers and turquoise shirt with brass buttons down the front did not look as worn as they should, having traveled half the breadth of Demona and back again. His white jacket was as spotless as ever, and only the black shoes looked a little worse for wear, covered with dust and scuffed on the sides.

Too preoccupied with recent events to put attention on the flurry of activity around him, Cedar was trying, and failing, to figure out what to do about this world. For the last few years, it seemed to be continually falling apart or being turned upside down at every opportunity, like an old cart made of half-rotted wood with faulty axles. Cedar rubbed the bridge of his nose and pulled a face to ease the tension from his muscles. He didn't often wish for peace, quiet, and no one bothering him, but he was closer to that than he had ever been before.

"Cedar?" a woman's voice called.

He looked to the side to see the Witch who had journeyed with them since D'Ohera, S'Aris O'Pac of Lii, traces of hesitation in her expression.

"Yes?" he replied, turning to face her fully.

"The others suggested I call Berria and Liæna and tell them of what has happened," S'Aris said, looking at him for final confirmation, the Nyican inflection on the words giving her speech an appealing, foreign quality.

The Witch was young and pretty. Her shoulder-length dark blonde hair was tousled by the harsh wind that had accompanied the Demon Rift which appeared a few moments ago and wisps stuck out at odd angles. The sleeveless white dress fell to her knees, and the hem had been torn off in several places to provide makeshift bandages to patch up wounds that the Guardians and the girl had sustained.

The girl. The thought of her brought back the flurry of uncertainty and anguish at the danger Cedar had placed her in, a danger increased immeasurably by the appearance of the Nine. The irony was salt in his wound - he had been sure by removing her from this land and his influence, she would be safe. Now she was far away, gods knew where, and he was unable to protect her.

Cedar shook his head, banishing her from his thoughts. It would do no good to dwell on it. Only action would save her, and the longer he remained inactive, the more likely it would be that Ria of the Other World would find her end at the hands of these Demons and the Sorcerer, or the Placer of Pieces, as he was called by the Men in White.

"Cedar?" The Witch grew more nervous, her fingers twined in the folds of her dress, then going to the beads of her belt for comfort.

Cedar took a moment to appreciate the courage of the young woman. She had left the Coven and everything she knew four years ago, at only sixteen years of age. She had just witnessed eight of the most powerful Demons, foes of Demona banished eons ago, return to this land. Most people would have run in fear, or cowered, whimpering in a corner, afraid to face what their eyes beheld. Not the Witch. Though shaken, S'Aris chose to stay beside the Guardians, just as the Witch who was the namesake of her order had stood by the First Guardian so long ago.

"Yes," Cedar said. "Tell them. They should know."

The Guardians had parted company with the princess Berria In'Orain of Ghor and Liæna Nati, the assassin of Spyne, less than a day before. The two women had their own problems to solve, and there was little use in their staying after their failure at the Crescent Temple. The Witch had remained with the Guardians after fashioning a scrying glass to which the princess and the assassin carried matching counterparts. S'Aris looked apologetically at Cedar.

"I'm afraid I will be the only one to see and hear in this," she told him, holding up the shard of mirror, which glinted like an ordinary glass in the light. Her eyes narrowed in sudden inspiration. "Perhaps you may see something if you held my hand, but I have never tried that."

Cedar nodded. "There is a first time for everything, they say."

"Hopefully not *everything*," the Witch replied as she took his hand with one of hers and cupped the magyc mirror in the other. She gazed at it for a long moment, preparing herself, then she took a deep breath.

"Liæna," the Witch called out in a clear, commanding tone.

Cedar waited. Nothing happened, and he wondered if the Witch was correct in her assumption that he would not be able to see in the mirror, but her frown said something was not right.

"Liæna!" she ordered again, in a louder voice.

Cedar looked between the mirror and the Witch's pinched face.

"She's not answering," S'Aris told him.

"What does that mean?" he asked.

"Either my scrying spell didn't work, or she's not near the mirror," S'Aris said.

"Try the princess," Cedar suggested.

"Berria," S'Aris called in the same commanding tone.

The mirror shimmered, then went dark. Light flickered and shapes formed in the darkness. Vertigo made Cedar feel unsteady as someone moved the mirror on the other side, and then the face of princess Berria materialized. As S'Aris had predicted, it was faint and blurry.

"S'Aris!" Berria exclaimed, her voice distant and warbled as though she was speaking under water. Her happy smile turned to a frown. "I had hoped for good news, but your face tells me not."

"Something has happened," S'Aris told the other woman, her voice heavy. "The Nine have returned to Demona."

Berria gasped, the color draining from her face, brown eyes going dark. "When? How?"

"They came through a Rift a few moments ago, and as to how, we can only guess," S'Aris said.

"After all this time, they have finally found a way to break their chains of banishment," Berria said in a wondering voice, then her eyes snapped forward and her voice took on an urgent concern. "Is everyone alright?"

"No one was harmed," S'Aris reassured her, and the princess's clouded features smoothed.

"What are you going to do now?"

The Witch glanced at Cedar. "The Guardians think it best to find the girl. The Demons will be looking for her. And should they find her-" S'Aris shook her head with a grim expression.

The princess nodded. "What should I do?"

Cedar spoke up, pitching his voice louder on the chance the princess would be able to hear him. "Find your family. Make sure they are safe. We think there may be a way to find and go to the girl. We will contact you the moment we find out anything."

"Was that Cedar?" Berria asked, tilting her head, and S'Aris nodded.

"Tell him I will do as he says, and I will keep my eyes and ears open for news of any kind."

"Thank you," S'Aris said. "Good luck."

"And to you."

The princess's face faded, and the Witch returned the scrying glass to one of the many pockets of her dress as the other Guardians wandered over.

"I have told the princess what happened," the Witch reported dutifully.

"Now on to the Dale," Cedar said, glancing at Timo.

The tall, blond Daleman did not look happy, his

handsome face set in an expression of resigned determination. He gave the others a weak smile when he saw they were looking at him.

"On to the Dale," he repeated in a lackluster tone.

"We have no time to waste," Jæyd said, a grim set to her features making her sharp elvish beauty darker and more lethal. "The Eight will be here, causing whatever mischief they can while we are looking for her."

The elf had taken the change in the Nine more readily than the others. Saying *Eight* instead of *Nine* still felt wrong, as if it would jinx it and bring the last back to life.

Timo nodded. Pale blue eyes were veiled, though a slight frown gave some indication to the doubt in the Daleman's head. Cedar knew Timo had not set foot in his home for over ten years, and this would be the first time he had returned since taking up the mantle of Guardian. *It cannot be easy for him being a Daleman,* Cedar thought. *But that is the life of a Guardian. Sometimes one must do what one doesn't want to because that is the only way.*

Cedar tried to cheer himself with this thought, but it only furthered the tangle of doubt which had begun upon meeting Ria.

"Lead the way," he told Timo.

The Guardians set out east, running swiftly in a line, Timo at the lead, followed by the Witch, the elf, and Cedar with Luca bringing up the rear. Jæyd called on the Path with her flute to speed their journey, and gold light chased their steps across the plains.

The music helped keep Cedar's head clear. He focused on following the lithe form of the elf, her auburn plait swinging in time to her steps. He also kept half an eye on Luca behind him. The dark Guardian kept up, his eyes clear, but Cedar was alert for any sign of that cursed rock the elf termed a Demonhärt showing in the Guardian's manner.

The sun rose higher over the plains and somewhere in the distance the O'Rente sparkled like sapphire and diamonds. The singing of the river filled their ears long before they saw it, and the rushing water grew louder and louder until the Guardians stood on the bank. They followed the curves of the mighty ribbon of water until they came upon the ferry. Without the princess's deep pockets, the fare was difficult to scrape together from Luca's sack of Melbori, but they made out, and the ferryman allowed them to board his crude but proud vessel.

The Guardians sat on the wooden planks, saying nothing as they were poled across the surging waters. Jæyd sat cross-legged, her eyes closed, her hands resting featherlight on her knees, her lips moving as she silently chanted an elvish meditation mantra to herself. The Witch was in a similar repose, her finger going over her beads, first the white one, then the larger green one, then a yellow one, and a brown one, then a deep purple one, back to the brown one, up and down. Timo stared at the sky unblinking and Luca, for once, was not trying to annoy everyone with mindless prattle or off-color jokes.

For this, Cedar was grateful. Though he was willing to cut his fellow Guardians some slack regarding the black demonic object he carried, Cedar's patience only went so far. Cedar sat at the far end of ferry, watching the opposite shore come closer at an agonizing pace. When gold sparks sent water flying behind them in white waves, Cedar smiled.

He turned back, expecting Jæyd, but it was Luca who had his fiddle out, playing some heartbreaking tune almost too softly to hear. He caught Cedar's eye and threw a mischievous wink at him. The lightheartedness was short-lived. Cedar knew under Luca's carefree and flippant exterior, he cared for the girl's well-being as much as Cedar did.

Ria and Luca had spent some time together after the Maker's tunnel had collapsed around them as they fled the Justice Trem Descal and his Men in White. Though at first the girl had taken a dislike to Luca, he had grown on her and the two had come to some understanding. Cedar had mixed feelings about this, but he could not explain to himself why he should begrudge the others the girl's affection.

When the ferry bumped against the bank, the Guardians were off in a flash, running once more. With both Jæyd and Luca working together, Cedar felt the Path carry them along on its smooth, flowing arms. After the sun set and the moon rose, they found a small rise and a little copse of trees that would offer shelter to spend the night.

Cedar's dreams were filled with red-eyed Demons and a little girl who sang a song darker than the Demons. She called them to her, and they grew larger. She smiled, and her eyes were red as she stepped through an acrid Rift towards him, opening her arms. Cedar woke with a gasp, sweat drenching his skin and his chest heaving. He lay back down, but sleep eluded him.

They were running as the sun came up, and by midmorning, the Dale appeared before them. The mountains looked like something out of a dream, as though they were made of colored glass. Cedar slowed and then stopped.

Stories and fairy tales abounded regarding the magyc of the Dale. They told that the ring of mountains preserved and protected a time of the past, and that only those invited could pass. Creatures could be found within which were not seen anywhere else. It was both exciting and terrifying to think of venturing into the forbidden realm.

"Where do we go from here, fearless leader?" Luca asked Timo.

Timo gave him an irritated look, belying fraying nerves, for even the most barbed taunts from Luca rarely got beneath the Daleman's skin.

"We must go through the outer passes. Those are Tanor, Sern, and Arr," Timo pointed to the three largest of the peaks in front of them. "The easiest is just north of Wrena, but I can take you through here."

"Well, doesn't that just inspire great quantities of confidence," Luca frowned. "Why the long face?"

"These mountains were built to keep things out," Timo said.

"But surely not you," Luca said. "You're a Daleman."

"I was," Timo said. "But I am not certain the mountains would see me as such anymore."

"It's not like they know who tries to climb them," Luca commented, then paused. "They don't know that, do they?"

"The mountains are wise," Timo said. "Let's go."

"Okay," Luca said, taking a deep breath, then marched after the blond man. The rest followed. Cedar came last, unable to tear his eyes away from the mountains. Timo's trepidation did not bode well, but all Cedar could do was hope for the best. At this point, he had no other choice.

Cedar felt it as soon as he stepped foot inside whatever sphere the mountains had. It was like stepping from shadow into the sun, or perhaps from the sun into shadow. The rock hummed with magyc so strong Cedar imagined himself floating on it. Despite his assertion that he was no longer accepted by the Dale, Timo found the paths with ease, leading the others with sure steps through the mountain. The closer they got, the more the young Guardian relaxed. *It was true what they say*, Cedar thought. *Once of the Dale, always of the Dale.*

"When we reach the hamlet on the other side of the ridge, let me do the talking," Timo was telling them as they walked. "I will introduce first myself, then the men, and finally the women, in order of ascending status. Do not speak unless the Head of the village bids you to."

"That sounds really complicated," Luca complained.

"Keep your mouth shut," Cedar said. "That's not complicated at all."

"And what then?" Luca asked Timo, ignoring Cedar.

"We will be invited to eat with them. It is still early in the spring so the fare will be sparse, but I believe they will honor us with the best they have."

"We cannot stay long to tax them, or ourselves," Jæyd said.

"It would be impolite to arrive, impose on their hospitality, and then rush off," Timo frowned. "We must let them do their honor to us. Then we can ask them where the Man of Tongues can be found."

"Oh, that's right, because you don't know where this magycal man is," Luca groaned. "This is sounding worse and worse by the second, you do see that, don't you?"

"The Man will help us," Timo said firmly. "I will see to it."

"Very well," Cedar said, believe the ardent words of the Daleman. "Is there anything we need to do at this feast?"

"Eat at least one bite of anything offered to you," Timo said. "And do not drink until everyone's mug has been filled and the Head has toasted the health of the guests and the blessings of the gods."

"Um, maybe I don't want to know this, but what happens to us if we mess up any of this?" Luca said.

Timo shrugged. "It depends if they judge you mean to insult them or not."

Cedar clapped Luca on the shoulder. "Like I said, just keep your mouth shut."

Luca glared at him. Timo did not deign to comment and pushed ahead, leading them up the peak. They came up, clustering around him.

"Behold. The Dale," he said, his voice hushed with reverence and a hint of pride.

A blue jewel of a Lake spread out in front of them, so vast they could not see where it ended. It may well have been the sea. Emerald mountains ringed the water like fearsome teeth, guarding it like a gaggle of women over a newborn.

"It is beautiful," Jæyd said, her voice soft for a different reason. Her eyes were sad, home-sick, as she took in the magnificent view.

They could have easily stood for the next three days, just taking in the view, but time pressed them on.

"Let's go," Timo said.

He led and they followed. They went back the other way, and when the path forked, and Timo took the branch sloping down, Cedar frowned.

"The Mountains are like a maze," Timo explained. "I told you, they were built to keep things out. If we tried going straight down, we would undoubtedly run into a dead-end, or worse. Trust me, this is the way."

"How do you know?" Luca asked.

"I am of the Dale," Timo said, with a helpless shrug at the inadequacy of the explanation.

True to his words, the Daleman's route took them

deeper into the mountain, and they emerged above a small valley. The sides were steep, but not impossible, and at the far end, the Lake was visible. Luca walked out to stand next to Cedar and peer down the side.

"I name this hole of a valley…Timo's Hole," Luca said grandly, spreading his arms as he perched at the edge of a lethally beautiful precipice.

"This Valley had a name - a much grander name - long before you or I were born," Timo muttered, still not in the mood for banter.

"Oh, I don't know," Luca replied with a grin. "I'm quite spry, but I was born a long time ago."

"Signs of dementia are already showing," Cedar said. "Which way from here?"

"Down," Timo said, with a hint of a smile.

"Is there a path of some sort or are we just going to sort of crawl down?" Luca asked. "Or perhaps fly?"

"There is always a path," Timo said.

"Right, because of the magyc mountains," Luca said, nodding with a sage look in his eyes, a look which disappeared when he rolled them at the sky.

"Do not belittle the mountains," Timo warned, and the rest of his words were banished by a rumble across the way.

It grew, vibrating in their bones, and Jæyd pressed her hands against her more sensitive ears. A huge chunk of rock fell from the peak and plummeted down, smashing on the valley floor with a ripple of thunder.

"Good thing you weren't standing under that," Cedar told the dark Guardian with a small smirk.

Luca was wide-eyed and silent, staring at the shattered boulder and the dust still rising from the shards.

"Let's go," he muttered. "I don't think I like this place."

Cedar couldn't help it. "I don't think it likes *you* either," he whispered as he walked past him and followed Timo down into the valley.

The Guardians camped in the crack that opened out to the lake. Timo went to collect the firewood from under the trees in the valley. When Cedar and Luca offered to help, he declined with a silent shake of his head. Cedar couldn't decide if it meant the Daleman simply wanted to be alone, or if the wood was sacred and an outsider collecting it to burn would bring another chunk of the mountain crashing down, this time on their heads.

The Dale was alien, with a strange aliveness. The air tingled with electricity, and at any moment, Cedar expected trees and rocks to simply grow legs and walk away. He checked that the large, flat rock he had chosen to sit on was nothing more than a rock before planting his bottom on it.

When the sun disappeared, long before the stars came out or the moon became visible, a chill made steam rise off his skin and his breath mist in the air.

"It's not usually this cold," Timo commented, crouching in front of the fire, his hands held out to the warmth.

"Do me a favor," Luca spoke up from where he lay, staring at the grey sky through the trees. "Don't say things like that."

Timo chuckled. "Weather is just a phenomenon, Little One. It means nothing, but the winter has been hard and doesn't want to let the land go."

"I'd still prefer not to know," Luca said. "Now all I can think about is the fact that this hole in the land is trying to freeze me to death. On purpose."

"You would have died much earlier today if the Dale truly meant to keep you out," Timo said.

"What did I say about saying things like that?" Luca turned to glare at him.

"It was supposed to make you feel better," Timo protested.

"I feel just fine without your help, thank you," Luca grumbled. "I'm going to sleep."

He rolled over, and, true to his word, was asleep in moments, one arm under his head, the other in his pocket, clutching the Demonhärt wrapped in cloth to protect him from its touch.

Cedar shivered. It was an abomination to have that thing, yet they had no choice but to keep it. It wasn't something one could bury and forget about. For better or worse, Luca would continue to carry it. Cedar just hoped that Luca could control and contain its power.

Looking at the peaceful expression on Luca's face, Cedar thought he had. Cedar glanced up to find both S'Aris and Jæyd watching Luca as well. Cedar smiled. No matter how much trouble they got themselves into, the others were always there to pull them out of it. *But who would come get them out of the trouble they were all in?* The word *Aethsiths* was foremost in his mind.

"The Guardians as named, though Strong and True, cannot rekindle a dead fire," Cedar whispered to himself.

He lay down and tried to sleep. He did not have as much luck as Luca did. The ground was hard, and it was cold. Luca's trepidation about the Dale leached into Cedar's strained mind, and he began to harbor suspicions the Dale had some grand purpose for depriving him of sleep this night. Cedar tried rolling onto his other side, but the same root or pebble dug into his hip. He squeezed his eyes tighter, willing himself to sleep.

Blackness enveloped him. He was no longer aware of his body or the hard ground under it, or the strange Dale.

Within moments of examining the darkness around him, Cedar determined he was dreaming. He waited for more to come, but nothing happened. Just as he was about to give up on the dream theory, a bolt of green lighting struck from the invisible heavens. Cedar dove to the side, narrowly escaping the destructive power of the energy as it tore apart the darkness.

Then he was inside the green. He stepped into a familiar world that was appealing despite its alien and suffocating pressure. There were others with him, vague shapes next to him, behind him, in front of him. Seven of them, but he didn't count them, or think of them as a number. They just were, as he was. They moved, and he moved with them, his attention not on what was, but what would be.

Foremost in his mind was a girl. She stood in front of him. Cedar's heart sped up when he saw her, and in an instant, he was looking at the world through another set of eyes. His chest struggled to remember how to breathe.

She was about twelve years old, small for that age. Her brownish hair was disheveled, and bright grey eyes looked into his soul when he met them. A golden light gleamed all around her and beat with her own heartbeat. She started to fade. He reached out for her, but she was gone.

Cedar woke up with a start, shivering in violent spasms. He was frozen to the ground, unable to move save for the desperate attempts of his body to regulate its own temperature. In painful inches, he moved closer to the coals. Through chattering teeth, he blew on them, coaxing a small tongue of flame to come to life. He blew harder and felt the muscles in his face and his arms relax slightly.

Timo had left the pile of wood close by, so Cedar sat up and added sticks to the fire. It took a long time for him to become warm again, but he didn't want to go back to sleep. He fought to keep his eyes open, but they dragged down. His head sagged, his chin sinking to this chest.

He started awake again. This time he wasn't alone. A man sat next to him. The others still slept, so soundly their chests didn't even move. Then Cedar realized the fire was no longer flickering. It had frozen, a red-orange gem. Tentatively, he held out his hand, and they passed through the flames without harm.

Jerking his hand back as though he *had* been burned, Cedar took a deep breath and turned to the figure. The man stared at the fire, a pensive expression on His face. Cedar waited, unwilling to speak first.

"Hello, Cedar Jal," He said, finally turning to face Cedar.

Cedar nodded. It seemed the respectful thing to do.

"You recognize Me, I see," Death said, the ghost of a smile flitting across His face.

Cedar nodded again. Death choosing to visit him now was not a good omen in his book.

"There's no need to look so frightened," Death told him. "It is not your time."

"You sound very practiced at saying that," Cedar said, then cringed, hoping Death wouldn't take offense at the accusatory tone.

Death sighed. "Unfortunately, I have had far too much opportunity to use that comforting phrase in the last few weeks." He looked at Cedar, a trace of reproving in His blue eyes. "More than a few times with you and yours, I might add."

"I can't honestly say I'm sorry about that," Cedar said.

"And you shouldn't be," Death chuckled. "Oh, before I forget. I spoke to Ria recently. She's fine."

All Cedar's words stuck in his throat. He blinked back a wetness in his eyes, relief as heavy as the worry which had plagued him threatening to crush his lungs.

"Thank you," he managed to get out.

"I have Marked her," Death said, as though commenting on particularly pleasant weather. "And put her under the protection of My power."

Cedar blinked. Why Death was sharing this information with him, he didn't know. Death's Mark was a great thing - but also a terrible thing.

"What's done is done," Cedar said, unsure that was the correct response.

"That is a wise thing to say. Now, on to why I'm here," Death continued. "We are at a very special turning point in the confluence of the worlds. Events which are beyond you, and even beyond Me, are upon us. There have been Omens in this world and others like it. I am doing what I can to prepare for Chaos or Revival, the only two outcomes at the End."

Cedar blinked, trying to keep up with the greatest power in the universe after the Builders themselves. "What does that mean for me?"

"You understand the concept of Chaos?" Death inquired.

"A little," Cedar said, the inflection on the word assuring him his grasp of it was not broad enough. "War, famine, end of worlds."

"A limited description, but it will do for the moment," Death said. "You will undoubtedly learn more when you finally meet whom you seek."

"The Man of Tongues!" Cedar blurted out. "You know where he is?"

"No," Death said, frowning at Cedar. "And please don't interrupt further than absolutely necessary. I am very busy, and actually have better things to do than…" He trailed off, then took a deep breath. "Don't interrupt more than absolutely necessary," He iterated. "We don't have much time."

Cedar nodded, staring wide-eyed. Death's hair was brown and long, swept to the side, and a sharp widow's peak made His face narrow. Bright eyes, a hooked nose and a mouth equally prone to smile or anger made for a handsome countenance. *If you didn't know the person you were looking at was Death*, Cedar amended.

"What do you expect of me?" Cedar asked quietly.

"As you have always done." Death surprised him with a wide smile. "You recall the circumstances of our last meeting, I trust?"

"How could I forget?" Cedar said, for the first time feeling somewhat equal in the conversation.

When he had been trapped in the quasi-void between worlds, Ria had followed his music and come to rescue him, calling a Door to Demona by whatever strange magyc or will she possessed. Cedar had resorted to Blood Magyc to transport them through the Door, not a fact he was proud of, but he had managed to stave off Death and keep Ria from Him that time, firmly stating he would bring her back. Cedar now figured that Death had let the girl go because He saw a power in her and not due to Cedar's vehemence.

"Good," Death said. "I need you to keep that girl alive."

Cedar's jaw dropped. "How...but..." he spluttered for a moment, then pulled himself together enough to shout. "You're Death! Why am *I* keeping her alive?"

"A common mistake people make regarding Me is thinking that I am the cause of the condition known as death," the namesake of the condition said. "This is erroneous. I am merely present at the time of demise to take the person to My realm."

"But why can't You just not take her if…if…" Cedar couldn't bring himself to finish the thought.

Death regarded him with a fathomless sadness in His deep eyes. "If it were only so simple," He said.

"And why isn't it?" Cedar demanded.

Death sighed. "You ask many questions, Cedar Jal, and that is a good thing. However, you ask them at inopportune times, and this we must work on."

"Time doesn't appear to be a problem at the moment," Cedar said, pointing at the fire, which looked more like a picture every minute.

"You speak of things you do not know," Death frowned. "Yes, I have stopped time here. But this is a piece of My realm. The living do not belong here anymore than the dead belong in your realm."

Cedar was put in his place.

"I cannot refuse into My Realm those who have died. The Dead belong rightly to the Voide, not the Path, and they must pass through to return to the Path. I am known to the people of the realms of the Path as Death. What I truly am is the Keeper of the Walls. When Path and Voide meet, the result is Chaos. The Walls keep Chaos at bay. That, Cedar Jal, is the entire reason for My existence."

"Reincarnation?" Cedar asked.

"If they choose, in this world or another," Death said. "Some choose to live in My realm. Some choose to pass through the Voide to what lies beyond."

"And what lies beyond?" Cedar said.

"A good question at an inopportune time," Death replied, a smile playing over His lips. "And it will be answered in time. But what you must now turn your attention to is your task as Guardian of the Path. This Prophecy of yours, the Prophecy of *Aethsiths*, soon it will be fulfilled, or Demona will fall."

"Is the girl *Aethsiths?*" Cedar said, a reckless desire to resolve the spinning uncertainty of her identity causing him to ask the dreaded question. For a split second, he wanted the truth, then waited with bated breath, wishing he had never asked.

"The girl is no more and no less than who she chooses to be," Death said. "But whatever she chooses, she is important. She must be protected from those who want to send her to My realm."

"The Nine," Cedar said.

"Among others," Death agreed. "They are powerful and of the Voide. They disrupt the Balance in worlds of the Path and so breed Chaos. It has already begun. The First Guardian staved off Chaos for thousands of years, but his work is coming undone. This I am sure you know."

Cedar grimaced. He thought Death may have been teasing him. How could he possibly *not* know that? It was Cedar's responsibility to do something about it, ever since he had followed Chesko to Akorgia and watched his friend die in fire and his own blood. It had just grown and gotten worse from then, and now Death Himself was here, adding to the Guardian's problems. It made Cedar's head hurt. Death saw his expression and smiled.

"Cedar Jal, I believe now you feel a shadow of what My existence is like," He said with a chuckle.

"Do you get used to it?" Cedar asked.

"Never." Death stood, and the fire flickered once before falling still again. "But would you rather return to the life of a farm boy in Torin?"

Cedar pursed his lips, then sighed. "Of course not."

"And I feel the same," Death shrugged. "The life of a Guardian is not easy. Trust me when I say I know this, Cedar Jal. The weight of the world rests on our shoulders. We can only do the best we can do."

"Why are you doing this?" Cedar asked, curiosity getting the better of him.

"My Mandate does not allow me to interfere with the workings of the worlds," Death said, a faraway wistful gleam coming to His blue eyes. "But there is nothing which prevents Me from offering encouragement in difficult times." Cedar got the distinct impression that was a loophole, but Death continued before Cedar could say anything. "It is time for Me to return you to your realm. Try to get some sleep. You have much work ahead of you. The Dale will not eat you as your Demonhärt-bearing companion believes."

Cedar stifled a grin. "Okay."

Death smiled at him, and a stray strand of hair blew across His face as the wind returned and the flames began to jump again. "May the Path keep you and yours, Cedar Jal."

"Thank you," Cedar replied. "I have one last question."

"Of course you do."

"When we killed the God of Blood in D'Ohera," Cedar began with a tentative expression, "did You come to ferry it to Your realm?"

"Yet another good question," Death said. "And also one you will learn the answer to. But not from Me at this time, I'm afraid. Good night, Mr. Jal."

With not another sound, He was gone.

Cedar opened his eyes. The sun was shining over the mountains, dressing them in pink auras. The songs of birds filled the air as tendrils of mist dissipated, revealing a pale blue sky, exactly the same color as Timo's eyes. Cedar stretched, more rested than he'd been in days, and looked to find his companions still sleeping soundly.

"What?" Jæyd started when Cedar touched her

shoulder. She leapt lightly to her feet, and gazed at the clearing with unease. "Who had the watch?"

"I don't think a watch was necessary," Cedar replied, a bemused lift to his brow as he roused Luca then Timo.

"And why is that?" Luca asked, his speech slow with sleep.

"I had a visitor last night," Cedar said. "Death."

"I find that hard to believe as you're very much alive in front of us," Luca said, sitting up and rubbing his eye with a fist, yawning widely. "Were you dreaming?"

Cedar shrugged. "I could well have been, but somehow I don't think so."

"I don't think so either," Timo said slowly, his voice heavy and his face awed.

The others gathered around him. In the ashes of the still sleeping fire, a Mark was drawn in the ashes. Cedar's breath left him, and he was momentarily speechless. He wondered how close Death had come to branding that Mark on him. *He told me it was not my time.* Cedar shivered, and wished the thought away, but it clung with uneasy fingers.

"What did He say?" Jæyd asked.

"He told me many things about the Path and the Void and Chaos. He said He had seen Ria, and Marked her..."

An uproar of questions assaulted him.

"Why would He do such a thing?" Timo's baritone rose above all the others.

"He said it was to put her under the protection of His power," Cedar said in a soothing tone though he didn't quite understand it himself. "And then He told me that I had to keep her safe, that He was the Keeper of the Walls, and He could not pick and choose who to take and who to leave."

"Did He say we were right to come to the Dale?" S'Aris

said. "Is this how we will find Ria?"

"No, but He didn't tell me to turn around and head back either," Cedar said.

"Did you happen to ask if she was the one who will fulfill the Prophecy?" Luca asked, narrowed eyes and tight lips suggesting he expected a tongue-lashing from Cedar.

"Of course," Cedar said. "He told me she is who she chooses to be."

"Sounds helpful," Luca said.

Cedar shrugged. "It was Death. I wasn't going to tempt my fate and provoke Him."

"That sounds like a sound course of action. I approve," Luca said. "Now what about an even sounder course of action - breakfast?"

THE MAKER'S FRIEND

Llaem Bli, Maker of Marks, stood upon the grassy plains which spread for some distance in three directions then dropped away to the sea in a dramatic plunge of stone cliffs, blinking away the mild confusion of a strange dream.

Two Thaumaturgists in tunics of the colors of their respective orders, black and vivid green, came up behind Llaem, nodded their greetings, and passed by. Llaem hoped he only imagined that they looked over their shoulders at him with identical expressions of suspicion. The Maker had no idea if they could see the golden dream - those ways of the Path of Guardians and the Thaumaturgists were not known completely to him, as he was sure his way of Making Marks was not known to them.

Llaem adjusted his grip on his faithful walking staff and leaned on it, a thoughtful frown on his face. In this Path-dream, the Guardians of the Path had appeared. With some distress, they had relayed what had happened to Ria, the girl from the other world, and then asked if he had been wrong in his Making of her Mark.

Llaem Bli was not a humble man, but he was quiet in his conceit. He was content in his own good opinion of himself and did not need other to share it, nor confirm it. Yet he was not offended when the Guardians had asked this of him, despite his mild rebuke. The Mark had been odd in too many ways. Even now, a week after he had Made the Mark, it still intruded on his thoughts at odd times.

He would not second-guess himself though. It was the right Mark. The girl was satisfied with it, and that was all a Maker could ask for. Others did not know it, and Makers did not make it common knowledge, but a Maker was inhibited by a person's own unwillingness to acknowledge a part or parts of themselves. A very good Maker could pierce the shadowy shroud and reveal something of whatever lay obscured, but not always and not always faithfully.

The main benefit of Makers had been to establish that a person was truly who they said they were. But Makers were rare, rarer than Guardians of the Path, rarer than Witches, rarer even than nymphs who chose to show themselves. And so the Makers devised a way to have each person prove they were themselves. A Mark which would reflect the essence of the person was Made. However, this had some unforeseen, and negative, side effects.

When some who may have wished their secrets remained unknown had those secrets revealed so starkly, they campaigned against the Makers of Marks. Never mind that the full meaning of the Mark remained hidden to any who did not possess the gift of the Maker or only the magyc of the Mark was visible; never mind that everyone had parts of themselves and their history that they considered best forgotten and unmentioned; never mind any common sense or decency.

The Makers were shunned. People came to them for Marks and sent their children to them for Marks only on tradition or superstition. In the present day, it was considered somewhat old-fashioned. Some had even taken to the signing of their name, rather than a Mark, to affirm their identity.

Llaem shook his head. He looked down at his companion, the tree nymph Kwik. Before, she had been stuck in the loss of her tree and was the shadowy reflection of a nymph. When Llaem had sent her after the girl, he had not expected the resurgence. But Kwik had regrown her hair and rekindled some of her spark after she had returned. Now, in order to disguise her true face when she went among ordinary folk, she wore a pendant with a glam-Mark, something of Llaem's own devising. He had used another like it to disguise his house before the Men in White destroyed it.

In the ruins of his house, Llaem Bli had come to the conclusion that the Guardians he had sheltered and their three companions, the Witch, the princess, and the assassin, could not achieve their ends on their own. So he and Kwik had gathered what could be salvaged of his most treasured possessions, packed his old traveling bag, and set out on the road east. With Kwik's knowledge of the land, gleaned from what the trees and other plants told her, they made good time. Now their destination sat within sight.

Samnara, the City of Iniquity, sat at the extreme northeastern part of Demona at the end of a tiny finger of land protruding into the Sea. It is unknown whether the peninsula took its name from the city or the city was named for the peninsula. The majority of the city lay up and down the near-vertical cliffs, though over time the city had spread back along more hospitable ground. The wharves at the bottom of the plunging cliffs were the heart and soul of the city, and everything behind them depended utterly on their existence.

The wharves were as old as the land itself. Stone foundations had stood the test of time against the onslaught of the Sea. Not wave, nor wind, nor typhoon had washed them away. Stores, taverns, and nautical shops pressed against the base of the cliff, and steep streets led upwards to the rest of the city. Along the top edge of the cliff, grand houses of the Magisters and Very Important People of Samnara stood in ostentatious parody of their owners.

The streets widened as they made their way back along the relatively flat ground of the cliff. The establishments were brightly colored and of varying sizes and shapes, making Samnara like a patchwork quilt draped over the cliff. Two great arms of stone embraced the outer edge of the city. The gates stood open much of the time, flanked by watchtowers of the same stone. Streetwardens in uniforms of indigo trimmed with silver and black, under the Magister of City, stood upon the wall.

Llaem and Kwik continued their brisk pace. More people joined them, coming from the farms and homesteads in the outlying. Woodcutters with cords of firewood stacked on wagons lumbered behind farmers bringing crates of eggs or vegetables. A tinker with a mound of pots and pans on his back walked beside a shepherd herding a modest flock of eight sheep before him.

Llaem nodded politely, then moved off to put distance between them. A nymph could not walk the streets of any city without attracting attention, and since attention was precisely what Llaem Bli did not want, he had dressed her as his daughter and given her the glam to hide the iridescence of her hair and her eyes. Nothing he could do could hide her manner however, and the nymph's direct and piercing gaze turned many eyes away from her. Llaem did not like how the eyes returned, covertly, and marked their progress.

He lifted his chin and walked forward when the line outside the gates permitted it until he passed through the gates. Expecting to walk right on through, Llaem was bemused when the line halted at a table set up in the shade of the towers. He stood, waiting with growing impatience until he could hear what was going on.

"Papers," a surly Streetwarden with a double chin demanded of the person in front of him.

Short white hair left bare pointed ears and midnight skin with rich purple undertones marked the person as a goblin. He reached into his richly embroidered tunic, pulled out a bundle of parchment, and presented them. The Streetwarden undid the ribbon and examined the papers for a long time. Then he laboriously filled in the ledger in front of him before handing the packed back to the goblin and waving him on his way.

That doesn't look like something I'm wanting to go through, Llaem thought.

He tugged on Kwik's hand and the two escaped the line. They walked along the wall until they reached the northern cliff that plunged down into the foamy waters nipping at the rocks. Kwik looked at the lifeless minerals with distaste.

"We're going down there?" she asked.

"No," Llaem smiled. "This is a city of pirates, smugglers, and generally unpleasant sorts of people. There's bound to be ways to get in and out without passing under the watchful eyes of the Wardens."

"And how will we find these unpleasant sorts of people?" Kwik asked. "And how will we get them to help us?"

"Well, they usually find you, and I believe money works well," Llaem told her. "Although, I'm not above the idea of using pain as a method of gaining cooperation."

Kwik gave him a look. "You mean you'll want me to do something to them."

He knelt so he was eye to eye with her. The glam did not work on him, as he knew it was there, so he could see past it. Also, he had made it, so it couldn't fool him. Her iridescent eyes showed more fire: reds and oranges and deep yellows, indicating she was annoyed.

The Maker was reassured when a glitter of purple surfaced. The nymph was not beyond being reasoned with. This was fortunate for him, for a nymph was a primal force of nature in a deceptive pint-sized form and could wreak amazing quantities of havoc when she felt like it.

"Sometimes," the Maker began, "you have to do things which you would prefer not to because the bigger picture demands it. You have to act now and ask forgiveness later."

"There is no forgiveness," the nymph countered. "There is Growing and there is Ungrowing."

"But what about the boring beetles that weaken the tree?" Llaem asked. "When you take measures to get rid of them, is that Growing? Or Ungrowing?"

Kwik thought about it for a brief moment. "Boring beetles only plague a tree that is already weak. They take the wood and turn it to dirt to nourish the other trees. That is the Cycle, and the Cycle is Growing."

"But what if the boring beetles are attacking a healthy tree, a tree that you don't want to die just yet?" Llaem pressed.

That gave the nymph pause. "You mean to say Trem Descal is the beetles and Demona is the tree?"

"Exactly," Llaem said, pleased his analogy had worked so well.

"And what of these men who will help us get into this city?"

"They are like the rain which washes away the poison you have put down to get rid of the beetles," Llaem said after a moment to think of how to continue the analogy. "A nuisance that cannot be avoided, but must be dealt with if you want to get rid of the pests."

Kwik wrinkled her nose. "Poison is Ungrowing. It is much better to nourish the tree with minerals and magyc. The rain will come eventually, and the poison will wash into the soil and the water."

Llaem blinked, feeling his hold on the situation was slipping. Kwik stared at him, her large eyes wide. She moved her mouth from side to side, then sighed.

"I see what you are trying to say, Llaem Bli, and I see the wisdom in it." She wrapped her thin arms around herself, and hunched down, a morose expression on her pointed, pixie face. "I have been among men for too long. I understand how they think, the reasons behind what they do, and what they say. I, too, can think like them now."

Llaem embraced the little nature being, pressing her waifish form to him, hoping the gesture would comfort her as his words would not be able to. He found himself speaking them anyway. "We will return you to your people and your home when this is all done."

"I cannot go back." Her voice was soft, muffled by his chest. "I have lost my tree. There is nowhere for me to go back to."

She pulled away, and wiped away a pearlescent tear with her overlong sleeve. "Now, how do we bring these men-like-the-rains-that-wash-away-the-poison to us?"

Llaem stood. "I'm not sure." He raised his hands to his mouth and shouted. "Halloooo!"

"That will probably bring the Streetwardens," the nymph commented.

Llaem ceased shouting. He picked up a pebble and began hurling them at the wall. The wall gave no response. The Maker spun in a circle, his snake-toed boots scuffing up the grass. He had to get into the city and could not pass under the scrutiny of the Law. What to do, what to do?

"What's the point of making all this racket then?" a snippy voice called out.

Llaem spun back, delight lighting up his face. The delight turned to surprise. In front of him was a short, stocky man with a dark red beard and eyebrows to match. His curly hair was more brown and a large nose dominated his rough-hewn face. He wore leather breaches and chain mail.

"I was expecting a goblin," Llaem said. "A Yelndel, to be more precise."

"Well, you got me," the dwarf said with all the characteristic warmth of a frozen rock. "Did you want something, other than to annoy and disturb me?"

"I want to get into Samnara," Llaem answered.

"Gate's that way." The dwarf jerked a thumb over his shoulder.

"Yes, I'm aware of that," Llaem said. "I'd like to get in without scrutiny. Actually, I'd like to get in completely unnoticed if that's possible."

"Anything's possible for the right price." The dwarf gave a thin smile.

Llaem looked at Kwik. She looked back up at him. Llaem jerked his chin in a subtle nod. The nymph turned her eyes to the dwarf, then back to the Maker. Llaem coughed. Kwik pursed her lips, then turned to the dwarf.

"We would like to get into Samnara. Please."

The dwarf stared at her, then burst out laughing. Kwik blinked, but her expression did not change. The dwarf's laughter was cut off by a tangle of fibrous roots exploding out of the ground at his feet and twining around his neck. His eyes bulged as the roots tightened.

"I said we would like to get into Samnara, *please*," the nymph iterated.

Llaem put a hand on her shoulder. "I don't think he'll be able to point out the door if he's unconscious." *Or dead*, he added silently.

The roots loosened their hold, but only a little. The dwarf spluttered and choked.

"I think he's trying to say something," Llaem said, crossing his arms and looking interested.

"He does not need to say anything," the nymph said. "He only has to point to the door."

The dwarf began waving his arm frantically.

"I can't quite tell exactly where he means to be pointing," Llaem said, looked at the wall.

"There. *There!*" the dwarf croaked.

Llaem still could not see anything, but he felt the point was made. "Let him down."

Kwik looked at him for a long time, then the roots withdrew as suddenly as they had appeared, dropping the unfortunate dwarf to the ground. Llaem thought he might make a run for it, but found his suspicion was uncharitable and unfounded.

The dwarf, who Llaem noticed had failed to give his name, stood up and straightened his mail. He beckoned them forward, his eyes clouded with resentment. Without waiting to see if they would follow, the short man stomped towards the wall. Llaem blinked and the dwarf disappeared from view. After a moment, a disembodied voice floated out, saying something inarticulate in a grumpy tone.

Kwik went over with dainty steps, setting herself at the edge of the hole, and slipped down. Llaem was less graceful. He threw his walking staff down first, then his pack, and then he followed into the dirt tunnel. He watched the dwarf pull the rope which raised the plug of turf again, concealing the entrance.

"Clever," Llaem nodded approvingly.

The dwarf grunted, clearly in no mood to accept compliments. He finished his job, picked up the lantern that now lit the stone corridor, and led them under the wall. They emerged in a modest armory. Gleaming bayonets and pikes lay in a rack. Bows stood against the far wall, and a table held various hammers, maces, and other implements whose main purpose was to smash things.

"Nice place," Llaem said.

The dwarf gave him a dirty look. "The door's over there."

Llaem nodded. As he was about to turn the handle, a thought occurred to him.

"We don't have to do anything to ensure you won't go running to the Wardens and squeal, do we?"

The dwarf rolled his eyes. "Not the sharpest sword are we?" he said. "What would I tell them? Sorry, mister Warden, sir, but I have this secret tunnel under the wall and I let these two people in and they're running through the streets of the city with no papers?"

"Right," Llaem said. "Well, thank you."

Kwik tugged on his sleeve. "You should pay him."

Llaem walked back, dug some money out of his purse, and placed the coins on the table. The dwarf looked at the silver and gold, and though his face was suspicious, avarice made his hand dart out and claim the payment.

"Thank you," he said, only a trace of resentment in his voice.

The dwarf's door opened to a little alley shadowed by the great wall on one side. Only two doors came into this alley, the dwarf's and another rounded green door with a shoemaker's sign hanging above it. A thin orange cat lounged against the wall, eyes half closed, tail twitching.

"We have reached Samnara," the nymph stated. "Now where are we going?"

"I have a friend who used to live here, before he took to the wandering-road at duty's call. I imagine he has returned here. At least, I hope he has."

Kwik looked bemused. "We came all this way to see a man who might not be here?"

Llaem shrugged. "It seemed to be the most logical course of action at the time."

He tried to come up with a plan for finding his friend. They had last seen each other twenty years ago. This was the City of Iniquity. Any number of people came here to disappear. They would not be pleased if their past came a-knocking to disturb their new life. *I have no idea where to begin, so I'll just start.*

"I think we should go this way," he pointed.

"That is a good idea, as that is the only way out of the alley," Kwik said and started down the street.

The Maker hurried after her and caught up her hand. "Don't run too far ahead, my young daughter. These streets can be dangerous."

"I am older than you are and can take care of myself," the nymph replied primly. "Father, dear."

Llaem smiled. The nymph had a strange grasp of humor and significance, but she was learning. Some of her jokes even made sense now. The pair continued through the colorful streets of Samnara.

In the middle hours of the day, in the high light, the City was full of people going about the daily business of their lives. Streetwardens numbered one for every twenty people. Their indigo uniforms stood out even among the riot of color. Electric tingles of mild panicked suspicion ran over Llaem's skin whenever he saw them, and keeping his breathing even required constant effort.

A pair of them coming towards Llaem and Kwik gave the Maker an additional queasy feeling in his stomach. Looking at a person's Mark was so natural and unthinking an action, much like breathing, Llaem had seen, analyzed, and put away for later both men's Marks before he had registered what they looked like in body, form, and feature, and before they had taken one and a half steps in his direction. It was his knack, his gift, his talent, his power. Whatever one called it, it was what he could do.

It was an interesting business, seeing and interpreting Marks. What he saw and the Mark he Made corresponded much the same way a song and the musical transcription of that song correspond. The Maker's eyes saw what they saw and his fingers drew what they drew. Those two things were identical yet entirely different. He called them both *Mark* to simplify things.

The Wardens' Marks were similar enough in nature. Both were clouded, like the bottom of a lake after a storm has lifted the silt. Both these men were trying to hide who they were from no one else but themselves. That they hid that self from others was a mere byproduct of the first. Despite the murky nature of the men, the Maker could yet see enough.

It could be described as an amalgamation of shapes and sound and light and color, like a rainbow cloud, flickering with lightning and grumbling with thunder, but that was more inaccurate than it was accurate. Lines and angles made notes unheard by any ear, pure sound cast shadows and made light, shapes moved into colors and colors into crystalline forms. It was dynamic and alive and vibrant and confusing and delightfully, undeniably, a single distinct person.

Llaem Bli had no use for cynicism. He did not have to believe the worst, or the best, of people. He was advantaged in that he saw exactly what they were, good and bad. Most Makers looked only when they were asked to, being unwilling to deal with the knowledge and the consequences of their power, afraid they would be tempted to misuse it and so lose it.

Llaem saw no need for such trepidation. In the worst people, some good was always present to temper the bad, and to date Llaem had yet to find a person who had no flaws.

Unfortunately, good people could and would still do stupid things. The bad were not always able to be avoided, and Llaem, as powerful a Maker as he was, did not possess the innate persuasive skills necessary to turn people from their chosen path with no more than a well-placed suggestion. Nor did he have the telepathic powers such as the Silent Ones were said to have, which could alter a person's course without the use of words.

So he tried to move discreetly to the other side of the street, watching the Streetwardens gravitate towards him, hoping they would pass by without paying him undue interest, right up until they stopped in front of him.

The one on the left was older, grey coming into his dark hair, and a nose like a hawk. The Warden next to him was much younger but almost exactly the same height, dark yellow hair and nondescript eyes which could be grey or brown. They both wore swords at their sides.

"Good day," Llaem said with a nod as he too stopped, planting his staff in front of him and leaning on it with both hands.

The elder Warden looked him up and down with a look of distaste.

"Papers," he ordered.

"I'm afraid I don't have any," the Maker confessed with a pleasant smile. "I've just arrived."

The Warden glared at him suspiciously. "How did you pass the Gate?"

"Oh, the Streetwardens had their hands full with some fuss about a crate of inebriated chickens and some contraband. They waved me through. I suppose they thought I must look a harmless sort of fellow." Llaem continued his bland smile.

Accepting his explanation with a mildly bemused nod, the Warden put a hand on the hilt of his sword. "That's fine then, but you'll have to come with us to the Papers and Records to have papers drawn up."

"Of course," Llaem nodded. "What about my daughter?"

The Streetwarden looked down at Kwik for a long time, his head tilting from side to side. "How old is she?" he asked at last, rubbing his chin.

Llaem would have stumbled on his answer, but the nymph saved him. With all the imperiousness of a child who knows how to pull the strings of the much bigger and probably more stupid adults around them, she looked up at the warden.

"I'm nine," she declared.

The Warden was taken aback, but he gave his best charming and fatherly smile. "I would have guessed at least thirteen."

"I'm big for my age," Kwik told him with a reproving

pout.

"I'd say so," the Warden agreed. "That's fine then. Only twelve and older must have papers."

Llaem bowed his head. The older Warden started down the street, and the younger gestured for Llaem to follow. The Maker took the disguised nymph's hand, and complied, while the young Warden took up the rear.

The City of Iniquity, Llaem Bli thought as he made his way up the narrow winding street, sandwiched by the Streetwardens, *is aptly named. Though who is being wicked is a matter of viewpoint, I think.*

The Maker was not a young man. Though he did not look it, he was fast approaching his eightieth year of life. Path-magyc did strange things to the days and years and time in general. Llaem Bli did not enjoy the burdens this imposed on a man, but he accepted the gift as it was. He rarely wondered what it would be like when Death came for a final visit, but now, feeling as though he were being led to the gallows, the thought popped into his head. He squeezed Kwik's hand, and she squeezed his back.

Papers and Records was a small, pale blue building, with two gold columns flanking the white door. Two Wardens stood on either side of the door. The pair leading the Maker nodded at these two and they nodded back, an unspoken and arcane communication and agreement. Llaem sighed. *They're going to be asking for my papers on the way out.*

Llaem was ushered inside more as a prisoner than a guest. The first room was long and narrow with a marble bench running from wall to wall along the back. Iron bars cut the space into sections and separated the front from the back.

Bored, pale faces stared out from behind the bars, looking somewhat in the general direction of the faces of those at the front of the lines. A babble of voices tripped and stumbled over each other and several high-pitched voices pierced through the background noise, carrying tales of lost papers, unfair assessments, unregistered changes in name or address, and other such things.

"It's a bit small," Llaem commented, his staff providing a counterpoint to his boots on the stone.

The Wardens looked uncomfortable with the fact that he was talking to them. The younger one mumbled an answer.

"The previous Records were decommissioned and refitted as barracks." For whom, he didn't say. "Three new separate Records were commissioned to handle the workload. This is the last one."

"Ah." Llaem raised an eyebrow. How three separate places Papers and Records were held could exist was beyond him, but he wasn't going to press the Wardens for details.

Said Wardens nodded curtly and left. It may have been the Maker's imagination, but he could swear they dumped him at the end of the longest line. His eyes flicked to the glowing signs, lighted with thaumaturgic fire, above each cubicle.

In Common, Elvish, Ozbian (the language of the dwarfs), and the weird pictographs of the Islanders, each sign authoritatively directed a person to the correct line depending on what they wanted and who they were. The first said *Papers - Samnaran Domestic and Resident.* Next was *Papers - Demonan Domestic and Resident. Papers - Other Landers. Records - Personal (Birth, Death, Marriage, etc.). Records - Requests and Updates. Records - Public, Communal, and Commercial.* And finally *Records - Historical.*

Llaem was indeed in the longest line. He counted twelve people ahead of him. In the time he had been standing there, three people had joined the line behind him, a solemn looking elf and a man in rich robes bearing a merchant class sigil, arguing with his wife in whispers.

"You're lucky," a voice to Llaem's left spoke. "You missed the real bottleneck, when they made up the requirement two weeks ago. The line stretched halfway to the wharves."

It was a pirate, at the end of the much shorter line for *Papers - Samnaran, Domestic and Resident*. Bright red hair was subdued somewhat by a black bandanna. A silver hoop dangled from one ear, a row of pearls graced the other. An open jerkin of brown suede showed a tattoo of an anchor around his neck and a hairless chest.

His personal thundercloud from which his Mark could be discerned was so bright and stark it gave Llaem a flash of a headache behind his eyes. This man was not hiding who he was, he was so afraid of being no one, he asserted himself with forced disregard for the opinions or standards of others. It was like a heavy curtain thrown over a darkness to keep it from drowning out the light.

"And how is it you're here so late in the piece?" Llaem inquired, pitching his voice to be heard across the distance which separated them.

"They divided the city up into precincts," the pirate explained. "Nothing logical like doing it by districts or sectors of districts. No, they had to go and redraw up all the lines, and a timetable for the precincts to come to Papers and Records to register so they weren't overrun.

"They did such a good job, I heard one man went in three days before his wife because the precinct line went right down the middle of their bed."

Llaem was sure the man was exaggerating, but he appreciated the sentiment. Corruption and bureaucratic nonsense were not limited to princes, the Maker knew, a fact most people forgot after living with the illusion of freedom given by electing their princes and calling them Magisters.

"They got to the wharves last, thank Seidon, and it's on a ship by ship basis, so it's relatively quick to get your papers if you're on ship's company. One fellow had to stand in line for almost two days. He went home for lunch and lost his place. You can be sure he didn't go off again no matter how hungry he got."

Llaem was sure that was also probably exaggerated, but he made an agreeable face and nodded anyway. By this time, the *Papers - Samnara, Domestic and Resident* line had moved up, and the pirate turned his attention to the plain girl behind the counter. She gave him a bored greeting, and he flashed her a wink and a gold-plated smile.

Llaem's line had moved not at all. The man in front, in the dark blue coat, was leaning on the counter and gesturing furiously. The elderly woman behind the bars was glaring at him through square glasses, spots of color growing on her cheeks. She moved in a sharp jerk forward, and a bell sounded with shrill urgency. The room momentarily fell silent, then the babble continued, somewhat louder and now with a new frantic undertone.

Two Wardens came out a dark doorway in the back corner, pushed through the lines, unhooking and reattaching the rope cordons, making sure to bump and disturb as many people as possible, though the people moved away far in advance of the oncoming Wardens. The people moved back into place after the Wardens had passed like the waters of a puddle which has been disturbed by the boot of an excitable child.

The Streetwardens came up behind the man in the blue coat and he fell still. In a business-like tone which carried farther than was necessary, they informed him he was to accompany them at once. He did not protest or resist.

"That's probably going to happen to all of us," a morose voice came from behind Llaem.

He turned to find the elf looking with moist eyes at the man being led away. Brown hair cropped close made his pointed ears look a little ridiculous. He wore nondescript Demonan clothes, boots, trousers, and buttoned shirt under a coat. His voice held none of the musical lilt and timbre usually associated with elves; he most likely had never seen the trees of Carallión, being Demonan born and raised.

His Mark was faded, grey, almost tired and devoid of motion. This man was not just hopeless; he had abandoned all thought of the possibility of hope. It made Llaem nauseated, like a meal which did not agree with him. The Maker started. *As an elf, he can probably see something like my Mark, except he calls it an Aura,* he realized.

Though the elf had never seen his racial homeland, that did make him less an elf. The elf, however, did not look like he had enough interest to even register an Aura. Llaem suspected Auras and that part of a person he saw as a Mark were the same thing, but he had no way to prove it, save finding a Maker of Marks who also happened to be a member of the Old Races. He had never heard of such a one - it was as though the Old Races, seeing Auras as they did, had never needed Marks.

Llaem, out of mild curiosity, had asked an elf, a goblin, a dwarf, and a troll, all on separate occasions, what they saw when they slipped into what was called Old Sight. All their stories were similar enough to be considered the same. They described a cloudy, colorless word, broken by golden glows.

When pushed further, they told him the lights generally appeared within the person's chest and head, somewhat less often nearer to the stomach.

But that wasn't exactly right, the members of the Old Races had hastened to clarify. It wasn't any*where* really. It just *was,* and was all around, in front, behind and inside the person. It moved, floated almost, without moving at all. That matched Llaem's perception of Marks, minus the grey world, in the seeing-that-was-more-like-feeling-with-the-eyes way he perceived them.

Llaem was about to open his mouth to answer, thinking he would offer some banal comfort or platitude, when Kwik turned, stepped up to the elf, and wrapped her arms around his leg, squeezing hard, her eyes shut tight. Her lips moved, and a breath stirred about the room.

The elf's mouth fell open, but no words came out. Llaem was equally shocked for a different reason. He felt the impression of force or power, the same spark or jolt when a storm broke not drop by drop, but with a heavenly downpour, or whatever energy was required to push a seed from dormant and lifeless to the wellspring of life.

He felt this not so much from something the nymph did - the nature Guardian was still a mystery; he could see a little of her, but it went over his head - but from the rapid change in the elf.

It was brief and faded as quickly as it had come, but for an infinitesimal span of time, the elf remembered, no - *became* someone who knew what it was like to be happy, to live, to have a bright world around him for the taking, to hope.

Kwik released him from her hug-of-life and he blinked, looking around in confusion. Llaem looked around as well, expecting people to be gaping and pointing, exclaiming over the spectacle which had just occurred in their midst.

No one was looking their way. No voices were raised in wonder. It was as if nothing had happened. Looking at the elf, it seemed nothing had happened. *No, not nothing,* Llaem corrected. The man was different somehow. In a flash, the Maker saw what the nymph had done.

She changed him from Ungrowing to Growing. Whatever downward spiral he was on was halted if not turned back. It might not go all the way, but there was a spark. Of what, I surely couldn't say, but where there was nothing before, now there was something.

Kwik took his hand again, staring ahead as if she had forgotten anyone stood in line behind them.

The line continued to move forward in agonizing steps. Eventually Llaem and Kwik stood before the bench. The woman looked like she could be someone's grandmother, if they liked bitter tea and nettles more than a warm hug and cookies.

"Name," the poor woman said.

"Wiliem Hiddles," The Maker replied cheerfully. "This is my daughter Rose."

The woman gave him a look to say *I don't care what her name is. Why are you telling me?* "Place of birth?"

"Little town east of Torin called Grindlwald." Such a place did in fact exist. Llaem had spent some time there early in his life though he had not been born there. But if they were inclined to check a map or other records they might have on hand, Grindlwald would appear in one or the other of those.

The woman slid a beige piece of parchment folded in three onto the bench. "Mark."

Llaem smiled. He drew a small loop, a squiggle, and two dots. He returned the paper to the woman. She glanced at it and was satisfied he was who he said. At least, he imagined she was satisfied. Her expression did not change, but she made an official mark in red ink next to the Mark he had made.

Llaem's smile widened. One could not lie with a Mark; it was built into the magyc of Marks. But as a *Maker* of Marks…Llaem fought to keep his smile from becoming a grin or an outright giggle.

The woman looked up, now with a *what could you possibly have to be so cheerful about?* twist on her forehead. "Reason for visit?"

"I'm here to see an old friend."

"Name?"

Llaem paused. He knew what he would call the fellow, but he would eat his boots if the man was using that name now in Samnara. "Lyan Tovin."

The woman spun her chair around and called the name into a brass tube in a black hole in the wall. Others like it were spaced behind the other tellers. A moment later, the tube vibrated as a voice somewhere else answered. The woman made another mark in red.

"Length of visit?"

"We'll just be here for the day. Two at most."

She gave him a long, measured look.

"Two days," Llaem said. "We'll be here two days."

The woman marked that down. "Are you bringing anything into the City?"

"Well, I've already brought myself and my daughter," Llaem said, rubbing his chin. "As far as I know, there were no gremlins hiding in either of our jackets..."

He had been going to elaborate, but chose not to when he saw the slow simmer in her eyes and the pink flush in her cheeks. The last man to cause that reaction was having what was no doubt a very friendly conversation with the two Wardens summoned by the malicious little bell.

"No," he stated.

"What's in the pack?"

Llaem kept a straight face as he answered. "Clothes,

soap, handkerchiefs, comb, personal and traveling sundries, and several family heirlooms."

"And what is the nature of these heirlooms?"

A large portion of the Maker's eclectic collection had been damaged or destroyed by the Men in White who attacked his house; what little he had salvaged had to be further pared due to necessity. He owned only the one trusty pack, and he was not a Witch with the magycal talent necessary for fitting a small general store and an apothecary in one dress.

"A pendant, two books, a carving, and a somewhat oddly tuned harmonica." He chose not to mention the knife. Or that the pendant was in fact a Ducuore. Or the rough yellow crystal, the spyglass, and the vial of thick red liquid which looked like it could be blood - which would be because it *was* blood, but Llaem didn't feel like inventing a halfway plausible story for how that could be in any way a family heirloom. "The pendant was her mother's," Llaem said with an appropriately mournful glance at Kwik.

The woman's eyes remain hard as flint. "And what is the size of your purse?"

Llaem was not going to tell her how much money he had on him; she probably wouldn't believe him and call the Wardens to arrest him for his insouciant dishonesty, or she would believe him and would call the Wardens because he had robbed someone. He did a quick mental calculation. He couldn't give a figure too little to be believed either.

"One Anar and seven, and change. Silver," he said, trying to look both pleased at the sum, and dissatisfied at the same time. *I'm becoming quite the actor*, he thought. *Perhaps I'll try my hand at the stage after this.*

The woman wrote down the number, then spent some time doing something else behind the counter where Llaem couldn't see, though she glanced up from time to time.

Then she took a great bronze stamp and with a sadistic flourish, her hand hovered over the paper as if debating whether or not to officiate it. Finally, she stamped it with a loud thud and handed it to Llaem.

She had drawn a rough portrait of him. It was a fair likeness, though the Maker fancied his jaw was squarer than she credited.

"Three Katon, silver," she said.

Llaem dug the fee out of the ready coin he kept in his jacket, debating about making a comment on extortion. He handed over the money without a word.

"Haveanicestay," the woman said, running all the words together. "Next!"

Llaem pocketed his very expensive permissions to walk the Streets of Samnara, then walked around the little pole, along the indigo rope cordoning the lines, and towards the door. He paused at the second to last cubicle, *Records - Personal (Birth, Death, Marriage, etc.)*. There was no line.

After a quick look around, Llaem marched up to the teller. It was another woman, slightly more pleasant looking than the first two, perhaps because she was younger and the frown lines had yet to indent themselves permanently on her face. She was reading something, pale strawberry-blonde hair covering her face, and did not look up. Llaem tapped on the bars. Pushing something under the lip of the counter to hide it from view, she lifted her eyes.

"Can I help you?" the woman asked with a polite expression.

"Yes, I hope so," Llaem smiled. "I'm trying to find a friend of mine, Lyan Tovin. It has been many years since I've seen him, and he may have moved. I was wondering if you could check the records for me?"

The girl looked uncertain. "Um, well, mister…"

"Wiliem Hiddles," Llaem widened his smile. "And my daughter Rose."

Kwik stood on her tiptoes and peered over the counter. She offered the secretary a tight-lipped smile, eyes unblinking.

"I am hungry," she announced. "Father promised me Mr. Tovin would have wonderful food for me. It has been over three hours. I would very much like to leave now."

The teller's expression faltered, and she blinked rapidly, perhaps to make up for Kwik's unblinking stare. "Very well. Let me just have a look. Lyan Tovin, you said?"

Llaem nodded. The woman filled in a form and put it into a narrow slot under the brass mouthpiece behind her. It disappeared, sucked in on a current of air. She waited, her hands clasped together, a nervous smile on her face. Several moments later, another piece of paper shot out with a hiss. She picked it up and read it.

"It seems Lyan Tovin was in residence in the Silver District for several years, but this says he sold the house to one Harvard Madsen," she said. "There's no forwarding address."

"Thank you," Llaem said.

"I'm happy to be of service, Mr. Huddles."

Llaem did not bother to correct her, just smiled and turned away. As he'd guessed, the Wardens at the door checked his papers upon his exit. They seemed much happier with the papers than he was, but he returned their smiles and stepped back onto the street.

"Make sure you keep them," a familiar voice advised. "You'll get a reduced fee if you present them the next time you come back."

The Maker turned to see the red-headed pirate lounging against the wall of the Papers and Records. His attire clashed with the modest blue paint.

"Thank you," Llaem said. "How did you know they weren't permanent?"

"The color. Blue is permanent. Brown is temporary."

He waved his own papers at Llaem, a faded purple-blue.

"I see." Llaem paused. "You wouldn't happen to know where the Silver District of Samnara is, would you?"

"Of course. It's that way, north of the Business District, beyond the Coinage."

Llaem nodded a thanks at the pirate. Without invitation or permission, the pirate fell in step beside Llaem as the Maker started in the direction the man had indicated would take him to the Silver District.

"Name's Sceleb," the pirate told him. "Sceleb ObdaSea."

"Wiliem," the Maker responded. "Wiliem Hiddles. This is my daughter Rose."

"Lovely little thing. Must take after her mother." It was not an insult. *Nor was it a question*, Llaem noted, *though it smacked of prying.*

"She favors her grandmother, distaff side," Llaem said.

"Ah," Sceleb nodded. "And what brings you to our fair city?"

Fair was a word few would use to describe Samnara, pirates and cutthroats among those few. This Sceleb was on the shady side, the kind of shade one got before the sun disappeared behind the thick, grey wool of stormclouds that will stay for days before they rain themselves out. He was conniving and interested primarily in himself and his own well-being. Despite this, Llaem saw no outright malice or ill-intent.

"Visiting an old friend."

"Ah!" Sceleb exclaimed. "Yes, I heard you asking about him. What was his name again? Loam Trovan?"

"Lyan Tovin," Llaem gave the name he had given in the Papers and Records, keeping his expression pleasantly bland though a small flare of anger at the extra attention threatened to ignite his tongue. "Do you know him?"

Sceleb appeared to think on it, then shook his head with a sorrowful expression.

"I didn't think so," Llaem said. "My friend's a private sort of fellow." That was an understatement - the person Llaem was calling Lyan Tovin was the personification of whatever the polar opposite of *gregarious* was.

"Well, there are ways and means of finding someone even when they don't want to be found," Sceleb confided, "If one knows the right people to ask."

"I take it you know these right people?" Llaem asked.

Sceleb shrugged. "A poor sailor gets around."

Poor sailor, my pen, Llaem thought. "And would a poor sailor be inclined to help a poor traveler and his poor motherless daughter to find one such person?"

"He might indeed!" Sceleb exclaimed. "If the traveler was willing to exchange a small object of small value."

"I don't have much money," Llaem lied.

"No, no, I wouldn't dream of parting you with your much needed coin. I wouldn't want your pretty daughter to go hungry," Sceleb hurried to assure him. "I was thinking something much smaller and of less value."

Llaem waited, leaning on his walking staff.

"You see," the pirate continued after a pause, "I am a collector of unusual things, things oft overlooked, those sorts of things. I happened to see the pen you used to make your Mark. It seems quite worn…"

"It's not for sale or trade," Llaem said, a warning bite in his tone.

The pirate fell silent, a shrewd squint morphing into a disarming smile. "It is quite dear to you, I see."

"It was a gift from my late wife," Llaem said.

He was surprised when a very real tear sprang up, and he brushed his cheek with the back of his hand, feigning neither the emotion or his embarrassment at displaying it. It didn't happen often anymore, but sometimes it managed to sneak up on him at random times.

"Ah," the pirate voiced his favorite syllable in a more subdued voice and an uncomfortable expression. "I'm sorry."

"It's just a little sentimentality," Llaem said, clearing his throat. He concentrated on the false personality of Wiliem Hiddles and pushed his own past back where it belonged. "Nothing to be sorry about."

"Perhaps there is something else we can trade?" the pirate said, turning the conversation back to more important things.

Llaem thought for a moment.

"I have an idea," he told the pirate. "You say you are a collector of unusual things. Well, as a matter of fact, my friend is quite a collector too. I can promise he will have something which will more than compensate for your troubles."

The pirate frowned. "You must be good friends indeed if you can indebt him so."

Llaem smiled. "We are indebted to each other."

Sceleb pursed his lips. "And how do I know you are speaking the truth?"

"Do I look like a person who would lie?" Llaem asked, spreading his arms.

Sceleb considered. "Not really," he said, but he did not look entirely convinced.

"What do you have to lose?" Llaem pressed.

"You're right," the pirate beamed. "Come with me."

The pirate took him along the streets to a small square.

The Other World

In one corner, a man in a Streetwarden's uniform lounged, buttons on coat undone, a cigarette dangling from the corner of his mouth. Llaem gave the pirate a doubtful look. Sceleb clapped the Maker on the shoulder and sauntered towards the dilapidated Streetwarden, who smiled when he saw Sceleb. They greeted each other, shook hands, and spoke for a few moments. The pirate waved Llaem over.

"This is my friend Wiliem Hiddles," he introduced the Maker.

The Streetwarden gave him a once over. "And you're the one looking for the person who doesn't want to be found?"

Llaem nodded. There were two types of people who came to Samnara: those who wanted their deeds to be remembered, and those who wanted their deeds to be forgotten. Only a fool sought out the latter; one was more likely to be killed than rewarded for their efforts. The Streetwarden was silent, waiting.

"Him you'll need to pay," Sceleb prompted.

Llaem handed over coins, at first bronze Melbori, then silver Varyen. When the Streetwarden did not appear appeased or impressed, he took out one shiny gold Varyen, the hexagonal coin glinting in the sun. The Streetwarden gave a small nod, and Llaem dropped the coin on the pile in the Warden's hand. The money disappeared inside his jacket and the man took a drag on his cigarette, then blew it out in a blue-white stream.

"Lyan Tovin hasn't been around these parts for years, but you already knew that."

He saw little point in denying it, so Llaem nodded.

"He moved. Up to the Stacks."

Llaem looked at Sceleb. "The Stacks are up yonder, just below the Magisters' homes," the pirate explained. "Everything stacked on top of each other, you know."

"That was half a dozen years ago. I haven't heard from him since."

"Thank you," Llaem said.

"So, on to the Stacks then?" Sceleb asked.

Llaem gave a single nod. The pirate took them to the beginning of a steep street that jerked back and forth down the cliff. The buildings looked precarious, but they had stood there for ages, and like barnacles on the hull of a ship, they kept growing and crowding each other.

"The Stacks," Sceleb announced, with a grand sweep of his hands.

Llaem looked around with a duly impressed expression and started down the street.

"So now what?" the pirate asked, hurrying after Llaem. "How are you going to find your friend?"

"I'm going to wander," Llaem said. "He usually turns up."

And wander they did, but not for long. The strains of a harp floated through the air. Llaem stopped.

"What was that?"

"A harp," Sceleb said. "Most of the sailors play."

Or like to think they do. Llaem kept the opinion to himself. No half-drunk sailor morosely serenading a long-lost love had created *this* song. It was simple, too simple, but the notes were sure, firm, as if you could catch one and squeeze it in your hand. Llaem turned, trying to pick up the sound.

"I don't hear anything," Sceleb complained.

"It is that way," Kwik pointed, her pale face like a flower opening to a spring day.

Llaem followed the music. It led him to a building at the bottom of the Stacks, before the shops, taverns, inns, and traders' places of the Wharf Row began. This building was two stories high with a door the color of faded sunshine, and red stones lined the path leading up to it.

A man sat in a rocking chair on the porch beside the door.

Old age had given him a paunch and steel in his brown hair and beard. His eyes were closed in a leathery face, and tanned hands caressed a harp in a restless manner. Llaem smiled, listening to the slow march of notes, some just out of place enough to keep the ear interested.

A growl from beside Llaem turned his head. The pirate looked like he had swallowed a peach pit and was choking on it. He rounded on the Maker.

"This is your Lyan Tovin?" Sceleb almost shouted. "Lyan Tovin is old Cobb Drammer?"

The man beside the door opened his eyes and looked at the pirate. His eyes were hazel with a hint of blue showing around the outside. He yawned and stretched, then looked again at his visitors. When he saw Llaem, he leaned forward, his face a picture of shock.

"Llaem Bli, under the sun above, I never thought I'd see you again!"

"And so now you're Llaem Bli?" Sceleb said. "Great. I'm Prince Irdem of the Northernlands."

"So you do know him?" Llaem asked the irate man.

"Yes." Sceleb directed a glare at the old man. "If you had asked me to take you to old Cobb, I would've known the person in front of us. And I would have said *no*," he added, waving his finger for emphasis. "He's a leech. And a drunk. But mostly he's a cheat, and *that* I can't abide."

"That was just the one time," Lyan, or Cobb - who was really Hejjer Oduram - protested.

"There's never *just* one time," the pirate said and made a sound of disgust. "You can have him."

The pirate turned and trudged up the street, muttering

to himself. He did not look back.

"I may have promised him a token for bringing me here," Llaem told Hejjer, twirling his stick and thumping it on the ground. "From your collection."

Hejjer rubbed his beard. "How long have we known each other?"

"Oh, about half a lifetime," Llaem said.

"Some live longer than others," the old man countered with a smile and a pointed look at Llaem. "You haven't changed a bit."

"And you've changed a lot," the Maker said.

Hejjer's face clouded with memories of a past. "What do you want?"

"To talk," Llaem said. "And to pick up what you owe me. Starting with that man's payment."

Hejjer pulled a face and heaved himself out of the chair. It creaked in protest and settled back into place as its former occupant stretched the creaks out of his own muscles. He went inside and was gone for a while.

Llaem kept half an eye on the door and half an eye on the retreating back of the pirate. Sceleb turned the corner just as Hejjer came out and thrust a hand in Llaem's direction. The Maker leaned forward to pluck out the offering. It was a wooden carving in the shape of single-sail skiff. The sail was painted blue.

"Fitting," Llaem said. "Should I tell him what it does?"

"That," Hejjer said, displaying a complete lack of interest, "is up to you."

Llaem turned, cupped his hand around his mouth and gave a yell. "Oi!"

So fast Llaem suspected he had been waiting there, the pirate came back around the corner, one eye narrowed in a mistrustful manner, and a scowl on his lips. He did not come any farther.

"I have what I promised you!" Llaem called. "If you care to come and collect it."

The pirate looked one way, then looked the other. With a great sigh, he started back and took his time coming. He looked at the boat and though he tried to show a skeptical disdain, a light flickered in his eyes as they roamed the details of the carving.

"That's fine; that's fine," he said, and took it from Llaem.

Llaem opened his mouth, meaning to tell the pirate what the carving would do, but then thought again. *It will give him a chance to grow as a person if he figures it out for himself,* the Maker thought and smiled. *And teach him a lesson about life if he does not.*

"So we're square?" the Maker asked.

The pirate hesitated before nodding his head. Llaem stuck out his hand. The pirate hesitated even longer but then shook hands. Llaem beamed.

"It was a pleasure making your acquaintance."

Sceleb looked doubtful and cast a long glance of dislike at Hejjer before he turned away. This time, he had a little spring in his step when he walked. The Maker turned back to his old friend.

"So what do you want to talk about?" Hejjer asked.

"Aren't you going to invite me inside for a drink?" Llaem returned in a mild voice. "It's been a long journey."

"One you shouldn't have made," the old man muttered.

"But I have made it," Llaem said. "And if not for the sake of old times, then for the sake of future times, I would like to be invited inside."

Hejjer sighed. "Fine."

Llaem smiled broadly. "You're a good man, Hej."

"I was," Hejjer acknowledged. "Come in then. But I'm

not offering you a drink."

Llaem nodded and followed the old man through the faded door. It opened to a faded room, and Hejjer took him to a faded kitchen. The tile on the wall was chipped in so many places it seemed to be an intentional design. The stove was dull from layers of grime, and a wooden table and four wooden chairs, all in need of a good sanding and polish, stood in the middle of the room. Llaem put his bag and his stick in the corner and began opening the cupboards.

"What are you doing?" Hej protested.

"As you're not going to offer me a drink, I thought I'd better find it myself."

Silence from behind him prompted the Maker to turn around. A subtle smirk on the old man's lips told Llaem everything he needed to know.

"Except you don't keep it in the kitchen, like a normal person."

Llaem made to go upstairs, but Hejjer waved him towards the table.

"Sit, sit," he told Llaem. "I'll get it."

The Maker sat. Hejjer left and returned a moment later with a dark blue bottle. Gold twine looped around the long neck. Llaem's eyebrows went high in a surprised and impressed gesture.

"You flatter me," he said.

Hejjer shrugged, a flush making his face even darker. "Said I wasn't going to offer you a drink. Didn't mean I wasn't going to give you one. For old time's sake."

He got two glasses, poured generous drinks for the both of them, and then seated himself across from Llaem.

"Who's the child?" Hejjer finally asked, with a jerk of his chin in Kwik's direction. "Is she yours?"

"No," Llaem smiled.

He glanced at Kwik, who removed the glam pendant from her neck. Hejjer choked on his drink and blinked rapidly, his eyes tearing up from the alcohol fumes going up his nose.

"Hej, meet Kwik. Kwik, this is my friend Hejjer Oduram. He answers to a variety of names but is partial to Hej."

Kwik nodded solemnly but didn't say anything.

Hej's throat worked, and his mouth was having trouble forming words. "Is that a…a…"

"Nymph," Llaem supplied. "Yes."

Hejjer blinked again, took another sip of the drink, and studied his glass with a pensive frown. "You've got some tales to tell, I see."

Llaem sighed. "Unfortunately, I don't have time for the telling of all of them. I do have one tale that you should hear."

"Let's hear it then."

"A rather surprising guest dropped in on me the other day," Llaem said. "A man by the name of Cedar Jal."

If Hejjer had been surprised by the appearance of a nymph in his kitchen, this news floored him. He regained his composure and glared suspiciously at Llaem.

"And?"

"You know him then?" Llaem smiled.

"Of course. Well, I know *of* him," Hejjer clarified. "I never met him."

"Did you know that he had left Demona for a time?" Llaem continued in a conversational tone.

Hejjer snorted. "That's an interesting way of putting it."

"How would you put it?" Llaem asked.

Hejjer gaped and realized the trap he had walked into. Llaem smiled politely, encouraging Hej to speak with his silence.

"I heard he went messing with Demons. Magyc was involved; I'm not saying of what kind," Hej hurried to add, "But he got himself killed, was the story. And in doing so, set the Demons loose on the world."

"Well, I can attest to the fact that at least one part of that story is not true," Llaem said. "He appeared on my doorstep, quite alive and well, despite the Men in White chasing him."

The Maker saw the old man's hand spasm around the drink. Hej took a long swallow to hide it, but an anxious tightening of his brow he could not hide.

"You've heard of these Men too, I see," Llaem commented.

"Their numbers have been growing in the City. First came around a month ago, just before Papers were mandated," Hej said in a quiet voice. "They work under the Magister's blessing, asking about people with certain talents, and then they started on about a girl, detaining whoever they wanted." He shuddered. "Came here once, a fortnight past. At first, I thought they had come for me. I thought I could feel Death's hand squeezing my heart." He rubbed his sweating hands on his pants. "Turns out they wanted to talk to this goblin, one of them Yelndel fellows, or so it was rumored. Haven't seen either the Men or the goblin since."

"Did you tell the Men in White where he was?" Llaem asked.

"Demonfire no." Hej glared at the Maker. "What sort of scoundrel do you think I've degenerated into? I told them there were no darkies here, but there were some up along the Wharf Way." He chuckled, but the sound was caught by a net of fear choking up his throat. "There are too. Hundreds of them, coming and going on the ships. I figured they'd never be able to search all of them and find the one they were looking for."

"I wouldn't count on that," Llaem said, but he relaxed. The man before him had not turned rotten, like the Maker Adar Kerstel in Catmar, who had lost his ability to see people's Marks when he lost his hold on the Path through dishonesty and gods knew what else. "There is some sorcery at work which makes them more than mere men."

"You looked?" Hej raised his eyebrows.

Llaem shrugged. "I tried. They were not totally of the Path, so I couldn't see very well. Couldn't see much of anything at all."

"Usually you go all high and mighty and lecture me on the ways of righteous men when I ask questions about what you see."

"I do not go all *high and mighty*," Llaem said with a frown. "A Maker can't go around talking about other people's Marks. That's not the point of Making Marks."

"But not for these people?"

"I couldn't see their Marks," Llaem told him. "I'm not breaking the rules."

"Stretching them, then?"

"I'm not stretching them either. Could we please stay on topic?"

"Cedar Jal?"

"Yes!" Llaem threw his hands up in exasperation.

Despite himself, Hej was intrigued. The old man leaned forward. "What did he want?"

"He didn't want anything," Llaem said. "I offered him help, which he accepted. We had an interesting two days. Men in White were chasing him out of D'Ohera and the Justice of the City had some problem with him and his companions."

"There were more with him?"

"Yes, three others."

"Calling themselves Guardians?"

"It doesn't matter what they call themselves," Llaem said. "I know who and what they are."

"What are you telling me for?" Hej asked. "I gave up the life many years ago."

"I know," Llaem nodded. "But you never gave up on the others. Even when Cedar Jal made a name for himself, and everyone disappeared after he did."

Hejjer gave a slow nod. "That's true. I take it there's more to this tale?"

"There is. He brought with him a girl."

"A girl?" Hej repeated. "Let me guess: this would be the same girl the Men in White are so interested in?"

Llaem shrugged. "I would guess the same thing."

"And this girl is special?"

"Indeed."

Llaem took out a scrap of paper and for the first time in his long life broke the most sacred rules of the Makers: he Made the Mark of a person for another. It had been his plan all along – it was the only way he could think to make the man sitting in front of him believe what he was saying – but even so, a moment of unease accompanied the first motion and made the pen waver. This action was not a small or insignificant thing, and Llaem did not try to convince himself of that falsehood, only that the consequences were dire enough to warrant what he was doing. His mind more at ease, his pen now slid in a circle of effortless grace. The girl's face jumped to mind, as did her silent yet musical thundercloud which conjured this Mark. He slid the paper across the table to Hejjer.

"This is her Mark," he announced in a quiet voice. "Recognize it?"

Hejjer stared at it for a long time. "It's not complete."

"No, it isn't," Llaem agreed.

"So what have you come to me for?" Hejjer growled, aggressively refilling his glass from the bottle and just as aggressively emptying it in a single gulp. "I *was* a Guardian. Even if I *still* were, that doesn't mean I can conjure up *Aethsiths* for you."

"I'm not asking you to," Llaem said.

"Are you asking me to go back?" Hejjer asked this as if he had left a physical place which could be reached by a number of days of travel.

"No," Llaem shook his head to give the word emphasis. "But I do need your help."

"To do what exactly?" Hejjer was becoming more jittery, his fingers moving restlessly, his feet shifting under the table. He couldn't hold the Maker's gaze.

"I have to tell the Guardians," Llaem said. "They have to be ready."

"For what?" Hejjer's face said he already knew.

"For *Aethsiths*."

"You told me you can't tell what a person will become, only what they are," Hejjer said with an accusing thrust of a finger at Llaem's face.

"And I can't," Llaem said. "But I can have a hunch."

"A hunch?" Hejjer pulled a face. "You came all this way on a hunch?"

"I've done more on less," Llaem said.

"Tell me about this hunch that made you come all the way across Demona, then," Hejjer said, looking as though he'd rather hear about anything else, including the agony of the Blood Plague.

"Only halfway across. It's a hunch," Llaem told him. "What more is there to say?"

Hejjer gave him a look.

"She is…well, as you said, special," Llaem said. "In an

undefined way. This Mark..." he tapped the paper, "is the Mark of a person who hasn't decided who they are yet. At some time, I don't know when, she's going to have to make a choice. It could be soon, it could be many years from now, and it could go any way at all."

"So you're saying she could save us or leave us to be destroyed?" Hejjer asked.

Llaem nodded.

"And you think she's going to save us?"

Llaem nodded again.

"Because of your hunch?"

The Maker continued to nod.

"And why are you telling me?"

Llaem held his tongue.

Hej's eyes widened. "You didn't tell Cedar Jal this, did you?"

"He was there when I Made the Mark," Llaem said. "He saw what you do now."

"But you didn't tell him your hunch."

"No."

"Why ever not?!"

Llaem thought back to his meeting with the Guardian Cedar Jal and what he knew of him by the Mark which was as plain to Llaem as the nose on Cedar's face. The Guardian was a strong man, a man of principle, but he was lost in a storm of confusion, no longer sure where he could he place his feet lest he be sucked down by treacherous ground, stranded in a land where no compass recognized north as north. His view of the girl he supposed chance had thrown in his lap was clouded by his own insecurities and doubts and even his fellow Guardians could not apply to him to see it in another wise.

Llaem Bli thought it was not chance that had brought them together; chance was fickle. Something greater had intervened. The Maker would not say it was Fate or Destiny, or something of greater intention. He was sure then, as he was sure now, that if he had attempted to tell Cedar Jal what he believed of the girl, he would have lost the willingness of the Guardian to listen to anything he said. And so Llaem had let them go into his tunnel, trusting to the Path to keep them, as they were entrusted to keep it.

"We never had the time," Llaem answered.

"Where did he go?" Hejjer wanted to know.

"When he left my home, he was going to the Sister Cities, to take the pieces of the Amber Torch to the Crescent Temple."

"The pieces have been found?!" The old Guardian leaned forward, a feverish gleam lighting his eyes.

"By three industrious women, also traveling with the Guardian."

"They've remade the Amber Torch?"

"Not yet," Llaem said.

"But you think they will?"

"I do."

"But you didn't come to Samnara to tell me that."

"No." Llaem pulled a world-weary grimace. "I think there are forces that would be pleased if Cedar Jal failed."

Hej considered this. "Cedar Jal got us into this mess. It's only right he should get us out."

"Cedar Jal is also special, in that he was caught in the center of the storm, and his actions may have contributed to the turbulence, but he alone is not responsible for the trouble this world is in," Llaem chided. "You should know that, my friend. He is a Guardian of the Path, yet the Guardians do not protect the Path from an outside enemy destroying it; they protect it from fading from the hearts of the people of this land."

"And what is your plan?"

"My plan was to come to Samnara and see if you were still alive," Llaem answered with a smile. "From there, it was a bit hazy in my mind."

"What you mean to do-"

"You and yours must be awakened," Llaem said quietly. "You know this, Hejjer Oduram, Guardian of the Path, son of princes-"

"Okay, okay, don't start with that again," Hej interjected. "I only know where a few of them are: Zaira, Navardamen, Temm. They were my closest companions, and they're still around, here and there. They've managed to avoid getting papers, as I have. But I can send you to them. They should be able to give you more names."

"And what of you?" Llaem asked, tilting his head and gazing at the old man with a fond twinkle in his green eyes.

"What of me?" Hejjer tried to slip sideways from the question.

"You are speaking to a Maker of Marks," Llaem said in a breezy tone. "Don't expect to fool me."

"I never expect to fool you. I was just stalling for time," Hej said.

"Will that make it easier?"

"Not really." Hejjer Oduram drew in a great breath and breathed it out. "So it's time then?"

"Yes," Llaem declared. "It is time."

DESCENDANTS OF THE SEVENTH KING

Jæyd Elvenborn admired how Luca could turn a conversation about Death Marking the girl who could potentially be *Aethsiths* around so quickly and simply to a subject as mundane as their next meal. She suspected that he was being even more insouciant than usual, not only to fight the Demonhärt he carried, but also to fight the empty hole Liæna Nati left when she parted ways with the Guardians.

Jæyd's stomach reminded her that it had been a long time since she had eaten, and though sometimes it seemed as if she could subsist forever on only the Path, it was not truly so.

"Breakfast does sound good," the elf admitted.

She stretched to take the heaviness of sleep from her muscles. Though her rest had been dreamless, she sensed the remainder of a presence which had settled over them in the night. The news it had been Death Himself come to visit was not as disquieting as the others thought, and Death's Mark in the ashes was not an omen of blood and pain. His Mark was both light and dark for a reason. Luca groaned when Timo shook his head in response to the talk of breakfast.

"We must make haste for the village," Timo told them. "They will feed us, I promise you, but the Dalefolk do things in their own time, and if I were to guess, you will not be happy with their speed of choice."

"I think you mean their lack of speed," Luca said.

The dark Guardian stood up, dusted leaves from his jacket, and settled his violin on his back.

"Lead on, noble leader," he bowed to Timo. "Breakfast awaits!"

Timo did not smile and Jæyd saw his inner conflict reflected in the lines of his clenched jaw and the crease between his eyes, a conflict she understood but did not share. *What I would give to return home.*

With his grim expression, Timo turned and led them out of the narrow ravine into the Dale proper. A thousand shades of green blended to create a jewel which was more breathtaking than the Elves' Emerald, ringing with life, and reminding Jæyd that though the elves were of the Old Folk, there were things older still, closer to the pure magyc of Before.

The vast Lake was still, a deep steel blue with the reflections of white clouds scuttling across the surface. On the shore, a small collection of houses stood wreathed in grey smoke.

Dogs greeted the Guardians as they came to the fringes of the village, and blond, blue-eyed children stopped their playing to gaze at the strangers as they walked through. Several big men dressed in leather and fur stopped them at the edge of the rough square, shaggy blond hair waving in the breeze, staffs of thick oak grasped in sinewy hands. Two of the men had neat beards streaked with red.

The man in the middle stood a step ahead of the others, his beard longer than the others and more grey than blond. He wore a circle of beaten bronze on a braided leather string around his neck, and his staff was the longest, topped with a crystal orb in metal filigree.

He spoke only to Timo. "Greetings. From which King do

you descend?"

"My father is Askor, descended of the Third King," Timo replied, his voice raised to carry to the dozens of ears listening eagerly.

"We are of the Seventh," the man said. His blond hair was edged with white, and he wore a spotted-fur cloak about his shoulders. "We bid you welcome."

"I accept your welcome," Timo said.

"My father called me Doman." The old man raised his chin with a proud look.

"My father called me Timo," the Guardian responded, the words a dance of sound, and each knew the steps well.

Although he has been away from home for so many years, he still has the grace and bearing of a Daleman, Jæyd thought, her eyes roving over the villagers, who though still wary, were relaxing as Timo spoke the familiar words of greeting. They nodded and talked amongst themselves, some with smiles, others with solemn faces but not unfriendly. *How fortunate for us.*

"You travel with company," the chief said, and only now did his eyes acknowledge the others.

"These are my companions," Timo said, stepping smartly to the side and gesturing at each as he named them. "Luca of Isos, Cedar of Torin, S'Aris of Lii, and Jæyd of Carallión."

The elf noted the stress of importance. The last were always the most important, and women were always introduced after men. It was unlike anything else the long-lived elf had experienced in any other realm among any other people, and it always made her smile. She waited until the chief turned his blue eyes to her, then she bowed. It was not her traditional elven bow, but straight at the waist, with no flourish or whimsical additions.

"Greetings, Chief of the Seventh King," she said as she rose.

The Witch caught on at once, and when the chief looked at her, she copied the bow with grace and a solemn face. "Greetings, Chief of the Seventh King," S'Aris said.

"Greetings, Chief of the Seventh King," Cedar bowed.

Luca was pale, and he looked nervous when the chief looked at him.

"Greetings, Chief of the Seventh King," he said, his voice breaking twice.

Jæyd watched him closely out of the corner of her eye. This would be a terrible time for Luca to have one of his episodes. The dark Guardian swayed on his feet, bowed faster than was proper in the Dale, but not too fast to be insulting. He straightened and breathed in. Jæyd saw him relax, and she did likewise.

"I see you have been traveling long," Doman said. "I extend the hand of hospitality to you and your company. We will prepare a meal in your honor."

"I accept this gracious offer," Timo inclined his head. "And you have my thanks for inviting us into your home."

Timo bowed again and made a discreet gesture for the others to do likewise. They did, and Jæyd smiled while her face was turned to the floor. She enjoyed the theatrics of the Dalefolk. The elven way was simpler, yet more complex in other ways, and it gave her continual pleasure to discover the similarities and differences between the two. Doman returned the bows, then turned and walked down the street to the largest house, which stood in the middle of the hamlet.

Though the house was twice the size of the others, it was just as plain. Three separate suites of white stone walls, thatched roofs, and windows of thick thaumaturgic glass, which distorted the visage slightly, had a weathered look, as if daring another storm or season to attack.

Doman took them through the entrance in the middle suite to the left wing. He held open the door to the room at the far end of the passage. It was an austere sleeping room with six pallets on the floor, blankets folded at the foot of each.

"The water of the Lake is most reinvigorating," Doman said, still in his formal tone, leading Timo to the next movement of their verbal waltz.

"Then we will take time before we join you in eating to clean our bodies," Timo said.

"My family will bring soap and towels."

With that, Doman bowed and left, shutting the door behind

him. Luca sank onto the nearest pallet with a dramatic sigh, slipping the violin off his back so he could flop back and throw an arm over his eyes.

"That was *exhausting*," he said through the fabric of his jacket. "Do they do anything here that's not rite and ritual?"

"Yes," Timo said, smiling for the first time in days. "There will be no more *rite and ritual* like that until we leave."

"Is that supposed to make us want to stay longer?" Luca said.

Jæyd laughed softly and lowered herself onto the pallet next to his. "The Dale is a world apart, Luca. You get accustomed to it and even come to enjoy it."

"Don't tell me you actually like all that," Luca lifted his arm and gazed at her in disbelief.

"I did," the elf said. "It is like a dance, the steps even and precise, one move for each of the other."

"That was like a funeral procession. Dancing is more fun and spontaneous," Luca countered.

"Then you will enjoy the feast," Jæyd told him with a playful shove and settled next to him on the pallet.

Luca looked horrified. "They don't expect us to dance, do they?"

"Dancing is optional," Timo said. "You all did well and brought honor to my father and the Third King."

"It sounds as though we've been adopted," S'Aris said.

"In a way, you have, until you leave," the Daleman told her, moving to the window and peering out. "They are preparing a space to bathe for us. Washing in the Lake is…"

"A ritual?" Luca butted in, arching an eyebrow.

"An honor," Timo corrected. "The waters have many beneficial properties. And not just for the body," he added with a significant glance in Luca's direction.

The dark Guardian pulled a face at the Daleman but offered no retort. The bathing was another thing Jæyd enjoyed about the Dale. It was not as sophisticated as the bathhouses in Torin or Catmar, nor was it as sylvan as the elves' bathing practices. It, like the Dale, was unique.

She was the first to follow Timo out a back door. A low wooden building sat close to the edge of the lake with a dozen swinging doors on the long side.

"What is that for?" Luca asked, eyeing the building mistrustfully.

"To remove your clothes," Timo stated.

Luca stared at the blond Guardian as he disappeared into the building though the closest door, emerging several moments later completely naked. He carried towel and a wooden cup to the water's edge and then waded into the Lake until the water was up to his chin, where he ducked under the surface and splashed about like a happy puppy.

"Do you think that much frivolity is allowed, or are we being a bad influence on him?" Luca asked.

Jæyd smiled and went to undress herself in the second stall over. It was tight, a narrow bench along one side taking up most of the space, with a basket under it to leave her clothes. Sitting on top of the bench was a stack of soft towels and a wooden cup, which held a thick, jelly-like soap. She picked these up and went to the lake.

Immersing herself in the water, she sighed as contented bliss took away the worries of the world. In the shallows, it was warmer than expected and effervescent against her skin. The soap didn't lather, but cleaned her skin and hair until they squeaked when she pulled her fingers over them to rinse it away. The elf didn't spend more than a few minutes in the water, though she would have liked to spend a few hours soaking. To the frugal Dalefolk, it would have been impolite.

When Luca saw her and Timo leaving the water and wrapping their towels around themselves, his face fell. He began throwing soap over his head, dunking down to rinse it off, and heaved himself out of the Lake with the grace of a beached whale, following the Daleman and the elf to the changing stalls.

Their clothes had been taken away and replaced with soft suede breeches and jerkins in the same style Timo wore. Luca came over, his fingers fumbling as he tied the strings of the jerkins, his eyes panicked and his hair still dripping.

The Other World

"They took my jacket!" he cried.

"Don't worry Little One," Timo said. "They didn't steal it. They are only cleaning it."

Luca hardly spared a moment to give him a withering look. "I'm not worried about them *stealing* it. I'm worried about what they might find *in* it."

Jæyd, Cedar, and Timo stared at him, then they rushed off in a body. The chieftain looked slightly alarmed at the group rushing up to him. Timo composed himself first and presented himself to Doman.

"There are objects of special value in the jacket of Luca of Isos," Timo told him. "It must never leave his side."

"I apologize," the Chief said, his face distraught. "We meant no offense."

He took them to where their clothes had been placed to be laundered. Luca gave a muffled squeak, pounced on the black jacket, rifling through the lining until he found the securely wrapped package containing the Demonhärt. He searched his breeches for pockets, then gave up and turned to Timo, throwing his arms out in question.

"In the jerkin," Timo said.

After the Demonhärt was safely stowed away, the Guardians relaxed. The remainder of the morning was spent wandering the hamlet, nodding in grave courtesy to the Dalefolk. A crowd of blond children followed, pointing and whispering at Luca.

"What do they want?" the dark Guardian asked, getting more and more agitated as the children's interest became more pointed.

"I believe they are fascinated with your hair," Jæyd answered.

"What about it?"

"The color is probably something they have never seen."

Luca ran a hand through his black mop. "What about it? Cedar has dark hair too."

"His lacks a certain...sparkle," Timo said.

Luca sighed. "They're not going to leave me alone, are

they?"

"Few visitors come to the Dale," Timo said, folding his muscled arms across his chest. "Can you not indulge them?"

Luca turned to look at the children and made a face, pulling his lips back with two fingers to show his teeth and rolling his eyes back in his head. The children shrieked and ran for cover.

"Luca!" Jæyd chided. "Giving their offspring nightmares is no way to win the favor of the Dalefolk."

"I think referring to their children as offspring might offend them more," Luca said with a smirk. "They're not dogs or chickens. Besides, it didn't scare them a bit. Look."

True enough, the children were peeking out from behind walls, troughs, barrels and whatever else they could find to hide behind, eyes sparkling. Timo beckoned them over. The bravest few darted out, slowing as they neared the Guardians, eying Luca with suspicion.

The dark Guardian gave a theatrical bow, parodying the formal Dalefolk. "I am Luca," he announced. "But my father likes to call me something less polite."

"They heard the introductions Timo made to the Chief," Jæyd whispered to him.

"Maybe some of them need reminding," Luca smirked again.

"Why is your hair different?" the closest of the children said, a boy of eight or nine, with dark blond hair and blue eyes ringed in darker blue.

"Because I'm different," Luca said. "In a very acceptable way," he amended at Timo's expression.

"How do you make it like that?" a girl asked as she came up, keeping behind the boy.

"It grows like that," Luca knelt down so he was eye to eye with the girl. "What's your name?"

"My father called me Timma," she said, smiling.

"That sounds like a good name," he said and looked over her shoulder at Timo, wiggling his eyebrows.

"It is a good name for a daughter," she agreed.

"What does your tattoo mean?" another child behind the

others asked S'Aris.

She looked down at the interlocking triangles on her hand and smiled. "It is the symbol of my faction in the Coven."

"You're a Witch?" the boy asked, tilting his head skeptically.

"I am," S'Aris nodded.

"Do a spell," he commanded with great authority.

Timo, Cedar, and Jæyd opened their mouth to brush away the request, but the Witch knelt down and held out her hand, fingers closed tight. The boy reached out and pried it open and gasped when several bright butterflies fluttered out.

"Do another!" the children clamored, crowding close.

"Perhaps later," the Witch said as she stood.

"Why have you come to the Dale?" another voice piped from behind.

The Guardians spent the next hours entertaining the children and answering questions about the fearsome beasts that terrorized the land outside the Dale, pirates, lands beyond the great water, what sort of food they liked, and other such questions children placed great importance in.

When the sun was directly above, Doman came to fetch them. Tables had been set out in front of his house and down the street. All three hundred villagers gathered for the feast, and the Guardians saw Timo had predicted correctly. The fare was as lavish as the villagers could spare from their diminished winter stores.

The descendants of the Seventh King laid out smoked hams, fish stews, a thin broth with carrots and string onions and course, dense bread. Jellies and candied fruits came next, and after all were satisfied, a strong coffee sweetened with honey and cream.

"I thought coffee only grew in the Wild Islands," Luca said, moving his cup under his nose with a beatific expression.

"That is true," Doman said and smiled. "We prefer to remain undisturbed, but we do trade with outsiders and other villages in the Dale." He closed his eyes, took a sip, then opened his eyes and looked at the Guardians. "Now, tell me what you have come for."

"We are searching for a man," Timo said.

"Tell me his name, and I will see if I know him," Doman said.

"I don't know his name," Timo admitted. "He is called the Man of Tongues."

Those seated nearest to the guests of honor looked up at the name, faces filled with shock, some with horror. Doman quickly collected himself as only a practiced leader can, lowering an indecipherable mask upon his face.

"I see." He paused, and set down his coffee. "This is not the place for this talk. Come."

Doman took them into to his house, and in the middle room, seated them around a small hearth. He lit the fire, and a sweet aromatic smoke drifted about the room. He sat with the Guardians and the Witch, his face grave.

"This man you speak of," he said. "The Man of Tongues. He is not a man."

"Perhaps," Timo allowed. "But still we must find him. He can help us."

"Tell me what you need," Doman urged. "Perhaps there is a more wholesome way to fulfill your need."

"I thank you for the offer, but I don't think you can help us," Timo said. "What we seek is in another world entirely."

"And that is why you seek the Man of Tongues," Doman said, sadness on his face.

"Why is that so bad?" Luca spoke up.

Doman turned to look at him. "You are outsiders, so you cannot know much about us. We are sheltered, but still we have heard of the Guardians. Some of our own have even come to the calling of the Path." He nodded at Timo. "Our sheltered existence comes with a price. We are not advanced as some cultures and do not enjoy some of the conveniences or pleasures, but there is a purpose in the seclusion, a purpose set forth by the Seven Kings from which all Dalefolk are descended. We do not bend to the whims of men or time. We have heard of what has happened to the Guardians, but we do not take part in the censure of that which we don't know. I trust you mean my family no harm, but you must know the Man of Tongues is dangerous. They say he holds with demons."

"This I know," Timo said. "But there are few ways to cross the barrier between worlds. We *must* do this. Every second we delay is a second in which the enemies of this world, and others, grow stronger."

"The Man of Tongues was banished, many hundreds of years ago," Doman said. "No one has heard from him. At least, no one living."

Timo's shoulders slumped.

"But there is someone who could help you," the Chief continued. "Our shaman, who does not live within our village. Perhaps he may be able to use his powers to find this Man of Tongues."

The other Guardians looked heartened, but Timo looked put-out. Jæyd knew why - shamans dealt in magyc, and the Dalefolk did not hold with magyc, at least magyc wielded by men and mortal. Those hopeless and crazed by magyc were sent into the mountains because their kith and kin did not know what else to do with them.

"Thank you," Cedar said.

"Do not thank me yet," Doman held out his hands to ward off the gratitude. "I have only made the suggestion. The shaman may refuse to aid you. But we will see."

"When can we see him?" Cedar said.

"Not for three days. No," Doman said before they could protest. "He is in meditation in preparation for the First of New Days. To go to him before he comes out of his seclusion would be a terrible omen and bring bad luck to the whole year."

The Guardians looked at each other. Timo, who had brightened at the chieftain's words, gave a small shake of his head. They could do nothing but wait.

"Do not fret," Doman said. "After his spiritual cleansing, his power will have grown, and he will be that much abler to help you if he chooses."

The Guardians and the Witch slept in Doman's house, and the next day, dressed once again in their own garb, they were absorbed in the activities of the Dalefolk. Jæyd and S'Aris mended clothes and blankets, cooked meals, and tended the fires of the village. Timo, Cedar, and Luca were set to work chopping firewood and repairing damage the winter snows had wreaked upon the houses and boats of the village.

The villagers continued to be gracious, though the children were conspicuously absent, and idle chatter was sparse. Jæyd missed the openness of the first day, when it had been like old times, and the appearance of the Guardians was a blessing on a town and celebrated, even in the Dale. Cedar threw himself into his work, to forget that every passing moment was a moment the Nine could find a way to get to Ria, and the others followed in his wake, hard pressed to keep up.

"I don't understand it," Luca announced when they finally stopped for the day to eat the last meal. "How is it not even the first day of spring yet? Everywhere else spring is almost half over."

"The Dale is not in sync with the rest of the world," Timo said, spooning venison stew thickened with an odd root which imparted no flavor but a magnificent creaminess. "It was built after Demona and the rest were formed and remained a world apart."

"How do you figure that?" Luca asked. "Have you ever seen these Seven Kings, the Seven Builders?"

"No, but they are said to live in the mountains," Timo said, with a pointed glance. "You can go look for them if you like."

Jæyd knew it was an empty offer, a bluff, but Luca didn't argue further.

That night, Jæyd could not fall asleep and lay staring at the ceiling, listening to Cedar tossing and turning on his pallet. Eventually the elf pulled the cover back and crept over to Cedar, touching him on the shoulder. He stood at once and followed her to the common area of their small wing.

"I cannot stand much more of this waiting," Cedar said,

rubbing his hand over his head, over and over, until his hair resembled a hedgehog.

Jæyd shrugged. "We must not fret about what we cannot change."

"How can they not understand how important this is?" Cedar asked. "Worlds are at stake, and they quibble over one year."

Jæyd did not answer, but her silence was reply enough. That was the way of the Guardians' life, it had always been that way since the time of the First Guardian. People did not consider much outside their own lives, homes, or families, and unless a Demon was sitting on their doorstep, it was a far-off terror that did little to stimulate them to action.

The man and the elf watched the stars' light creep in through the warped glass and move across the room. The moon shone down at them, a thin slit which looked like an elven blade, reminding Jæyd yet again of Carallión, the forest home of her people. The light made a faint rainbow in one corner of the window, and Jæyd made a wish, though she did not believe in that childhood fable of the elves. Rainbows were pretty, but they were not magyc, nor could they grant wishes. *May the Man of Tongues appear to us and send us to Ria.*

Jæyd was not unfamiliar with the term Man of Tongues, though to the elves, this creature was more myth than fact. It was said he could speak all languages and even had the ability to converse with animals, a skill even the elves did not possess. *Yet who will I turn to if the Man of Tongues is unable to send us across the barriers to where we need to go?*

Her father would be a good first choice. Serene and sharp, he would have an idea about what to do, and he had the ear of the Elven Council. However, to reach Carallión, it would take a great deal more time spent traveling. Time they did not have, pointed out by the grey dawn sending the night's shadows back to where they lived out the day.

Jæyd glanced at Cedar's face. His eyes were narrowed and his cheeks were flushed. He kept his knees tight against his chest, breathing deeply through his nose. He tried to hide his thoughts, but Jæyd did not need a down-turned mouth or a frown to know that he was preoccupied with Ria and her part in their predicament.

Just as she opened her mouth to offer comfort or commiseration, she had not quite decided, a startled cry from the other room brought both the Guardians to their feet.

Jæyd dashed into the sleeping room with Cedar on her heels. Timo was crouched between mats, his hands squeezing his head as if trying to crush it, his face screwed up in torment. Luca and S'Aris knelt behind him, but the large man shook off their hands when they attempted to touch him.

"What happened?" Cedar demanded.

S'Aris's gentle blue eyes flicked to him, her brow furrowed. "I don't know. He looked like he was having a bad dream, tossing and turning…" she moved away as Timo lunged to the side, still grasping his head, then continued. "Then he yelled out, and I went to wake him. He woke before I reached him, and I saw that something was wrong with his eyes."

Timo slammed his fists down on the ground, and his face snapped to Jæyd. His eyes were clenched shut, but bright gold light seeped out through his lids. Timo began to shake, his fingers twitching, then his head flew back, and his eyes opened wide. The glowing golden orbs darted back and forth with frantic energy, holding Jæyd transfixed. *Of all the things I have never seen before, this is the most unusual.*

"What is the matter with him?" the elf whispered.

The Witch could only shrug helplessly as the Daleman muttered, frowning. When he arched his back and fell back, jerking on the ground in a fit that would break bones, Jæyd started to move towards him.

"Don't touch him," S'Aris warned, and it was then the elf saw the dark bruise in the shape of a hand on her forearm.

The Witch shrugged at the question in Jæyd's eyes, a sheepish smile twitching on her lips as she prepared to make an excuse for her mishap. Just then the door opened, and Doman stepped inside.

"I heard noises," he said, then the whisper of accusation was overshadowed by concern when he caught a glimpse of Timo. "What is going on here?"

Jæyd stepped forward and grasped the chieftain by the elbow. "He could not sleep and has some pain. He will be alright."

The chieftain tried to twist around to get a clearer look at Timo, but Jæyd put her other hand on his shoulder and steered him through the door, closing it behind him. She watched his shadow linger for a moment, then move off. With a sigh, she turned back to Timo and the others.

"Has he ever done this before?" the Witch asked in a quiet voice.

Jæyd shook her head, and without realizing it, she started pulling at her bottom lip with her teeth. She knew Timo was uncomfortable with returning to the place of his birth, but she had thought it was just his pride or imagination. Apparently, she was wrong. Both the elf's and the Witch's gaze fell to Timo when he spoke.

"Paper," the Daleman rasped, rubbing his eyes with one fist as if he could wipe the light from them, the other waving for the requested item.

Moving with fluid grace, S'Aris handed him a piece of paper and a stick of charcoal and snatched her hand away before her fingers could brush his skin. The paper was thin and whispery, like solid moonlight. Timo closed his eyes again, and the golden light darted back and forth, in time with his lips as he wrote in slow, even strokes.

The Guardians held their breaths, unable to read what he was writing until he stopped and held up the piece of paper in a shaking hand. Then, as though a fire in his body had been suddenly doused, Timo relaxed. His head lifted, and he looked up to gaze at the Guardians, eyes blazing with golden fire.

Though disconcerted, the Guardians and the Witch leaned closer to see what he had written. Pretty swirls with the odd jagged slash across crossed the paper, in regular lines Jæyd recognized as poetry, though she could not read it.

"What does it say?" she asked Timo.

The strange light was fading from Timo's eyes, and when they had returned to their usual sky-blue hue, he looked confused at what he had written. The Daleman shrugged helplessly.

"I have no idea. Did I write that?"

The elf nodded, a questioning look in her eyes.

Timo shifted with disconcert. "I don't remember doing that."

"Where did the words come from?"

"I believe," Timo said slowly, "the Man of Tongues sent me them in a vision."

"And what makes you think that?" Luca asked, breaking the brittle silence with a hammer.

"Because he has done it before," Timo said.

"When you thought about going to the Dale to get Ria?"

"Yes." Timo continued in the barest of whispers, "And one other time." He looked up. "When I decided to leave the Dale, to become a Guardian, he showed me a vision of *Aethsiths*."

"Why have you never said anything about this?" Luca demanded, once he had gotten over his shock.

"Have you told me the story of when you became a Guardian?" The question was gentle, but Luca closed up at once.

Jæyd understood the rebuke, and Luca deserved it, though she too was surprised by the revelation. It was true, the moment one chose to become a protector of magyc was personal and not lightly shared. Jæyd knew Cedar's and Luca's stories, only because she was a character in those tales, but Timo's she had never heard, and never asked.

Cedar nodded and, dismissing the awkward silence, stepped forward, took the paper from Timo, and held it up for everyone to view.

"Does anyone know what is it?" Cedar asked, looking at everyone in turn, pausing when he reached Luca and the other Guardian flinched. "Luca?"

The dark Guardian was looking at the writing like it might bite, but his eyes moved across the lines of symbols, jumping from one to the next with long pauses as he struggled to take in the meaning.

"Luca?" Cedar prompted again.

"It's the language of Lii," Luca said, his voice at once disgusted and awed.

The Witch leaned over and verified the identification with a surprised lift of her brow and a nod.

"You mean Nyican?" Cedar asked, a frown growing on his face from Luca's theatrical antics.

Luca laughed, a touch of mania in the sound, and shook his head. It was the Witch who explained.

"No. Nyican and the language of Lii are two very separate languages. One is the common language of the land, the other is spoken only by those of the Coven. They bear no relation to each other."

Luca stopped chuckling long enough to add, "Liish bears no relation to any tongue in this world, perhaps any world. Good luck with understanding *that*."

S'Aris frowned at the mocking tone, then pulled the paper closer. "Let me see if I can translate it."

She took it and moved her finger under the first line, stopping every now and again to reread a group of glyphs. Before she had reached the end of the second line, she was shaking her head.

"This is old, very old High Liish," she said. "There are books at the Library which I could use to translate it, or it is possible a Darkrobe who was versed in Etymology and Semantics could tell us what it means, but this dialect has not been spoken in the Coven for centuries."

"Perhaps this Man of Tongues is toying with us," Cedar said, looking at Timo, whose eyes had returned to their normal sky blue color.

"If he is, he has a very warped sense of humor," Luca added. "One even I can't approve of. We'll never find him with this."

"He is the Man of Tongues, not the Man of Shadows," Jæyd said firmly. "He is flesh and blood of one kind or another, and he *can* be found. A tongue is only so useful as it can be understood, and I trust we have the combined wits among us to figure out what he means to tell us."

She stared Luca down, until he sighed and rolled his eyes like a spoiled adolescent.

"Oh, fine then. Give it here."

The three Guardians turned to Luca, who grabbed the paper and frowned at it. He did so for a long time, the other Guardians becoming more restless the longer he stared at it without moving his eyes.

"Well?" Cedar prompted.

Luca looked up, a puzzled glint vying for supremacy with the stubborn look in his eyes.

"It's definitely the language of Lii," he said. "And it makes no sense at all."

"You can understand it?" S'Aris asked, blinking.

"No, but I can *read* it," Luca glared at her, daring her to contradict him. "My mother was of Lii, before she came to Isos. Even though she gave up her Blacks, she made me learn."

"Your mother was a Dark*robe*?" S'Aris said, incredulity animating her face and frown.

"Yes," Luca snapped, and shifted uncomfortably. "What of it?"

"Nothing," the Witch said, stepping back. She looked at him with an intensely thoughtful expression.

"Your parentage is all very fascinating, but what does it say?" Cedar demanded.

Luca cleared his throat and chanted out the verse in hesitant syllables.

"An arrow swift...no, wait - an arrow true as Death
Twixt the two teeth rising
Over the shifting mirror
which has trapped the sky
The silent draping falls
and then you will find the rest
Three steps to follow
First comes second
Second is first

And the final clue lies beneath the sky."

Luca looked up as he finished reading, a disgusted expression on his face. He muttered something that sounded like *Liish, smeesh* under his breath. S'Aris's eyes flicked to him, but instead of the usual affront, they held only the same thoughtful look.

"It's a riddle," Cedar said.

"You think so?" Luca asked, arching an eyebrow. "I was having difficulty deciding between that or a recipe for flat cakes. Whatever it is, it still makes no sense."

"That is why they call it a riddle," Jæyd smiled. *A riddle is good. A riddle has an answer.*

"What are we supposed to do with it?" Luca grumbled.

"Solve it, of course," Cedar said, echoing Jæyd's thoughts. "It will lead us to the Man of Tongues. Look. The first part is easy. There are three steps to follow and six lines. So each step is two lines…"

"Very well," S'Aris chimed in, catching on to his reasoning. "Let us take it one step at a time. The first step is the third and fourth lines…"

"Over the shifting mirror that has trapped the sky," Luca read out.

"I know that," Timo said, looking up. "A lake."

"Which one?" Cedar asked.

Timo stared at him as if Cedar had suddenly become a simpleton. "This is the Dale. There is only *one* Lake."

"Of course." Cedar gave a sheepish shrug. "So, across the Lake, then what?"

"Second is first, so a*n arrow true as Death, twixt the two teeth rising* is the second step."

Silence grew heavier the longer it stayed.

"Look," Luca said suddenly. "If the first part is direction, this is continuing the directions. A landmark of some kind-"

"Monuments, or statues, something of a pair," Jæyd agreed.

"Two teeth could be mountains…" Timo mused.

"Now would be a good time to ask *which ones*? We're surrounded by them!" Luca said.

"Maybe it is a reference to the name of the peak?" Jæyd suggested.

"Perhaps, but I know none by that name," Timo said.

"Are there old names for the mountains?" Cedar asked. "Names they were known by before?"

"Everything in the Dale is old," Timo replied. "And their names are as old. The problem we have is they do not have *new* names."

"Are you sure you translated correctly?" Cedar gazed at Luca intently.

"Of course I'm not sure!" Luca snapped. "It's Liish. There's only about ten different meanings for each word!"

The others stared at him.

"Okay, most of them don't have that many," he amended. "But most words have more than one meaning. Depending on the context of the whole piece, and the meanings you take for the other words, the meaning of the word will vary." He paused, and made a face. "And how sick and twisted the writer is influences things as well. It's rather brilliant, and *infuriating*, to put a riddle in Liish, because there *is* no context."

"Don't you think that might have been important to mention?" Cedar said, throwing his hands up.

"Sorry," Luca muttered. "Next time *you* read it."

"Fighting is not going to get us anywhere," S'Aris stepped in. "He must have had a reason for choosing the meanings he did."

She looked at Luca, and he was thrown off by the unexpected encouragement from this quarter. He pointed at one glyph.

"This one means Death. It's one of the few that has only one meaning, because, it's…well, *Death*."

"And then you worked out from there?" the Witch asked.

"More or less," Luca said.

"That's rather brilliant," S'Aris said.

"Thanks," Luca replied, still not trusting her newfound appreciation.

Jæyd, watching quietly, noticed a strange flicker across

Luca's face, reminiscent of when she had first reunited with her friend at the Crescent Temple. He had been hiding something from her, his possession of the Demonhärt, and had evaded her then, but he would not do so now or again. She fixed her gaze on him.

"Luca?" the elf asked in her sweetest melodious voice. "Is there something more you would like to tell us?"

Luca glared at her. A flicker of worry tickled the elf's stomach. Luca could be cantankerous, but his mood swings became worse when the Demonhärt gained sway over him. Luca saw the concern in her eyes and tried to smile.

"It's nothing, I think," he reassured her. "I have a feeling."

"What sort of feeling?" Cedar demanded.

"Like my head is about to explode with dragon flame and my toes are going to fall off," Luca said. "I don't know. It's just a feeling. Don't you ever get those?"

"I do, and usually I should pay more attention to them," Cedar said, controlling his tone with effort.

Luca glared but kept the retort from jumping out of his mouth; instead he paused and chose his words with care. "I don't like that this riddle is in Lii. I think you're right: we're being toyed with, and we don't have time for that. Too much is at stake, and he's making light of it."

"What choice do we have?" Jæyd asked, knowing her words were small comfort, true though they were.

"And I like that least of all," Luca said.

Jæyd shared his feeling, but she attempted a confident smile. "When have we ever allowed such a small thing to deter us, my friend?" She put a hand on his shoulder. "Come, tell us the other meanings of these words of Lii. We have not gotten this far to be thwarted."

DEATH'S FIRST CALL

Death was sitting in the library, in the chair which was the most comfortable, because over the spans of His existence He had carved and guided it to all the right contours, when He felt the warning tingle of a person ready to be guided through the next part of their cycle.

His heart clenched in His chest, and for a moment, He was afraid it was *her,* then realized it was not and felt a small measure of shame - Death was supposed to be impartial. He had been watching the beckoning light that those who served Him called *candle* grow brighter and brighter the farther she strayed from the Guardians. It was still bright, but not bright enough. She had time left to her. Which meant it was another.

He looked down at the book He was reading and toyed with the idea of sending Fynairhon or Reviel in His stead. The feeling grew stronger, until it was like standing too close to a fire, and Death realized this was someone He should see to personally.

He set the book down and made His way down to the stables. His beautiful Akhal-Teke horse was called Halalen, meaning *starfall* in the forgotten tongue of the Desert People who built the city which became the ruins of Larnn, before the time of Damon Rok or even Dymitri Spyne.

"We have a long journey and must make all haste," Death told the horse, who understood the words though it lacked the capacity for speech.

It was times like these when Death wished He had the foresight necessary to include a clause in the creation of His Realm to provide loopholes. The pleasures of life such as sunlight, eating, sleeping, exertion of physical effort to move from point A to point B, and the creation of family were grand things for breaking the monotony of the repeating Cycles of Forever, and Death would not be denied this simply because He was Death, and so He had stipulated these pleasures would remain in His Realm.

Before He was known as Death, He was Northirion Fynstaer, and by the Builders, He deserved some recompense for His service. In His Realm, He was unburdened by the realities - such as Time and distance - of other realms, and by this He could see more; by the same token, in His Realm He could not circumvent His own version of those realities simply because it now suited Him, which made such things as horses necessary. But sometimes that compensation was a burden He would rather forgo.

Saddling His mount, Death took off for the shores of the Great Waters and the piers. Once there, He set Halalen loose to make his way back to the stables, and untied the boat that would take Him across the Great Water to the Wall between His Realm and others. The small craft sped over the water, sending spray back into His face. Far from being annoyed, Death found the sensation refreshing.

Arriving in one of the many realms of the living, traveling became immensely easier. No longer bound by the constraints of distance and speed, Death appeared precisely where He was needed. The house was a smoking ruin. Men in White and men in red uniforms milled around or stood in attentive ranks.

Death took a moment to observe the Men of the Rose. He could see through what the Sorcerer had done to them, to the people they were, and the people they would return to at the moment their life ended and they came to Him. Death shook His head. In countless years, He had never come up with a way to convey to the man-who-was-now-the-Sorcerer that he was going about this all wrong.

The fact of the matter was, should the Sorcerer wish to be reunited with his wife and son, all he had to do was embrace Death. After so many millennia, it would be a comfort to be released from the endless Cycle he had created and maintained with his sorcery. *Perhaps* Aethsiths *will get through to him*, Death thought without much hope. *If the Guardians ever manage to find her.*

Death continued into the remnants of the house, past smashed stone and glass, and wood lying in splinters around shattered doors and furniture. The Witch waited for Him with an impatient expression on her face.

"What took You so long?" she demanded in a rough, throaty voice.

Death resisted the urge to roll His eyes. Witches were so overbearing at times; it took a saint with more patience than any one man could ever hope to possess to deal with them. Instead of berating her for her rudeness, Death tried to be understanding. She had, after all, just died.

"What happened here?" He asked.

"What do You think happened here?" the Witch

snapped. "Cedar Jal and his interfering Guardians happened, and then the Men in White happened. Then a fyr-spell went wrong, and…" The dark-skinned, white-haired goblin woman waved her hand at the mess surrounding her.

"I see," Death said. "Well, I'm sure you know how this works. Are you ready to go?"

"Not a bit," the Witch glared harder. "I have work to do."

"As do I," He reminded her, His voice hardening ever so slightly. The question had been meant as a nicety, a courtesy, nothing more binding, but it seemed she needed reminding of that.

Immediately she became more deferential, though not by as much as He would have preferred. "Of course. But my work is Your work at this time."

Death sighed. *It is always so taxing when people try to weasel out of this*, He thought.

"You know that is impossible," He told her, holding out His hand, willing her to take it.

She crossed her arms and smiled at Him smugly. "Not if you're a Witch, Northirion Fynstaer."

Now Death did roll His eyes. Blackrobes liked to use that name when dealing with Him, perhaps due to the outdated and erroneous belief that if one knew the true name of a person or thing, they had control and power over it. Or perhaps it was because they thought they could impress Him with their knowledge the Way of Things of the past. Or maybe, it was like a mother using the full given name of a disobedient child in the hopes they would obey forthwith. It never worked.

"I think we should leave now," He told her. "I was in the middle of a particularly good book."

The Witch gaped at Him for a moment, then closed

her mouth with a dark look. "You were in the middle of a *particularly good book*? Oh, I'm sorry to inconvenience You then. I was merely in the middle of trying to maintain the Balance of the worlds and keep the Sorcerer from snuffing out the Path in this one, but that can be dropped now, in light of Your *particularly* good book."

Death sighed and gave a helpless shrug. "What do you want Me to do?"

"You know the girl Ria?" the Witch asked.

"Of course," Death replied. "What about her now?"

"I sent her home." The Witch told Him this with an understated pride.

"Good for you," Death said, and though He was pleased, He didn't want to swell her head further. "What does that have to do with Me?"

"She will have to come back here, of course," the Witch continued.

"And?" Death drew the word out, hoping to encourage her to state her point, concisely and with simple words.

"And there is her mother to take into account," the Witch said, a smug twist to her mouth.

Death heaved a great sigh and rubbed His brow. He felt a headache coming on. *Why does all of this have to involve Me? Why couldn't things just be simple for once?*

"What are you proposing, M'Rella D'Ral of Lii?" Death asked and cringed when He realized he had used the exact same tactic as she had on Him.

"The Way of Things is not done for me yet," the Witch stated.

Death held back a sigh. He half suspected the Witches used that phrase - *the Way of Things* - for their own personal benefit, without relation to anything real or concrete. Born of Fyr and Ayr, the shifting, changing, mutable essences, the Way of Things was never still and ever-changing, and the Witches exploited it to its full potential for their own ends.

Just as she is doing in this case, Death grumbled to Himself. *Who is to say the Way of Things is one way or another, or will be one way or another? Surely she does not know any more than I.* And yet, while the Way of Things was related to, and approximated Death's own magyc, they were different and distinct. *So it was, and so it is, and so it will be. Until the End of All Time, And the End of Worlds.*

"If it makes You feel better, I have made the necessary preparations, the amendments to the Contract, if You please."

Death did not please, yet the Witch held something out. Death didn't touch it, but He looked at it for a long time, assessing it with a silent gaze. The Witch shook her hand impatiently, demanding He take what she held.

"Just until the time runs out, during which time I will continue my part in the Way of Things," she coaxed. "Then I will come with You willingly."

Death wanted to remind her that her willingness did not matter. He wanted to tell her that everything was under control, and that the Balance would be restored without any further extraordinary measures. He wanted to tell her that her staying here after the true end of her cycle was not the answer. The words would not come.

He wanted to remain outside of it, as He believed His Mandate required, but He could not stand by a second time. Now, He had to put His preparations into action so this situation could be more rapidly resolved, resulting in a faster restoration of the Balance. *At which time I can return to My book,* Death thought wistfully.

"We do not have much time," the Witch added in a quiet voice. "For me or this land."

"Let me think," Death said, trying to keep the bite out

of His voice.

In the end, He was forced to admit the Witch had taken the decision out of His hands, as mortals were wont to do. Still, He needed to keep a professional attitude, and at least the semblance of being in charge of the current circumstances. He glanced again at what the Witch held.

It was a clever piece of Witchery and showed just how skilled she was. The object that held the spell didn't even belong in this world and how she had come by it - Death shook His head. That did not concern Him. He sighed and held out His hand. The Witch smiled and placed the object carefully in His palm, and He looked at it with traces of astonishment or what might be called awe if He were a lesser person.

It was called a pocket-watch in the world of its origination. The cover was inlaid with a fantastic design, a dragon curled around a spherical world. It opened to a round face, with three gold hands, the numbers one through twelve depicted in dark gems. Gears were visible behind the glass in the center. The chain had been severed, leaving just a finger's length. On the back, a small bolt for winding the gears pressed into His palm.

The spell the Witch had woven into it was not visible but no less tangible. Like the beads the members of the Coven wore around their waists to store spells for a later point when they may not have enough time to create the temperamental things, the watch held a powerful magyc, though Death sensed it was yet incomplete.

It was a spell to counteract the effects of Time while still allowing Time to pass. The Witch's body was dead; whatever had motivated it had passed. But this would allow it to go on for however much time the spell held.

Usually an hourglass would have been used, giving the user hours. With this other-world object, the witch would have - Death didn't even know how much more time: days? A week? More? *She had prepared for this eventuality a long time ago*, Death saw, and even He was impressed with her mastery of the Way of Things.

"How much time?" He inquired, as if this were pertinent to the fundamental issue at hand. It was not. The Cycle would be broken by a minute as much as a year. *As it has already been broken.*

This was troubling. He finally gave into the nagging thought that it was time to put His preparations into more concrete form. He had plans, and if He could manage to pull them off and bring them to fruition without use of His own powers, He considered that somehow circumvented breaking His immortal bindings and Mandate. *Semantics and technicalities.*

For that, He would need a Witch, a Blackrobe. He considered M'Rella, but she was going to be busy, and she was too overbearing for His taste. He did not dwell on those few left at the Coven for a single moment - the Blackrobes there would not help; even the faction of V'Ronica, the *Eohl-din,* would only pay lip-service and give tokens. He could send the Traitor V'Ronica herself, but that would defeat the point if He meant to put things more to the right as opposed to skew them further.

And there has to be a way to do it without straining the Balance further. He started as the answer struck Him. *There was one...*

"Are you listening to me?" the Witch snapped.

"What?" Death turned to her.

"I said, sixty days," the Witch told Him. "One for each degree on the face."

Death did not know what she intended to do in those days, and He did not want to know. The less He knew, the better He would feel. At least He tried to tell Himself that. *To Watch Over the Walls, and to Nurture and Oversee the Cycle -*

that was His Mandate, given to Him by the Builders.

Perhaps a small nudge, nothing more than a breath in the Winds of the Worlds, in the grand scheme of things, or the Way of Things in their parlance...

"I must keep the Balance," Death said quietly and drew in a deep breath to explain further, but the Witch gave a tetchy grunt.

"Do all who try to take their fate into their own hands receive the same lecture I'm getting about Your Mandate and such?" she asked. "Or am I special?"

Death refused to give her the satisfaction of a reaction to her not-so-subtle rebuke. "In these times of uncertainty where the Balance is called into question, we will be called to unusual actions. This is one of these."

"Does that mean yes?" she asked, hope lighting her eyes.

Death regarded her. "Perhaps."

The Witch narrowed her eyes, and a shrewd smile pulled her lips open. "You want something in return."

Death gave a curt nod, though He knew not what He needed at this precise moment. He cast out for the memory, the memory of her candle lighting, the steady flame telling Him she was bound for His land. Each time a candle was lit, in that brief instant, He was granted some foresight in the where, how, and why of their fate. That brief glimpse gave Him the information to help Him determine the precise moment He should intervene.

His part required a little more thought. They were - all of them - getting in not over their heads exactly, but over their expectations. They were not prepared, and in no way could they ever be prepared. *And that is exactly what I will give them - preparation.*

"The Witches are said to carry magyc in the beads of their belts."

M'Rella said nothing, and He took her silence to mean He was not wrong. "I require three from you."

It was a good number, neither too many or too few. "Which ones?"

Death looked at her belt. The beads were numerous and all different colors, shapes, and sizes, accumulated over the Witch's substantial lifetime. He had no idea what any of them did.

"I need something to give more time - which I doubt you'll have a problem with," He added dryly. "I need something to escape. I need something to make another do as you will. And above all, I need them to be potent and to work."

The Witch gave Him an irritated look. "You think I keep weak, dud spells on my belt?"

Death shrugged, and the Witch bent to examine her beads. He knew she knew it like her own name, and her intent study was somewhat disconcerting. *What was she looking for?* As if in answer to His question, the Witch spoke.

"I have many spells, and if I had time, I could make you something exactly to Your requests. As I do not have time, I will have to give You what I have that most closely approximates what You've asked for."

She pulled three beads off the belt on her dead body and held them out. A bright orb of silver with a dusting of white sparkles sat with a dark green oval circled by two lighter green stripes, and between the two sat a blood-red bead with countless facets like an insect's eye.

"The silver one will pull one outside the reach of Time. The green one is a compelling spell - it will make a Thrall of someone, but it is not forever, and they cannot come to harm while under this spell. The red one will send you to the last place you felt safe. I caution you that the fact of your safety is not the point, only your feeling on it."

Death accepted the beads, still not entirely at peace with what He was doing. The Witch remained silent, which was credit to her intelligence. He might have changed His mind if she was going to be smug.

Death turned the pocket watch over and began to wind it with slow deliberate motions, imbuing it with the next component of the spell, which could be described more or less as His permission for her to remain without the bounds of His Realm as long as the clock ran and sealing it with His Mark. Then He handed it back to the Witch.

"There is something missing from the spell," He told her. "It won't go into effect without the final piece, and you cannot linger long between worlds. And I *cannot* take you back the opposite way, so don't ask."

"I know," she assured Him. "I have plans for that."

"And do you understand it must be done by a person who *truly* serves Me, not just any priest?" Death asked. "One who knows both the white and the black?"

She smiled and patted Him on the shoulder, her face as earnest as her words. "I know. Don't worry about me."

Death gave a final nod and left the Witch standing over her own body, while He walked past the Men in White without being seen, the Witch's beads clutched in His hand. He thought about His book, the story He had been so fascinated with only moments ago, and found He had lost the desire to continue reading.

Who needs books when Life and Death are so complex and engrossing? He blinked and was back at the shores close to the Wall to wait for the next part to His preparations.

MAN OF TONGUES PART I

Timo's whole body ached from the dull throbbing in his head to the raw tenderness in his fingertips. His eyes smarted, the image of the ancient message still burned into his retinas. He sat on the mat, glad not to have to hold his body up, and watched the others pace the room, faces alight with determination and excitement.

The Daleman's usually placid lake of equilibrium was choppy and dark, and he was quick to find fault with his companions' optimism. Though he kept his thoughts to himself, Cedar noticed the scowl on Timo's face and turned to face him. The full intensity of the black-haired Guardian's piercing gaze irritated Timo even more.

"What?" he snapped.

Cedar blinked in surprise, and a twist of guilt sprang into Timo's gut.

"Are you alright?" Cedar asked.

The Daleman sighed. They would never be able to

understand, being outsiders. The deepening cloud of mistrust was tangible, hanging above the chieftain's home like a choking blanket. Though Timo had been all but blinded by the golden light, he had seen Doman come in during his - *what did the Witch call it?* - episode. Timo felt a belated flash of gratitude for Jæyd's quick-thinking action of leading the intruding man out.

Timo knew they wouldn't have much time before Doman returned and requested that they leave. The Dalefolk tolerated magyc much as they tolerated the other peoples of this world: they did not deny their existence, but wished them to stay far away and not to intrude on the Dalefolk's own existence. Even the descendants of the First King, with their *Ándahs' Éllahd* - the "second-sight" - did not indulge in the gift if they could help it, and when they did, it was quietly and discreetly.

Cedar was still looking at Timo with a questioning squint, waiting for an answer.

"Oh gods, he's not having second thoughts, is he?" Luca piped up, his eyes never leaving the paper covered in the writing Timo did not entirely remember making. "That's a comforting turn of events."

For a split instant, Timo wished a horrible fate on his small friend, but then the ill feeling vanished. *This had little to do with the here and now. This had to do with before.*

It was as Timo had feared - coming back had only stirred up the uncertainties from when he had left. *This was why I became a Guardian in the first place*, he told himself. *The reason I forsook my home, my family, the values of my father, and the security of what was known for the terrible, mercurial unknown.*

The Daleman had no desire to dwell on that, any more than to dwell on the possibility that the Man of Tongues was a siren's call to lure them to the rocks of defeat and leave them stranded. The others were looking at him, waiting for him to speak. He could only shrug and nod at the paper, which Luca read out again.

They debated through the small hours of the morning, questioning Luca and the Witch, and Luca explained his long, overly-well thought out reasoning behind choosing the meaning for each word. By the time he had done this for the third time, Timo understood the look on Luca's face when Liish was mentioned. It was enough to give even the most steadfast thinkers a headache.

When dawn's light crept in, the knock Timo was expecting came at the door. The others looked to him for guidance.

"Come," the Daleman said in a heavy tone.

The door opened and Doman entered, his face set against revealing any thought or emotion, but Timo knew what was in his mind, what would be in the mind of any true Daleman. Timo stood, though every bone in his body protested, and his muscles felt like mud. Doman did not blink as he gazed at the Guardians.

"I understand I cannot ask for an explanation of what happened," he said. "But you cannot stay here any longer."

The Guardians' faces fell, but Timo was confused. *He did not say we were no longer welcome.* Timo saw Luca get ready to mouth off, and he cuffed Luca on the shoulder to stop him. No protocol existed for this - and he chose his words like walking on the last ice of spring, seeing a faint hope that he may make it across, and the chieftain may yet retain a sliver of willingness to help them.

"I understand, and thank you for the honor you have shown us," Timo said. "I offer sincere apology if we have disturbed you."

Doman nodded, the only sign of his troubled thought was a small frown. "You spoke much during the night," he said. *So he had been listening.*

Perhaps unaware he was breaking protocol, or perhaps he did not care, Cedar stepped up to the chieftain, snatching the riddle from Luca on the way, and held the paper out to Doman.

"Does this mean anything to you?"

Doman looked as though he'd rather eat thorns than look at it, but his good grace prevented him from such. He gave it a cursory glance. His brow furrowed more deeply, but he shook his head. Cedar deflated, his shoulders slumping.

"Ask him if he knows of any other lake," Luca took the opportunity to be snide.

"There is one Lake," Timo said firmly. "We must cross it now and no more burden the descendants of the Seventh King with our presence."

With her knowledge of the Dalefolk, Jæyd understood the gravity of the situation and made ready to leave at once, bowing to Doman with the proper formality. He looked uncomfortable with her quiet acceptance, as though bitterness or resentment would give him some justification. He appeared to struggle with himself, and then came to some understanding, but whether it was surrender or vanquishment, it was hard to tell.

"There is another lake," Doman said, his voice so soft Timo almost did not hear it.

It was only Jæyd's sharp gaze fixing on the chieftain that told Timo he had not imagined anything. He stared at Doman, trying to figure out which lake the man could be referring to.

"The *mandalin*," the chieftain elucidated.

Timo straightened, his eyes trained on the other man's. "That is not a real place."

"What's not a real place?" Luca asked, looking between the two Dalemen.

"The *mandalin* is a lake in a story. It floats on a cloud above the Dale and is home to the Queen of the Water people, those known as merpeople," Timo explained. "And everyone knows where it is. The Elderidge - the tallest and oldest of the Dalemounts."

"And probably the scariest and most likely to kill us," Luca said. "We'll be going there now I'm guessing?"

"It's the only thing we have to go on," Timo said, with a glance at Doman. "The Elderidge is on the other side of the Lake and is flanked by two mountains."

"Wait a moment," S'Aris said, her words coming faster as she pieced her thoughts together. "In Liish, words all have several meanings depending on the context and other things. Perhaps..." she trailed off, tapping her chin as she thought. "Perhaps it is several riddles in one. After we get to the Elderidge, if we translate the words again, with their different meanings, it will lead us to this *mandalin*."

"But how would we know if we were translating it correctly?" Cedar wondered. "It sounds like we could be going off on a wild goose chase far too easily."

"The words rely on the context," Luca explained. "This is the translation which makes the most sense based on *this* context. When we get to the mountain, the mountain itself may become the context for the riddle."

"That's brilliant," S'Aris said.

"Thank you," Luca replied and smirked.

"This time I was referring to the person who wrote the riddle," S'Aris said.

Luca looked put out and stomped towards the door. "Well, what are we waiting for? Let's go visit those old gods in the oldest and baddest mountain."

Timo made to go after the other Guardians, then turned back to Doman, who gazed at him warily.

"Thank you," Timo told the chieftain. "The

descendants of the Seventh King are most generous."

"I will pass on your thanks to my family," Doman said. "Fair skies, fair tides to you, Timo of the Third King."

"And to you," Timo said. He hesitated, then lifted his chin. "And may the Path keep you."

Timo half stepped through the door when the chieftain spoke again.

"The fastest way to reach the Elderidge will be by dori. You should ask Nano if he can take you. His is the largest boat and will fit you and all your companions."

Timo looked at him, surprised by the volunteered help. He still had mixed feelings about coming back, but perhaps he did not give his own people enough credit. He bowed his head. Doman returned with the stiff, formal Dalefolk bow. He said nothing further as Timo joined the others.

"We will go by dori," Timo announced.

"What's a dori?" Luca whispered.

Jæyd pointed. The boats the Dalefolk used to fish the waters of the Lake and cross the expanse of water bobbed serenely. A rowboat with simple lines and a narrow, flat bottom, planked up with wide boards along sides which flared out, known for seaworthiness and rowing ease, they embodied the spirit of the Dalefolk.

"We must find a man called Nano," Timo said as he set off for the water.

"And how are we going to do that?" Luca asked, determined to be querulous.

"He will have the largest boat," Timo said.

Luca muttered something crude, but dutifully followed the Daleman to the fleet of dories bobbing in the water. It wasn't hard to see the biggest boat - it was at least twice as long as the others and as the Guardians approached, they saw the reason for this.

"And I thought you were unnaturally tall," Luca said.

Nano was a hand above seven feet, with long white blond hair to his waist, a beard of the same color plaited on his chest, and blue eyes hinting of green. He was working on his boat, knocking in the wooden planking with an odd shaped hammer, but when he saw the group coming up with Timo in the lead, he put down the tool and bowed.

"Greetings, Timo of the Third King," Nano said in a voice that sounded like rocks shifting under the pounding of the sea, looking down at him with a serene expression.

"Greetings, Nano," Timo replied, returning the bow. "I have spoken with Doman, and he has advised me to ask if you would take us across the Lake to the Elderidge."

Nano looked up at the sky, eyes narrowed, and breathed in a great lungful of air, keeping it for a moment, as if gleaning the secrets it held, then let it out. "The weather will be fair all day, though the water is still cold," he said. "It is a long journey, but because Doman has advised it, I will take you."

"Thank you," Timo said. "We are ready to depart at once."

"It will take some time to prepare," Nano said. "I will bring back fish tonight."

His manner was slow and steady, and infused a calm in the space around him. The Guardians helped him haul piles of nets into the boat, then loaded themselves in around the nets. Jæyd and Luca sat in the middle, Timo and Nano took the back, and Cedar and S'Aris were in front. All held oars, patterned off the webbed flipper of some creature, with triangular fins up the shaft. After the Daleman taught the foreigners how to row properly, instead of countering the efforts of the others, they augmented each other and the dori sped across the water.

The Lake was still, but currents pulled at the boat. Luca looked uncomfortable, and Timo knew he was thinking about something under him, lurking unseen and unfamiliar. Years ago, Timo would have laughed at him, unconcerned with anything in the water. But Timo had left and was more a stranger to this place than he would like to admit.

He concentrated on pulling the oar in time with the others. Kelpies, Nixies, serpents, and other things which lived in the water and wreaked havoc on those that walked the land shouldn't bother Luca - he was from Isos, a City sired by the sea.

This lake, however, guarded by these mountains which could be living things crafted of stone and time, was nothing like the sea, and that set Luca on edge, so much so he flinched when the spray hit him. Around the middle of the day, Nano pulled out some food, offering it to them, and they stopped to eat the coarse bread and hard cheese. Timo ate his simple meal, enjoying the gentle motion of the drifting boat.

Luca splashed some water on his face, being careful not to let his fingers linger in the water any longer than they had to. Dark shapes below them played tricks on the eyes, and Luca turned to look at blue sky above so he wouldn't have to look at them.

Jæyd touched him on the arm. He looked at her, his face already protesting what she would want him to do, namely, look at something in the water. The elf was pointing down, her face alight with rare wonder. Luca glanced down, and his eyes widened. Timo followed their gaze. Swimming in lazy circles not more than a dozen feet below in the clear water was a mermaid.

Her tail was blue and green, flashing in the light, and tresses of the same color hung over her shoulders, waving in the water. She smiled, then blew a kiss at them, and with a flick of her tail, she was off. Luca looked at Jæyd, bemused awe overtaking his trepidation for a brief moment.

"She's prettier than the fish-maids I grew up hearing about," he said. "But I thought the merfolk were supposed to live in the *mandalin*," he added with a pointed glance at Timo.

"In legends, their Queen dwells in the *mandalin*," Timo corrected. "The fish folk go where they will, in river, lake, or sea."

Luca looked like he didn't like the sound of that.

"I do not think she plans to cause mischief," Jæyd said, giving him a comforting smile.

"How do you know that?"

"The same way I know all people," she replied.

"You could see her Aura?" Luca asked, dark eyes flashing with curiosity. "What did it look like?"

"Water," the elf said, and it was hard to tell if she was being serious or not.

"And what did it tell you?" Luca pressed.

"That she was like the water itself. She can read those around her; she knows when to approach and when to hold back. The merfolk are powerful, but shy."

"And bring good luck," Nano added, nodding sagely. "Your journey is blessed this day."

They said no more as they rowed. Soon, mist obscured the far end of the Dale, even though the sun was high in the sky. They rowed to this bank, trusting Nano to steer them true, and eventually a shape began to appear, then fade, and appear again. The mist grew thicker, the air still, watching their approach with hidden eyes

On no apparent signal or sign, the huge Daleman turned his dori, and then the gentle lapping of waves on the shore reached their ears. The sandy shore materialized, and the dori came aground with a crunch, paused, and was lifted by the next swell.

"This is as far as the water can take you," Nano said. "From here the Mountains will carry you."

"Thank you," Timo said. "Fair tides, fair skies to you Nano."

"And to you, Timo of the Dale."

A rush of gratitude for the simple acceptance heartened Timo as the Guardians disembarked, splashing through the shallows to dry ground. Within four paces from the water, the mist thinned, then cleared completely, revealing this side of the Dale with crystal perfection. The Mountain in front of them dwarfed its companions, its peak lost in a swath of clouds.

"The Elderidge," Timo said, his voice hushed and respectful. "The two beside it are Damante and Irn."

"And there is our arrow," Cedar said, pointing at an old road into the mountain.

His shoulders slumped as he looked up to where it was lost in the rock and stone and trees, and the vast expanse of the mountain still above it.

"Let's go," Luca said. "Despite what Nano insinuated, that mountain isn't carrying anyone anywhere."

Jæyd ran easily behind Cedar and Timo, and while Luca tried to keep pace with them, he was sluggish. S'Aris stayed at his side, lending the dark Guardian moral support with her pale form flying lightly at his side. Though the distance looked not too far, it was more deceptive than a chameleon. The more they ran, the farther the mysterious mountain seemed.

After they had been going for an hour, Cedar stopped and bent double, his hands on his knees as he heaved deep breaths. Luca took advantage of the time for a reprieve of the grueling pace and dropped onto the ground with a groan of fatigue.

"The Dale may not be the grandest place, but it's not small either," Cedar said. "And I think it grows with every step we take."

"How much further?" S'Aris asked, wiping the sweat streaming down her face.

"To the foothills of the Elderidge?" Timo said. "Another hour at this pace. To the Man of Tongues? It is anyone's guess."

Cedar glanced up at the stone giant towering into the sky. When you stood among them, inside them, these mountains were more formidable than the Mountains between Demona and Prrus, and the Elderidge was king of these.

"That is quite a mountain," Cedar said softly.

"Naturally, we have to find this Man of Tongues in the largest mountain here," Luca remarked. "How do we get ourselves into these stupid, mad missions?"

"By being stupid, mad people," Jæyd said. "Come. We have a Man of Tongues to find."

"If he is a man," Luca muttered, his face weary as he stood.

"He is a man," Timo said, to convince himself as well as the others. "Albeit a strange one."

"Standing here talking will not carry us any closer," Jæyd said. "Cedar, if you have got your breath back…"

"Right," the tall Guardian said, brushing sweat-damp hair from his forehead. "Let's go."

Timo took up the pace again, trying to banish any doubts regarding the wisdom of further pursuing this course and the Man of Tongues. *Perhaps it was wiser to turn back now and cut our losses.* But that was impossible, and Timo was left hoping Luca knew what he was doing with this riddle.

THE ASSASSIN OF SPYNE

The moon hung low in the sky, magnified by the Mountains until it was a gold plate floating in a sea of ink. Scraggly clouds blocked most of the stars but could not stifle the moonlight. Muted sounds of revelry pattered through the night as though afraid if someone heard, it would be stopped at once.

Liæna Nati of Spyne entered the northern city of J'Erd as a shadow of the night, a figure hidden underneath a dark cloak. The Lost City was an apt name for this poor, forgotten place. It did not truly deserve the name "city" for it was more a motley amalgamation of collections of buildings separated by the sheer stone of the mountainside, joined by worn trails not wide enough to be granted the dignity of the name *road*. If Samnara was where people went to find a new life, J'Erd was where they came to die.

Liæna made her way up one of the few steep streets which was actually paved for most of its length. Her destination loomed above her, a tavern built in drunken tiers up the near-vertical side of the mountain. A sign, the fresh paint glaring on the eyes, depicted six indistinct figures and one man standing in front with a roguish smile and a wink on his face. She took a deep breath, stilling her beating heart, reminding herself of the Triad of Strength. *Conviction. Perseverance. Serenity.* At the moment, she lacked all of the three.

She thought of the Guardian with purple and green streaks in his hair and the matching jacket. *Luca Lorisson.* Even his name was pleasant on her tongue and in her mind. He intrigued her, and the call of delving into the mysteries of his world was hard for her to ignore. *But I cannot get distracted so near to the end. Just a few more hours and it will be over.*

She couldn't stop a small smile coming to her lips at what he would think if he knew the thoughts in her mind. She tried to focus on the here and now, but with the tumult of her thoughts and memories, it was difficult not to dwell on their conversation after his mysterious journey to his past in Isos on their way to the Crescent Temple only a week ago.

The assassin tried to remember the last time she had let anyone else inside the wall of duty and commitment she had built after her father had been murdered. Berria and S'Aris had broken through, after a fashion. They were companions, partners in a shared mission, and had become friends even, but Liæna had never imagined they would be part of her future. She had never imagined a *future* beyond her mission until Luca came along.

In short order, this Guardian had found some way through the impermeable cracks and captured her attention. As much as she tried to forget him, he managed to pop back in when she least expected it. *Conviction. Perseverance. Serenity.*

The thing was, what he had said had shattered the iron logic she had held onto for years.

And what do the assassins say about forgiveness? Luca had asked. Liæna had barely been able to bring herself to answer, the words salt to a wound, when they should have been a balm. *The Triad of Forgiveness: Look, understand, and* Solu, *a word that means not fight, yet neither succumb. It translated roughly to* acceptance *or* peace.

Solu. She had tried to find it, for months after the fire destroyed the only home she had ever known. Every time she had closed her eyes, she prayed for it, but she only saw fire, and the rose, half black and half red. She saw the smear of blood on the ground, all that was left of her father, and the calm center he'd promised would come with *Solu* never came to her.

Night after night, she fought to attain it until she no longer believed it was possible. She had thought for a long time, thought about her father, and everything he had taught her. She'd thought about the Theory of Three and what it had taught her.

Then, as though on a message from the gods, the Triad of Weakness had popped into her mind. *Hate. Ignorance. Indolence.* She hated the people who had done this. She was ignorant of who they were or why they had done what they had. And she was doing nothing about it by sitting in the old, creaky bed of the Magister of City's Orphanage in Balmar.

In order to preempt her decline into weakness, nine-year-old Liæna had done the only thing she could. She could not stop hating the monsters who had taken her father, but she would no longer wallow in indolence or ignorance. Thus had begun the quest which had consumed her every waking and sleeping moment for the last 22 years.

And now the resolution to the quest was staring her in

the face, and she wasn't sure she was ready for it. *Conviction. Perseverance. Serenity.*

Liæna looked down at the letter she held from the Maker of Marks. It was brief, but the few words took the assassin to the brink of knowledge, a hair's breadth beyond ignorance. As she looked into the black abyss of the future, the thought occurred to her that ignorance might be the easier to bear of two evils. *Conviction. Perseverance. Serenity.*

She unfolded the note again, afraid the words would have changed, or that she had somehow read them incorrectly. The note said the same thing it had the last time she'd read it and all the times before that.

Dear Miss Nati,

Before he died, I saw some of what the Man in White was before he became the pawn of the Sorcerer. If the leader of these Men is truly the same man you are seeking, then that man is in J'Erd, in a tavern called the Seventh Son, under the name Moun Zette. I would caution you he is a dangerous man, but I think you already know that. Wherever your path takes you, I hope you find Solu. L.B.

It still surprised her how worldly the Maker was. How he knew about the Desert People and the epics of Damian Rok, she couldn't even begin to guess. It reminded her of her father, the way he could bring up a story or parable from any one of seven different lands whenever she had a question about anything.

"Papu, I am almost there," the assassin whispered, rubbing the bejeweled pin in the shape of a scorpion on her shirt, her fingers enjoying the roughness of the gems and the comfort it gave.

Hardening her resolve, she continued and a few more steps brought her to the entrance of the tavern. Liæna pushed the hood from her eyes and stepped through the door of the Seventh Son. It was as tall and narrow on the inside as it was on the outside. The bar took up half the first story, and above it were three levels of balconies crowded with rickety tables and chairs. In front of the bar, only half the tables were occupied. Most of the people wore hoods like Liæna, and she blended in without strain.

The room was lit with blue-fire lanterns, the luminescent stone found in the foothills between Ghor and the Wasteland giving a soft, flickering light which was used throughout J'Erd. The floor was worn and the bar was carved with the artistic ramblings of a hundred years of drunk men. Liæna waited for the barman to serve a white-haired man with a flaming red beard and silver rings on his thick fingers, then coughed to get the barman's attention.

"What can I get for you, missy?" he asked as he came over to Liæna.

"Nothing to drink, just some information," the assassin said.

"It'll cost you the same," the bartender replied, looking at her with blue, wary eyes shadowed by a furrowed brow.

Liæna pulled out a silver Katon and slid it across the pitted bar. The bartender did not look impressed. She sighed and pulled out another, and then another.

"How much does a drink cost in these parts?" Liæna snapped.

"Depends how old the bottle," the bartender said. His smile showed two gold teeth.

"I'm looking for a man named Moun Zette," she stated.

The bartender said nothing, and the assassin took out a silver Fenn. The man reached for it, but she held it down with her finger, sliding it back and forth with an enticing smile at the corner of her mouth.

"I might have heard the name," the bartender said, tugging on his ear.

Liæna pushed the coin a little closer but kept her finger

on it. The bartender leaned across the bar. He smelled like beer and smoke and something less savory.

"A man who calls himself that comes here now and then," the bartender whispered to her.

"And where can I find him now?" The coin inched closer.

"He might be in for dinner in a bit," he said. "He always sits in that corner table."

Liæna glanced to where he indicated. The table was as yet unoccupied. She nodded to the man and flipped the Fenn at him. He caught it with a fumble and tucked it into the pouch on his belt. The assassin walked to the table, seated herself with a view of the door, and prepared to wait.

She recognized him the instant he stepped over the threshold. Something in the set of his shoulders and the subtle grace with which he moved marked his physical prowess. Liæna sat up, her stomach clenching. She became lightheaded before she realized she wasn't breathing. The figure came closer, but stopped when he noticed the table was occupied.

Liæna gestured for him to join her. The figure hesitated, then took several more steps forward. Liæna waited until he stood beside the table before she spoke.

"Moun Zette?" the assassin asked, hoping her voice didn't waver.

"I am he," the figure acknowledged with a nod.

His voice was low and pleasant and not at all how Liæna expected him to sound. Her mind went blank, unsure if she should continue with her plan. *What was her plan? To confront him? To force a confession? To kill him?* She reminded herself that even if it looked and sounded like a man, a monster hid beneath.

"Sit," the assassin ordered.

Moun Zette complied, his hands in his lap, his head bowed so his hood obscured his face. This infuriated Liæna, and she fought to maintain her composure. *Conviction. Perseverance. Serenity.*

"Do you know who I am?" she asked, her voice flat in a mockery of the serenity she sought.

For a moment, the assassin thought the man was not going to answer. Then his chin lifted, and she looked upon his face. It was not easily apparent how old he was, but he was a handsome man, a blond beard defining a masculine jaw and strong, grey eyes. His nose was crooked, and a thin scar ran from the corner of his left brow to just below his eye. "Liæna, daughter of Nharen Nati."

Taken off guard, she blinked, and the shreds of the plan fled. "And do you know why I am here?" she asked, her heart beating in erratic thuds.

"To exact revenge for the murder of your father," Moun Zette said, his voice as even as hers.

Liæna remembered the way the Man in White in Balmar had known about what had happened to her father. This Moun Zette had the same uncanny knowledge they had, which confirmed her suspicions and also meant he had the answer to a single burning question.

"You know what happened that day and the reasons why," the assassin said.

"I do," the man replied.

"Tell me."

"No."

"Why not?"

"It is not for me to tell."

His voice was ominous, a warning not to travel any further down that path lingering in his light eyes. They were odd, too bright, yet haunted by shadow. Liæna shivered.

"Who are you, really?" the assassin asked, then realized too late she didn't want to know.

The man did not answer for a long time, and when he finally did answer, his voice had a thick, hollow sound to it. "Nobody."

The single word raised the hair on Liæna's arms and she knew, as surely as she knew she would die if she could not draw breath, that she was in danger. And not just in danger of losing her life. She was in danger of losing herself, becoming nobody, like the thing called Moun Zette in front of her. In an instant, her father's calm instruction filled her, and she knew she had a chance to save herself.

She stood, the movement fluid. Dancing on the balls of her feet, she banished all thought from her mind but for self-preservation, survival, and escape. Her eyes mapped the best route through the maze of bodies, chairs, and tables. Her heart pounded in strong, even thuds, sending adrenaline-spiked blood to every cell.

Light and color became so sharp she could walk upon them like a bridge. Each sound stood separate and distinct, the closest man chewing broth-soaked bread, the protest of a stool as someone shifted, the clink of coin being dropped onto soft flesh, the rough hawk as someone cleared their throat, and the purr of the scruffy cat dozing with one eye slitted open, the other closed permanently by an old wound. Smells crawled into her nose, thick and wet, beer and dust and sweat and tobacco.

"Sit down." His voice was loud in her heightened awareness, though Moun Zette spoke softly and did not look at her.

His head was bowed, and only half his face was visible, muscles lax. He looked as though he didn't have a care in world. Her body was urging her to flee, her skin tingling in protest that she wasn't moving. In a cold instant of epiphany, she saw her whole premise for avenging her father's death was never based on the Theory. She had molded the Theory to justify her desire, not formed her course of action per the Theory, as was right.

"Sit down," Moun Zette repeated.

Without knowing why, the assassin sat. Part of her was curious, but her mind was strangely devoid of anything articulate. She didn't know what to do now that the burning embers of anger, the desire for revenge, and slow burning hate had been extinguished in a heavy spring downpour.

The man sitting across from her watched with an impassive face as Liæna settled down on the edge of the chair. She thought of Luca and the way he saw through her and her justifications. *He would probably make some joke about it, and it would be so wrong but so right in the twisted way only he could manage.*

"Well, it appears I've come all this way for nothing," she heard herself say, the absurdly chipper, Luca-esque phrase threatening to send her into hysterics.

"Your friends will fail," the man told her.

Liæna was thrown further off balance by the non sequitur statement, the inflection suggesting the man was pointing out it was raining and she would get wet if she went outside. *This was not how this was supposed to happen.* The assassin waited for more, but the man just sat and looked at her. She was struck by the sudden cold thought that he was not breathing, and that he did not need to.

"Fail at what?"

"They cannot overcome the power of the Sorcerer."

"You don't know that," Liæna stated, the conviction automatic, but no longer unshakable.

"You do not know what you are going up against," Moun Zette continued as if she had not spoken.

"Why are you telling me this?"

"The world is built on balances, Liæna Nati. It is at a tipping point, and it has tipped too far for the Guardians to right it."

Faster than a striking snake, he grabbed her wrist, and through the cruel pressure of his fingers, thoughts and images were pressed into her mind. *Berria, unconscious, tied to a chair, blood seeping from a hundred wounds inflicted with inhuman precision, bones crushed inch by inch, the muscles around them swelling until the skin burst, flesh twisted and maltreated in small ways, compounded into wordless agony, suffering only Death could cure...*

The assassin tore out of the man's grip, breathing heavily and struggling to erase what she had seen. It didn't matter, the pictures kept coming back in greater detail.

"I don't believe," she whispered.

His silence only served to convince her of the truth of what he had shown her.

"I should never have left them," she said, heavy dread settling in her stomach. "I should have stayed with them at their side." *I was blind and selfish.*

"There is a way for you to stop their suffering," Moun Zette said.

Liæna suspected a trick and a trap before the man had finished the sentence, but she had no choice but to listen.

"The Placer of Pieces searches for a sword, a blade of Starheart, forged before Time began. The princes of Ghor wielded this sword, but it was lost in the Moonlight War."

Facts began to align in the assassin's mind, memory furnishing story and imagination connecting them in a chain of events, leading to the conclusion which fell from her mouth before she could stop it.

"You're Lan Holdun," she stated, an awed horror dawning on her face, and the final piece fell into place. "That's why you attacked Erridon during the peace talks at the end of the Moonlight War. You were to retrieve that sword."

The man did not deny it, nor did he confirm it. Again, his silence was testament to the truth behind the words.

"What do you want from me?" she asked. "I do not know where this blade is."

"The princess of Ghor never spoke of it?" Moun Zette or Lan Holdun inquired.

Liæna shook her head. "Never." She took a deep breath. A lie was like a blade - if it did more good to lie, then that was the right thing to do. *Conviction. Perseverance. Serenity.* "The princess and I were companions on the road, little more. I agreed to help her because I thought it would lead me closer to the answers I wanted. She had lost all ties to her family and did not speak of them. She carried no blade. She does not have what you seek."

Lan Holdun regarded her impassively. She held his gaze, concentrating on the truth within the lie - the princess carried no blade.

"Then we are done," Lan Holdun rose and turned away without another word.

The picture of Berria's battered body leaped into Liæna's mind. She didn't have the vaguest concept of a plan; she only knew she would figure something out. Before Holdun had taken two steps to the door, Liæna rose as well, drawing her scimitar, the ring of the metal reassuring.

No one in the tavern paid any attention, but Lan Holdun stopped and gazed at the sword, and for the first time an emotion stirred. What was it? It was not fear, or desire. Could it be sorrow? The assassin didn't think so, but she couldn't be certain.

"How did you come by that blade?" The question was not the one she expected him to ask, and she blinked. But it gave her time to think. She needed a diversion. She would never be able to find out where Berria was or get to her without this man. And the princess did not have time for Liæna to track her down. The assassin's story was easy enough - it was the same one she had been telling herself for almost thirty years.

"It doesn't matter," Liæna said. "I must speak with the person who can tell me what happened the day my father died, why he was killed! You know where he is. Take me to him."

"You wish to go to the Placer of Pieces, the man people call the Sorcerer?"

Liæna gave a single, firm nod. Lan Holdun watched her with fathomless eyes, but she did not blink or look away. Eventually he nodded in return. "Very well."

The assassin of Spyne lowered her borrowed elven blade, then pain exploded at the back of her head, and everything went black.

MAN OF TONGUES PART II

The Guardians followed the road into the mountains. Though it had been straight when looking at it from the lake, in truth it wound up the sides like a snake. The slabs of stone were long, huge rectangles that did not crack with age, though in the gaps between the rock, greenery took hold with great gusto.

Gravity dragged at Luca's feet with every step. Sometimes he swore the mountain shifted, trying to throw him off like a bad-tempered horse. He blacked everything out except the next step and used the bitter-sweet memory of the assassin to draw himself along. His surroundings were an unremembered blur of green and brown as the road took them through small vales and across ridges until it ended abruptly at a triangular overhanging, leaving them nowhere to go but empty space beyond the cliff.

"What now?" Cedar asked, looking at the cliffs around them.

His face said what they were all thinking: if this was the end of this path and they were forced to go back, they would have wasted days of precious time. The clench of Cedar's jaw suggested he would subdue Time to his will sooner than be defeated by the Man of Tongues' riddle, but they hadn't run out of options yet.

"We try the Witch's idea," Luca said, dragging himself out of the grey haze growing in his mind like the mist that concealed the Elderidge. "Give me the paper."

The Witch retrieved it from her robes and handed it to him. He stared at it for a while, turning in a slow circle as he held it up, translating the complicated double and triple meanings of the words with a distinct lack of confidence he hoped didn't show on his face, placing them within the context of the cliffs, and then the abyss, and finally the sky above.

"I can't tell if it's supposed to fit anywhere," he said at last.

"Well, let's assume we have to go up that way or grow wings and fly," Cedar said, pointing at the cliff walls surrounding them. "What would it say then?"

Luca turned to face the sheer stone wall once more, and grimacing, he looked down at the ancient language staring up at him. *Man of Tongues indeed. Why couldn't it be the Man Who Tells Us Everything We Need to Know Simply and Plainly? How hard would that be, really?* His resentful thoughts not helping, he turned his attention back to the riddle, running through the possible meanings again, sure he was forgetting a few.

"Well, it doesn't change a great deal," he said. "Though it was a good idea."

"We can't just wait here - we have to go *somewhere*," Cedar retorted, barely controlling his impatience.

They waited, no one willing to be the first to suggest it

was a dead end. Then Jæyd's head came up, her abrupt shift of attention drawing all of theirs. She marched purposefully to the wall, proceeding to walk along it, her fingers trailing across the surface like a lover's caress. In the very middle of the wall, where the rock seemed most formidable and impenetrable, her hand disappeared and the elf smiled.

"Or we could go through here."

Here turned out to be a narrow stone pathway, concealed from view by clever lines and shadows. It looked natural, and though Luca doubted this to his core, he could think of no force which could shape whole mountains like that. *The Builder Kings of the Dale could do that,* a voice irritatingly similar to Timo's baritone said.

Luca did not appreciate the idea that the mountains could hear his thoughts and answer them, and he folded the paper and put it in his jacket, then hurried into the crack after Jæyd and Cedar. The sides leaned in and threatened to collapse on any unfortunate traveler. The Witch followed Luca in and turned to gaze at the tiny sliver of light leading to the open behind them.

"How did you know this was here?" S'Aris asked Jæyd.

"I heard a breath of air," the elf smiled and touched her pointed ear. "These come in handy at times."

They went single file through the tight pass, and Luca held his breath, sucking in his ribs so he didn't touch the stone. He had no wish to wake it and have it crumble down on him. On the other side, the road did indeed start again, but the stone was different. It was reddish, as though rusted.

Or colored with blood, Luca thought, *of those the mountain has devoured.*

"The Red Road," Timo said, his face a mask of uncertain shock. "Also from the story of the *mandalin.*" A look of wonder overtook the shock. "The word is not *arrow*, it's *pointing*! *Pointing true as Death* describes the Red Road," he said. "It will lead you to the Realm of the Cloud King if you walk it full."

Luca examined the riddle and saw that *pointing* did indeed fit the context and translate for that glyph.

"Another story?" Luca huffed, irritated by his mistake and quickly changing the subject. "What is it with the stories?"

"Stories are where we keep the magyc of knowledge," Timo said.

"The magyc of words," S'Aris acknowledged. "In the Coven, we believe the same."

"Only now do you tell me I should've paid more attention to my father's bedtime fairy tales," Luca shrugged. "Shall we?"

He bowed and made a flowery gesture at the Red Road. The Road took them higher into the craggy maze of the Elderidge where the air began to thin, and the sweat steamed off Luca's skin. His body was growing heavier with something black and dragging, tightening around his chest and his eyes.

He gasped, pushing himself to keep up with the others, but he blinked and they disappeared around a corner of stone. Luca froze, clutching at the wall to remain upright. Using his fingertips to coax his body forward an inch at a time, he stumbled around to find his four companions arrayed in a line, looking up.

A crumbling arch supported by equally crumbling columns hung with dead vines marked the end of the Red Road. A narrow ledge leading on hung over a drop into thin air. Across the abyss, mountain peaks rose up above them, and in the distance smaller peaks popped from a cotton blanket of clouds. Timo took a deep breath, squared his shoulders, and took the first step onto the ledge, hugging the wall. Cedar swallowed, then made to follow.

"You've got to be joking," Luca groaned, leaning on his knees, his head hanging down.

An arm on his elbow helped him stand straight again. It was the Witch, and she smiled at him.

"Come on. Just don't look down."

"I don't think I can do that," Luca said, images of falling endlessly and coming to a sudden stop pummeling his mind.

"For Ria, we can cross mountains, journey to Cloud Realms, and as Cedar was ready to do not too long ago, grow wings to fly if necessary."

"Don't give them any ideas," Luca said, a jerk of his head indicating the other Guardians creeping across the very narrow pathway. "They just might go chasing after a way to do just that if they thought it was even vaguely possible."

"Oh, it is possible. I think I could do it if they needed me to," the Witch said. "It's just very, very painful."

"Great, but that wouldn't deter them. In fact, they'd probably think that made it an even better option," Luca said. "Ladies first."

S'Aris gave him a gentle squeeze on the arm and slid onto the ledge, her back pressed against the stone. She smiled at Luca one more time, then looked up with a determined expression, jaw clenched, and inched along. Luca mimicked her, sliding along with tiny motions of his feet.

The fiddle on his back shoved him further forward than he was comfortable with. Never before in his life had he ever wished it was not on his back. That he did so now scared him almost as much as the void of air lying a hand's breadth beyond his nose.

Near the middle, the ledge narrowed, and Luca took deep breaths with every step, being careful not to rush, despite the overpowering desire to be away from this place as soon as possible. The small pebbles and dust that his feet dislodged threw torments and jeers back at him as they fell, promising him a certain death if he followed.

He almost did. A lip of rock separated the ledge from the comforting solid shelf on the other side, and his foot caught on it. Pitching forward, he swung his arms in an attempt to catch his balance. His knees buckled, and he began to tip out of control.

In the instant before he fell, his thoughts turned to Liæna and a spike of regret for words unspoken made dying almost bearable, and living more important than it had ever been. Then strong hands closed on Luca's arm and pulled him back, and it was only his cry which fell, echoing in the void.

Luca collapsed to the ground, pressing his cheek against the comforting solidity, and refused to open his eyes for a full minute, sweet relief coursing through his blood and making him tremble. The vision of the assassin's smile infused him with a deep warmth that did funny things in the stomach and turned the knees weak and finally convinced him to open his eyes. When he did, he was staring at the bluest sky he had ever seen. It was too full and rich for this world, so…

"Am I in Death's Realm then?" Luca asked no one in particular, feeling the blue suck him in.

"The air does something to the color," Timo said. "But you are very much in the realms of the living."

"What's that sound?" S'Aris said, tilting her head.

A steady thrumming, like a thousand far-away drums singing in time drew their eyes to the far end of the valley they were now looking out over. From an unseen point above, a large cascade of white water grumbled down the mountain to some underground chamber.

"Where to next?" Cedar asked, a brief glance to admire the land all he could spare when he was on a quest.

"There," Timo said.

He pointed to a path leading down to the green meadow and behind the Daleman, the Guardians traipsed down. As Luca walked, between concentrating on moving his feet, he wondered how much longer this journey was going to be. Then he wondered if the Man of Tongues would have food for them, and what sort of food it would be. *I hope it's pie with peas and carrots and lots of gravy.*

As a Guardian, he would be able to subsist on the magyc of the Path for great lengths if he needed to, but his belly always appreciated the solidity of real food. Luca sustained himself all the way down with a parade of delicious meals he imagined gorging himself on.

The valley floor was pretty, almost magycal. Green grass spread like a velvet carpet and small white and yellow flowers clustered against the white and grey boulders littered around the valley. Once more, Luca pulled out the paper with the Man of Tongues' riddle.

"The silent draping falls," Luca read out the next line, then he glanced around at the others.

"The silent *draping*?" Cedar said, eyebrow raised. "Is that even a word?"

Luca sighed. "This is the last time I reveal any of my *many* hidden talents, if ridicule is the thanks I can expect." He blinked at the word. "Draping, drapery, curtains, wave, veil, blanket. This combination of glyphs could mean any of those. *Falls* could means *fall, falls, falling, fell, downward, to happen upon, happens, comes, to become, hides, veils.*"

"Two veils," Jæyd pointed out. "Perhaps that is the clue."

"*When the silent veil veils?*" Luca said, mimicking Cedar's unimpressed expression.

"The 'silent veil or curtain' means night," Timo said. "When night falls."

"Not *when*," Luca said. "Just *the silent...*" he glanced at Cedar. "*Draping-veil-blanket-curtain-thing falls-happens-comes-becomes.*"

"Surely it must mean *when*?" the Daleman said.

Luca shook his head, then shrugged. "It's easy to be ambiguous in a language as complex and infuriating as Liish. My grasp of it isn't good enough to say one way or the other."

"What's the next line?" Cedar said.

Luca read it four times, making sure each word was a right as it could be. "And you will find the rest."

"And you will find the rest," Cedar repeated.

"Perhaps the rest will be revealed in the darkness," Jæyd suggested. "A sign only visible in starlight."

It was all they had to go on, so they made themselves comfortable sitting or lying in the grass. Luca took the opportunity to doze, and his disjointed dreams of an alien world which felt like home was broken by dreams of a dark-eyed woman with a curved blade and a scorpion pin. He was rudely awakened by a prodding finger and he slapped Cedar's hand away.

"Wake up!" Cedar said. "It's night."

"One is *supposed* to sleep at night," Luca mumbled, but he rolled over, sat up, and looked at the sky.

His eyes widened. A full moon shone out over the valley, lighting everything in brilliant silver. Like great ribbons, colored lights danced and writhed in the sky, blue and green and pink. Stars were visible behind the heavenly hues, tinted by the lights.

"What is it?" Luca asked, his voice soft.

"The Builders' Fires," Timo said. "They are magnificent."

"Well, according to the riddle, the final clue lies beneath the sky," Luca said. "Maybe the riddle refers to that?"

"The lights are *in* the sky," Cedar muttered.

The Guardians thought and searched, but they could find nothing to solve the last part of the riddle. Luca fought the numbing exhaustion suffusing his bones and muscles, but his eyes lost the battle as the lights faded with the glow of the approaching sun. He must have dozed off again because he started awake, stretched, and gave a great yawn. He stopped with his mouth wide open when he saw Cedar's lethal look.

"What?" Luca mumbled.

Cedar threw his hands up in an inarticulate frustration. Luca gave an unsympathetic shrug.

"If Jæyd cannot find any hidden passages in the stone, then this is where we will find the Man of Tongues," Timo stated, his chin lifted in stout confidence.

"Are you out there, Man of Tongues?" Cedar yelled into the valley, his voice bouncing back to him from all angles.

They waited, but the cry was not returned. Luca felt they were missing something. He looked again at the riddle. "And the final clue lies beneath the sky." He looked up. "That's a bit unspecific isn't it?" he muttered to himself. "Lies *under* the sky? Lies *ground* the sky? Lies *lower* the sky?"

He continued to insert meanings, one after the other, then stopped, looked up, then down, then up again. "Under, ground, lower, below," he muttered to himself, repeating the sequence again.

The page taunted him, the glyphs of the word unchanging. "Under...under...under *the sky!*" Luca cried out, as he fit it together.

He placed his finger on the word that lay under *the sky*, and eagerly showed it to his companions.

"Under the sky!" Luca crowed. "*Falls* is under *the sky*!"

One by one their eyes moved to the waterfall.

"The final clue lies beneath the sky," Luca was now chortling, approaching hysterical glee at having figured it out. "The *words* 'the sky', not the *sky* sky."

"Not so silent, is it?" Cedar said, peeved at having overlooked something so simple.

"It would be if you were far enough away," Timo said.

"Or deaf," Luca said, still seething with pleasure and seeing no reason to inform them that particular glyph could also mean *quiet* or *distant*.

"Let us have a closer look," the elf said, swinging her plait over her shoulder and striding with graceful steps towards the falls.

The Guardians and the Witch gathered at the edge of the small lake that the water plummeted into, the sound thundering in their ears. It was narrow in length, greater in width, and black. Despite the volume of water spraying them with mist, the water was undisturbed at the edges. Timo reached down, plucked a flower, and tossed it into the water. With a frightening speed, the water sucked the flower down into its black depths.

"That must be deep indeed to have such a thirst," Timo said, voice raised to be heard.

"We have to get behind it," Cedar said.

"Preferable without killing ourselves," Luca added.

"What about those?" S'Aris pointed.

Flat grey stones were placed in even jumps around the one half of the pool, disappearing behind the shower of water. They did not appear on the other side of the bank. Cedar readjusted his guitar on his back and marched to edge where the stones began, his face set.

"Only one way to find out," he said.

Before anyone could stop him, he had hopped onto the first stone, and then the second and the third in a blink. The closer Cedar came to the edges of the fall, the more drenched he got. His clothes clung to his thin frame, and his hair was flattened against his pale skin. He wiped at his eyes constantly, blowing water out of his nose and mouth. When he reached the final stone, a shadow of uncertainty settled on his face. Then his eyes narrowed and he jumped into the waterfall, disappearing from view. The others waited with bated breath.

"Did you hear that?" the elf said, cocking her head.

The others shook their heads.

"It sounded like Cedar," Jæyd continued.

"Are you sure?" Luca asked. "You're not imagining it?"

"No Little-One, I am not imagining anything," the elf said, but the doubt in her eyes gave feet of clay to her words.

She waited one moment more, then made to follow in Cedar's footsteps. The Witch was the next to follow, two paces behind the elf. They disappeared behind the waterfall. Then only Timo and Luca were left. Luca forced a grin.

"What do you think, oh strong one of the Dale?" Luca asked, trying to quench the apprehension in his stomach with gaiety.

"I think we must follow our friends," Timo said.

"Of course, they could've drowned and we could be the last ones left to fulfill this quest of fools," Luca countered in a conversational tone.

Timo gave him a look, and Luca rolled his eyes. "Fine, fine. It was just a thought. After you, mountain man."

Luca watched the blond giant make his way across the

path of stones. His legs were so long he was able to step from one to the next without the ungraceful hopping of the others. Luca watched the place where Timo disappeared, forcing himself not to blink. Nothing moved. Luca glanced over his shoulder. The valley was empty, not a bird nor blade of grass stirred, and the sound of the fall drowned out all other sounds. It looked like a beautiful painting, but the stillness spooked Luca.

He went to the first stone and stepped onto it without thinking. It was firm under his feet, and though water ran over it, he did not slip. He jumped onto the next one, almost fell, and righted himself, hear hammering in his chest. Mist got in his eyes and clung to his lashes. The stone wall was too far away to touch, and though he wanted to reach out and feel the comforting solidity, he fixed his eyes on the next stone, and jumped.

The last stone was the only one embroiled in foaming water, but it was as solid under his feet as the others. Though he had not stepped through the waterfall, he felt as if he were standing in the middle of it. It was like standing out in hardest of the spring rains in Isos, during one of the tempests Seidon, the Lord of water and Waves, sent to the shore.

Luca's vision was taken up by white water, his ears by the roar of the same. He breathed at the wrong time, sucking in a lungful of water, and started to choke. He pitched forward, into the wall of water, and was floundering, trying to find something to grab onto, to hold him back from black wetness…

…and strong arms did that for him. After Luca coughed and recovered his breath with the help of hands pounding him on the back, he looked around to find the other Guardians and the Witch. All were as wet as he, grinning at him in the odd light.

"We thought you weren't going to come," Cedar said, his light tone heavy with relief.

"*I* thought I wasn't going to come," Luca replied, wringing out the water from his jacket.

It didn't help, and he let it fall in disgust. He looked instead at where he found himself. The walls of the cave glittered, the light of a million trapped stars shining out of the rock, responding to the glowing orb dancing at Cedar's fingertips.

Luca concentrated and found that he too could call the magycal light into being. It was easy here, taking not more than a thought - so unlike the effort required in Demona, a land of dying magyc - and the light hovered willingly above his outstretched hand. Luca sent it floating away, and saw that the cave gradually widened until it became a huge cavern, giant teeth rising up from the floor and hanging from the ceiling. The Guardians circled the cavern, guided by the Path-lights, then S'Aris called them to one side. Another tunnel, this one black as night, beckoned them forward.

It was a long journey, their lights lonely protection against the darkness. Twice Luca heard the telltale drip of water, the sound desolate in the stone confines of the mountain. Luca pushed away claustrophobia and continued. Eventually the tunnel took them to another cave, small and round. Timo's head brushed the curved ceiling, and the only place it was comfortable for him to stand was in the middle of the room. Luca didn't have this problem, and without fear for the continued wholeness of his skull, walked around the room.

For a room it was. A small bed lay in the back, beside a desk. A hearth had been dug into the wall. An iron pot hung over a few coals, and a table sat in front of the hearth.

"We should search the place for the next clue," Cedar said, his voice quiet for no reason they could articulate, but all felt on an instinctive level.

Luca began his second circuit of the room, dreading what he would find. He was half afraid something would leap out at him from a dark hiding place, half afraid they would find nothing. Something unfriendly was watching him, he was sure, baleful eyes making him shiver, and he wished he could tell the others. Part of him didn't want to alarm them, but another part didn't want to deal with the disbelief he was sure would come his way so he turned all his attention to his search.

This Man of Tongues lived sparsely and simply. His larder held tubers and some dried meat, but Luca suspected it was from many years before the harvest of last spring, and visions of hot, succulent pies faded from Luca's mind. A square chest beside the bed held a waterproof cloth, an extra blanket and sundries.

Luca knelt down and tapped the bottom of the chest in different places, his knuckles protesting at the hardness of the wood and the force with which he rapped. A resounding solid thud came back after each tap.

"No false bottom," he said to himself, the sound of his voice reassuring to his ears.

He looked up to see if the others had found anything more promising. Jæyd toed the ashes in the hearth with a frown, Timo hunched in front of the larder, moving the pitiful supplies to see if something hid behind them. Cedar was pawing through the things on the table. An old pen and some charcoal in a small box sat on several sheets of paper. It was different than the paper the Witch had, browner and less supple, almost as if the pieces were very thin slices of wood.

From his vantage closer to the ground, Luca saw what

Cedar did not. A piece of this paper was stuck to the underside of the table. Luca crawled over, his still-wet jacket making a swishing noise behind him.

It took doing to get the paper free, and the others clustered around to see what he was working so intently on. Eventually Luca called one of his dirks to hand, an easy thing to do in this place of old magyc, and pried the paper off. A yellow stain of resin appeared where the paper had been.

"What did you find?" Cedar asked, his face appearing at Luca's level.

"I'm not sure," Luca said, turning it over in his hands before handing it to Cedar.

"It's blank," Cedar said, disappointed.

"But the resin is still clear, and the ashes are warm," Jæyd said. "Someone was here recently."

A breeze stirred in the room.

"Someone is *still* here," Luca said, bile rising suddenly in the back of his throat.

It was the sour taste of something soon to be dead, and it threw him back to the Isos of his childhood and the nightmarish trip he took there to witness the murder of his friend Wind, the one-legged fiddler. Jæyd took a searching look of the room.

"There is no one here," the elf said, her voice gentle. "What do you see?"

"I don't see anything, but something is not right," Luca said, eyes flitting back and forth, searching for something he was sure was there.

He found himself caressing the Demonhärt, taking comfort in the cold, pulling vacuum. It soothed the sour heat in his throat, and he relaxed. Some part of him recognized what he was doing was dangerous and unnatural, but the movement helped him focus.

He turned in a slow circle, once, twice, and then again. Each time, the figment became clearer. The Guardians followed his gaze, but they saw nothing. When Luca turned for the third time, he gasped and stumbled backwards. In the middle of the room stood a figure, shrouded in darkness and the same acidic taste Luca sensed on his tongue.

"Guardians," it said, the voice resonating somewhere below the rib cage. "I see you have solved my little riddle."

They all looked at each other, then Cedar and Jæyd pushed Timo forward. He stared at them over his shoulder, eyes wide. Cedar gave him a *this-was-your-idea-this-is-your-show* look and motioned the Daleman onwards.

"You are the Man of Tongues?" Timo asked, his foot moving forward and back again, unwilling to take another step.

The figure bowed his head in affirmation. The indistinct features resolved into a face and a man's body. He was slight, and average height. His eyes were an electric blue the laws of nature and refraction of light could not explain, and his hair was a tousled blond so dark it was almost brown.

"We need your help," Timo said. "Please."

"What is it you need?" the Man asked, head cocked as he looked up at the tall Daleman, regarding him with bright eyes.

"We need to travel to another world," Timo said. "To find someone."

"The girl called *Aethsiths*," the Man of Tongues said and smiled a long, slow smile which stretched his face in odd ways.

"Yes," Timo said. "Can you help us?"

"Walking between worlds is the Way of the Witches," the Man said. "And you have brought a Witch with you."

"The Way of *Things*," S'Aris corrected. "And I am not skilled enough to do that."

"You know where this girl is?" the Man asked.

Timo shook his head. "We were hoping you would be able to help us find her."

A flash of anger crossed the Man's face. "How impudent."

Timo was taken aback, but could not think of anything to say. Luca swayed on his feet, suddenly unsteady. He tried to speak, but his tongue and his lips were no longer connected to any part of his mind. In fact, his entire body seemed to be curiously separate. With an icy splash of fear, he realized he was not doing anything. Something else was holding him like this.

Using all his concentration, Luca moved his fingers around the Demonhärt and squeezed. Just like when he was on the plains with Ria, and then again on the journey to the Crescent Temple when he closed the Rift the Eight Demons had come through, he found he was able to control the consuming blackness. He was now able to move his mouth and his toes, but his voice would still not work. Luca swallowed, and tried again, to no avail. The Man of Tongues was still talking.

"You have nothing I want. I will not help you."

Thunder was growing on Timo's face, and mirrored in Cedar's. Only Jæyd remained calm, though her blue-green eyes were narrowed slits. Before anyone could blink, the sharp edge of her rapier was out, pointed at the Man of Tongues.

"Who are you?" she asked, her voice hard.

"Jæyd, don't hurt him," Timo said, though his voice suggested he wouldn't mind if she hurt him a little. "We need him."

"He said he would not help us," the elf said. "And he

is not who he says he is."

The air was frozen as the Guardians gazed at the childlike face of the Man of Tongues. Cedar and Timo squinted at him, but their faces showed nothing but confusion and the remnants of their displeasure at being refused. Then the Man of Tongues, or what had been such a Man, turned to look at Luca.

Luca's fingers spasmodically gripped the Demonhärt, and the sharp, uneven edges of the black stone sliced into his flesh. The cuts burned, and Luca's vision expanded to include a field that was not of this world. His stomach turned. The Man was not a Man. *So this is what a Demon Thrall really looks like,* Luca thought, part of him dazed with revulsion, part of him pleased to see an old friend.

Behind the human face, a black cloud broiled. When the Man turned to gaze into Luca's eyes, the Guardian saw into the heart of the cloud, the bright spark of intelligence and cunning. *Demon.*

The Man's face made the gruesome parody of a smile and began to transform before their eyes. Luca was not startled, but the others cried out in shock. In half a second, golden weapons were unveiled. The cave was too small for the monstrous creature now looming over them, one of the Nine-now-Eight, the creature who called itself God of Metal.

It was shorter and squatter than its companions. It stood only a head taller than a man, but its girth was thrice that. Red eyes flashed like baleful stars in a dark face of ridges and angles. The Demon bared its abundant teeth at them and growled.

Luca had the absurd notion it was remembering the God of Bones, which the Guardians had killed. *That was only because the girl was there,* Luca thought hysterically. *You couldn't kill a god, not really, even a god from the Void.* The thought came from something beyond Luca, and the moment it was gone, he could not remember thinking it. The Demon's eyes settled on Luca, and the Demonhärt heated to unbearable temperature. Luca yelped but could not unclench his fingers.

The Demon darted for him, reaching out six-fingered hands tipped with black nails like scythes. The other Guardians closed in, forming a protective wall around Luca. *Which is good, because I'm really in no condition to do that for myself,* Luca thought, a single gold dirk held in limp fingers. Jæyd's silver rapier sang as she brought it up en garde, as was the golden arrow nocked in Cedar's bow.

The Demon was not looking to fight the Guardians, and what Luca carried was apparently not worth that much to it. With a flick of its massive shoulders, it stepped into a biting Rift which appeared behind it and disappeared. The Rift closed with a clap. Luca pulled in a great gasp of air, and sank to the ground. The Witch rushed to his side.

"I'm fine," he said, pushing her away.

"Look at your hand," the Witch countered.

Luca winced when he beheld the angry red lines in his palm. He submitted to the Witch's ministrations, though he still felt grumpy.

"Well, now what?" Cedar said. "The Man of Tongues is lost to us."

"That was not the Man of Tongues," Jæyd said. "Only a demon wearing his form."

"In any event, it killed the man we are looking for," Cedar said.

"I'm sorry," Timo said, sighing. "I've led you all this way for nothing."

"Not for nothing," Luca said, as his eyes lit on a sliver of hope. *Well, maybe not* hope *exactly, but at least not cause for complete despair.* "He's not dead."

The others did not know what to make of Luca's odd statement.

"What do you mean?" Cedar demanded.

Luca nodded towards the paper the golden-eyed Guardian had dropped in order to draw his bow. Runes were etching themselves across the hard surface, in black and gold. The other Guardians stared at it until the message had appeared fully and no more was forthcoming, then turned their gazes to Luca, staring at him for a long time.

He smiled. "See? There's more to me than just my good looks and intelligence."

Cedar rolled his eyes, picked up the paper and held it out to Luca. Luca's face fell when he did not recognize the writing. He could not even begin to guess where it was from. It looked like a series of twigs crossed and scattered across the odd paper. He shook his head, gloom settling in his stomach.

"This means nothing to me," he said.

THE PRINCESS OF GHOR

Her Majesty Berria In'Orain of Ghor strode down the streets of Elba as if she owned them. They were home in a sense, but never in the same way as Ghor. Though she had been only twelve years old when she had been forced to flee the former principality in the north, Berria remembered her homeland well and with longing.

Everything in Demona was a reflection of its lack of self, a land with the pedigree of a mutt. *A mutt with mange and fleas, if the analogy was to be entirely accurate*, the princess thought and was then ashamed at her lack of charity. Her mother and father had not taught her to sink to such petty thoughts of acrimony and resentment.

Still, Ghor *was* superior in so many ways, and no amount of charity would change her mind. In Erridon, the Ghoris style of design and architecture made for pleasing lines and curves, where nothing caught the eye as out of place, and nothing jarred the attention in a way to provoke headaches. Columns and tall, arching windows gave a sense of space and peace, and white and grey marble or pale brick was soothing on the senses.

In any city of Demona, including the cities more pleasing to the eye - Catmar, the City of Light, or Torin-before-it-fell, the City of Stone - there were too many colors and shapes jostling for attention to be considered pleasing. The influence of elves, dwarfs, trolls, goblins, Desert People, the mountain men called Cantons, Dalefolk, Islanders, Wild Men, Nyicans, and yes, even the influence of Ghor and her people mingled in Demona in a blend which could no more be untangled than a roomful of yarn after a hundred cats had gotten into it.

Elba, the City of Trees, was not bad as far as Demonan Cities went, Berria granted. The Elbans built their houses and shops to blend with the trees and though they did not do as well as the elves were reputed to, it was distinctive, homogeneous, and not entirely unpleasing.

Berria walked down the main thoroughfare, nodding at those she passed with an automatic gesture which was seldom returned, her eyes trained ahead with unflinching purpose. Mulch had been pounded down into a surface almost as hard as stone to surface the streets of Elba. Roots had been sculpted to mark the edges of the street, and to form steps up to the houses built around the trunks and stretching up into the boughs.

Berria turned down a side street, continued for a short distance, then turned again. Her circuitous route was a precaution, but when she rounded another corner and saw the white uniforms ahead, she wished she had been less diligent.

This street was sparsely peopled. Most people were inside, at work by the ovens or the forges or the looms of their trade or in the markets to sell their wares. A few figures passed by but did not look Berria in the eyes, and they gave the three Men a wide berth. Suddenly, Berria was acutely aware how much she stood out in her red satin and the Ghoris cut to her long cape.

The princess missed a step but continued almost at once, her heart beating fast as she came close to the Men. If she stopped, turned, or gods forbid, ran, they would be on to her in an instant. She measured her pace, debating whether it would be more suspicious to look directly at them or look away.

At the last moment, her eyes fell to the ground, and she passed the Men, who were blurred shapes in her peripheral vision. She could feel their eyes following her as she went past, and her heart pounding in her ears obscured the shout from behind her.

It came again, more insistently. She stopped and turned slowly, her mind blank but her lips twitching with an excuse she had yet to make up. Looking up, she froze. The three Men in White had surrounded a short goblin, who looked torn between terror and wanting to rip off their faces. One of the Men held out his hand, and the goblin was forced to relinquish the woven bag he carried.

As she watched the Men in White rifle through the contents of the bag - several spools of sewing string, four brass buttons, a package of sugar, a mesh bag of potatoes, and a cake of white soap - a feeling of helpless rage infused Berria. She wanted to go over and stand up for the persecuted goblin, she wanted to *do* something more than stand here and watch or skulk away thankful she was not the one.

The Man closest to her turned and looked over his shoulder, straight at Berria. She saw the empty, fathomless nothing in his gaze, through which a malevolent entity watched without blinking. Cold ice shot into her stomach, and she dropped to a crouch, hastily fumbling with her boot for a moment as if something had come undone, then stood and walked away as fast as she dared.

She hoped she had done enough good in this life to make up for her cowardice, but her justification fell on empty ears. She was right, she knew, but it felt so wrong. *This couldn't be the way the world was meant to be.*

She pushed the thought away, threw a glance over her shoulder to make sure the Men in White weren't watching or following, and broke into a trot, abandoning caution and making her way directly to the address she had memorized but never been to.

Berria stopped in front of a small, nondescript house, the brown wood of the walls matching the color of the trees on either side exactly. A thatched roof came down in three levels, and a soft green door was flanked by two green windows. The princess stood for a long moment before ascending the steps and knocking on the door.

An elven girl opened it. Her hair was very blonde, and warm brown eyes looked out at the world with a quiet watchfulness that was not quite mistrust, but almost. Berria's heart leapt to her throat. This person was too young to be the same as the one who had charge of her younger siblings.

"Can I help you?" the elf asked the princess, her eyes widening slightly at Berria's distress.

"Yes, I am looking for my...for a sister and a brother. They lived here, last I knew. Their names are Marga and Damson." Those were the names Privere and Degan lived under since fleeing Ghor, and they felt strange on Berria's tongue.

"Oh." The elf's face fell still and closed, her tone guarded. "Well, they left some time ago."

"When will they return?" Berria asked, fighting to keep

her voice even. *If something has happened to them…*

"You misunderstand," the elf said. "They *left*."

The meaning took some time to sink in, and Berria's heart began to flutter with tentative hope.

"Where did they go?" she inquired.

"I couldn't say," the elf said. "It was quite sudden, and then they were packing and saying it was time to go."

"Thank you," Berria remembered her courtesy as she began to turn from the door.

Another face, this one elderly, appeared behind the young one. The elven woman's dark hair was greying at the temples, and fine lines appeared at the corner of her eyes when she smiled. "Hesaya, who is this?"

"She has not given her name," the young elf said.

"Cara-" The princess paused and changed her mind half-way. *They should know my true name.* "Berria."

The older woman scrutinized the princess's face, and though it was impossible that the elf would know her, Berria thought she was searching for something familiar. The older elf's eyes widened when she found what she sought.

"A child of Ghor. You should come inside," she said with a furtive glance.

Surprise froze her thoughts, but Berria nodded and followed the elves inside, and the young girl shut the door behind them. The house was quaint with an elvish touch which made everything finer.

"I am Raela, and this is my goddaughter Hesaya," the elder of the two said, putting her hand on the girl's shoulder.

"Pleased to meet you," the young elf curtsied.

"Why don't you go put some tea on?" Raela told the girl. "I'm sure Berria is hungry."

The princess was about to protest that she had no time,

but her father popped into her head, his face wise and patient as he leaned over the Venture board, his eyes unhurried as they went from piece to piece, picking his next move. *Those who do not have enough time rarely spend the time they do have well. Stop. Breathe. Take the time to look, to listen, and to think. If you rush, you risk missing something important. If you miss something important, you risk losing the game.*

"Thank you," Berria said instead. "That would be wonderful."

The elves set the table and brought out simple sandwiches of cold meat and relish on brown bread, along with a pot of strong, hot tea which smelled of cinnamon. The elf poured two cups of tea and sat down opposite the princess. Berria took a sandwich, and it was only when she started to eat that she realized how hungry she was.

"How did you know me?" Berria asked, wiping crumbs from her lips with a napkin.

"About three months ago, your brother appeared at the door. You share his eyes," Raela explained, and then her face clouded. "He looked bad, Berria, as though Death Himself had personally carried him the last few paces."

Berria listened, her hands clenched around the cup of tea to keep them from shaking, as the elf continued.

"I tried to convince him to stay here, to heal and regain his strength, but he would not listen. He said they had come for him and your sister in Samnara and would be here any moment."

"Who?" the princess asked, her throat tight, already fearing the worse. "Who was coming?"

"He called them the Men of the Sigil of the Rose."

Berria closed her eyes, willing the emotions welling up inside her to quiet.

"You have heard of these Men?" Raela asked softly.

Berria looked up at her and nodded. "We call them the

Men in White. Did they come here?"

Raela shook her head. "They have never come here, not while your brothers and sisters were here."

A wave of relief made Berria weak. "Did Haman tell you anything more?"

Raela sighed. "He was sure he was being followed and seemed afraid they would find him through some sorcery. He did say they had come for *Jormyda*."

Berria frowned. *Jormyda* meant "of light" and was the name of the sword the heir to the title In'Orain carried. "Why would they want such a thing? It is a family heirloom, worthless but for its sentiment."

"Your brother seemed to think this was the sword the Men of the Sigil - or the Men in White - wanted," Raela said. "He wouldn't let it out of his sight. He thought they could somehow see it or follow it."

Berria shivered. Sorcery was powerful, and because it was forbidden, few knew what it could or could not do. Perhaps they could trace magyc. *Hadn't they followed the girl to the City of Light?* Berria realized, her dread growing.

She looked up when the elf held something out. "He did not want her to, but your sister left this for you."

It was a scrap torn from a piece of fine clothing, a simple thing, but it brought tears of nostalgia stinging to her eyes. Berria blinked the wetness away, turned the cloth over, and began to count the stitches while the elf watched quietly.

"When we were children, we would leave each other hidden messages," the princess explained, running her fingers over the scrap. "Messages hidden in stitches."

Her fingers had to find the tiny length of thread because her eyes could not - the thread was almost the same color as the cloth. The bumps revealed themselves slowly, and she went over it twice to be sure. It was a simple message. Running stitches and Basting stitches in one of the first codes they had developed formed the words *dorga undal ve.*

"Dorga undal ve," Berria whispered.

"What does that mean?" Raela asked.

"It means *become the sun*, or *be the sun*, in Ghoris," Berria translated.

"Does that tell you anything?"

"It might," Berria replied, her tone hesitant though the answer was gaining solidity in her mind. She continued her thoughts aloud, the sound of her voice making a foundation of certainty that she could build on. "When we were children, we would play hide and seek. The Orain estate was so large, we would leave clues so we weren't hiding for days, waiting to be found." A faint smile came to her face as she remembered. "For example, if we were hiding in a high place, like a tree, or the bell tower, we would tell the others *be a bird*. Or if you were hiding under the table, you might say, *be a crumb*," Berria mused, her thumb running over the stitches again and again.

"So if she was telling you to be the sun, they are hiding in the sky?" the elf guessed.

"Or behind the horizon?" Berria said.

"Perhaps they have left this land? Perhaps he means to say they have gone to the Wild Islands?"

Be the sun, be the sun, the princess chanted. *Where would the sun go? No,* she realized, *where would the sun* hide? *It was too big and bright, you could always see it, except perhaps when it was behind a cloud, or...*

"In the night!" she exclaimed. She began to run through the names of alleyways, taverns, and streets in Samnara and Elba having to do with the word *night.* The Dark Day was a tavern in Samnara's Gold district. There was an inn called The Nightingale, and she knew of a district near the gates called Knight's Pass…and then she realized the cleverness of the code.

"Not *night or knight*," Berria said. "Nite."

Raela gave her a bemused look.

"Nitefolk," Berria whispered. "They've gone to the Nitefolk."

It was impossible but she knew it was right - the place where hunches were born and intuition lived told her so. She didn't know what Haman was thinking - the Nitefolk did not take in outsiders, even if they could find their way that deep into the Mountains alive. *What did he think to gain?* She stopped trying to reason it out before she started.

"Thank you," Berria told Raela. "For all your aid."

The elf gave a gracious nod, accepting the implied debt and dismissing it. "What will you do?"

"I don't know precisely," the princess said, standing quickly. "But I must leave at once. They already have a head start."

She stood straighter, tucking her blouse into her trousers, arranging her cloak about her shoulders. Putting the loose curls of dark hair behind her ears, she considered her next choice. *I have no idea where to find the Nitefolk. But if I go to Samnara, maybe I can trace Haman from there.*

She clung to that hope, tugging it around her as a blanket to ward off a chill, but a taunting doubt that no trace of her brothers or sisters would be found in Samnara slipped through the cracks. She had not spoken to them in four years, or seen two of them in thirteen, and this placed a veil between Berria and the memory of her siblings.

"I'm sure they will be alright, princess," Raela said, reading her face. "All the children of Ghor are strong." A fond smile softened the elf's face. "If the others are to be judged by the youngest."

Berria looked around, trying to imagine a small Privere

and Degan playing here. The princess tried to see her younger sister doing lessons here, or needlepoint, but it was hard. After the dwarfs' willingness to shelter the In'Orains grew thin, they were split up. Samnara was too dangerous for the youngest; Elba was a better choice. Privere had been eight years old. She would be 21 now, and Degan a full man.

Berria needed help to find them, and who better than the Witch? She had come to rely on the Witch in lieu of her siblings since their meeting almost four years ago. Berria reached into the purse at her waist, her fingers searching for the sharp edge of the broken mirror. She pulled it out and stared at her pale reflection, her dark thoughts haunting her eyes.

"What are you thinking, princess?"

Tapping the glass against her fingers, Berria spoke in a faint voice. "I feel I am walking further into darkness. I want those I...those I love and those I have come to love with me, but I don't want to bring them into the darkness. S'Aris is *Ehol-Din*. Sent by her faction the *Ehol'Di*, the Traitors and the faction of V'Ronica, S'Aris was to help the Guardians, not the royal family of Ghor...ouch!"

Berria moved the mirror to her other hand, the reflection of the cut on her finger wavering in the shaking glass. A smear of blood marred the shiny surface for a protracted moment, then it disappeared. A red light sparkled around the mirror like a crystal mist and then faded. Berria frowned, trying to work out what had just happened.

First Magyc, or Blood Magyc as it was still called in some parts, had never disappeared in Ghor like it had in Demona, for the good reason that it had never been abused in Ghor like it had in Demona. But Berria didn't think she possessed that particular magycal power.

"What is that?" Raela asked, gesturing at the glass, her elven eyes bright with the recognition of magyc.

"A scrying glass," Berria said.

A shadow fell over the elf's face. "Perhaps you should leave that, princess."

Berria's other hand fell over the mirror, loathe to lose it. "Why?"

"Your brother suggested that the Men of the Rose could sense magyc. That was how they were following him."

"Haman was always good at jumping to conclusions." Berria shifted in her seat. "He couldn't know that. He was simply guessing." Her ears told her the words were feeble even as she tried to believe what she was saying, unwilling to part with her safety line to the Witch.

Raela looked at her, the expression of timeless wisdom elves seemed to be born with making Berria feel like a stubborn child who wouldn't accept that the wind had taken her kite just because she wanted it to be so.

The Men in White can track magyc - they follow Ria as if they know where she is going to be before she gets there. Perhaps they can sense magyc. She recalled the eyes of the Man she passed on the street and shivered.

"I will take it," Raela said. "If it makes it easier for you."

"I don't want to endanger you," Berria protested. "I will find another place for it."

"Princess, I was endangered the moment I fostered two children of Ghor under my roof," the elf said, holding out her hand. "But if it makes you feel better, I have a place away from here where it can be hidden safely."

Berria handed over the glass. A feeling of being sail-less and rudder-less in a storm trickled into her stomach. Now she was truly on her own again. *Much as I was before I met S'Aris,* she told herself. *I did just fine then. I will do so now.*

"Thank you," she told Raela.

"May the Moon watch over you," the elf said. "And your family."

Berria nodded, and silently added her own prayer to the elf's well-wishes. She stood to leave, and another thought occurred to her.

"May I borrow a cloak of a plain color?" she asked.

She traded her plush satin cape for a soft brown cloak. Leaving the safe-house feeling more comfortable in her ordinary looks, the princess asked the first person she met for directions to the nearest carriage station.

The carriage for Samnara would not depart for another hour, so after she purchased her ticket, Berria seated herself on the low bench, and thought of Ghor to keep from thinking of what could have befallen her siblings.

She thought most about her parents. Her mother and father had embodied everything a prince and princess of Ghor should be. They were proud; self-deprecation was looked upon as a form of weakness which could be exploited as surely as arrogance. But their conceit did not taint their understanding of their place in the world or their relationship with those who shared it with them.

Princess Ennia, Berria's mother, was wise and kind. She knew when to speak her mind and when to disguise her thoughts. She supported her husband, prince Thalev, with sage advice and a steady presence.

Thalev wielded his power well. When the princes met in council, he listened more than he spoke and did not try to force the world to his own design. He counseled temperance, patience, and foresight. *Demona could have learned much from them,* Berria thought wistfully.

Somehow, the seven princely lines of Ghor - Orain, Delfae, Trant, Holen, Klemor, Parn, and Dorr - had managed to remain true and unsullied by the madness, greed, or pettiness which afflicted princes from father to son and could cause them to lose their seats and crowns. Demona had passed through their Time of Princes and grown weary of that cycle. Shrugging off the burden of such leadership, the Cities had chosen to be independent and autonomous, electing Magisters to see to their leadership and public affairs.

And now the Magisters have begun to lose view of their place in the world. In her many dealings of the Magisters of Samnara, Elba, Catmar, Balmar, and D'Ohera, Berria had too often come upon the dishonesty and underhanded dealings of those with the public trust.

The clatter of horses' hooves and the rattle of trappings drew the princess from her remembrances. The carriage came, an old brown thing with brass rivets, covered in dust and listing to the left like a wandering eye. Berria noted all this with dispassion. Her title may be majesty, but she was accustomed to life at many strata of society.

Handing the grizzled carriage-driver the ticket with the mark showing she had paid, Berria grabbed the bar beside the door and hoisted herself into the carriage. She sat in the corner and stared out the window, though she did not see the small station or the trickle of people passing.

She jolted out of her reverie when the carriage started. Only one other passenger was traveling with her, an elderly man who had put his hat over his face and was snoring under it. It seemed only moments before the Gates of Samnara were towering over her, casting the carriage in shadow, and then they wobbled to a stop. Disembarking from the carriage, Berria shielded her eyes and squinted. A line of people snaked out of the Gates like a tongue moving sluggishly into the city.

Berria joined the line, drawing her brown cloak tight about her, and after a long wait stood before the

Streetwarden behind the table. She wrote her Mark for him, he issued her temporary papers without smiling, and she walked into the First Square of Samnara.

Here she stopped, unsure of the direction of her next step. *How to find a Nitefolk?* she wondered. *It was the task of a master of all skills and magycs, so impossible to do, one would be considered crazy for just thinking of it.*

The Nitefolk was the name given to the strange creatures who lived in the mountain region of Pruss. Diminutive people with cat-like features - stubby fingers and toes reminiscent of paws with retractable claws, wide amber eyes with a slitted pupils, coarse fur, whiskers, and fangs - the Nitefolk were rarely seen outside of their mountains. Berria didn't even know how to communicate to them, as to her knowledge they did not speak. After the rumors of their attack on Demona, even fewer of them had shown their furry faces south of the Mountains.

As the princess stood around looking at nothing in particular, she failed to see the figures moving towards her. They stayed to the sides close to the walls, and their white uniforms were hidden under brown cloaks much like hers. She gasped when a hand grabbed her shoulder, and something harsh and sweet-smelling was pressed against her face. Fighting strongly at first, then weakly, she finally floated away from the world on a black cloud.

The blackness dimmed to a dark grey. Pounding in Berria's head made hearing difficult, but she thought voices were speaking somewhere nearby in the greyness. When she attempted to move, she found she was tied to a chair, her hands behind her. The rope bit into her skin, and she couldn't feel her fingers. A crick in her neck made turning her head an effort, and her throat was dry and sticky, just like when she would eat too many desserts and sugary drinks at banquets as a child. Her feeble stirring attracted attention - the voices stopped and things moved around her.

"Hello?" she called out.

Her voice was muffled by the cloth over her head. Someone pulled the cloth away suddenly, and the dark grey became more the color of storm clouds after they had dropped their load of rain. Figures blurred in front of her, white forms. One of them knelt down in front of her, and Berria forced her eyes to focus.

He was older than the other Men in White the princess had seen, at least forty years old. His hair was brown, just darker than his tanned skin, and his eyes were the color between green and brown which could never be accurately described as either. On his shoulder was a rose, half wilted and black, half vibrant and red. Berria noted for the first time that no definite line divided the two - the wilted half grew into the red half, or perhaps the red half faded into the black. Tiny jewels simulating drops of dew dusted the outer petals. On his sleeve were two pale bars and a chevron. *A captain.*

He held a glass of liquid to Berria's lips. Her thirst overcame her suspicion, and she drank eagerly. When she had drained the water, the Man handed it to another, who retreated into the gloom, the click of his boots on the stone following his ghostly form.

"What do you want?" the princess asked the captain, her voice clearer now.

"You already know that," he said. His voice was low and raspy, not unpleasant in tone, but still it made the hair on Berria's arms stand up as revulsion rolled over her skin. "Your family. Where are they?"

"I don't know," she replied.

He looked at her for a long time. Berria wondered if he could sense untruth like Ria of the Other World. It didn't matter. She truly didn't know where Haman and the others were.

"Would you tell me if you did know where they were?"

Berria was still, her gaze unflinching even as her heart thudded erratically in her chest. "No."

"Then you are of no use to us," the Man in White said, unblinking, the strange presence clearer in his eyes than in any of the others.

With the silent animosity of a trapped and wounded animal, Berria watched as he rose to his feet and walked away. He stood with his back to her for a long moment, then turned. His arms hung loosely at his side, his feet a comfortable distance apart.

"But there are ways to persuade you to change your mind."

The sack was put over her head again, and movement became blurs of dark and light. Berria felt the chair tip back, and someone dragged her across the floor. Then the feet of the chair hit the floor, sending a jolt up her bones, and the chair rocked back into a steady place.

Silence descended. Crisp footsteps marched towards her, in a slow, metallic tattoo, and then stopped, the silence punctuated by her ragged breaths. A faint whistle reached her ears, a scant moment before pain shot down her arm as the rod slammed into her shoulder, and the princess screamed.

MAN OF TONGUES PART III

When Luca pointed out the magycal writing, Timo's heart had swelled with hope. Now it looked to be another long, arduous quest to find someone to translate it for them, and the Daleman glanced wearily at the paper.

His eye widened, and hope came flooding back to him. He snatched it from Cedar's grasp, not minding the other Guardian's surprised glare. Timo's pale blue eyes traced the lines of the glyphs and a smile grew on his face. *All is not lost.*

"This is not Liish," Timo stated, a triumphant ring to his words. "This is Dalespeech."

"Dale...speech?" Luca said, drawing out each word as he rose from his place on the floor. "Is that an actual thing?"

"It is," Timo said. "All our oldest and most important stories are told in Dalespeech. Though, it is a long time since I have seen or heard it. Give me a moment."

They waited for him to figure the meaning, and then he began to read aloud.

"To find the one that you seek
Into your own eyes you must peak
The crying mountain will sing to you
Follow the song, it will lead you true
Always right then left
but for when they come abreast
Through the maze of starless night
And then like a dragon take flight…"

"Great, now not only is he a riddler, he's also a poet," Luca groaned.

"There's more," Timo said.

"Of course there is," Luca said. "Please. Go on."

"The first is as the first
and the first is last
Last comes after the first."

"What did the first riddle say?" S'Aris said immediately.

"The first comes second," Luca said, his expression saying he'd read the words so many times they would be permanently ingrained in his memory until he died, and probably after.

Timo reread the riddle. "The crying mountain will sing to you. Follow the song, it will lead you true."

"The first comes second, but first is last as well?" S'Aris said with a confused glance at the Daleman.

They all stared at each other, silently mouthing the words.

"There's too many *firsts* in that riddle," Luca complained.

The statement was accepted with discouraged nods.

"There *are*," S'Aris said suddenly, her eyes lighting.

"Are what?"

"Too many *firsts*," the Witch said, waving her hands.

"How does that help us exactly?" Luca asked.

"Look. If the first is as the first, then the first clue comes in the middle." S'Aris pointed. "And the first *lines* are the last *clue*."

"What about *last comes after first?*"

"The last two lines come after the first clue," S'Aris said. "It's true and useless. But if we know where the first and last clues are, the one that is left is the second clue."

Luca stood up and hugged her. The Witch stood, blinking and not moving. She raised a hand and patted Luca on the back with an awkward expression. Luca squeezed her, picked her up and set her back on her feet, grinning from ear to ear.

"So where to from here?"

"We have to find the crying mountain," Cedar said with a bemused grimace. "Any ideas?"

"We could beat it up, maybe break one of its fingers," Luca said. "That'd make it cry."

"We do not have time for games," Jæyd snapped.

Timo was taken aback at the unusual lack of patience, but when he saw the elf's eyes dart in wary motions to the stone enclosing them, he understood. Luca did not.

"Just trying to lighten the mood," he said with a dark sneer.

The elf rubbed the bridge of her nose, and gave him an apologetic look. "I am sorry. I just want to be out of these mountains."

"Don't we all," the Witch said.

"So what's a crying mountain?" Luca said, traces of resentment in his tone.

"And one that sings," Cedar reminded them.

"Tears," Timo said, when the answer came to him. "Weeping water."

"A spring!" S'Aris said.

"There were at least two in the tunnel getting here," Luca said, and shivered. "Wonderful. More cold, wet water. It's like being hugged by your least favorite aunt, only worse."

With Cedar in the lead, a golden ball of Path-light floating in front of him, they retraced their steps. The first spring was no more than a wetness leaking down the tunnel wall.

"Tears maybe, but not exactly an opera," Luca commented.

The next was more promising. The sound reached their ears long before they felt mist on their face. The nearer they got the more the water resembled the chime of bells. Haunting voices were added to the melody.

"It was *not* doing that before," Luca said.

"No, it was not," Jæyd agreed in a soft voice.

When they came upon the second spring, exclamations of surprise echoed through the tunnel. The spring cascaded from the wall. It ran down a series of holes and gaps in the rocks, producing the "voices" before flooding down the rest of the tunnel.

"Where are the bells coming from?" Cedar asked, looking around.

As if in answer, a particularly strident tinkle came floating up to them.

"It will lead you true," Timo said.

They looked down the watery path, none eager to start, but they slowly moved towards it, sloshing through the water, the ripples gleaming in the glow of the Path-light.

"Wait," Jæyd said, stopping and holding up her hand to stop the others.

"What is it?" Cedar asked.

"Quiet. Listen!" the elf's voice was low and urgent.

At first their ears could hear only the gentle sound of

water lapping against the wall, but then a rumbling began and grew too quickly for comfort, and they turned to see water galloping towards them on silver hooves and foaming manes.

They had but a moment to draw a breath and brace themselves before the stampede crashed over them, sweeping them off their feet and carried them straight into the stone. Timo shut his eyes, expected to break his nose on it, but the water continued to carry him along and deposited them in an underground pool of black water in tremendous splashes.

Coughs, splutters, and yells echoed through the chamber as one by one they surfaced and slogged out onto the smooth stone shores. Somehow Cedar had maintained his Path-light, and they were drawn to the comfort, arraying to look up at the mountain cage they found themselves in. It was so huge they could not see the ceiling or other walls, swallowed by the darkness, the Path-light a tiny pinprick of gold in the black. The light illuminated the wall in front of them, and etched in the dark rock were five giant doors with red tracery along the borders and fearsome carved creatures for handles.

"Which door?" Timo said, his voice tiny in the vast space.

They examined them, alone and in pairs, walking between the stretches of blackness.

Luca snapped his fingers. "Logically, the one with the dragon on it," he said, pointing. "Otherwise, why would this Man of Tongues put the word dragon in his poem?"

"Perhaps it is a trick, and he meant to warn us away from the door with the dragon on it," Jæyd suggested, looking uncomfortable with the idea of going through any of them.

Luca sniffed. "I like my idea better."

They all turned their gaze on the door with the dragon handle, but as they looked, the figure morphed, losing its scales and horns and growing fur and ears.

"That's a bear." Cedar stated the obvious in a tone of disbelief.

"It *was* a dragon," Luca countered.

Timo walked the length of the pebbly shore, looking at each door, stopping when he reached the door on the other end. A familiar reptilian countenance of myth and tale stared at him from the handle of this one.

"Here's the dragon," Timo called.

The others came over, and when they were crowded around him, he reached out, hand poised to turn the handle, but again the scales disappeared, to be replaced with the profile of a horrible woman with snakes for hair, snarling at him with broken teeth. She snapped at Timo's hand, and he jerked away.

"Well, that's just great," Luca said. "How are we supposed to go through the dragon door?"

"I think one must not linger or hesitate," S'Aris said, peeling her wet dress from her legs, but when she let it fall back, it only stuck to her skin again.

"We have to..." Cedar began, but the Witch was already moving.

She strode with determined steps to the third door where the dragon now glared out. Without stopping, the girl gripped the handle and turned. The door flew open, and a gust of hot wind blew her sodden hair back. Still she didn't pause and stepped through. It slammed behind her, leaving the Guardians in silence.

Timo felt a wrench in his chest when the Witch disappeared. The longer this went on, the less certain the Daleman was that they were on the right path, and the more he leaned towards full thought, and less towards rash, unplanned action, such as the Witch had just shown. *She'll be alright,* he told himself.

"Beaten by a girl," Luca was telling Cedar with a grin. "*And* a Witch, no less. Losing your touch a bit, Cedar?"

Cedar gritted his teeth, golden-eyes searching out the dragon handle. It now resided on the fifth door, at the other end of the stone beach. Cedar sprinted for the door, hardly slowing to pull it open and fell headfirst through. The door slammed behind him, and the remaining Guardians were left in darkness as his Path-light flickered out.

Jæyd called another, her Path-light different than Cedar's, the gold tinged with the green of sunlight shining through leaves on a spring day, but it was pale and its light caught the drawn angles of her face, making her look much older.

"Right-o," Luca said, rubbing his hands. "Here, dragon, here-here dragon."

He jumped through the door with the dragon. Jæyd motioned for Timo to follow. Timo shook his head, meaning for her to go first. She deferred, leaving her Path-light hovering just above the surface of the pool as she stepped through the door. It winked out when the door slammed.

In the instant it took Timo to call a light, the dragon had moved, and Timo's eyes followed the dragon from the first door, to the fourth, back to the first, and to the third. The thought that it may disappear for good and leave him trapped in this prison banished his hesitation and sent him at a dead run for the third door.

The handle was rough and warm enough to bite - *like a true dragon*, Timo thought - and turned by itself as if it sensed his intention and did not need further coaxing. The hot air stuck in Timo's nose and throat, threatening to choke him, and he was pulled through the door into blackness and then light.

The Daleman was standing solidly on his own two feet. Cedar and Jæyd were conferring nearby. The Witch sat cross-legged on the ground, a bit pale but still smiling. The tightness was banished from Timo's chest in a rush that left a warmth.

The feeling was pleasant, but short-lived. Luca was whistling, and the cave threw it back at him. The sound raised the hair on the back of Timo's neck. A black void faced them. From the look on Cedar and Jæyd's face, the prospect of crossing that did not appeal to them either. Only Luca seemed truly carefree, and Timo knew that was only skin-deep.

"Through the maze of starless night," Timo whispered.

Night-ight-ight-t the cave whispered back.

"Looks like a picnic, doesn't it?" Luca said and sent a piercing whistle into the darkness, which came back three-fold to assault their ears.

"Please stop," Cedar asked, his voice strained. "You're not being helpful."

Luca shrugged. "We have to go. Through the maze of starless night and all that. There's no use crying about it."

"I know that!" Cedar snapped. "But you don't have to make it unpleasant."

"I really don't think *I'm* making this unpleasant," Luca said. "I think it's just unpleasant all by itself."

"We can't keep a Path-light going in there," Cedar told Timo.

"It is as though a slice of the Void has materialized inside this accursed mountain," Luca said. "If any one of us was truly inclined to sorcery, now would be the time to try it."

"Or we could light a torch," the Witch announced.

The Other World

The Guardians turned to her. She held four slim twigs in her hand.

"Those look more like matches than torches," Luca said. "How long will it burn for?"

"These are of wishwood and will last longer than you think," S'Aris said. "But we should not tarry."

"Right. Not tarry in the maze," Luca agreed. "Because that shouldn't be hard to do."

The Witch ignored him and handed all four twigs to Cedar. "It won't burn you. Each will last about ten minutes. When it starts to fade, look ahead and memorize the next few steps. This will give us a few moments more, and perhaps that will be the difference between success and failure. Single file; don't lose the person in front of you." She placed her hand on Cedar's shoulder to demonstrate.

Her words instilled a shadow of order and calm, and the others followed suit, Luca gripping the Witch's shoulder, and Jæyd gripping his. Timo took up the rear, trying not to squeeze the elf's shoulder with too much force. She looked at him with a reassuring smile, though her face was pale.

"Ready?" Cedar asked.

Timo nodded, sure his face must look much like Jæyd's. Cedar stepped right up to the line of total black. In one hand, he held three of the Witch's wishwood twigs and in the other he held the remaining twig. The muscles in his jaw worked as he looked down the line of people behind him. Nothing was visible more than a hair's breadth beyond the beginning of the crevice. Cedar took the match, struck it against the rock surface.

A brilliant purple-blue light sparked and spread into the crevice, a steady half-circle that illuminated several paces ahead. Cedar did not linger, marching into the darkness as fast as he dared while not losing the rest of them in his haste. The crevice was wide enough to walk comfortably. Timo kept one hand on Jæyd's shoulder, the other trailing along the wall to right. The stone was dark and tinted by the light of the wishwood, jagged and creased while the floor was smooth.

When the first match went out, the world was plunged into an inky blackness. The dark seeped into Timo's eyes and nose and mouth and clogged his pores. Pressure began to build as he fought the oppression, and his heart hammered in his chest. His fingers slipped from Jæyd's shoulder as the line kept moving forward, and he grabbed at her shirt as if it were the only thing tethering him to hope. Cedar had heeded the Witch's words. He led them four paces more through the dark, then they stopped, and the sounds of breathing and feet shuffling on the stone were the only indication anyone was there.

The second twig flared to life, and they were moving again. They didn't waste breath or thought on conversation. After the wishwood went out, Cedar continued for seven paces. When the third match was lit, tensions rose, adding to the dark. *Almost gone, almost used up the light,* the sinister chant seemed to whisper within the rock and follow them through the maze.

The third match went out. They continued for twelve paces before they stopped. They stood there in the darkness for several long moments. Timo's eyes began to play tricks on him, placing phantoms in the black around him, ghosts with horrible faces and monsters he and his younger brother Haldar used to scare each other when they were small.

"This is the last one," Cedar's voice floated back. Though he tried to be strong, a waver belied his trepidation.

"Well, we cannot go back. We must go forward," Jæyd's voice issued after Cedar's.

The claustrophobic elf did a much better job of hiding what must be something close to terror at the prospect of being trapped in the dark innards of the stone giant. The purple flare of the match banished Timo's spectres, but not his anxiety. Twice the match spluttered, flickered, and died, only to spark to life again. Cold sweat ran into the Daleman's eyes as they progressed, but he would not wipe it away for fear of losing Jæyd or his hold on the solid wall which kept him from floating off into the black.

Then the final match went out.

Timo waited for it to brighten again, praying for the light to come back, but it did not. Cedar led them six steps farther, then drew to a halt.

"I can lead no farther," he said in a strained voice. "I don't know where to go."

"Always right then left, except when both come abreast," Luca's whisper crept through the blinding dark with eerie similarity to the ancient voice in Timo's head.

"Okay," Cedar said. "Don't lose the person in front of you."

The going was halting. Timo's muscles were tense, fighting to keep the fear at bay as his fingers went numb in a petrified attempt not to lose his grip. The scraping of Cedar's hand against the wall was like snakes slithering. They went right, then left, then right, and left, then left again. A faint kiss of air blew from a passage on the right. *When both come abreast,* Timo chanted in his head, blinking, his breath tight in his throat. The dark clutched at Timo's feet with sticky tendrils, trying to make him stumble and fall.

As he made his way into this new passage, one hand

on Jæyd's shoulder, the other glued to the invisible wall at his side, he lost his grip on the elf. She simply was no longer there.

"Jæyd?" he called out, frozen. "Cedar?"

He received no answer. They had disappeared. They were dead - *or perhaps this was the way out of this accursed maze.* Timo gritted his teeth and took one more step forward. Then he was falling, his scream left behind in the growing air above him. He fell, and fell, and continued to fall even when he no longer had breath to scream. *Like a dragon take flight.*

On a childish impulse he could not explain, Timo rolled in the air and spread both arms in a ridiculous parody of wings, the air running through his fingers, arms straining to remain at right angles as the rushing air tried to pull them up, his shoulders growing weary after just moments…

…and his feet hit solid ground. Though he did not know how, his feet were now under him, his arms still spread. White light surrounded everything, driving into his eyes like spears. Timo's knees gave out, and he caught himself in a crouch, his arms still held out. He blinked, and the light dimmed, then became bearable as his eyes adjusted. Looking up, he saw Luca there, picking himself out of a similar pose, face white, blinking eyes clouded with terror.

"Where are we?" Luca asked, his voice a squeak

Timo recovered his wits enough to glance around, glad to have the use of his eyes back, but he trusted nothing they told him. He and his companions may not be on the Elderidge anymore or even in the Dale. They may have left their world completely. He saw what appeared to be a cavern. Only one entrance was visible, the mouth of another tunnel, triangular and gaping, stalactites and stalagmites poised like uneven fangs. It felt real enough, but this didn't convince the Daleman.

Timo opened his mouth to answer Luca's question, but didn't get a chance to speak, as Cedar appeared at that moment. Being a dragon did not come as naturally to him, and he fell and hit the ground with his shoulder. Grunting with pain, he rolled away and came up, shielding his eyes with one hand. Jæyd was next. Her breath hissed out in pain when the light assaulted her. Luca was rapidly recovering, and as his terror faded, anger suffused his cheeks with red, and his mouth worked in silent and inarticulate rage.

"Like a dragon take flight!" he finally exploded. "By all that is holy and all that is cursed, when I get my hands on this Man of Tongues, I'll…I'll…" He could find no threat good enough, and he crossed his arms with a sulky expression.

"Where is the Witch?" Cedar asked, looked around.

The others looked and worry grew on their faces when they didn't see her and she didn't appear.

"She hasn't figured out she's supposed to mimic a dragon," Luca said, his anger abating.

"Do you think we can tell her somehow?" Timo wondered. "What if she doesn't figure out the riddle?"

"That was never a riddle," Jæyd said, her voice soft. "It was a spellchantment meant to keep things out. We were only able to get here after every step was fulfilled, including walking the maze in starless night. She must do the same, or the spell will not release her."

"Do you think she'll just fall forever?" Cedar asked with an uncomfortable expression, as though he had swallowed something which disagreed with him.

Jæyd did not answer.

"How long do we wait?" Luca asked at last.

None of them wanted to answer that either.

"I have an idea!" Cedar exclaimed, his eyes brightening. "We find the Man of Tongues and he can get her out!"

"Only if he cast the spellchantment," Jæyd warned. "The spellchantment will only answer to the one who cast it."

"And who else do you think cast it?" Luca said, his voice dripping honey sarcasm.

"If not, then we can come back here and figure a way to get her out," Cedar said.

"We may not be able to get back here once we leave," Jæyd warned again. "We may still be in the throes of the spellchantment."

"I could stay," Timo said. "And continue when the Witch finds her way out."

Luca barked a laugh. "You're the one who started us on this crazy path in the first place. What are we supposed to do when we get out? We don't know where to go from here!"

"He's right," Cedar said. "We leave together or not at all."

"The Witch is resourceful. Spellchantments are right up her alley," Luca said, his face confident. "She'll find a way out."

Timo was not fooled by the dark Guardian's trick. Nor was either of the others.

"Just because you say it like you believe it doesn't make it true," Cedar snapped.

"Naturally," Luca said. When he grinned with clenched teeth at Cedar, it looked like he was considering if he should eat him or not. "It's true no matter how I say it." His expression softened. "And maybe the Man of Tongues *will* let her out. If we ask nicely and say please."

"Then you should leave the asking to me," Cedar muttered and brushed by Luca with an irritated huff. "Let's

The Other World

go."

He did not get far. A burst of red and orange light from the tunnel blew him back, accompanied with a great roar. At first Timo thought it was fire, but no heat accompanied it. A shrill cackle echoed around the chamber, bouncing off the sides until Timo was convinced someone was actually flying around like a bat. The light faded, and a figure too small to have created such a racket emerged from between the lumpy base of two stalagmites.

The figure shuffled and hopped, favoring first one foot then the other, his cackle continuing to reflect and rebound. He came closer, and Timo saw it was a wizened man who wore a loose grey robe. The man looked something like a shrunken version of the form the Demon had taken.

He was half the height of a man. Fluffy brown hair sprouted in irregular tufts. His lips were too red, and his skin too pale. His eyes turned from blue to green to yellow depending on the angle of his head, which changed frequently. He looked like a bird eyeing an unsuspecting worm. When he spoke, his voice was high and childlike.

"Hello, hello! Did you like my game, little Guardians?" he asked.

The Guardians looked at each other in shock, and the creature's smile widened. Timo saw two sets of teeth, one normal and the other hiding behind and between the first, sharp pointed needles like the teeth of the fish that lived in the farthest depths of the lake. Timo blinked and the second set disappeared.

"Quiet quiet little Guardians, did you leave your wits behind?"

"Are you the Man of Tongues?" Cedar asked, taking a step forward.

The wizened creature stared at him, then burst out

laughing again. He doubled over, hissing and wheezing with manic mirth. He pointed a hand at the Guardians, the other clutching at his heaving stomach, tears streaming from his eyes, which flashed between green and yellow.

After a few moments, he fell silent, but the laughter continued reverberating through the air much longer than was natural. He looked up at the Guardians with a smile which took up half his face, stretching his jaw and cheeks too far, and Timo tried not to look for more teeth.

"Engman of Elderidge, though some call me the Man of Tongues," the Man cackled, dropping into a low bow mocking respect. "At your service."

Timo stared at the Man, unsure what to make of him. This Man was nothing like he had expected. *But then I didn't know what I should expect,* Timo thought, unable to come up with words. Cedar had no such problem.

"The spellchantment was impressive, but one of our friends is still stuck in it," he said. "You have to let her out."

"Too easy to impress you, I think, and I did not make it to impress, no, no, no," the Man said with a frown as disproportionate as his smile had been.

Cedar sucked a breath in through his teeth, and seemed to remember Luca's advice. "Please let her out?"

"Aha! The magyc word. Of course I will. Or maybe I won't." The Man tapped his nose and scrunched up his face.

The Guardians held very still, watching him consider. He looked back at them with wide eyes, blinking slowly.

"No words? No pleas? No begging?" he said at last, sounding disappointed. "Do you not love this friend of yours? Perhaps I'll leave her there."

"No!" Cedar exclaimed.

"What will you give me if I bring her out?" the Man said.

The Guardians shared uncertain looks. Cedar looked around as if something of value would be lying on the ground nearby. Luca felt his violin, and his shoulders slumped, but his expression was set and determined.

"No, no, no," the Man said before the dark Guardian could offer his precious instrument. "That is no good to me. I am not a Guardian." He looked from one to the next. "Nothing? You have nothing?" He looked up at Timo, craning his neck to meet the much taller man's eyes. "Not even you Daleman? I know you have. What brought you to me, Daleman? Have you lost that? Did you lose it in the dark? I think not, think not, think not I do."

Timo sighed. He pulled the statuette from his jerkin and held it in his extended hand. The Man's eyes widened and his fingers twitched.

"You know what this is?" Timo said.

The Man nodded, reaching eagerly for the statuette, but Timo held it back. The Man pouted and withdrew his hand, twisting them against his chest.

"Pretty, pretty. Where did you come by that, Daleman?"

"A woman in Torin made it," Timo said, and thought perhaps the Man already knew that.

"Powerful magyc," the Man said. "First Magyc." He closed his eyes and chanted.

"They who wield the First,
Sacrifice the most
The hunger, the thirst
For the power they boast."

"He speaks of the Conhaime," Jæyd murmured, her head tilting as she frowned in confusion. "But this woman could not have been. The Conhaime are extinct."

In all his life, Timo had never heard of the Conhaime, but now was not the time to go down that side trail.

"I do not believe Eselma was whatever you are referring to," Timo said, holding the statuette out to the Man. "But this is yours if you bring back our friend and help us."

The Man of Tongues cocked his head, eyes shining. "Always more, always more. More, more, more. What can I do for you Daleman?"

"We have to find someone," Timo said. "In another world."

"Ah-ha," the Man clapped his hands, childlike, and did a little dance, capering about in a circle like an absurdly large monkey.

Timo waited for him to say more, but the Man just looked at him brightly, one eye twitching slightly. The Guardian began to regret his hunch about coming here, but they were invested this far and all he could do was push on.

"We need your help getting to the other world," Timo continued.

The Man laughed.

"I can send you from here to there
But I ask you first there is where?
In another world, another time
To what you seek, or what you find?"

"I wish he would stop with the whole speaking in verse thing," Luca muttered. "It's giving me a headache."

"From verse one can learn
That which he cannot see
From song one discerns
What to do, or what to be,"

"I shouldn't have opened my mouth," Luca said.

The Man prepared to launch into another fit of singing,

and Luca gave him a warning look. The Man froze, then stepped closer to the dark Guardian, his mouth now agape in wonder.

"What is it that *you* have, sparkly man? Show me now. Show me!"

Luca drew back, repulsed, and Timo watched intently. Both Luca and the Man of Tongues were unpredictable and volatile when on their own, and Timo wanted to be ready to step in before a potentially dangerous explosion caused irreparable harm. Cedar and Jæyd were as watchful, leaning forward, poised to act in an instant.

The Man capered up to Luca and though Luca was not a tall man, he still stood two heads taller than the Man. He looked down at the Man with the same revulsion he would a grubby child. Quick as lightening the Man's hand shot out, going for Luca's jacket, but even faster was Luca's hand, which darted out to close around the Man's wrist.

The Man yelped but couldn't extricate himself from the Guardian's grip. Luca bared his teeth at the Man and the Man stuck out his tongue, then disappeared in a puff of purple smoke. He reappeared behind Luca and tried again to get his fingers into Luca's pocket, but the pickpocket wasn't quick enough. Somehow Luca managed to grab him again.

The Man gave up after this second attempt, pouting. Two tears ran down his cheeks and splashed onto his grey robes. Luca did not look impressed. More tears followed the first.

"Stop it," Luca said. "I mean that."

"Or what will…" the Man fell silent under Luca's gaze, and his tears dried up at once. "Fine, find, little Guardian. Keep your little Demonhärt. I don't need it, no I don't."

"I don't know how you can call me *little* when you're the size of a half-starved cat," Luca said, throwing the Man away from him. "Now, are you going to help us or are we going to make you help us?"

The Man considered, tapping a long finger against his nose, eyes bright with avarice. His gaze kept sliding back to Luca, but he wouldn't meet the Guardian's eyes. Luca just glowered at him.

"Help you, I shall," the Man of Tongues said at last. "If you give me the Key."

Key was a new word to describe this statue the Daleman had acquired, and the way the Man said it rang in the air. Naming it such told the world it was in the presence of something extraordinary, and the world responded with the proper respect.

Timo cocked his head. "Key to what?" he asked.

"Key to whatever you need it to open."

Timo rubbed the statuette between his finger and thumb. He had not thought much about it since receiving it from Eselma, the Blood-Magyc-wielding sculptress in Torin. Jæyd's reaction to it, and now the Man's desire for it, made him reevaluate its worth. *It can be whatever you need it to be,* the specter of Eselma whispered in his ear and he started.

The Man was grinning at him, as if he too had heard the memory. Timo clenched his fist around the carving, and trying to convince himself he was not making a decision he would regret, he held the Key out to the Man of Tongues. The Man snatched it up, cackling and prancing about in a clumsy and erratic dance of glee.

"Ma...Engman," Cedar said with firm patience. "Time is of the essence."

The Man of Tongues stopped dead still and slowly turned to face the Guardian. Raising his skinny arms above his head, he chanted three syllables in an ominous voice. *Da Var Rüm.* Cedar glanced about with wary eyes, waiting for something to strike him down, but nothing happened. The Man tittered.

"No more games," Timo said. "I have given you what you asked for. Now you must help us."

"Help you, help you!" Engman grinned. "Yes, of course. With what?"

"First bring back S'Aris," Luca interrupted, before Timo could say anything.

The Man rolled his eyes, then he waved his hand and S'Aris fell out of the air. She hit the ground hard, and cried out in pain. Luca and Timo rushed to her and pulled her up. She winced, then attempted a smile.

"I'm fine," she said. "Just a little bruised."

Her face was white, but her eyes were calm. *Perhaps Luca was right and she was more than a match for a spellchantment*, Timo thought. *Or at least easier for her to tolerate,* he amended when the Witch shuddered.

"You were supposed to fly like a dragon," Timo explained, and held out his arms to demonstrate.

Surprise flashed on the Witch's face, then understanding. "Oh!"

"Well, now you'll know for next time you get caught in a spellchantment cast by an unstable sorcerer inside a magyc mountain," Luca said in a silver-lining tone.

S'Aris gave a weak laugh. "Believe it or not, I actually missed your horrible sense of humor."

"Not many of my jokes are worse than falling through endless blackness," Luca agreed.

"Though that one might be one of them," Timo said. "And a little of your humor goes a long way."

Luca twisted his lips in a sneer but saved his retort as Cedar turned to the Man of Tongues.

"And now the second thing," the golden-eyed Guardian demanded.

"What second thing?" the Man of Tongues said, his hands clasped behind his back, looking up with an innocent face.

"We must retrieve someone from another world," Cedar explained in a patient voice.

The Man wrinkled his nose. "No."

Cedar blinked. "But you said…"

"I know, I know," the Man looked behind him at the tunnel. "Got to go."

He dashed into the tunnel and without hesitation the Guardians and the Witch followed at a sprint. The Man of Tongues ducked into a side crack which the Guardians had to turn to the side in order to fit, which slowed them considerably. Timo sucked in his stomach, holding his breath as he inched along behind Luca, peering ahead with half an eye, afraid of losing the Man.

"Need to lose some weight around the middle, hey Timo?" Luca gasped.

Timo didn't have the breath to answer, nor did he have the range of motion to hit Luca. Instead the Daleman concentrated on taking shallow breaths and inching along as fast as he could. On the other side the Guardians spilled out into another small cave.

This was the Man of Tongues' home, Timo saw. *Or one of them.*

The Man of Tongues stood in the middle of the cave. A blanket on a rickety bed was bunched upon on end, spilling onto the floor. A rock with a more or less flat top served as a chair beside a ledge recessed into the cave wall. A few odds and ends decorated the natural table, a dried flower, the skull of some rodent, and a fork. A bucket in the corner was full of scummy water. Timo couldn't imagine what this Man ate.

"Your other place was a lot nicer," Luca commented,

wrinkling his nose.

The Man scowled at him. "Shouldn't make fun of those whose help you need, little Guardian. Bad things could happen."

Luca was unconcerned. "Why didn't you just send the Demons away? You're a sorcerer aren't you? Surely you could've done that?"

"Yes, yes," the Man of Tongues said. "Easy to think, easy to say, not so easy to do, day after day."

"They bother you that much?" Luca said.

"They think I can help them just like you think I can help you," the Man snickered. "Jokes on you all. I won't help them and I can't..." He paused and looked at Luca. "Maybe I can help you," he amended. "If the sparkly Guardian plays nice."

"I'm always nice," Luca said. "Now, about this person we need to find-"

The Man of Tongues cackled. "Going to find *Aethsiths*, little Guardian? Already found her, you did, then you lost her."

"What do you mean by that?" Cedar demanded, his head coming up sharply.

"The Girl from Another World," the Man of Tongues answered with a sly smile. "Too easy to see, for someone who has the right eyes. Right, Daleman?"

He looked right at Timo. Timo glanced away. Twelve years ago he had made a journey up here and been taken into a dream of the Path. He had met *Aethsiths*, or something that claimed to be her, a figure which was more light and movement than form. She had asked for his help, and at that moment, Timo knew deep down it had become his duty to find her. It was more than instinct. It was what his people called *Ándahs˙Éllahd* - the "second-sight". But only descendants of the First King possessed any measure of *Ándahs˙Éllahd*. And he was descended of the Third King. It did not make sense to him then, and it did not make sense to him now.

"Ria is not who you say," Cedar stated, his voice sharp. "Her Mark says so."

"No. Her Mark says what her Mark says, not what you want it to say. You just will not listen to it."

Timo gaped. How could he know that? The Man of Tongues was more powerful than his slight and disconcerting form would suggest. Timo was not too preoccupied with this to notice that Cedar didn't like what the Man said at all. As always, when Ria and *Aethsiths* were mentioned in the same sentence as interchangeable, he put up a brick wall.

"We are not here to discuss who *Aethsiths* is," the elf interjected before Cedar could comment. "Only to find her."

"Find her, find her, find her, but where is she?" the Man said. "What if she lives not in a different place only, but a different *time* as well?"

Timo had not thought of that. "What do you mean?"

"The past or the future. Not *now* but *then*," the Man said, his eyes wide. "What will you do if that is the case, Guardian? Flip the World's Hourglass and make the sand run backwards? Or break it and have the sand pour forward?"

Timo's eyes flicked to Luca. A fine sheen of sweat had broken out on the diminutive Guardian's face. Just a short time ago he had been thrown back to the Isos of his childhood, an Isos of two hundred years earlier. Though the tale stretched the limits of the mind to the breaking point, Luca was convinced. The haunted look in his eyes said as much, and Timo believed him and doubted at the same time.

S'Aris spoke up, her voice shaky. "There are rumors, whispers rather, at the Coven that some can traverse the Nexus between times as well, but only with…" she paused, searching for a word. "…forbidden methods."

"Yes, yes! Through space, yesss, and also time," the Man said, and cackled. "But can it be done be done be done they wonder."

His insanity was wearing on the nerves of the Guardians and the Witch, pulling at frayed threads and unraveling it further.

"Well, *can* it?" Cedar snapped, his voice cracking in the middle.

"Of course it *can* be done," the Man said with a sniff, somehow looking down his nose at Cedar while looking up at him. "Demons do it all the time, you know." He smiled, enjoying their skepticism. "Have been too, since before Time."

"That's impossible," Luca said. "How can they travel through time before there *was* time?"

The Man of Tongues looked surprised, then hurt. "Liar, liar, pants on fire, he says." He burst out laughing. "Right he is too. I lied. They didn't do it before Time, but they don't know Time like we do." He tapped his nose. "How do you think they knew who *Aethsiths* was before you did, little Guardians?"

"Ria of the other world was not, and is not, *Aethsiths*," Cedar said quietly. "Her Mark confirmed that, and Marks do not lie."

This sent the Man of Tongues into a fit of laughing so violent Timo was afraid he was going to hurt himself. *If he hadn't already hurt himself beyond fixing*, Timo thought with some pity.

Wiping his streaming eyes, Engman the Man of Tongues bit his lip to keep from bursting into laughter again and explained to the Guardians as though they were very small children.

"Not the Mark of *Aethsiths,* no because not *Aethsiths* she was," he said.

Cedar shifted. The sentiment was familiar to Timo as well. It sounded like what the Maker Llaem Bli had told the Guardians while they took shelter under his roof. *If the girl changes, then her Mark will change too.*

"So is she *Aethsiths* then?" Luca snapped.

"Not telling," the Man smirked. "You wouldn't believe me anyway, little Guardians."

Though he may not like the answer, Cedar asked the question. "Can you do it? Can you send us to Ria…if she is *Aethsiths?*"

"And the one with golden eyes asks the right question." The Man of Tongues regarded him. "I can, yes I can. Send you to find this girl, or send you to find *Aethsiths* I can. Not both, not both. *What?* they think. *Why?* they wonder. Not two of you, can't be in two times at once."

"You said Demons do it," Luca said, a querulous edge to his lilt. "We're smarter than they are, we should be able to do it."

"Different than a Demon, yes, smarter, no." Luca looked infuriated, and the Man clapped his hands. "Can you survive in both a world of the Path and a world of the Voide, hmm? The answer is no, no, no, definitely no. And why why why you say?" The Man looked about like a teacher who thought he had asked a very simple question and hoped one of his students was bright enough to answer. Like a teacher, his face fell when nothing was forthcoming. "Because born of Chaos are the Demons. You are born of the Path. Cosmogony, cosmogony."

The last syllables sounded like his usual nonsense, until he deigned to define it. "The origin of all the universe, lands, realms, worlds, everything. Where did it all come from? How did it all come to be?"

The tangent was not relevant, and Cedar shifted restlessly. "We don't have time for..." he began.

"Time, I can give you time," Engman said. He snapped his fingers and presented an empty palm to Cedar. "Lots of time."

Cedar stared at the outstretched hand, lines etched into pale flesh, tracery of purple veins showing through the papery skin. He took a deep breath, then nodded as he reached out and plucked some of the nothing from the Man of Tongues. "Very well."

A change came over the Man. His face smoothed out and he somehow became younger. The light in his eye dimmed from a febrile gleam to an adroit twinkle. Standing taller, he addressed Cedar in a clear and lucid voice, though he retained a hint of his childish sing-song. "There may be hope for you yet, Guardian, indeed, indeed. Would you like to know about the Chaos which birthed the Demons Nine?"

"Not really," Cedar said, tapping his foot.

"Closed eyes, closed mind, doesn't look, doesn't find," Engman chided.

"If you're going to lecture, speak plainly," Cedar retorted.

"Speak plainly, he says, and I shall, but in what tongue?" the Man grinned wickedly. "I know them all, I do. Do you?"

"Using a language I don't understand would hardly be speaking plainly," Cedar grumbled.

Timo was afraid that Cedar would sour the sorcerer's mood, and he would no longer considered helping them, but the Man of Tongues remained sedate. He began to speak, and as the words flowed from his lips, he was further changed. *There is a reason he is called the Man of Tongues.* The words and the magyc they held, magyc of the past, and of meaning, and of thought, held whatever insanity plagued Engman of Elderidge at bay. Timo was disquieted by the thought that while his mad counterpart was powerful, this other side was even more so.

"Now you speak of things that I know more about than any living and most dead. Languages. Tongues. The beauty, magyc even, of words. What do you know of these things, little Guardian?"

"I'm not sure," Cedar said, and hurried to add more, though he did not know what the Man meant for him to say. "I speak, and I read. If I don't know a language, I cannot do this."

"And what of words?" Engman asked. "What of the magyc of words?"

"I only know magyc as the Path," Cedar said. "It comes in golden light and music. I feel it here -" he pressed his hand against his chest. "But there are no words."

"That is akin to sight without color," the Man lamented. "Flatter, emptier, grey."

"But I'm not color-blind. I can see it if you show me," Cedar said earnestly.

"Then what does it mean, Cedar Jal of Torin-before-it-fell?"

"What does *what* mean?"

"The *word*. The *name*. The name for the one you seek."

"*Aethsiths*?" Cedar frowned. "It means *songstress*, the..."

Engman's quiet chuckle stopped him short. "That is not wrong. *The singer of songs* is one of its meanings, I grant you. But there are other meanings, older meanings if you like, though a meaning that is timeless is neither old or new."

The Guardians were still, tense, hoping to preserve the spell. Timo didn't know exactly what was happening, and he half expected the Man to suddenly revert to the half-mad trickster, gibbering riddles with answers only known to him.

"Do you know how many tongues there are and have been and will be?" Engman continued.

"A lot?" Cedar tried.

"An overly simple answer, but again, not wrong. Do you know which is the oldest of all of them?"

"The elves?" Cedar guessed.

"No. The language of the VarHaynei," Jæyd countered. "Before they were destroyed."

"Wrong. And wrong." The Man grinned with malicious delight at the pronouncement.

"The Builders," Timo said.

"Not quite right!" the Man said, his eyes lightening further. "Think, think, my pretty blond friend, what is older than even the Builders?"

"The Path!" Cedar cried.

"Half right!"

"The Void," S'Aris said softly.

"Half right again is the Witch," the Man said.

"What is the full right answer?" Luca said.

"Put them together and what have you got?" Engman hinted.

He received five blank stares.

"Something," the Man proclaimed, holding out his hands as if presenting a priceless piece of wisdom.

The blankness did not abate.

"Just something?" Luca asked. "What sort of something?"

"Not something - *Something*," the Man said.

"Before The Beginning was Nothing,
"Dark and Solitary, Empty and Silent.
"And it Existed
"Without Light or Time or Counterpart,
"And it Was.
"And it Was All.

"At The Beginning
"Came into being Something,
"Which in Truth was Two.
"The First of Two, the Impulse of Life,
"Which in Time would be known as the Path.
"The Second, Twin to Life, its Equal yet Opposite,
"Which in Time would be known as the Voide."

"It is the Legend of the Builders," the Man said, his voice reverent and wistful.

"What does that have to do with us, here, now?" Cedar said, his tone pleading.

"First came Sentience. Then came Understanding. Then came Thought, and only then came Words; The Thought Word, The Spoken Word and then the Written Word. Demon magyc, including the magyc of their words, is magyc of the Voide, which came at the very beginning of sentience, before you and your kind, and that is why the Guardians cannot understand it."

"So you're saying the word *Aethsiths* is a...a *Demon* word?" Cedar gaped.

"You're skeptical, Cedar Jal. What you must understand is that your namesake, Cedar Rün, was just a man. A great man, but just a man. He saw things through a man's eyes, with a man's perspective. He was shown *Aethsiths,* but the Demons know *Aethsiths* better because it is they who named her."

"She is chosen by the Path," Cedar asserted.

"Chosen maybe, but named still by the Nine," the Man said serenely.

"Eight," Luca muttered.

"Pardon?" the Man said, his voice turning sharp.

"We killed the God of Blood some time past," Luca said, matter-of-factly, though his eyes held the glint of a boast. "Only Eight to go now."

"Oh, you foolish, foolish, young creature," the Man lamented, passing his hand over his face. "It was never meant to be that way."

His sadness vexed the Guardians. He explained, and his tale made him old, again a thing of the forgotten days only he remembered.

"In the beginning was Chaos, when the Path and the Voide mixed freely without barrier. Gods - yes, Gods, for that is what they were - of the Voide, and Gods of the Path came to be within this Chaos and existed there. How long this was so, I cannot say, for how long can someone live when there is no time through which to pass in order to measure how long? Then the Gods of the Path created worlds, separate from the Voide, and put up Walls to keep it so. Some say this was the birth of Time, and yes, of Death. You, born only of the Path, dislike the feel of the Voide on your skin and in your lungs."

"Hang on just one moment," Luca interjected. "I can see where you're going with this. You're going to say the Nine never meant any harm and never wanted anything with any of us, but I would just like to point out they have been trying to kill us for several thousand years, starting with the First Guardian."

"And before that?" Engman commented with mild interest.

Luca's mouth hung open, but no words issued so

Engman answered his own question.

"Before that, Demons did not plague the world, as you would describe it. Sometimes yes, they found a way here, but there is no malintent, no desire to come here, just as you have no desire to go to their cold, dead world. Where they thrive and you find only discomfort. But there is no death there, for in order for Death to be there must be Life, and the Path is Life and the Voide is..."

He left the question hanging in the air.

"Death?" Timo ventured.

"Not Death," Engman pounced. "Death came after. The Voide is the opposite of the Path, the opposite of Life. What is the opposite of Life? The antithesis, the converse, the counterpart, the inverse obverse reverse?"

"Death," Luca said firmly.

"That is the end of life, the absence of it, but what is the opposite of it? The Voide!"

"What's your point?" Cedar asked.

"You think you know everything, but you only know what you know, and what you know does not even begin to touch the faintest edges of everything," Engman said. "You must remember that when you look at the world. There may be little or much that you don't know. Now I ask you. Where shall I send you?"

"Maybe two of us could go to Ria, and the others could go to the time and place of *Aethsiths*," Jæyd said.

The Man of Tongues shook his head. "To the girl or to *Aethsiths*. Only one, not both. You must choose a place to arrive, or lost between worlds you will be forever."

The others looked to Cedar. His face was tight, and emotions warred in his eyes, disbelief, distrust, anguish, hope and despair. Timo knew if Cedar still truly believed that Ria was not *Aethsiths,* all his heart would be crying out to go to the girl and protect her.

Cedar looked like he would rather stab his eyes out than choose between the two. He was a Guardian of the Path, a protector of the magyc that is the lifeblood of the world, and to forsake that was counter spirit, mind and body of a Guardian. Something like the Heartbeat of worlds runs parallel to their own heart, and when he made the pronouncement, the honor of the First Guardian was untarnished, and their own honor would remain so.

"We go to *Aethsiths*," Cedar said.

MAN OF TONGUES PART IV

When Cedar's words fell upon his ears, Luca sighed to himself. Part of him had hoped Cedar would've chosen to go to Ria and bugger the whole *Aethsiths* problem. *It's not like we have to babysit* Aethsiths - *she's powerful and capable enough to take care of herself. Demonfire, she's supposed to come save us!*

Still, Luca's gut told him Cedar had made the right choice, though it was also the hardest choice. He comforted himself with the hope that Ria and *Aethsiths* turned out to be one and the same. *Even if Cedar doesn't wish it so, I do.*

Luca looked to the Man of Tongues to see what he thought. The Man saw Luca's glance, and Engman grinned slyly, his eyes beginning to shine with an odd gleam as he hunched back over to his favored twisted posture. Luca frowned, then rolled his eyes. He suspected the inanity was a ruse, something to throw off the eye and any suspicion.

Engman of Elderidge crossed his eyes, threw his hands up and screeched, startling the other three Guardians. *Crazy's back.*

"To *Aethsiths!* You come with me," the Man of Tongues shouted, waving his hands in the air. "I will send you to her!"

He shuffle-hopped to the back wall and passed his hand through the air in front of it. The rock rippled, then parted like water. A tunnel appeared, the mouth triangular in shape, and Engman spun in a circle, threw his head back, and laughing maniacally, disappeared into the black. The sounds of his progress diminished, and still the Guardians stared at the wall, unwilling to move.

Without warning the Man popped back out, running full tilt at Timo. The big Daleman did not have enough time to move and Engman's head plowed into Timo's midsection. Like a comic routine, Timo and the little Man fell back onto the bed against the wall, and it splintered under his weight. The Man of Tongues was quick to jump up, but the Daleman was not so. Timo picked himself out of the debris, his face growing redder by the moment. The muscles in his jaw worked, but he said nothing.

"Come, come!" Engman sang, and once more disappeared.

Silent as stone, Timo made to follow him.

"Are you sure that's a good idea?" Luca said.

"The sooner we are gone from here the better," Timo said, grinding the words out between clenched teeth.

The Guardians followed the Man of Tongues along the serpentine passages. They emerged into a round cavern just in time to see him disappear into yet another hole. Jæyd shuddered.

"It can't be much longer now," Cedar tried to comfort her.

She smiled at him gratefully, but did not look comforted.

"How do we get up there?" Luca wondered, gazing up.

The hole the Man had disappeared into was set in the stone half a length again as tall as Timo. The Daleman tried to reach it with his fingertips, but he was too short, even when he jumped.

"That's not going to work, big man. Give me a boost," Luca said.

Timo laced his hands and made a step for the svelte Guardian, and sent him flying into the hole with an enthusiastic heave. Luca landed with a muffled grunt, and when he tried to come to his feet, his violin emitted a bang of protest when it hit the ceiling. Luca turned back and stuck his head out the hole, directing an unimpressed look down at Timo, who shrugged a careless apology.

"Who's next?" Luca asked, gesturing for someone to step up.

"Ladies first," Cedar bowed at S'Aris.

The Witch was hoisted up, in a gentler fashion than Luca had been, he noticed. She was followed by Jæyd, then Cedar. Timo tossed Cedar's guitar to him, and then his own drums. The tunnel was tight, but now a hint of sunlight trickled back, shining off the fine sheen of sweat on the elf's brow. Cedar turned back and hung the front half of his body out of the opening.

"Don't let me fall," he called back to Jæyd.

The elf grasped his ankles. This time when Timo leaped, Cedar was there to catch him and pull while Timo used his legs to propel himself up the wall. Jæyd pulled the both of them back, then leaned against the curving wall, bent over and winded.

"I see an opening!" the Witch's voice floated down to them.

The elf looked up, pure determinism making her eyes flinty. Massaging her side with a wince, she started towards the Witch's voice. The light grew brighter and brighter, as did Jæyd's face. The others came close behind her, footsteps thudding on the floor. Soon the sound of water trickled to their ears and the air cooled, fresh draughts chasing away the memories of stale, suffocating breaths. They came upon the Witch gazing with delight at a picture out of a fairy tale.

Moss-covered rocks framed a portal to an enchanting vale. White water sang as it splashed and dripped its way down to a pristine lake which sparkled in dappled sunlight, and yellow and pink flowers grew in abundance, creating a fragrant carpet.

Partially ruining the effect, the Man of Tongues splashed madly in the shallow water, moving in the direction of the waterfall. He walked through it, gargling and spitting the water as it ran over his head and became a vague shape on the other side before disappearing completely.

"We'd better make sure he doesn't accidentally drown or something," Luca said, starting out of the rock archway. "I don't want to have gone through all that for nothing."

The Guardians followed the Man, the cold water leaving them breathless, skin flushed and tingling from the kiss of ice. The mountain pool glittered like a sapphire and reeds and lilies grew at the edges of the water, giving way to maple and magnolia. Blue sky peeked through the foliage, and sunlight shone down in white gold spears, liming silver and gold motes drifting in the air. Rocks covered in silver and blue lichen formed a stairway beside the waterfalls, and up these the Man of Tongues scrambled to the lip of rock overhanging, where he struck a grand pose.

"Welcome to the Wellspring of Doors!" he announced.

"I don't see any Doors," Luca said after an unimpressed survey of the glade.

"Wellspring of Doors, Wellspring of Doors," the Man chattered. "Wellspring, spring, spring of Doors; not *Vault* of Doors, silly little Guardian. They spring forth when called, but one must do the calling before they do the springing."

Cedar was flushed, a fanatically hopeful gleam in his eyes, ready to claim the prize they sought. "What do you want us to do?" he asked.

"Stand there, be fair of form and face, and Engman shall do the rest."

"I have a bad feeling about this," Luca muttered. "And he's not doing much to put my fears to rest."

"I can heeeeeeeear youuuuuuu," the Man hollered, making the Guardians start.

He leapt down from his pulpit on the rocks, looking like a skinny, hairless, flying squirrel and landed in front of the Guardians in a surprising graceful manner, surprising mostly because he did not hurt himself. "Look there," he commanded.

Hanging over the little fall, like a bridge of glittering cloth, was a rainbow. Red, yellow, blue, and green swirled like ribbons of smoke, blending into colors which did not have names where they met. It appeared solid enough to walk upon.

"It's lovely," Cedar said, nonplussed. "Now what about that Door?"

The Man of Tongues made a "tsk" of disapproval. "Every child of this realm knows the story of the secret rainbows hide at their ends," he said. "A disgrace, I think, that you do not."

"A pot of Living gold," Timo spoke up. "Watched over by a gremlin. If you are able to catch it..."

"No gremlin. None! Nor imp or little demon!" the Man said fiercely. "It is a metaphor."

"A metaphor for what?" Cedar asked.

"Alchemy." Luca rolled his eye. "It's nonsense. If ever a person existed who could change lead to gold, he's gone from these realms."

The Man sang, "What is gold, not only seen, but felt and heard in a dream, takes you places far away, or tomorrow or yesterday, belongs to all, yours and mine, existing since before all time?"

"The Path!" Jæyd breathed.

"True, true," the Man agreed with a proud smile at the elf, his star pupil.

"So you're saying the legend of Living Gold at the end of a rainbow refers to the Path?" Luca asked.

"Not the Path, the *power* of the Path." The Man cackled, and scrambled back up to stand at the top of the ledge, under the rainbow, waiving his hands at it as if he could reach it or pull it out of the sky.

The Guardians looked at the rainbow with new eyes.

"So what do we have to do?" Cedar asked, his tone growing more urgent.

"Ask too many questions too many times," the Man shouted, waving his finger at the golden-eyed Guardian. "I have already told you. Stand there, and remain fair of form. Except this one."

He pointed at Luca, and Luca's heart started drumming double-time. The Man of Tongues beckoned him, and Luca came with heavy feet, climbing the slippery stairway until he reached the Man of Tongues. Luca was not a tall man, but even at five and a half feet, he was head and shoulders above the Man.

This must be what it feels like to be Cedar or Timo looking at normal people. His mind was compressed by a dull terror, not a knife to cut coldly to the marrow, but a blanket to wrap him up and smother him. *Here it comes,* he thought, and though he could not put words to what *it* was, part of him knew.

He looked down into the almond eyes of the Man. They were as curious as the Man himself, now hazel in color with pale flecks throughout. Sometimes these flecks appeared gold, sometimes blue or purple or white. The pupils dilated and contracted in no relation to a change of light, and at times even elongated so they resembled the cat's eyes of the Nitefolk.

"Are you ready, Luca Lorisson, the man with the Demon's heart?" the Man of Tongues asked, his voice oddly gentle.

His words solidified the terror into a pit in Luca's stomach, until he figured out the Man had actually said *Demonhärt.*

"No," Luca said honestly.

"True, true," the Man said, voice still soft.

"What are you singling me out for anyway?" Luca asked.

"I already told you this, little Guardian, in the Legend of the Builders," the Man chided. "You carry the Demonhärt. This will guide you where you need to go."

Luca tried to swallow and speak, but his mouth was too dry. He nodded instead. He turned to find the other Guardians clustered around the Witch and conferring with great intensity. After a moment, Cedar noticed Luca staring.

"S'Aris is staying here," he said, his voice carrying to Luca.

"Why?" Luca demanded, then regretted his tone. *It*

probably has something to do with the falling in darkness. She doesn't want to risk that again. Not that I blame her.

"The princess has not answered again."

"This is the tenth time I've tried to contact her," S'Aris said, biting her lip. "I'm afraid something terrible has happened to her. I was sent to help you, Guardians, but she is my friend, and I feel I must go to her. She has no one else."

"Of course you must go to her," Jæyd said, with a glance at Cedar and Luca, and both men nodded in agreement.

"You are not bound to us," Cedar told her. "Luca, will you please tell her?"

Luca stared at him, trying not to think of Liæna, and the way she left so abruptly. "Why would she listen to me? She's smart enough to figure out what to do. But really," he added quickly before Cedar could say anything. "You should go if you think the princess needs you."

"But the princess is a capable woman," Timo said, placing a comforting hand on the Witch's shoulder. "I wouldn't worry about her."

S'Aris nodded with a weak smile, yet she did not look convinced. She frowned, as if trying to remember something, then her eyes widened in pleased recollection. She reached into the innumerable pockets of her Witch's robe and brought out another small mirror, like the one she had used to make the scrying glass for the princess and the assassin. This one she broke in half.

"I'm going to need an eyelash," she told Cedar, the same instruction she had given the two women before.

Cedar complied, and the Witch spelled the glass, and handed him the larger piece.

"We may not be able to use this where we're going," Cedar said, his fingers loose around the sharp edges of the scrying glass.

"For when you return then," S'Aris replied and briskly tucked her half back in her dress, smoothing it into place.

Then the Witch stood there, her hands fluttering as if she wasn't sure where to put them. She suddenly moved forward and threw her arms around Timo for a brief second, then Cedar. She paused in front of Jæyd, almost bowed, hesitated, and would have carried on like that for who knows how long if the elf had not stepped forward and put her arms around the Witch.

"Farewell," Jæyd said, eyes closed as she embraced the Witch tightly. "We will meet again soon."

S'Aris took in a shaky breath and gave a brave smile as she stepped back. "I hope it is sooner rather than later. I will miss you all."

"I can make you wish you'd never see me again, if you'd like. Or at least not miss me while you're gone," Luca called down to her, not wanting to be forgotten in the farewells.

S'Aris gave a choked laugh which came out as a snort through her nose and turned to look at him. "I will miss you too, Luca Lorisson, Son of a Witch."

Luca grimaced, but inside he was not displeased. The Witch walked up to where he stood with the Man of Tongues. Luca gave her a hand over the last and largest step, balancing with his feet wide apart on two sturdy stepping stones and accepted the Witch's embrace. She pulled away, staring at the strange sorcerous Man blinking happily at nothing over her left shoulder.

"How do I get out?" S'Aris said. "Please don't make me go back through that mountain."

Luca looked at the Man of Tongues. "Can you send her straight to the princess Berria In'Orain of Ghor?"

"Too far, too far," the Man said, still staring over her

shoulder. "Too too far far."

"It's not even out of the world," Luca protested.

"Too. Far."

"Fine. Can you at least send her out of the Dale?"

The Man of Tongues thought for a moment. He tapped his chin, then his nose. He pulled on his right ear, then tried to balance his head by pulling on his left ear. "Yes. Yes, I think I can do that. Come here, come here."

S'Aris stepped closer. She was a head taller than he was. Her white dress blew around her knees, the short sleeves crossing at the back. Her bare arms were un-tattooed, unlike the traditional style of Nyica, though on her hand right hand was the symbol of her faction, the faction of V'Ronica, the *Eohl'Di, the Traitors* in the language of Lii.

The Man of Tongues plucked a flower from between his feet and held it out to her. She reached for it, but he snatched it back. They repeated this five times and the Witch fought to keep the growing exasperation in check.

"Do you want me to take it or not?" she finally demanded.

The Man of Tongues thrust it into her hands and gave her a wicked grin. "Hold tight."

He gave her a shove, and with a high-pitched scream, the Witch fell into the lake, bobbed once, then disappeared. The water frothed and spat and began to spin. Luca leaped down and splashed into the water but a great wall of force pushed him out, and he fell back against the other Guardians who had rushed to the edge. They looked down at the water, now moving faster, and the noise rose to thunderous levels, but no sign of the Witch remained.

"What do we do?" Cedar yelled above the growing roar of the spout.

"We have to trust him," Jæyd replied, though her face was pale, and she did not look like she had her usual strength of conviction behind her words.

In a flash of light, the spout went black and disappeared. The water gave a last shimmer, then settled back into its lazy rippling. The Guardians continued to watch, both hoping for the Witch to reappear, and that she had been safely sent on her way.

"Ready, ready, are we now, little Guardians?" the chattering voice called out. "Don't have all day, we don't."

The Guardians looked back. Though it did not seem possible, the sunlight was dimming and the rainbow was fading.

"It's now or never," Luca said. "And right now, never is looking better."

"Let's go," Cedar said grimly, as if he had not heard him.

"After you," Luca said, giving a great sweep of his hand and marching after Cedar.

The Guardians stood arrayed in front of the Man of Tongues.

"Engman!" Cedar called out. "We are ready!"

The Man of Tongues cackled and bounded up to where the refracted light started. He looked out and caught Luca's eye, then beckoned with a long finger. Luca pulled a face, his hope that the Man had forgotten he was needed dashed, but clambered up once more to stand beside the Man.

With a wink, the Man reached out and began to pull the color from the rainbow. More shades appeared, shades of blue-yellow and purple-green that words could not describe though the eye could see them in all their brilliance. He wove them together tighter and tighter, the colors coming together to form even more complex and unique hues.

Only the suggestion of an arc was left when the Man had finished, grey and white and silver, and in his hand, he held a shining ball of iridescence. It illuminated his face, making him look different, not younger exactly, but more real. Its light fell on the Guardians, making their Auras visible, glowing gold arcs surrounding their body.

"Are you ready, Guardian?" the Man of Tongues asked Luca.

Luca reached into the pocket of his jacket, and gripped the Demonhärt tight with his hand and the image of *Aethsiths* with his mind. "Ready or not, here we come," he whispered and the Man grinned.

"And you, Guardians?" he called to the others. "Are you ready?"

The three stood firm together, looking much like their portraits in the Guardians' Hall, which served to make more solid the picture in Luca's mind. Cedar gave one grim, firm nod.

The Man of Tongues turned to Luca and kicked him in the rear, launching him towards his fellows. Luca caught Cedar in a flying tackle, and the two went down. Luca turned to see the Man blow upon his globe of shining color and ignite it in a ball of flame. As he raised it over his head, it looked as though he held the sun between his fingers, red and gold.

"Fare thee well Guardians!" he called, his sing-song voice augmented by magyc, undulating through the glade. "Come visit me again soon!"

With those words he heaved the singing ball of flame at them. Luca flinched, anticipating the impact. None came. Instead the light enveloped them, growing brighter. Then they were swept away on an invisible wave, plucked off the ground and hurtled along. Spinning, tumbling head over heels in a cyclone of gold...

As he tumbled through whatever it was he was tumbling through, Luca tried to keep the picture of *Aethsiths* fixed in his mind, but other faces kept getting mixed up. His sister and his mother came and went, and the one-legged fiddler named Wind hailed him before fading. Liæna was with him the whole time, though he couldn't always make out her form. Others were there, people Luca couldn't name, and it was only the thought of getting lost among them which kept him holding onto the image of the silver-eyed woman with the jet black hair.

The journey was disorienting, but not painful. The same could not be said for the arrival. After a period of time - which was like a blink stretched out so the colors and shapes were distorted and impossibly thin, and everything moved with agonizing slowness - being carried through a dark tunnel where *things* brushed by, soft, squishy things with an ephemeral touch which raised the hair on the neck, the Guardians were dumped onto a solid, flat, and very hard piece of something.

The tacky darkness was attacked and vanquished by a harsh yet insipid light. Luca groaned and wondered not for the first time why the world hated him so. Every muscle felt as though it had been peeled from his bones, twisted and pulled, and put back in the wrong place. His brain was too large, his skull was too small, and his extremities were thick and clumsy.

Someone was poking him in the eye, and someone else was digging an elbow into the tender flesh on the inside of his thigh. Luca yelped, a high, injured sound that set the whole world into motion. The movements were blind and uncoordinated, accompanied by grunts and exclamations, but at last the Guardians extricated themselves and stood to confront the world.

It was not a pretty sight and only the fact that they were all together kept Luca from acting on the desire to find a small, dark, corner, curl up and forget everything. It was flat, dead, and uninviting, like a badly preserved painting of a hostile terrain. Stark lines were brutal, like chips of flint in the eyes, and it all looked like a mirror in danger of cracking.

"What is this place?" Luca asked, trying to get rid of the stale taste of the air on his tongue.

"I have no idea," Cedar said. He looked much older in the light, or perhaps it was the look in his golden eyes.

A strange weight on his back vexed Luca. He entertained the notion that he had become a hunchback then dismissed it. Shrugging, he found the weight moved. With a grateful sigh, he pushed it off his shoulders. Something fell to the ground with an undignified bang.

Luca looked at the case, failing utterly for a moment to recognize it. Black and purple in hue, overlaid in silver and green, he knew that it must belong to him. It was in the shape of a fiddle. It reminded him vaguely of what he usually carried on his back, in the way the smell of food will remind a starving child of a good meal and a full stomach. Luca reached behind him for his fiddle, but it was no longer there. Vexed, his heart pounding in his throat, he groped for the comfort of the magycal musical instrument, craning his neck to get a glimpse of it. After a few moments, the truth began to sink in.

Before, he had taken his fiddle from his back without thinking or looking. It simply was. The case, as a supernatural extension of an equally magycal object, had appeared when needed and disappeared for the same reason, much as he had seen Cedar's guitar do, and paid equally no mind to.

When Cedar carried his guitar or set it down with no

intention of playing, it was sheathed in a case of red and gold. When he took it to hand, the case was gone, as though it had been no more than a mirage.

Luca had never given thought to the fact that his own instrument would act in the same way. In this new land, where the glint of magyc did not show, his instrument was as immutable as its mundane cousins. A prickle of apprehensive revulsion stayed Luca's hand when he reached out to touch it.

He bit his lip and plunged, expecting his fingertips to burn or bleed when they contacted. They did neither. Instead, the grain of wood and the patterns were comforting. The suggestion of warmth lingered, but even as Luca caressed the case, the warmth began to fade.

He flipped the silver catches and the case opened, revealing the familiar fiddle encased in a nest of purple velvet. Luca knew by looking at it that no matter how he tried or called, neither gold music nor gold dirks would come to him. The sense of betrayal was swift and cold, like a knife into flesh, and it fled just as swiftly, leaving Luca haunted and anxious.

Luca picked it up and dropped it when it slipped from his fingers. For the first time since it had been remade into a weapon of a Guardian, Luca was afraid it would break. The fear scared him in a deeper place, one that was not so easily reached.

He caught it before it hit the ground and held on to it with a death grip which turned his knuckles white. No longer an extension of his being, it no longer contained the inner spark which held the promise of music. Nor was it feather light, but heavy and cumbersome, something pulling it down and threatening to rip it from his grasp. Had he been asked, he would have said he had never seen this thing before in his long life.

The Other World

Grief began to overwhelm him. Tears squeezed from the corner of his eyes, and the memory of home slipped from reality to the dim recess of a secret imagining. Luca clutched at the memory, drew it back, and calmed himself with the thought of Demona; grand Torin; colorful D'Ohera; clean, sweet air; blue skies; and golden music. When he opened his eyes, a world so removed from that as to be alien assaulted his vision but did not throw him.

He placed the violin back in the case, closed it, and slung it over his shoulder. The neck banged against his shoulder blade and the case dug cruelly into his side. Luca looked at his companions and found no comfort in their shared misery.

Timo shifted with a distraught look on his face, unable to find a comfortable place to leave the straps of his drums. Jæyd was turning her flute over and over, her hands unaccustomed to the nervous gesture. Only Cedar looked unperturbed, though far from happy. With his usually pristine clothes sullied by foreign dust, dark hair awry, he hefted his guitar experimentally then put it upon his shoulder with a shrug and a grimace.

"Not the first time this has happened, so I suppose this must be no great shock?" Luca said and winced at the jealousy that laced the words.

Cedar smiled without joy. "When I was in the Void between worlds, my guitar did this same strange thing. It was off-putting, but I became used to it, and when I returned to Demona, it reverted to its original state. Until it was smashed by that Demon."

Luca took a step forward, staggered, and caught himself before he fell. He tried again and gradually his body and wits became accustomed to the strange forces of this world working upon him. The faces of the other Guardians mirrored his distaste and dismay.

Luca didn't want to be the first to ask the question, but someone had to. "What are we going to do? We have to find *Aethsiths*, and presumably she's here...somewhere." Luca gestured at the empty landscape.

"We should figure out if these work here," Timo patted the drums gingerly, like he might try to calm a screaming baby.

Again, no one wanted to be the first. The possibility of failure hurt too much, but Jæyd lifted the flute to her lips, settled her fingers, then resettled them. Everything was still for a moment, then she blew into the reed. A note rang out, pure as quicksilver. It shimmered in the air, molding the world to its sweet simplicity before it faded. The world did not care that it had come and gone. It didn't even remember the sound.

"Well, that settles that then," Luca said, but he could not continue as the thought of Demona becoming as this world - harsh and magycless, uncaring of beauty or warmth - choked up his throat.

Jæyd looked equally shaken. "This is like the Wasteland," she muttered, squinting and blinking. "At the farthest northern reaches of Carallión, the horror that ended VarHayne was stopped by the elves' trees. But just beyond them, all life drained from the land, so even though plants and birds and beasts remained, they lacked..." she searched for the word for a long time. "...vitality."

"So we just made it to the Wasteland?" Cedar said, and disappointment and frustration overtook his dismay.

Jæyd shook her head. "I said *like* the Wasteland. This is not that place."

"How do you know?" Luca asked.

"I do not believe the VarHayne ever created something like that."

The Guardians looked to where the elf pointed and

came together in an attempt to draw strength and comfort from the nearness of something familiar and trustworthy in the presence of such hostile strangeness.

"What is it?" Timo asked, his voice catching in his throat and making him sound like a boy who could not yet grow a full beard.

No one spoke, and one by one they shook their heads, eyes never leaving whatever it was in front of them. Many poles were lines in rank and column, with metal barbs and ropes of metal thin as spider's silk stretched between them. Behind this, towers oozed oily grey smoke, and in the middle of all this, a squat building sat, a carcass the carrion had yet to discover and pick clean. The whole place was enclosed by a thin metal fence which didn't look like it would stop a mouse, much less a man.

"I think we should go check it out," Luca said, surprising himself as much as the others.

"Why?" Cedar asked.

"Because we're here and what else are we going to do?" Luca asked. "The Man of Tongues' spell sent us here. Unless *Aethsiths* is going to walk out of that bush, we are going to have to look for her."

"You think she's in that place?"

"Only one way to find out," Luca replied with grim cheerfulness.

The Guardians gathered themselves, squaring their shoulders and lifting their chins, then followed Luca as he made his way through the scrubby grass towards whatever this strange world had in store for them.

THE NITEFOLK

To the north of Demona, sheltered by the Mountains to the south, east, and west, was the little-known land of Prrus. Jagged hills and the remnants of the Mountains covered most of the land before it evened into grassy plains.

It was the home of the Dællaidwar, those the rest of the people of Demona and the surrounding countries knew as Nitefolk. The Dællaidwar were a small people, with short, dense fur covering their skin, whiskers, stubby fingers, dark, retractable nails, and cat eyes with varying proportions of green, blue, and gold.

Their main city of Ninas was a warren built under a series of hills - tunnels, burrows, and catacombs winding through the earth, invisible to the eyes above. In the innermost chamber, tallow candles in bubbles of cloudy glass illuminated the large, round room. Four entrances were placed at equal intervals, and the center portion of the room was protected by a ring of pillars that grew out of the ceilings and into the floor.

Princess Privere In'Orain of Ghor sat on a soft cushion, her legs crossed, and listened without speaking, as she always had. The youngest Ghoris princess, Privere favored her mother's mother, with fair hair, golden freckles on her pale skin, and eyes which were a dark indigo with lavender streaks. The remaining children of Ghor had come here more than two months past, but the princess still wore the simple clothes - a frock and knee-high suede boots - she had worn in Elba.

She held on her lap three small Nitefolk, and they were the cutest thing Privere had ever seen. Their fur was soft, and they would purr when scratched on the chin or behind their over-sized ears. The princess sat with her back against a pillar, watching her brother Haman pace the tight hall.

The Nitefolk had called an Assemblage at the request of their guests, in particular prince Haman In'Orain of Ghor. A dozen of the Nitefolk sat around the room, on cushions like Privere, though theirs were raised on blocks of crudely carved stone, in hourglass form. The stands varied in height, showing the hierarchy of the cat-like people, and from their perches, they watched Haman walk back and forth with lazy eyes.

Haman was a handsome man, thirty-one years of age. *He looks like father*, Privere mused. Dark hair, strong jaw, broad shoulders. His legs were long and lean and he made use of the length of his stride to express his frustration.

"Still we are just expected to wait?" Haman finally cried, rounding on the line of Nitefolk.

The Nitefolk upon the tallest pillar was the leader, Kaslane. Kaslane had ginger fur frosted with silver. His whiskers were black as night, as was his nose and the tips of his ears.

When the Nitefolk replied, his voice was rough and low, and contained traces of a warning growl. "We have extended our protection to you. If you refuse, it would be a grave insult to the traditions of our people and yours."

"I am not *trying* to be insulting," Haman replied through gritted teeth. "I am trying to protect my family. What's left of it."

At the unspoken mention of her sister Berria, an overwhelming sadness bubbled up in Privere's chest. They had not spoken since Berria left for the Sister Cities, four years ago. Because Haman disagreed with her reasons for going, they had become estranged.

Privere didn't know why the two oldest didn't simply compromise and work together to achieve what seemed to be the same end, but she had been seventeen at the time, and her voice was not listened to. Not that she had anything to say - she had been only six years old when they had fled Ghor. She didn't remember much of her home before Elba, nor why Haman wanted to take it back, or Berria wished to discover what had happened. *It doesn't matter,* Privere told herself. *It was in the past. What matters is what we do here and now.*

She looked at those gathered at the Assemblage and tried to think what to do to turn the uncertain outcome to something positive. Haman was silent, and the Nitefolk were looking at each other, their ears back, eyes dilated in agitation. *If Haman isn't careful, he is going to end up with a fight on his hands.* Kaslane spoke.

"As we explained to you when we brought you here, you are descended of the Builders. We are retainers of the Builders. We are obligated to do for you whatever you require, but we cannot endanger our own people. Or yours."

"My people are already endangered. You say you must

help us, but then you sit here, doing nothing," Haman tried to tell them, but they shook their heads.

A second Nitefolk spoke, a female with long auburn hair curling down her back in a luxurious mane. Her cushion was on a lower stand, but the stand was covered with a pattern of criss-crossed lines none of the others had. Her name was Ikati, and she was something between a healer and a mystic to the Nitefolk, a witch-woman called a *maerrilegus*. She was the one who had nursed Haman back to health after the children of Ghor arrived in Ninas.

"It is old, something deeper than instinct," Ikati told Haman, her voice smoother, and just a little higher than Kaslane's. "It is part of us. It is part of *you*."

"Fine," Haman said. "But then help us. We want to get back to Ghor, reclaim what was stolen from our fathers."

Kaslane and Ikati shared a look. "We understand. That is not wise at the present moment."

"Why not?" Haman demanded. "We have waited for fifteen years, running, and hiding. Demona is engrossed in its own affairs, tearing itself apart from the inside. Now *is* our time! I am heir to the last living line of princes. They are bound to follow me, and if we rise up *together* then we can reclaim what is ours!"

He stopped, his cheeks flushed with passion, gazing at everyone in the room, daring them to defy or contradict him. Privere bit her lip and kept silent. *I wish Berria were here,* she thought. *Berria was the only one willing to stand against their oldest brother.*

The two of them were like night and day in temperament and mixed like oil and water. Haman was rash and fiery, prone to action without thought. Berria was calm and steady, every action planned against its merits and price. The two of them fought, sometimes loudly and sometimes quietly about their fate and future, Berria holding the reins on Haman's un-thought-out headlong rush fueled by his fervidness. *And with Berria gone, there is only Haman's vision which to guide and motivate them,* Privere realized. The thought was not a comforting one.

The youngest princess glanced at Terryes, who sat next to her. She was beautiful, with a combination of features from their mother and father, strong lines in her face, and hair a shade lighter than Berria's, almost exactly matching the single picture of their mother that Privere possessed. However, the middle princess was timid, suited to needlepoint and history lessons, not war and Destiny.

If something was to be done, it was up to Privere. She straightened, so she now sat eye to eye with the lower of the Nitefolk. This felt as though she were intruding on their hierarchy, but she pressed back the compunction to shrink from their unblinking gaze and spoke.

"We must find my sister, Berria. She is in the Sister Cities, and-"

Haman cut her off with a scoff. "Berria is lost to us. She forsook this family when she chose to leave in favor of the *Guardians*." He wiped his lips as if the name left a taint. "She is the reason we are in this predicament in the first place!"

Privere was not so sure her brother's prejudice was founded. She knew the rumors of the Guardians and their deplorable actions, but with Berria's calm reasoning against Haman's turbulent emotions, Privere was questioning the truth of these rumors more and more frequently.

The youngest princess tried to hold on to what her father, prince Thalev, had taught her about leading - *listen to all options, do not close your mind based on preconception or pride; be willing to amend, to compromise, just as you must be willing to stand firm* - and what her mother princess Ennia had taught her about advising - *weigh the importance of what you're saying against the benefits - if it wasn't important, don't make a mountain of a pile of dirt; be patient; use words carefully and with thought: while one word would inflame resentment, a better word would be like water on a flame.*

"Berria will always be our sister," Privere countered, her voice firm but even. "And she did not murder our parents, or our uncles, or our cousins. You cannot blame her for everything."

Her argument was impregnable. Haman's jaw worked, but the stubborn fire in his eyes did not die. Privere was going to have to do better if she was going to bring him around.

"Perhaps," she continued slowly, "whatever Berria has discovered has caused this turn of events, but that is why we should reach out to her, find her, and learn what she knows. In this way we can better prepare for what is to come."

"I am done preparing," Haman said, his voice barely less than a shout. "We have been preparing for *fifteen years*. Now it is time to *act*."

Privere wanted to point out that it was Berria who had been acting while the rest of them remained in Samnara and Elba under the shelter of their assumed names, waiting for something to happen. They had no plan of action, but saying so would only make the situation worse.

Her mother's voice came to her from memory, of a time when she was four years old and had wanted to go with Haman, Terryes, and Berria to the orchards to play real-life Venture, but they refused to let her, saying she was too young. Little Privere had begged and pleaded and when that had not worked she had cried, then screamed. When they still refused to let her go, she had run to princess Ennia, demanding that she make them take Privere with them.

Her mother had taken her into her arms and gently explained that people did not like to be made to do things. It settled under their skin and chafed whenever they thought about it. It was a good way to sow animosity and cultivate enemies.

A much better way was to show them the merits of your view through well-formed argument and lead them to believe they had decided to do this themselves. Though sometimes, against some people's pride and stubbornness, you would never be able to find a way to make them see your point, even if it had merit.

"But there is nothing stopping you from going to the orchards and playing your own game." Ennia looked down at her young daughter with a kind smile. *"Perhaps, if you play well enough, they will come to join* your *game."*

Now Privere's mind worked overtime. Haman was blustering and bluffing; he wanted to act, but he truly didn't know whom to attack, and even if he did, he didn't know where to find them. He had no followers, no supporters, and most importantly, no army. The one thing he would not do was go to Berria or Dirsh in the Sisters.

He would not even answer the letters they sent, his reasoning being that it opened up their defenses to discovery. It was really because he was proud and refused to forgive what he saw as a betrayal. Privere's fingers brushed the empty place on the gold chain around her neck where her mother's ring used to be.

She had sent it without Haman's knowledge through the clandestine channels to the Sisters before the In'Orains had gone with the Nitefolk, partly as a gift for Berria's birthday, and partly as a sign that not *all* her siblings had turned against her and forgotten her.

Privere could not convince Haman to see another way, and she could not play by herself this time. Her eyes went to the oldest Nitefolk in the Assemblage, whose fur may have been black, but age had bleached it to white with a few dark hairs here and there. His eyes were blind, but with his whiskers and twitching nose, he knew more about what was going on around him than most people with perfect eyes.

His name was Rimbas, and he had been their prime voice and supporter when the Nitefolk were called to decide whether the children of Ghor would be accorded the honor and status of the Builders from which they were descended, albeit distantly, or left to their own devices. It was because of him that the In'Orains were sheltered here in Ninas.

Rimbas felt Privere's gaze on him, and his head cocked in her direction, white ears flicking back and forth, a small smile on his mouth. Privere was confident she could count on him again. Terryes would go along with whomever won, taking no part in the process of conquering the opposition, and though Degan was twenty, a man in his own right, he followed Haman with hero-worship in his eyes.

It all rested on the slim shoulders of Privere. The youngest princess wasn't sure she was ready to bear that burden. *But it doesn't matter if you are ready or not,* a little voice told her. *If you are the only one who is willing to do so.*

But there is Berria, Privere argued back.

And if Berria has departed these Realms?

Privere didn't know where the thought had come from, and she didn't like it. Shoving it away, she concentrated on what she had to do instead.

Berria held the key to this, and finding her would unlock at least part of the mystery. *I will find her,* Privere swore. *And together we will come up with the right course of action and bring Haman to sense.*

She looked at Rimbas, and the first stirrings of a plan

took shape in her mind.

THE OTHER WORLD

In the small town of Brooks, the street lights came on in flickering spurts and stutters of orange and white. A few cars drove down streets which were too narrow to be two-way, though the yellow line divided it clearly in two. Along the sidewalk of one of these streets, a solitary figure walked, bowed with the weight of four brown shopping bags, two on each side.

The figure passed under a street light and was bathed in harsh light, revealing a young woman. Her features were exotic, black hair pulled into a ponytail, and pale grey eyes wandering from window to window as she passed in a way that suggested she didn't really see what was displayed.

She passed a fitness center, a tattoo place, a quaint tea parlor, and a vacant office with a "for rent" sign on the door, then turned into the parking lot of an apartment building. Against the purple-reddish remains of the sun's light, it appeared as a black mass devoid of feature, dotted with white squares of lighted windows. The woman mounted the small flight of stairs and entered the lobby.

Two potted plants stood guard on each side of the elevator, and she waited, stretching out her shoulders but refusing to set down the bags she carried. The elevator dinged and the doors opened, letting out a short, elderly man with long grey hair combed back who smiled at her. He lived in number 182, five doors down from the woman.

"Buona notte, bella Maria," he greeted her.

"Buona notte, signore Martelli," she answered, and he beamed proudly at her words, though she still put the stress on the wrong syllables.

She got into the elevator and pressed the button with the faded "3" under the plastic with her elbow. The elevator struggled to ascend, groaning and pleading for sympathy, which she had no energy to give. The "2" above the door flashed, then the "3." The elevator shuddered to a stop, went still, and the doors opened arthritically.

The woman went out, turned right, and started down the hall. The latest owner had tried to spruce it up by painting it a bright and obnoxious yellow color, but the doors were the same drab green they had always been and that ruined the effect.

She stopped in front of a door in the middle of the hall. The numbers "192" were at eye level, and the brass reflected a warped version of her face, her nose too small and her cheeks bowing and bending like a sail. Only now did she put down the bags, so she could unlock the door. As she turned the key, she realized she had forgotten to check the mailbox. *Shit,* she berated herself, then sighed. *Well, it's not like I had an extra hand.*

The woman let herself into apartment number one-hundred-and-ninety-two. No lights were on; no one was home and she had the place to herself. She went directly to the kitchen, her mind fixed on her desire to get some food. The kitchen was a mess, dirty dishes still in the sink and the table had not been wiped. She sighed, and suddenly lost her appetite.

She set the bags of groceries on the edge of the table, and as she was surveying the mess that needed tidying up, an orange tabby walked into the kitchen and looked at her with big green eyes. His tail was held high, and he started purring like a freight train.

"Hey, Turbo," she greeted the creature. "I'm happy to see you, too."

She knelt down and scratched the cat behind the ears and his purring increased several decibels. After putting the groceries away, she looked for the easiest thing she could eat for dinner. Half a carton of Chinese takeout was her best option. It had been a long day at work and she was too tired to even turn on the radio for company, so she sat in silence, eating her cold dinner with mechanical bites, mulling over the current state of affairs of her life, Turbo sitting at her feet.

It was going to be a big weekend. Her birthday was tomorrow, and the following day, Nexus, the band she did PR for, had a radio interview with The Nameless, a big name rock band that had been at the top of the charts for almost a decade now. Nexus was opening for the Nameless on this leg of their world tour. After a month of looking forward to both events, she couldn't seem to muster any enthusiasm for them. *I think I just need to get some sleep.*

But that wouldn't help either. In fact, that was where her trouble had started, where the dreams she didn't quite remember started. It was only a week ago, but it seemed like months. Since then, everything had been called into question in an unsettling way, as if she was staring into a mirror and a face that was not hers stared back.

When she finished eating, she rinsed the dishes and put them in the dishwasher, put the rest of the food away, wiped the crumbs into the trashcan, and fed the cat. All the while, her thoughts went round and round.

She was so tired, her eyes burned as she forced herself to keep them open as she got ready for bed. Before she changed into her pajamas, she remembered she had to get the mail. The elevator took forever to get to the ground floor, and she zoned out, mumbling the latest hit from Starheart: "Lost in Time." At least the lyrics didn't remind her of things she didn't want to think about.

Three letters and a magazine were shoved in the box with the same number as her door. The magazine was for power tools and woodworking projects one could do in the living room, addressed to Richard Westerfield. Two of the letters were for the same. Only one was for her.

The name and address was printed in the harsh, unfriendly precision of a computer label:

Maria E. Westerfield
45 Redbury Way, #192,
Brooks, Southerton 4453Q

The return address was a company she had never heard of. Opening the letter on the way up, she found she had won a 12-day cruise to some exotic location. *Call this number to reserve your suite now!!* Maria rolled her eyes and put it in the trash can. The others she left on the table for her father.

She turned out the lights and retired to her little bedroom at the end of the hall. She washed her face, still feeling uneasy and preoccupied with the decision she had made today. It hadn't been easy, and she didn't feel entirely ready, but she couldn't put it off any longer. She practiced saying it in the mirror as she brushed her teeth.

"It's over. It's *over.* It *is* over."

Pausing, she considered the words. *That sounds a little*

harsh.

"It's just not working out," she tried, gesturing with her toothbrush.

As she looked slightly ridiculous with foam spilling out of her mouth, it was hard to take herself seriously and Maria finally cracked a smile, the first in what seemed like days. She knew she never should have agreed to go out with Matt in the first place, but it had seemed harmless enough at the time.

Maria felt like she owed him some kind of explanation. It was, after all, sudden, and Matt was a good guy. *But what the hell am I supposed to say? Sorry Matt, but I keep having these dreams of a mysterious golden-eyed man and being in a band just can't compare with magic music or fighting Demons and…and…who am I kidding?*

She spat and rinsed out her mouth. Matt played guitar for Nexus, and they were leaving early Monday morning to make it to Johnston for their first show. She had no time left; it had to be tomorrow. *My twenty-first birthday. Happy birthday to me,* she thought glumly.

"I'm sorry. It's over," she told her reflection one last time before she turned out the light and climbed into bed, pulling the cool sheets up to her chin and closing her eyes.

It took a long time to fall asleep and when she finally did sink into the blackness of oblivion, it was not warm and empty but filled with red eyes and the wind whispering in a sinister hiss a word she no longer remembered. She tossed and turned, sweating as she tried to run away and fell into the arms of a golden eyed man as her blood spilled from her throat.

Her phone insistently ringing made Maria bolt awake, the dream of a lush green forest fading before she could remember how she had gotten there. Rubbing her eyes, she glanced at the clock. It was seven o'clock. *So much for sleeping in.* Finding the accept call button was too challenging for this early on a Saturday morning, and it took her four tries before the light went green.

"Hello?" she said in a barely coherent mutter.

"Maria! I need a huge favor!" Betty Coleman's chipper voice rang out, making Maria wince. "I forgot I have an appointment to get my nails done, so I can't watch the store this afternoon. Can you *please* be here by three..."

"Sure, sure," Maria mumbled as she fell back against the pillows, draping an arm over her eyes.

"Great! Thanks! You're a doll!" The dial tone was a welcome reprieve from Betty's piercing voice.

Maria lay in bed with her eyes closed, drifting in and out of half-sleep for a few minutes. Turbo was a warm weight on her legs. Being seduced by the embrace of the bed seemed too good to resist but Maria pulled herself up. After a cup of strong coffee, she felt better, and a hot shower completed the job of waking her up.

Maria fried herself some eggs and cut a slice of melon. She ate alone again, feeling drained and lethargic, knowing that if she fell back into bed like she wanted to, one of two things would happen: she would just toss and turn or she would be out like a light and she couldn't be sure she would wake in time to watch the shop at three. When she realized that she had been making repeating circles in the puddle of egg yolk and melon juice on her plate she stood suddenly. *I have to do something. Anything.*

She attempted to lose herself in mindless tasks, making spaghetti sauce for dinner, vacuuming, scrubbing the too-short bath until it gleamed, and she was surprised and pleased to find the next time she looked at the clock it was 2:30 and time for her to leave.

Though the sky was clear, the air had that thick, electric

The Other World

feel which meant a storm was on the way. At an unnatural speed, the clouds moved in and the rain began to fall. She stole from cover to cover in order to keep as dry as possible, but even so Maria arrived at the store drenched to the bone. Luckily the owner, Giovanni Citara, didn't believe in air-conditioning, so she wouldn't catch pneumonia.

Maria smiled as she wrung the wetness from her hair. She had known Giovanni since she was a baby because the guitar-maker had always had a soft spot for her mother. The sign on the door was done in gold, curly font, and the door was unlocked. She stepped into the store, opening her mouth to call out a greeting to the luthier, who would be working in the back even though it was a Saturday, but was met instead with a deafening yell.

"SURPRISE!"

Maria gaped at the crowd of people crammed into the little front room of the shop. The faces blurred as she tried to take them all in, but she recognized them - her friends from the band, from school, from work. Even Giovanni had emerged from his workshop in the back, standing in the doorway, his arms folded over his chest, a varnish-stained rag still in his hand. Everyone was grinning and clapping, and she realized she was laughing as they crowded around to wish her happy birthday.

"How does it feel to finally be an adult?" someone called out.

"Twenty-one!" someone else kindly reminded her. It sounded like Mike, the engineer at the studio Nexus recorded at.

She smiled gamely. "Feels just like thir…" she stopped, suddenly unable to complete the sentence and everybody laughed.

"Happy birthday, honey." Betty's platinum hair was

done in a too-stiff perm and her fuchsia lips matched her long nails. "I probably don't have to tell you this, but I don't really need to get my nails done."

"I figured," Maria laughed as she returned the enthusiastic hug with as much fervor as she could muster. "How…when…"

"We've been planning it for a week," Josh Peters, the drummer of Nexus, said as he came up, gave her a conservative peck on the cheek and handed her a cup of something red. His dark eyes crinkled at the corners when he saw her look at the contents suspiciously. "Don't worry; it's not spiked."

Maria smiled back at him. She liked Josh and his simple sweetness which wasn't found often in your average human being. His mere presence usually did a good job of quieting her secret demons, but the demons were wired today and wouldn't stop jumping around inside her.

The red stuff in the cup was overly-sweet fruit punch and she spied an elaborate and colorful cake which had been enthusiastically doused in Yellow 4 and Red 20 sitting on the reception desk. Someone had thrown a paper tablecloth patterned in balloons over the table. Everything was too bright, imprinting itself on the retinas with a burning brilliance.

"Hey birthday girl!" Adam Lake, the keyboardist sauntered over, his tattooed arms open wide as he enveloped her in a warm hug. "How d'you like the party?"

"It's wonderful," Maria said. "You really shouldn't have."

She relaxed under the charm of Adam's broad smile. His happy nature was infectious, and no matter how stressed out she was, he made her feel calmer just by walking into the room.

Adam laughed. "I knew you were gonna say that. But

you're a special sort, you know, and totally worth it. Happy birthday!"

Josh squeezed her arm. "I got you a present."

"That's sweet," she said as she took the carefully wrapped box. The bright orange paper was held together by so much tape it was practically waterproof. After a moment spent trying to find a seam with her nail, Maria gave up and handed it to Adam who pulled out an intricate pocket knife which sliced through the impermeable covering with one swipe.

"Hey! Be careful! That could be delicate!" Josh exclaimed.

Adam laughed and handed the present back to Maria. Now she could open it, and she pulled out a small, leather bound journal with blue lacings. It had her name etched on the front in gold lettering similar to the sign outside the shop.

"For your sketches and lyrics," Josh told her with a smile and a wink. "Which I don't know about."

Maria blushed. "Thanks, Josh." She held it up to her nose, smelling the clean, musky scent of leather and old-fashioned parchment. "This is lovely."

"I got you something too, sort of," Adam said. "Here." He handed her his phone and the attached earphones, wriggling his eyebrows suggestively. "It's the new one from The Next World Over."

"Sweet!" Maria grinned as she put the earphone in.

The anticipation faded as the chords washed over her. It was a cool song, but no more. Adam watched her, and she could see her flagging interest reflected in his falling expression.

"Not one of *those*?" he asked and she shook her head. He managed to look sad even as he grinned at her. "Damn. Pretty close though, right?"

"It's okay. It's a great song. Punchy. Nice solo, too."

"You're just trying to make me feel better," Adam laughed. "I know you won't take anything but the best."

Maria smiled. Adam was forever trying to find one of "those" songs, the ones Maria tried to describe and tripped over words which could never suffice. The ones that had something more to them than just the notes and the words, something that couldn't be heard, but *felt*. The ones that could pick you up and carry you away, make you more alive - the *real* ones.

"Thanks, Adam," Maria said. She looked for the person she was hoping wasn't there and hating herself for that, but she couldn't see him anywhere. "Where's Matt?"

Josh rolled his eyes. "In back. Composing. He said the whole yelling *surprise* thing was too melodramatic."

That sounds like Matt. She smiled, but under her happy exterior, regret and angst rolled into a bigger and bigger knot. She had already come up with a dozen reasons why she didn't have to do this before she realized what she was doing. *If I put this off now, it's only going to get harder.*

Her stomach clenching in a tight mass, Maria went into the back of the store to find Matt.

It smelled like wood and glue, and Maria breathed in the comforting scents. "Matt?" she whispered.

Hearing a voice and faint notes she crept to the back, bathed in the scent of the sawdust and lacquer, her fingers running over the velvety smooth neckboards. On a bench surrounded by boxes and half-finished instruments, Matt was gently strumming his guitar next to a bottle of beer and humming something. He took a sip and noticed Maria standing half in the shadows.

"Hey, babe," he said. "Come here."

She walked over, forcing a smile to her face. "Hey,

Matt," she said, her tongue and lips heavy and stiff. "You're missing the party."

"I know," he said and pulled her into his lap, setting the guitar on her knee and putting his arm around her to reach the frets. "But I didn't get your gift done, and I really want to give it to you before we hit the road. The thing is, I'm not feeling it now, you know? The words just aren't coming."

A curious sensation gripped her stomach. She almost felt sick. "I know what you mean," she said softly.

"But you don't write," Matt replied absently, looking down at the strings as he strummed a chord.

Maria stood up so suddenly Matt lost his grip on the guitar and his beer. The guitar fell to the floor with a discordant bang, and beer spilled over their shoes.

"Matt," she heard herself say in a detached way, floating somewhere above them and not really paying attention. "I've been meaning to tell you, but there hasn't been a good time. I just don't think this is working out."

"Wha…what are you talking about?" The blank look morphed into one of shock.

"We're over," she said simply. "We're not right for each other; we never have been."

"Where did this come from?"

This was the part she was dreading, and when it came to it, she took the coward's way. "I don't know."

"Are you…are you serious?" he stammered.

"Yes. It's just…better this way," she said.

"Wait…you have to at least give me a chance…" he started to say.

Maria wanted to run, to turn away from the hurt expression on his face and never look back, but she made herself sit back down. She put her hand on his knee and looked straight into his brown eyes. "Listen. I know this is going to sound like a cliché, but it's not you - it's me. I don't want you to change for me, but I...I'm looking for something. I always have been."

"And what is that *something*?" The hopeless look in his eyes did uncomfortable things to Maria.

"I don't know how to explain it," she sighed, so frustrated with the inadequacy of the answer. *What am I looking for?*

Matt looked even more hurt. "I don't understand. Why haven't you said anything before? Did I do something wrong?"

"No. No, you're okay."

He didn't look like he believed her.

"You're a great guy, Matt; you really are." She meant every word and hoped her earnestness came across sincere and not over-blown.

"Just not what you're looking for."

Maria bit her lip, then shook her head.

"What are you looking for then?" Matt asked again, the hurt on his face causing her to avert her eyes and remove her hand from his knee.

After a moment of silence, she sighed. Josh knew it as that which made her want to write or draw like the man with the magic marks. Adam knew it as the perfect song, the song which could do things to you, take you places, make you *feel* something. They were both right, and yet...

"You don't know the answer to that question, do you?" Matt said, and she was grateful that no trace of accusation slipped through in his tone.

"I...it's just difficult to put into words," she said. "I want you to be happy. And I know you will be. Have a good life, okay?"

She walked out, gave Josh and Adam warm hugs, wishing them well with words she neither heard or remembered. Then she went home and crashed in bed, too drained to even cry, but somehow tears still managed to spill over her cheeks. She felt them drip onto her pillow, making big wet circles, and then the circles began to disappear into light that hurt her eyes and she groaned, rubbing away the tears.

It didn't help and the pillow was the next to go. She tried to sit up as her bed followed the pillow, but her body wasn't obeying her orders, and she watched everything melt into a blinding gold, surrounding a man with eyes of the same color.

Maria awoke to the stained ceiling of her apartment gently lit by dawn's light filtering through the cracks in the blinds. She blinked and rubbed the crusted gunk out of her eyes. She felt drained and invigorated at the same time, and she couldn't fathom the reason. She had just broken up with her boyfriend, and though it was the right thing to do, she still felt horrible about it. She had cried last night, she knew. Then something had happened, but she couldn't remember what that was. She pushed it from her mind and concentrated on something more real.

Today is Sunday, she thought. *Something is supposed to happen today. Something big...oh! Right, the interview.*

Maria got out of bed, dressed in jeans and a blue three-quarters cardigan, brushed her hair and pinned it up, then went to the kitchen for breakfast. Her father was sitting at the table. He was tall and thin, and mostly bald with blue eyes. A fringe of greying blond hair fell over the rims of his glasses.

"Hi, Dad."

"Morning, Maria," her father said, his eyes flickering up from the newspaper he was reading. "How's my girl?"

"Good," she replied automatically.

She opened her mouth to say more, then changed her mind and dove into the fridge to pull out a container of yogurt and an apple. She paused, a vague wondering skating the edges of her attention. She felt like she was twelve again, and the sensation was disquieting.

"Good," her father repeated, taking another bite of his toast and beans and folding his newspaper in half. He looked up at her. "Happy birthday. For yesterday, I mean. I texted, but I wanted to say it in person."

"Thanks," Maria said. She hadn't even looked at her phone. "Sorry I wasn't up when you got home. I was exhausted."

"That's fine," his eyes twinkled. "Out partying with the cool kids?"

Maria rolled her eyes. "The gang threw me a surprise party at the store," she told him. "It was nice."

"That's good," he said. "You know, if you wanted to, we could do something today. Go to the movies; I don't know."

"Thanks, dad; that would be great, but I have a band thing with Nexus," Maria told him and gave him a kiss on the forehead. "Rain check?"

"Of course," he said. "And I still have to get you a birthday present. Have any particular wish?"

"Um, just whatever," she smiled, sitting down and opening the yogurt. "But if you want to buy me clothes, just get a gift card, okay?"

He laughed. "Still emotionally scarred from the attack of the yellow and purple polka-dot sweater?"

"Featuring a picture of Heavyweight Champion Donald 'the duster' Matter?" She pulled a face at him, then laughed. "I don't even like wrestling."

"I know, I know," he rubbed his face and looked bemused. "I don't actually know what I was thinking with that. I was probably..."

Maria knew what the end of the sentence would have been. *Drunk at the time.* He had been sober for almost seven years now, but it had gotten bad and worse before it had gotten better. She leaned over and kissed him on the cheek.

"Doesn't matter," she told him. "It's good for a laugh."

"Right," he smiled. "A laugh."

Silence crept onwards. He tried so hard, just like he had always tried hard, even when he didn't make the greatest choices. It would have been easy to feel sorry for him, but somehow Maria never did. He had a quality about him, a quiet strength which helped him pull back from the edge before jumping, and to always keep trying, no matter how many times he made a mess of it.

Maria thought that must be why women fell in love with him, what her mother must have loved him for. He had been endowed with average looks, soft spoken, not wealthy or sophisticated by any stretch of any imagination, and a large cloud of blackness which often obscured the light. Maria knew that light was an undying love for her mother and a desire to do well by her.

Mom. They didn't have any pictures of her because her dad had burned them all, one night in a drunken heap of tears, setting off the fire alarm and earning a warning from the building manager. There wasn't a lot to remind Maria that she even had a mother. Her one stepmother certainly hadn't left a lasting impression of anything good, and the girlfriends her dad occasionally brought over had never seemed to connect with anything motherly or even serve as a comparison to what was needed in a mothering capacity.

That train of thought went over bridges and through tunnels, over hill and dale, and somehow ended up at the dim, dirty end of the hallway Maria would hide in whenever her father fought with the woman who thought she was supposed to be a replacement for Maria's mother.

After Maria had run away, she had never heard him fight with another woman again. He divorced the stepwoman two months afterwards, and she couldn't remember him having a relationship longer than a year after that. From that time on, the first mention of Maria and anything wrong with her, and the woman who had the issue was gone without ceremony. It had taken Maria many years to understand what was really going on, that he wasn't being a playboy with a new woman every sixth or eighth month. He was trying to protect her, keep her from the reasons to run away again. *Speaking of that…*

"Dad," Maria began, turning the apple over and over in her hand. "I have a question."

"Yes?" her father asked.

"Do you remember when I was little and I…ran away?"

Her father froze, as she knew he would, then folded the paper in half again, then in again. She waited, unsure what his reaction would be; she had never brought it up before. He took a sip of coffee, and only then did he look at her.

"Yes," her father answered slowly. "What about it?"

"How long was I gone for?" she asked.

"A week," he said. "I was so worried when we found you sleeping at the end of the hall, all dirty with your hair all mussed and strange clothes." He paused, struggled with himself, then blurted out the next sentence. "You never told me why you ran away."

"I'm not sure," Maria said honestly, relaxing slightly now that there seemed to be no impending explosion or apocalypse. "I didn't really think about it or plan it out. I think it might have been an accident, and I just kept going, instead of turning back." *That was a lie.* She winced at the thought, but her father didn't notice.

He nodded, his mouth working as he struggled to understand. "Are...are you thinking about...leaving again?"

Maria stared at him, blinking. "Well, I don't..." she stopped, not knowing *what* she *didn't*. "I haven't thought about it," she told him and was pleased when the little chime of untruth didn't berate her this time.

"You'll talk to me before you go, if, you know, you do decide to?" he asked, a hopeful look on his face. "Decide to go, I mean."

"Of course," Maria promised, already feeling like she was breaking her word. "I'm sorry about before. I didn't mean for it to be like that."

"No, I'm sorry," her father sighed. "I was the one who changed, you know, after your mother died. I know that can't have been easy on you."

Maria smiled, hoping it didn't look forced. "I actually hardly remember her at all."

"You have her eyes," her father said. "They are so beautiful, like they're from another world."

Maria started. "What do you mean?"

Her father looked surprised at the sudden change. "I...I don't know, Maria. I was just trying to describe them. What's the matter?"

Her phone buzzed, and she looked down. The message was from Josh. *Hey! We're outside. Where are you?*

"Nothing," Ria said as she stood, already running through her mental checklist. *Lip balm; money; hairband and iPod, in case of emergency.* "I'm late. I love you. Don't forget to give Turbo food!"

"Love you, too," Richard Westerfield said, watching her run out of the kitchen. He was left staring at the empty room. "More than you know."

Maria had never thought her life fit well, but never before had she been so certain about it. The lobby of WBMN, the local rock radio station, reminded her of a bathroom at a highway rest stop.

No matter how clean the tiles looked, the idea that something foul had recently oozed over them, leaving a noxious residue, could not be banished. Florescent lights made everything glow a sick greenish white, like the effects on a bad sci-fi show. The abstract pictures on the walls and the odd shaped furniture were supposed to be avant garde or neuvu or some equally posh French term, but they really belonged in a nightmare with a clown laughing hysterically while brandishing a bloody knife.

All these thoughts went rapidly through Maria's head, and she tried to squash them because this was good for Nexus, and she wanted the best for them. She kept sneaking glances at Matt, both hoping to catch his eye and dreading it. She was relieved and disappointed when his brown eyes remained fixed on the floor between his shoes.

Josh and Adam were chatting with Ian Spencer and Connor Woods, the singer and bassist of The Nameless. Ian and Connor were both decked out in full rock star garb, black leather, chains and sleeveless shirts which showed a variety of tattoos down their arms. Ian had his platinum hair spiked and a generous line of eyeliner matched his black fingernails.

Connor forwent the makeup in favor of jewelry. A nose ring, a lip ring, silver gauges, two chains around his neck, several chains around his wrists, and a ring adorning each finger made him shine as brightly as his toothpaste commercial smile, which he flashed often with his easy laugh.

Maria thought about writing that down, but decided it wasn't appropriate and was more likely to be taken as a slur rather than the dubious compliment that it was. Connor was quite attractive, but not someone you should introduce to conservative, Ivy-league parents. *I can't put that in either.* Fiddling with the notebook and pen, Maria glanced around for something she *could* put down.

In the corner, guitarist Henry C. and drummer Finn Belle lounged against the wall. Finn spun a drumstick in each hand, and when he saw her looking at them, he flashed her a grin and a wink. She smiled back, and taking that as an invitation, stood and walked over. Finn's smile widened as she came closer.

"Hi. I'm Maria Westerfield," she introduced herself.

Finn hooked one drumstick through a loop in his belt, wide black leather with silver studs, freeing up a hand to shake hers.

"Finn. And this is my friend Henry, but we can pretend he's not here."

Henry was the most conservative of the rock band. He almost looked like he belonged in Nexus instead of The Nameless in jeans and a black t-shirt with a logo Maria assumed was a band she had never heard of or a brand of esoteric guitar strings. Dark hair swept low into bright blue eyes, and a single blue earring dangled from his right ear. He smiled enchantingly then grabbed the drumstick still twirling in Finn's hand and tapped a quick, hard beat on the drummer's arm, making him yelp.

"When you get tired of my narcissistic friend, you can come talk to me for some decent, intelligent conversation," he said, the slight hint of an accent instantly making him exotic and intriguing. *Now there's potential materiel.*

It reminded Maria of something, but she couldn't put her finger on it. "I can just talk to both of you at the same time, if that's alright," she replied. "I write some of the content for Nexus' social media and website. I'd love to ask you a couple of questions, if you don't mind."

"If all the interviewers were half as gorgeous as you, I think I could be asked questions all day long," Finn said, retrieving his sticks and starting them spinning again. "I could even be persuaded to give up drumming and become a professional interviewee." He grinned while Maria blushed. "Shoot."

"Well, my first question is actually for Henry. I noticed an accent."

"That's not a question," the guitarist teased, but his smile widened. "I've lived in this country since I was twelve, but I'm originally from Isos."

The blood drained from Maria's face and a wave of lightheaded dizziness threatened to topple her. The name echoed from a past which did not exist, a land that she'd dreamt of but did not speak of aloud. *It's not possible...he can't know that name...*

"Whoa there, are you alright?" Henry asked, his smile replaced by a frown of concern.

"Sorry, no, I'm fine," Maria croaked. "Where did you say you were from?"

"Ireland." His frown deepened. "Emerald isle, west of Great Britain?"

Maria drew in a deep breath and tried to hide her shaking hands. "Oh." She gave a breathy laugh. "Right."

"Most girls swoon over an Irish fella, but I've never gotten that reaction before," Henry said, a bemused smile beginning to surface again.

"My blood sugar must be low," Maria said and winced internally at the horrible excuse. *What am I thinking?* She thought she should stop, but words kept falling out of her mouth. "I didn't get a chance to eat breakfast this morning."

"Would you like a snack?" Finn asked, snapping to attention.

"No, really, I'll be fine," Maria protested.

"You sure?" Finn pressed. "They give us anything we want and more than we could ever eat. I'm serious. Nuts, chocolates, fruit, cheese, pizza, cookies, weird Italian food like olives and stuffed grape leaves…"

"I think that's Greek." Maria giggled at the face Finn pulled. "Alright, if you insist."

The drummer and guitarist gestured for Maria to follow. They took her back to a small room, inelegantly furnished with plastic folding tables and chairs. The tables were loaded with enough junk food and finger foods to supply a small city. Maria took a packet of cashews to avert suspicion as the two musicians sat. Finn put his black boots on the table.

"My turn for a question," the drummer said. "And don't ask me where I'm from because I can't top your reaction to Ireland."

"Okay," Maria agreed and pulled up a chair.

She had to push a giant bowl of bright orange cheese puffs to the side to make room for her notebook. "How did The Nameless choose Nexus for the opening act of this leg of their *Ten Years, Three Cheers* Tour?"

"We really like their sound," Finn told her. "They sound like they mean it."

"Great answer. And do you see any particular part or characteristic of The Nameless in Nexus?"

"They're not as good looking as we are," Finn said. "But they're alright."

"I don't know about seeing any of The Nameless in them, but I feel their style complements ours, in a bit of an unorthodox way, mind you. But I think that the fans will dig it," Henry smiled.

"Alright." Maria took a moment to check her notes. "Is there anything in particular you're looking forward to on this leg of the tour?"

The band members considered it. Finn looked as though he were going to make a dirty joke, then thought better of it.

"Just being on the road, on tour, on stage, after - what would it be?" Henry looked at Finn. "Two years? Yeah, two years in the studio. There's something magical about the interaction with the audience when you can see their faces and hear their voices. It makes the music something more, you know?"

"It's physically and emotionally exhausting," Finn added. "But it's also totally worth it."

"I can understand that," Maria said. "Any particular song you want to play?"

Finn and Henry looked at each other with *you first* expressions.

"Well, 'Can't Hide the Lie' is always a great song to play live," Henry said. "And it gives me a chance to show off a little. But I like those odd tracks we throw in there, mostly on a whim. Seeing those one or two people singing their hearts out while everyone else takes a breather, has a beer. That's special in a different way. Like 'Storm on the Horizon' or 'The Nameless' from our first LP. That's a great little gem."

"Back when we thought it was cool to title a song, an album, and a band exactly the same," Finn rolled his eyes, then he laughed. "Or 'Gonna Ride the Golden Rainbow.' Trippy and psychedelic, but an awesome song. It's one of those ones where even if you don't know the words, you can still get into it. And *I* get to show off."

"I'm sure you take full advantage," Maria smiled. "Any

The Other World

song of Nexus you'd like them to play?"

"'The Girl Who Came Back,'" they chorused without hesitation.

Maria's cheeks warmed, and she hoped they didn't notice. "Any particular reason for that choice?" she asked, keeping her eyes glued to the lines of her notebook as she scribbled.

"One, it's the audition they played and got the gig on," Finn counted off on his fingers. "Two, it rocks. Out of this world rocks. Raises goosebumps." He wiggled his fingers over his arm to demonstrate. Henry nodded silent agreement, and Finn continued. "It's like 'Empty Man' by Land Without Life. It sticks with you. Not like those annoying pop songs with the catchy chorus which repeats in your head more than they play it on the radio. This one gets *inside* you, becomes part of you, like you knew it *before* the first time you heard it," Finn explained, a febrile glint in his eyes, the drumsticks tapping double time.

"It's like someone who's been touched by the supernatural wrote that song," Henry added, the faint Irish brogue giving the words a sinister bent.

Or at least inspired it. Maria took a deep breath, finished the last word, and looked up with a big smile. A woman wearing a headset stuck her head in the room, saving Maria from having to continue.

"You're on in five," she told the guys from The Nameless.

They nodded at her and stood. Maria stood with them.

"Well, thanks very much for your time and willingness to talk with me, guys," she said. "Good luck with the tour."

She shook Henry's hand, but Finn wouldn't accept that, instead wrapping her in an enthusiastic and protracted hug.

"You'll be at the show tomorrow?" he asked, stepping

back.

"I'll try," Maria said, already mentally preparing her list of excuses. "Good luck!"

Maria paced the edges of the entrance room to the studio suites, her eyes flicking to the "on air" in neon red above the door every thirty seconds. It seemed like they were taking a long time, but she wouldn't know. She had never done a radio interview with a band as big as The Nameless.

They seemed like really nice guys, she thought, tapping her nails along the wall as she walked. The receptionist gave her a dirty look, and Maria pulled her hand back, then crossed her arms. After another long while, the door opened and the musicians spilled out. They were talking and laughing. *Looks like they found a rhythm*, Maria smiled to herself.

"Maria!" Adam called out. "We're going to grab some lunch. We're divided half-half between Cameron's Kitchen and Cafe 29. We need a tie-breaker."

"There are seven of you. How can you need a tie-breaker?"

"Matt doesn't care," Josh said, rolling his eyes. "So, which one?"

"I prefer Cafe 29," Maria said. "But I'm going to have to take a rain check."

"But it's not raining," Finn Belle protested.

Despite herself, Maria cracked a smile. "I know. I'm really sorry. I just have to get this stuff ready for the website and do some other things."

"All work and no play makes Maria a dull girl," Finn complained.

"I know, I know. It was a pleasure meeting you all." Maria smiled at each of them.

The Other World

"I can drop you off on the way," Adam said.

They piled into his SUV, Maria in the front, and Josh and Matt in the back. The air was thick. Adam kept giving her concerned looks. Matt was brooding, saying nothing but for monosyllabic responses to direct questions. Adam and Josh carried the conversation all the way to Maria's apartment. Maria had never been so pleased to get away from them as she opened the door and felt like she could breathe again.

"If I don't see you guys before you go on," Maria said, "have a good show."

"Why wouldn't you see us?" Josh demanded. "You're coming, right?"

"I'm not sure," Maria said. "I promised my dad we'd do something together. For my birthday."

"Come to the show," Alex said, in a tone that expected compliance. "You always come."

"I'll try," Maria said, but this time, the little bells warning of untruth stirred. *I will try,* she told herself fiercely and was reassured when the bells were silent.

"Fine," Adam said, who was not convinced. "We're driving to Jonston tonight, staying in the hotel with The Nameless. Text me if you want to come with. Or you can drive up with your dad tomorrow."

He was trying to laser-beam information, or an explanation, or something, from her head with his blue eyes trained on hers, intense and unblinking. She smiled at him.

"Thanks. I'll see you guys later."

She gave a little wave. Matt studiously avoided meeting her gaze, staring at the headrest in front of him. Maria wondered if he had said a word during the interview.

She went inside, made a cup of tea, and sat down in front of her computer. Turbo leaped up, trying to lie on her keyboard as she pulled out her notebook and arranged the papers. She pulled the giant tabby into her lap, and in careful, methodic motions, typed in all her notes. *There's some good stuff here*, she thought. *I can do something with this.*

She began filling in the meat and potatoes of the piece, not really paying much attention to what she was doing. Her mind kept returning to Matt's distraught and blank expression. She pushed it away for the twelfth time and focused on the paragraph in front of her.

Drummer Finn Belle was particularly enthused with the band's self-recorded single "The Girl Who Came Back," describing it as "one of those songs…that raises goosebumps." Henry C., guitarist and co-writer of the majority of The Nameless' most popular tracks, agreed, adding "It's like someone touched by the supernatural wrote that song."

She rubbed her eyes and looked up at the clock.

"Almost midnight!" she gasped. "Where did all the time go?"

She debated about getting a cup of coffee and pushing herself on, but in the next moment, all ambition drained out of her. She went to her bedroom, didn't bother undressing, and fell face-first into the pillows. Her eyes closed, and her breathing evened out, heralding sleep.

Then gold light began to creep under her lids. It was like the other night, Maria realized. She opened her eyes and blinding gold light made her wince. She tried to hold on to the world, the solid bed under her, but it was gone, carried away by golden notes of music…

…that after a moment began to retreat and her head cleared suddenly as her heart sped up.

Oh my god, it's happening! I don't believe this! Maria gazed around, feeling her heart-rate slow as no one appeared. A sense of profound disappointment filled her. In the gold light, she began to see shapes materializing. One became a large tree, the other a barn. A cow looked up at her and lowed before returning to its constant grazing. The sun was barely up - it was early morning.

She was standing in the middle of a field, certain she had never seen it before. In her dream, she allowed herself to think - and even to say the word - of that which she would never do while awake. *Perhaps this is Demona! That would explain why it's daytime here and night where I am.*

She hardly dared to hope, but then she saw the blacktop paved road and an old, rundown billboard with a familiar logo and the words *Get a fresh, hot quarter-pounder Exit 78b Chardc…* The elements had rubbed away the last few letters of the advertisement. For a moment, Ria thought she heard music, but then it was gone.

After standing in the same place for a moment, waiting for the music to return or something to happen, she grew tired of the nothing and walked towards the barn, figuring that was the most logical thing to do. She half expected the doors to open for her with just a thought, but they did not and she had to pull them open herself, grunting with the effort. She peered inside the dim, smelly barn, and her heart stuttered.

Curled up on a pile of hay was a large, blond man in rustic, fur-lined clothing, cradling a pair of drums as a baby would cradle a teddy-bear, though he looked like you wouldn't want to give that comparison to his face. Next to him was a smaller, darker man, a layer of dust almost obscuring the purple and green amongst the black of his hair and clothes.

Already awake, a slim woman with hair the color of flaming bronze was perched on the rickety wooden ladder to the loft, playing on a silver and ivory flute, almost too softly to hear. *That's the music I heard.*

Stretched out on the ground, shiny black shoes sticking out from under a roughly woven horse blanket, his red guitar case lying at his head, was the golden-eyed man of her dreams.

"Cedar?" Maria whispered and jumped when the man sat up suddenly.

"Did you say something?" he asked the woman playing the flute.

With a smile which revealed pointed teeth, the flutist shook her head. Cedar rubbed his eyes and stood, bending back and forward to put his spine into place. His grunts woke the other two men who stood as one, halberd and twin dirks extended. Cedar and the woman burst out laughing and Maria smiled.

"When did that get opened?" the tall blond man asked, gesturing to the door.

"Just now," the woman answered.

"Why did you open it, Jæyd?" the dark man asked with a scowl. "We're supposed to be keeping a low profile here."

"I did not," Jæyd smiled again. "It opened by itself."

The three men stared at the woman and Maria felt faint. *They can't see me*, she realized.

"By itself?" the big blond man said slowly. Someone may have thought him a bit mentally impaired, but Maria knew better.

"And no one came in?" Cedar demanded.

"That is correct, handsome." The she-elf leapt nimbly from her perch on the ladder, a smile shining on her face. "At least, no one entered that I could see."

Cedar's bow appeared in his hands in an instant, the red case lying open, but Maria hadn't seen him move.

"I would not be too concerned," the elf said as she strutted towards the still-open door. "If whoever entered wanted to hurt us, we would know it by now."

"And how do you figure that?" Luca asked.

"Look down."

The dark Guardian looked and saw the dirks in his hands. He beamed, then frowned. "Wait a moment. I tried this before, and it didn't work. This world is *not* of the Path. How is this possible?"

"Perhaps someone who could rekindle magyc is nearby and allows us to touch that which we could not before."

"*Aethsiths!*" Luca and Timo exclaimed.

"Perhaps," Jæyd allowed.

Cedar stood still as a pillar, and his bow faded, morphing into the guitar. He looked at it, turning it slightly so the strings and the runes over the frets gleamed in the light. His eyes moved about the barn, from the hay bales, to the loft, to the stalls at the back. His brow furrowed over hesitant eyes, a giant battle of wills behind the golden orbs making him tense.

"Ria?" Cedar called quietly.

Tears filled Maria's eyes. *No one has called me that since...since I was twelve.*

"Hi guys," she said thickly through the lump in her throat. "God, I've missed you."

The Guardians waited, expectant, and Maria saw with a sinking feeling they couldn't hear her either.

"Ria, are you there?" Cedar called, a little louder.

"Why can't we see her?" Luca asked.

"Perhaps because we are not looking," Jæyd said.

"I am looking!" three voices chorused in protest.

Cedar looked at her suspiciously. "Can you see her?"

"No," Jæyd said.

An idea struck Maria. She walked over and knelt by a patch of ground clear of hay. With one finger she wrote a single word in the hard dirt of the barn floor. *Hi.*

"Jeezuscryst!" Luca exclaimed. The other three looked at him and he shrugged. "What? I heard the farmer say it."

"Ria?" Cedar spoke hesitantly to the air. "Is that you? Can you hear me?"

Yes. And yes.

"Oh, great gods!" Timo whooped. "We've been looking all over for you. Where in this Path-forsaken land are you?"

Maria scratched her address in the dirt and received blank stares from Timo and Luca.

"What does that mean?" Luca demanded.

"It's an address," Cedar said immediately. "We say Samnara, two alleys left of the Drinking Monkey, next to the brick wall. This is how they say it in Ria's world."

"So what exactly is in Samnara next to the brick wall two alleys left of the Drinking Monkey?" Luca wondered, his black eyes bright.

"The most trustworthy purveyor of the finest apple pies in all of Demona," Cedar told him and Luca pulled a childish face at him.

Maria began to panic as the golden light began to fade. Hastily she scratched out: *Do you know how to find me?* And looked up to see four faint shapes. One of them, she thought it was Cedar, nodded. "But Ria, be careful! Don't…"

She never found out what she wasn't supposed to do because he faded from view along with the other Guardians, and she opened her eyes -

A frantic pounding pulled Maria from sleep. The pounding continued, louder and faster, urgently demanding her attention. Maria dragged herself up, pushed her hair out of her eyes, and shuffled to the door. For the first time she could ever remember, the latch caught, and she stared at it, fully awake now. It seemed like an omen. She pushed the thought away as she jiggled the latch. It came free.

Maria opened the door. Betty stood there, almost unrecognizable with not a stitch of makeup on, face white, eyes red and puffy. For a moment, the two women stared at each other, neither saying anything. Betty's throat worked, and her lips twitched, as if she was thinking what to say. As Maria watched, Betty's face cracked, and any semblance of keeping it together crumbled. With shuddering moan, the woman began to sob.

"What's wrong?" Maria cried, reaching out to clasp Betty's arm.

"You have to come now," Betty told Maria. Her voice was thick and croaky.

She resisted when Maria tried to pull her inside, her sobs intensifying. Tears soaked her ample cleavage, and a cold chill worked its way into Maria's bones. *I don't believe in omens*, she told herself. *I don't believe in omens*. Faint bells, as if they were just waking up from a long sleep, chimed in her ribs. *That's a lie.*

"What's happened?" she asked, trying to keep her voice as level as possible while her heart pounded in her chest.

"It's Adam," Betty whispered. "He...he...he..."

"He's what?" Maria asked, her voice shaper than she intended.

"He's been killed."

At first, Maria thought she'd heard wrong. The words didn't fit, like two pieces of a puzzle with no innies, only outies.

"How?" Maria demanded. "When?"

"I don't know," Betty shook her head, looking like she was going deeper into shock. "Josh is out in the car..."

"Is he okay?" Maria interrupted.

"Yes. Yes, he's fine," Betty reassured her.

She took a tissue out of her purse and dabbed her face. "He says to bring you down."

"Of course." Maria ran back into her bedroom, changed into a t-shirt and put on an old pair of sneakers, grabbed her warm black jacket, her keys and her wallet, then left the apartment without locking the door behind her.

She trotted down the corridor beside Betty, her head in a cyclone. Never had the elevator seemed so slow. Josh's car was idling in the middle of the parking lot, brake lights like eerie red eyes in the early morning. Josh was gripping the steering wheel as if it were the only thing tethering him to reality. *Or sanity,* Maria thought. *Because reality sucks right now.*

When he saw Betty and Maria, he leapt out of the car and ran over to them. His tugged at his hair, staring at a suddenly hostile world with wide eyes.

"What happened?" Maria demanded, hoping he would give her a different answer.

Josh just looked at her, and Maria started to lose it. *Not here, not now,* she thought. *I have to keep it together, for their sakes.* When Josh shook his head, it tested her self-control to the limit.

"I thought you were in Jonston with The Nameless," Maria said.

"It's a four-hour drive. We changed our minds, thinking it would be better to stay here last night and drive up early today, in time for the gig. Save a couple hundred bucks on the hotel." Josh's eyes were wide, rimmed in white. "We didn't…we couldn't… we didn't know what…Adam's life was worth more than that."

Maria gently rubbed his back as he took deep breaths.

Two tears slid down the side of his face. He didn't wipe them away.

"This morning, Adam didn't show up," Josh continued in a subdued voice. "He didn't answer his phone. I went over there…" Josh's face turned from grey to green, and he bit his knuckle. His haunted eyes made Maria ache. "I saw what happened and then I came to get you."

"I told him he shouldn't have done that," Betty fretted. "He walked away from a crime scene. It makes him suspicious. I mean, it makes him a suspect."

"You watch too many cop dramas," Maria chided, then stood helplessly. "What do we do now?"

"I can take you to…" Josh swallowed. "I can take you to where it happened."

Because she couldn't think of anything else to do, Maria nodded. Something told her she didn't want to go and see what was there. Something was waiting for her there, she was sure of it. *But Ria, be careful! Don't…* a phantom voice iterated the incomplete warning.

Maria ignored it and got in the car.

Adam lived on Lime and 43rd in one of the big apartment complexes, just behind Centennial Park and six minutes from downtown if you sped and ran at least two red lights, like Josh did.

Had lived, Maria reminded herself as she, Josh, and Betty climbed the white stairs to Adam's unit. This building was in slightly better repair than the one Ria lived in, smelled better and allowed more light inside. *Just like Adam.*

Though months had passed since Maria had last been here, and she hadn't come here that often, it was easy to tell which door was Adam's - the door was open and hanging slightly askew, the paint ripped off in large scrapes. *It looks like a wild animal,* Maria thought but did not voice to the others.

Inside was a strange combination of wanton destruction and pristine normalcy. Apparently the attacker had known exactly where to find Adam and made a beeline for the small bedroom behind the kitchen and living-room, shattering everything in its path and touching nothing else.

Maria stared transfixed at the obvious footprint in the carpet just in front of the bed: as long as her forearm, sharp claw marks in the floor ripped through the light blue fabric to reveal the dirty concrete below. She didn't notice Josh come up behind her until he touched her shoulder, making her jump.

"Hi," she said, her voice sounding strange in her ears. *Maybe if I pretend everything is okay, I'll wake up and find this is a bad dream.*

"Hey," he replied and swallowed. "He's…he's in here…"

Maria didn't want to follow him into the bedroom, and it was only with great effort that she moved her feet. She stopped in the doorway, eyes searching the dim room. Josh was standing in the middle of the room, and as Maria watched, he hunkered down, mesmerized by a form at his feet.

It was Adam, and in a dream, she walked over and dropped beside Josh, forcing herself to look. Maria had seen death and dead bodies in movies, but that was no comparison to having one in front of her. The television couldn't convey the cloying scent or the heavy presence that should be there but wasn't.

Adam's body was still and Maria had the urge to touch him, to prod him in the hope that his eyes would open and he would look at her in puzzlement before getting up like normal. She reached out, but Josh grabbed her wrist. Thankfully there wasn't enough light to see many details, but she could see more than she wanted to, like the dark pool of fluid he was lying in, the puffy discoloration of the flesh, and the wrong twist of his head.

For the first time, she noticed the bed itself. The body had been removed, but nothing would ever take the splashes of blood from the torn sheets or the mattress which hung over the side of the bed like a pancake that's been flipped too soon, with the batter running down the side of the pan. A faint, familiar buzz caught her attention, and her eyes roved until they fell on the black plastic shape in the corner of the room, half hidden under a pair of black jeans.

She walked over and picked up the iPod. Now closer, she could hear the song. The end faded out, and the beginning of the same song started up again. Adam had an annoying capacity for listening to one song on repeat for hours when he got in a certain mood. She attempted a smile, but her mouth wouldn't comply.

"'The End of the Beginning of the End' by Blackrobe," she told Josh. "It was one of our favorites."

Josh was slightly green, and he looked like he might at any moment start screaming or sobbing, but held himself together with effort, and tried to come up with a reply.

"We should call the police," she said, partly to save him the agony, and partly because she couldn't bear to hear what he would say.

Josh nodded, looking relieved to have something to do as he pulled out his cell phone and made the call. They waited, then the sound of sirens sounded in the distance and grew louder. Suddenly, activity erupted around them as tape was put up by people in uniforms and latex gloves. An officer took them aside, and Maria noticed that the tag on his chest said "Investigator Robert Jackson."

"I'd like to get a statement from each of you," he

requested.

"Of course," Josh said.

"When was the last time you saw or spoke to the victim?"

"Um…on Sunday, at the radio studio," Maria said, a lump coming to her throat as she recalled Adam's cheerful face.

"I saw him at the surprise party for Maria," Betty tearfully chimed in. "He left about five o'clock."

"I saw him last night," Josh said. "We were making some final preparations at my place…"

"Preparations for what?" the investigator asked.

"We were going on the road tomorrow," Josh said. "With the band. Nexus."

The officer wrote that down. "Is there anyone else in this band?"

"Matt!" Maria said with a glance around the small bedroom, as if he would be standing there. "Where is he?"

"I couldn't find him or get him on his cell," Betty told her, her fuchsia-tipped hands writhing on her chest. "I left him about ten voice messages, though."

"I'd like to speak to him," the investigator said. "If you could provide contact info…"

Maria showed the officer her contact page for Matt for him to take down the number and address.

"Thank you. Do you know of anyone who had a motive for the murder?" the inspector continued. "Anyone who was upset with him? An ex-girlfriend? Was he in any trouble with a gang? Was he dealing drugs, black market, prostitutes, anything like that?"

Josh looked shocked. "Adam? You've got to be kidding! The guy was the cleanest, happiest person you could find. His life was this band and his keyboard." Josh shook his head. "No. No one could have wanted him dead."

Maria and Betty nodded their agreement.

"Very good," the inspector said. "There is one last thing." He pulled a crumpled paper from his clipboard and held it out. "This was found on the body. Do you have any idea what it means?"

Josh leaned closer and looked at it with a frown. "No."

Betty peered over his shoulder and then shook her head. "No, officer, I'm afraid I don't know what that means. Is it hieroglyphics?"

"I'm not sure," the inspector said. "Miss?" he queried Maria. "Do you know what this means?"

Maria stared at the paper, noting the smear of brown on the corner, her hands trembling, feeling faint as the blood drained from her head. The paper held a Mark, two overlapping circles, one slightly under the other, and drawn in what was unmistakably blood. Each of the circles' left and right sides were slightly thicker than the top and bottom, giving them a distorted appearance. Underneath was a word that Maria had never thought she would see again.

"*Aethsiths,*" she whispered, her mouth dry.

"Yes," the inspector said, looking at her with a squinting glare. "You've heard it before?"

Maria moistened her lips, blinking hard at the Mark, feeling the faint warmth emanating from it.

"No," she heard herself say as she handed the paper back to the officer. "No, Inspector, I've never seen it before."

That was a lie, something in her head, or maybe it was her ribcage, chimed at her in an accusatory tone, loud enough to deafen her. She was just glad no one else could hear it.

Walking robotically out of Adam's apartment, Maria tried to come up with a way to get the paper from the police. She grabbed Josh's arm. "You guys go on ahead. I think I left my purse back there."

Without waiting for a reply, Maria turned and hurried back into the apartment towards the bedroom. She kept her head down, her eyes glancing about, trying to find Inspector Robert Jackson. Seeing him step into the kitchen, Ria veered to the right and collided with him just as he looked up from his clipboard. They both staggered into the fridge and he caught her as she fell, dropping the clipboard to the linoleum with a crash.

"Oh! I'm so sorry!" Maria said, extricating herself from his grip and kneeling down to retrieve the clipboard. "I think I left my purse in there."

The Inspector looked back at the room with a frown. "I see. Well, you'd better fetch it then."

"Thank you," Maria said and handed him the clipboard, the scrap of bloodied paper safely clutched in her hand.

The man waited for her to move, and when she didn't, he gestured towards the room. Maria bobbed her head, putting her hands in the pocket of her jacket and walked into the bedroom. She spent two minutes looking for her "lost" purse, so he didn't get suspicious. Finally, she shrugged and turned to him with a bemused smile.

"I guess maybe I left it in the car," she said. "I'm sorry to be a bother."

"Right." The policeman handed her a card. "If you think of anything else, don't hesitate to call, alright?"

"Yes, Inspector." Maria took the card, shoving it in the pocket with the paper and quickly made an exit.

Josh and Betty were waiting in the idling car, and Ria slipped into the back seat.

"Did you get your purse?" Betty asked.

"What?" Maria started. "Oh, no. I don't think I brought it up there."

"No, I don't think you did," Josh said, his gaze fixed on her in the rear-view mirror as he pulled out of the parking lot. "Because you don't carry a purse."

Maria avoided his gaze, the paper burning a hole in her pocket. She itched to get it out and examine it again, but she couldn't, not with Josh staring at her.

"Maria?" he inquired. "Are you going to tell me what's going on? Or should I turn around and take you back to the police so you can tell them what you know?"

Her eyes flicked to his warm brown ones, still fixed on her. "You should watch the road when you're driving," she said.

"You knew what that word was, didn't you?" Josh asked, his tone blunt and unforgiving. "On the paper? Athletic, or whatever it was?"

Opening her mouth to give some plausible story, Maria never got a chance to because Josh cut her off with a curt shake of his head. "Don't, Maria. I've known you too long. You can't lie worth a damn. Everyone in the room could tell you knew what it meant."

Maria felt her face flush. "I actually don't know what it means, not fully," she asserted, unable to keep the defensiveness from creeping into her voice.

"But you've seen it before?" Josh pressed.

Maria gave an unwilling nod. "Yes."

"Why didn't you tell the police?" Josh demanded, throwing his hands up for a second before slamming them back down on the steering wheel to make a sharp left a second before the light went red. "Adam's been *murdered*! Isn't that something they should know?!"

"It's complicated," Maria said, biting her lip. "I would

never be able to explain."

Josh sighed. "Fine. But Maria, just tell me this one thing: do you know who killed Adam?"

Maria opened her mouth but found no words there. Josh's eyes flicked back and forth between her and the road. Maria slowly took the paper out of her pocket and held it up.

Josh looked dismayed. "God, Maria, tell me you didn't steal evidence from a murder scene."

"This wasn't meant for the police. It wouldn't help them anyway," Maria said, tracing the mark with one finger. "It means *the Songstress*. The one in the Prophecy."

"What does *that* mean?" Josh cried. "Maria, that doesn't make any sense!"

"I told you I wouldn't be able to explain."

"You're being really cryptic," Josh said, his voice strangled to an even tone. "I'm scared, Maria. If this has something to do with you, if *Adam being murdered* has *anything* to do with *you*, what does that mean for me and Betty? And for Matt? Or your dad?"

Maria paled. *I hadn't thought about that.*

"Why didn't the neighbors hear anything?" Betty asked, sounding as if she were joining the conversation, but not understanding what it was about.

Josh and Maria stared at her. Her face was pinched in a puzzled frown, and her gaze was trying to find logic in a child's abstract drawing. "It happened sometime last night, right? But none of the neighbors noticed anything. Or else they would have called the police. How could that much destruction not be noticed?"

Magyc, the answer was on Maria's lips before she could stop it. Josh and Betty looked at her as if she had sprouted potatoes for ears or gone insane. *Which is probably more likely,* Maria thought, on the edge of hysterics herself. *This can't be happening like this. This isn't real; it has to be a dream.*

The thought prompted a memory of another dream, a vision she couldn't argue with even if she wanted to. It had the harmonious ring of truth she recognized in some deep part of herself. However, what she was going to do with that truth wouldn't make Josh any happier.

"Listen, do either of you know of any farmland near here?" she asked.

"We're surrounded by farmland," Josh snapped. "North, south, and west of here."

"It would be near a small town called Chardc-something," Maria said.

"*Chardc?*" Josh said. "Spelled how?"

"C-H-A-R-D-C," Maria replied. "The last few letters were missing though."

The three of them sat in silence trying to figure out what it could mean.

"Oh! It must have been Chardock!" Betty said from the front. "I have an uncle who owns a farm in Chardock!"

"Yes!" Maria exclaimed. "How far away is it?"

"About a hundred miles," Betty said. "Why?"

"Some friends of mine are there, and they need to find me. The thing is, they're probably going to have a little trouble because they're not exactly from around here."

Her eyes shifted, and her tone was light as she hedged. Josh was not fooled. "Do they have something to do with what happened here?"

Maria shrugged, unwilling to voice an affirmative to his question. His jaw worked, and a vein throbbed in his temple. Maria suddenly realized how much worse this must be for him. *At least I have my dreams and whatever happened to me when I ran away to help me make sense of this. He has nothing.*

"So what are you going to do?" Josh said at last.

"I'm going to go out there and find them," Maria said.

"How do you know you'll find them?" Josh demanded.

"It'll be really easy. I imagine they'll stick out like a sore thumb," Maria said. "They'll be carrying instruments and will be on foot, maybe on horseback. They don't have cars where they come from."

"*Where they come from?*" Josh's tone took on a more menacing bent as he interrogated her. "Does that mean they're from another country, and they decided the weather was better here so they got on a plane and came for some vacation? Or does that mean something different?"

Maria shook her head and shrugged, her face twisted in an expression of hopeless apology. She offered no further explanation, silently waiting for his next demanding question.

"Are we in danger?" he asked, his expression daring her to lie. "Maria, are they going to keep coming after us to get to you?"

Though it was hard to hold his gaze, Maria would not move her eyes from his. She couldn't say yes, and she wouldn't lie.

Josh watched her for a few seconds and then he sighed. "Okay, this is what we're going to do. You go, find your dad, then find Matt. Tell him what happened and get him to stay with you. I'm going to drop Betty off at home. Mike is there and she'll be alright with him and his shotgun…"

"I'm pretty sure a shotgun won't stop who…whatever did that," Maria said softly.

"Then she'll stick with you," Josh replied without missing a beat, his gaze hard. "You know what you're doing, right? You can handle this?"

A memory from long ago, a peppery man with purple and green in his black hair berating her - *if you're going to say you're certain, at least try to look like it. That would be more convincing for others, and sometimes, that's enough* - surfaced and

Maria put on a brave face.

"Yes," she declared. "I can handle it."

"Good," Josh said. "So I'm going to let you find Matt, and I'll go pick up your friends. Depending on how long I have to look for them once I get to Chardock, I should be back in four or five hours."

"Thanks, Josh," Maria said.

"Don't thank me yet," Josh said as he pulled to a jerky halt outside her apartment. "I have the feeling we're not in the clear."

Maria thought he was right, but she didn't voice her agreement as she slammed the door and watched him drive away, the taillights unpleasantly reminding her of red eyes.

"Let's go up," she told Betty. "We shouldn't be out in the open."

Betty didn't appear to hear her, and when Ria turned she saw what had mesmerized the woman. Something had torn a path through the weed-choked grass to the door of the apartment building, leaving a glaring trail of destruction, daring anyone to stop whatever was on that mission.

Exactly like in Adam's apartment.

"Oh my god, what do we do?" Betty covered her mouth with her hands, panic in her eyes. "It's here, isn't it? We're going to die…"

Maria grabbed her arm. "Listen to me. I just have to check and make sure my dad's not in there. Then we'll go to Matt's place."

She dragged the petrified woman to the nearest decorative shrub and pushed her behind it. "Stay here. I'll be back in a minute."

She tried to walked away, but Betty's death grip on her arm wouldn't let her go. She looked back and met the woman's pleading gaze.

"I don't want to stay here by myself," Betty whispered, the edge of terror making her voice grate more than usual.

"Fine," Maria sighed. "Come with me, and don't make any noise."

First, Maria checked the parking lot. She couldn't see her father's old cream sedan and she felt a little bloom of hope. Her eyes went to the window on the third floor and hoped her luck held out. Unlike in Adam's apartment, an urgent need to make sure her dad was alright drowned out her unwillingness to confront whatever horrible thing could be there. She hoped this was one of the days he wasn't home.

Following the path of destruction, her heart pattering in her chest, Maria made her way up the stairs and along the corridor. Four jagged lines of scraped paint at head-height on the wall guided her to the door of the apartment, wide open though thankfully still attached at the hinges.

Most of the furniture and fixings were intact and unharmed. Breathing shallowly, trying to be silent and invisible, Maria went from room to room, peering in and finding with relief no Demon and no dad. When she had gone through the entire apartment in this fashion and was standing in the kitchen debating whether to leave a note, she glanced down and saw the streaks of fresh blood under the table.

A rushing in her ears made it hard to think. She swallowed hard several times and took a tentative step towards the table.

"What is it?" Betty asked.

"Shh!!" Maria hissed with more venom than she intended to.

Her mind screamed at her to back away, get as far from here as she could, but she couldn't listen to it. Steeling herself, she knelt and looked under the table, preparing to flinch away before she saw what was there.

In the darkness under the table, two eyes glowed. But they weren't red - they flashed green in the light. Turbo slunk back, glaring at her, pupils huge and black, ears back, orange fur standing straight out. A gash on his leg bled profusely. She reached for him, and he hissed, paw shooting out with claws extended.

"Turbo!" she exclaimed, jerking her hand back, looking at the cat with a hurt expression. "It's me!"

At the sound of her voice, the cat calmed down. His ears came up a little, and he allowed her to touch him but yowled when her fingers pressed on his wound. Maria pulled him out from under the table.

"Oh, poor dear!" Betty cried, rushing over. "What happened to him?"

Maria examined the wound. It was deep and clean. She shook her head, wondering. "I think Turbo took on a Demon."

"A what?" Betty asked.

"Nothing, never mind," Maria said. "I should clean him up."

"Let me do that," Betty said, taking the cat from Maria. Once pressed against the softness of her breast, Turbo started up his signature purr.

Maria nodded. "Antiseptic and cotton is in the bathroom."

Betty left and returned with bottles and enough cotton balls to decorate the mall's Christmas Santa Claus display with fake snow. With efficient motions, Betty cleaned up Turbo's wound and wrapped him in gauze so he looked half-mummified.

"I was a vet's assistant in college," Betty told Maria, who stood by and watched, feeling useless and unneeded.

"Comes in handy whenever Mike accidentally nails his thumb to something."

"Mike doesn't really strike me as the type to accidentally nail his thumb to anything." Mike Coleman, Betty's husband, was a man's man who hunted, fished, and made his own furniture just as easily as having a beer.

"You'd be surprised," Betty said, directing a significant look at Maria. "That man would have died of blood poisoning twenty years ago if it wasn't for me. One time I-"

"What the hell happened here?" a voice shouted.

Maria looked up. Her father stood in the doorway, blue eyes wide behind his glasses, a box of pizza held up like a knight might hold out a sword to a particularly fierce dragon right about the time he was thinking it was a good idea to turn tail and run. When her father saw her, he dropped the box and sprinted over to her.

"Maria!" he gasped, grabbing her shoulders. "Are you alright? Are you hurt? What happened?"

"It's kind of a long story," Maria said, for what felt like the hundredth time.

"Adam Lake was murdered this morning," Betty reported in a matter of fact tone, one hand caressing Turbo's head. The cat was unconcerned with anything going on around him, his eyes half-closed in contentment. "We went to the crime scene and Maria recognized a symbol but didn't tell the inspector that she knew what it meant. Josh has gone to pick up Maria's friends from out of town, while we warn you and Matt."

Maria stared at her. Apparently giving Betty something useful to do had returned her equilibrium, and her propensity for talking. She was still pale, but her shaking had stopped, and her eyes had lost the glassy sheen. Maria's father was blinking as he assimilated this incredible tale. Slowly, his eyes turned to Maria.

"What did you recognize?" he asked.

Maria started. *That was the thing he fixed on, what I didn't share with the police, not that Adam was murdered?* That boded ill for her, but she didn't know exactly how.

"It was nothing," she muttered.

"It was some sort of symbol," Betty repeated, and Maria wanted to snap a sarcastic *thank you very much for that Betty; no really, thanks.*

Beads of sweat stood out on her father's forehead, and he stepped forward with measured steps, picking up the pizza box he had dropped and putting it down in the exact center of the table. This was the way he got when he didn't know how to handle a situation, but he was going to try anyway.

"A symbol?" he repeated in an equally measure tone. "What did it look like?"

"Two circles," Betty said promptly.

Maria's father relaxed, relief smoothing out the lines on his face. Maria stood straighter, all her attention now focused on whatever it was her dad was *not* revealing. She tried to catch his eye, but he would not meet her gaze.

"What did you think it was, dad?" she asked.

"Nothing," he answered.

I'd bet that's the same sort of nothing *I've been dishing out,* Maria thought, nausea cramping up in her stomach. Her father flipped open the lid of the box and the tantalizing smell of melted cheese and tomato sauce spread out like a balm.

"Anyone care for a slice?"

"Pizza for breakfast, dad, how many…" Maria started, but Betty brushed by, headed for the table, a woman on a mission. She shifted Turbo to one arm, unwilling to let go of her new purring safety blanket, took a deep whiff, then picked out the biggest piece of pizza and took a bite.

"Betty, now is really not the time…" Maria tried again, but Betty held up a manicured finger.

She finished chewing slowly and deliberately before she spoke. "I haven't had a stitch of wheat or dairy in four years, three months, a week, and six days - that brownie last Christmas doesn't count. We may all be about to die, and this could be my last chance to enjoy a slice of heaven, so now is *definitely* not the time to lecture me." She took another bite and spoke around the mouthful of mushrooms and sausage. "Besides, they've already been here and left. We can relax for two seconds."

The statement nagged at Maria. In Demona, the Nine Demons had tracked her with terrifying accuracy, mitigated only by a short delay, which was most likely the sole reason she was still alive. Here, nothing of that thing called magyc existed. *No Path magyc,* she thought, the terrifying belief in the actuality of that land and everything it held telling her she was not dreaming, this was really and truly real. *But what of that other brand of magyc, the stuff of demons and sorcery?*

Adam's iPod had been repeating "The End of the Beginning of the End" by Blackrobe. It was the first of *those* songs he had found for her and retained a special place in her heart, a reminder that maybe magyc did exist here, if faintly and sporadically. Maria's throat closed up.

No, she tried to tell herself. *It wasn't that. It couldn't be that.* The chime of untruth was louder this time, more insistent. With it came an inarticulate warning, incomplete but recognizable.

"We have to get out of here. Now," Maria said.

"Why?" her father asked. "Where do we have to go?"

"It doesn't matter…just away from here…" Maria's voice was shaky. "Dad, we have to go *right now.*"

"Okay," he said, but he brushed by her, heading in the opposite direction from the door. "I just have to get a few things."

He disappeared into the bedroom, and Maria waited, shifting from her left foot to her right, counting seconds in her head. When her father emerged a minute later, she grabbed his hand with one of hers, and Betty's with the other, and pulled them towards the door.

He followed without protest, bewildered but uncomplaining. Maria no longer worried about making a noise as they charged down the hallway. Betty started for the elevator. The thought of being trapped in a metal box while something with red eyes and claws made mincemeat of it - and them - made Maria's heart stutter. She tugged them in the direction of the stairwell.

"Where's your car?" she asked her father. "Dad! Where's your car?"

"In the parking spot," her dad replied with a bemused expression.

"Okay, listen to me. I need you to go out the back entrance, get the car, and come and pick me up by the dumpster. I need you to be as fast as you possibly can. Okay?"

Her father nodded and she squeezed his hand. "Okay, go!"

She watched him disappear through the door before she and Betty ran out the front. The woman froze, and Maria was jerked to a halt. Betty's terrified scream made Maria's heart catch in her throat. Both women were held frozen by the sight of the Demon stalking towards them, massive, muscular frame covered with spikes, huge horns gleaming in the sun. A yowl from Turbo, whom Betty had managed to keep a hold of in their flight, shattered the spell.

Maria rammed into Betty with her shoulder in a football-esque maneuver, shoving the other woman into motion and got them running around the side of the apartment, leaping over little rows of begonias and daisies which desperately needed a watering. Betty stumbled and Maria caught her.

"Don't fall!" she urged the woman.

Maria did not glance over her shoulder. She knew the stuff of nightmares called a Demon was coming, and she didn't need to know how close it was. Rounding the corner, the pair of women careened into the dumpsters with a metallic thunder. Tears were streaming down Betty's face, making her look very young.

A steaming wheeze from behind her caused Maria to stop and turn. The Demon was standing at the corner of the building, half a dozen yards away, massive ram's horns spiraling over its shoulders.

Turbo's ears were flat against his head, and his claws were out, digging into Betty's flesh. The woman gave no indication she felt it, her eyes riveted on the approaching monster as her mind tried to make sense of the same.

"*Aethsiths*," the Demon greeted with a bow of its head. Maria swore it was being sincerely respectful.

"Demon," she said. *The Nine, they were called in that place,* she recalled. "Which one are you then?"

"I am known as the God of Fire," the Demon replied, its voice burning and rusty.

Maria nodded, her gaze flickering behind her. *Where are you, dad?* "I take it you've come to kill me then?"

The Demon stared at her, then shook its head, a slow, regal motion, and Maria got the absurd idea it thought this was some kind of ritual, to be played out like a morbid dance. She took a step back. Betty was making quiet crying sounds and Maria tightened her grip on the other woman's hand. Somehow Turbo had managed to wriggle out of the woman's clutch and was nowhere to be found.

"It's going to be okay," Maria heard herself say, and with some surprise, she found that she actually believed it. "I promise."

Betty squeezed Maria's hand, and took a deep, trembling breath. "Honey, I never thought it would end like this."

"It's not going to end," Maria promised, absurdly elated by the adrenaline.

The Demon moved quicker than Maria expected, like a snake striking, and she barely made it behind the dumpster to avoid the claw that shredded the metal with a horrible whine which reverberated in Maria's head, making her teeth ache.

The wall was slimy with about a hundred years of grime but Maria pressed as close to it as she could. "When it throws the dumpster aside, we're going to make a break for it, okay?" she told Betty out of the side of her mouth.

"Okay," Betty agreed, a dazed look in her eyes.

Just as Maria had predicted, the dumpster flew aside as though it were made of paper, bouncing like a flat ball and coming to a crashing halt somewhere on the lawn but Maria was already running past the Demon. As she sprinted to the parking lot, the cream sedan skidded to a halt in front of her and Maria yanked at the door.

"Dad! Lock!" she cried out.

With a click, the door unlocked and Maria pulled it open, pushing Betty inside and tumbling in on top of her.

"Drive!"

The car peeled out of the parking lot before the door had closed. Maria pulled her legs inside the car and slammed the door shut. Scrambling over Betty's shaking body, Maria maneuvered into the front seat and with a glance at the side mirror, she saw that the Demon was not behind them.

"Maria," her dad said, his voice so calm it was flat. "What was that?"

Nothing for it now. "That, dad, was a Demon. One of the Nine. Sent for me."

"I see. Tell me, does this have to do with the conversation we had the other morning?"

Yesterday morning, she thought, and nodded, watching carefully for her father's reaction, unsure of what it was going to be. To her surprise, he simply rubbed his chin, a pensive expression on his face.

"Dad?" she prompted. "What's up?"

"Your mother told me something like this might happen," he said.

"*What?*" Maria couldn't believe what she was hearing.

"Before she died, she told me 'be surprised at nothing, and trust her,'" he explained. "She also gave me this, to give to you."

He reached into the pocket of his jeans and pulled out a small black box and a folded piece of paper sealed with black wax. In the wax, Ria saw a Mark, an 'x' with one straight line and one curved line and suddenly, Maria knew what symbol her father had been afraid she'd seen in Adam's apartment.

"This is her Mark?" Maria asked, feeling the dips in the wax with her fingertips, relishing the tingle that moved up her arm.

"This was the only time I ever saw her write that," her father told her. "She said it was very important that you get this, and told me I should give it to you when you turned sixteen." He paused, a contrite look on his face. "I think I should have given it to you when you were twelve, when you came back, but I was scared. But better late than never, you know." He gave her a weak smile. "I thought it would make a fitting birthday gift. Better than a yellow sweater."

"Do you want to know what it says?" Maria asked, her finger poised at the edge of the wax.

"I think it was meant for you alone," her father said. "I've never read it, though I thought about it many times. I tried just once, but for the life of me I couldn't open it."

Maria nodded. Whatever magyc had gone into the box and the letter that went with it worked here, and it gave her the same thrill as hearing one of *those* songs. She put both objects in her jacket. "I'll read it later. I've waited this long, a little while longer won't kill me." *But maybe the Demons might.*

Her father smoothed his worried look with an attempt at a smile. "So, where to?"

"I have to find Matt," Ria said. "And make sure he's okay." She paused, the next words the most difficult she had ever had to utter. "Then I have to go."

"Will you come back again, like you did last time?" her father asked, and his eyes sparkled wetly. "Or is it for good now?"

"I don't know, dad," Maria said, scooting closer to him and putting her head on his shoulder. "I really don't know."

Matt still wasn't answering his phone. He wasn't at his apartment, or at his parents' house. Neither his mother or father had seen him, or heard from him.

"What's wrong?" his mother asked, her brows tight with worry.

"Nothing," Maria smiled reassuringly and hugged the pretty woman with the beginning of grey in her dark blond perm, ignoring the clang of untruth reverberating through her bones.

I don't remember it being that annoying, Maria grumbled to herself. *Though, I suppose I didn't lie so much then.*

She thought it was slightly absurd that her inner-lie-detector acted up when she herself was lying, but maybe it just didn't like discriminating.

"Where do we go now?" her father asked.

"I don't know," Maria sighed. "Let me think about it for a moment, okay?"

"Okay. I'll get gas. We're running pretty low," he replied.

Maria nodded, staring out the window as he drove. *Where is Matt? And more importantly, is he okay?*

They pulled into the tiny gas station on the corner of two nameless streets and stopped beside pump number three.

"I have to go to the bathroom," Betty announced when the engine fell still. "Will you come with me? I don't want to go in there alone." She looked pleadingly at Maria.

Maria nodded, and the two women got out of the car and walked to the store. Betty disappeared into the single bathroom, and Maria stared around at the shelves half filled with junk food that was probably past its expiration date, but would last until the next century.

A T.V. was playing in the corner above the cash register. Maria's eyes gravitated to it as the most interesting thing in the room, then her eyes widened, and she dashed over, leaning across the counter to get a better look.

Yellow tape, red fire engines, and flashing lights made the scene on the television bright and morbidly festive. The building would have been beautiful, red brick and black ironwork imparting a rustic look. Now, most of the brick was covered in soot, a corner had crumbled, and one row of iron fencing had bent in half. Windows were broken and discolored by the inferno still spilling out of the gaping hole surrounded by rubble. A crowd of people milled around, displaced hotel residents, and trucks with a satellite

The Other World

dishes and a T.V. station logos painted on the side ringed the edge of the commotion.

Now, on the news story playing in the gas station, a woman with a perfect face painted on, wearing a pseudo-modest business suit, gazed at the world on the other side of the camera, her eyes narrowed as she delivered her edgy narrative.

"...just fifteen minutes ago in the Harrods Hotel in downtown Jonston. The multi-platinum rock band The Nameless were among the victims. Ian Spencer, vocalist, and Connor Woods are in critical condition at Saint Mary's Hospital. Guitarist Henry C. is still unaccounted for. Drummer Finn Belle was the first tragic fatality in the accident..."

A rushing in Maria's ears drowned out the next part. *Finn was dead.* His charming eyes and easy smile haunted her, now mangled and oozing thick blood and gore, blue and bloated like Adam's face. She squeezed her eyes shut, trying to banish the gruesome image, but it persisted.

Finn was dead.
Because of her.
Just like Adam.

Her eyes burned with suppressed tears of inconsolable shame and regret, and she forced herself to listen to the chipper yet somber voice of the newscaster.

"...thousands of fans mourn the loss of the flamboyant drummer, but the band's rep, Lulu Tahlia, has declined to issue a statement on behalf of the Nameless. In addition to the musicians, three other hotel guests have been killed, eighteen are missing, and countless were injured by the inexplicable fire. The police have no leads..."

"I'm all done," Betty's voice broke in. "Thanks for waiting."

Maria turned. The woman stood behind her, arms full of a variety of chips, three chocolate bars, and a packet of mini cinnamon-glazed donuts.

"Don't judge me," she said defensively when she saw Maria's look. "My blood sugar is dangerously low and I need comfort food right now…oh my god it's Matt!"

Maria whirled to the door, but Betty was pointing at the T.V. On the screen was Matt's picture, with eighteen others, the names of the missing people running in a ribbon along the bottom of the screen.

"Come on! We have to go right now!" Maria cried.

Betty gave a brief, longing look at her comfort food, then dumped it next to the magazine rack, and walked away despite the attendant's spluttering displeasure.

Maria hurried out of the convenience store into a cold wind that had blown up suddenly and was trying to sneak into her clothes. She huddled in her jacket, hugging herself and walking with her head down, but the wind seemed to have the upper hand.

Waiting impatiently for a dented pickup to inch past, Maria hopped from foot to foot and glanced down the road. She turned the other way then whipped her head back, certain she had seen something. But no, no red eyes were peering at the street from a dark alleyway. Maria shivered and ran to her father's car as soon as it was clear.

"We found Matt!" Betty cried triumphantly, as she slid into the back seat.

"Well, sort of," Maria amended. "He's in Jonston. Or was."

"That's four hours away," her father said.

"And we don't even know if Matt is there or not," Betty added. "Now I really feel like a private detective. Two crime scenes in one day and all this following clues. We could be in a T.V. show."

She didn't sound as excited about that as she would have a week ago, and Maria felt the beginning of an irreversible change to their lives take firm hold.

"So, private detective, what do we do?" Maria asked.

"We'll probably get into trouble if we try to go inside the crime scene," Betty said. "Do you have a fake badge?"

"Why would I have a fake badge?" Maria wondered aloud.

Betty shrugged, and a faint blush colored her cheeks. "I don't know. They have fake badges on the shows."

"I thought they were real cops," Maria's father put in.

"Some of them are," Betty said and declined to explain further.

Maria struggled and debated. She wanted to rush off to Jonston, but the chance of finding Matt that way was next to zero. *Unless by magyc,* she thought. *Which doesn't exist here.* Her head was fuzzy, and thoughts she was trying to put together kept slipping apart.

"I think the first thing to do is get something to eat," Maria said, looking at the clock. "It's almost three, and I haven't eaten breakfast. I can't plan on an empty stomach."

"You should have had some pizza and let me buy my snacks," Betty chided.

"There's a little restaurant nearby," Richard said. "Called something fancy, but I can't remember what it is."

Maria nodded, and the old sedan coughed to life and purred away. Two blocks down, they spotted the diner called Michaelangelo's. Betty debated for five minutes before she gave in and ordered lasagna and garlic bread. Maria forced herself to eat every bit of her cobb salad, even though it turned to ash in her mouth.

"Dessert?" her father asked when they were finished. "My treat?"

Maria nodded, to make him happy. She wanted

chocolate, but no restaurant could make a decent chocolate cake, something that wasn't picture-perfect yet tasted like sugared dirt, so she got strawberry cheesecake instead. Betty assured Maria she would only have a bite, then ate more than half of it. Maria didn't mind. After their stomachs were full, and the check was paid, her dad looked at them.

"So what now?"

"We can't go to Jonston," Maria sighed, the food in her stomach now weighing her down like a brick, but at least her head was clear. "We'll never find him."

"We should call the hotline they gave on the news report, and see if they've found Matt," Betty directed in an authoritative voice.

"I didn't note it down," Maria told her.

"Well, lucky for you, I did." Betty smiled.

Maria took the scrap of paper Berry handed her and dialed the number. She spoke to an officer who was polite though his voice was strained and took down her information and Matt's name, promising to have someone call as soon as they found out anything. Maria hung up and looked at her father and Betty.

"If you really want to go to Jonston, I don't mind driving you," her father said.

Maria shook her head. "Matt may not even be there anymore. He's not answering his phone, but I have a feeling he'll turn up soon." She didn't mention that it wasn't a good feeling.

"I'm going to stay with you until everything is sorted out," Betty said at once, and a horrified expression crossed her face. "I should call Mike! He's probably worried sick."

Maria watched as she dug her phone out of her pocket, called her husband, who hadn't noticed anything out of the ordinary, and assured him she was okay, and that she was going to be staying with Maria for the night. Maria thought about pointing out the idiocy of staying with someone who was a Demon-magnet, but thought that would just confuse poor Betty beyond tolerance.

"Where do we go to now?" Betty looked at Maria after she hung up.

"I don't want to go back to the apartment. It would just be weird, and I'd jump at every sound, even though it was nothing," Maria said, and her father and Betty's expression conveyed complete agreement.

"We could go to my house," Betty offered, though she had just told Mike she was staying at Maria's place.

Maria shook her head. "No, I don't want you to be put out because of me." She didn't add that she didn't want Betty and Mike to end up dead because of her either.

Betty waved her hand. "It's no trouble. Really."

"Betty, I don't think-"

"Oh, you don't have to if you don't want to," Betty said, looking put out. *She just wanted to feel useful,* Maria realized. *But that isn't worth the potential price.*

"We should find a motel," Maria said. "Close by. I think that will be safest."

"What about the one by the...by the thing?" Betty asked.

"The bowling alley?" Richard supplied, and Betty nodded, looking at Maria for confirmation.

A Motel 4 was on the other side of the small town, down the road from Brook's sole bowling alley and across the way from the empty lot that was supposed to have been a new shopping mall and ended up as a parking garage and a half-finished block of concrete rooms.

Maria nodded. "Sounds good."

On the short drive, she wondered how Josh was doing, and if she had sent him wandering around the boondocks for nothing but a figment of her imagination. She took out her phone and texted him an update, trying to be as un-alarming as possible when talking about the mysterious hotel fire and their missing friend. *Going to Motel near bowling place,* she ended the text. Then she leaned her head back and stared out the window.

In the monotony of driving, she dozed and dreamed again. This dream was different than the other ones. Golden light was present but not pervasive, and she was not participating but watching from a great height. Events sped by her, but too fast to make out details, like a time lapse videos of the seasons. Great tears opened and closed in the fabric of the world, showing through to its dark, smoky innards. With some effort, Maria recalled the names for these things: *Doors* and *Rifts* and the *Void*.

The difference between these things was easy for Maria to see. Doors leaked golden light and a glorious music was present when they appeared, growing louder when they opened. Though the Doors were beautiful, the Rifts were somehow neater, cleaner, the edges more formed and distinct. *Almost as if the maker of the Rift had more practice or was closer attuned to the makeup of the world.*

Then she was close, very close, her nose pressed against a window to this world as she gazed in at the scene unfolding. The sheath that kept the world whole and separate began to strain, bulging around invisible seams. A Door or a Rift, Maria couldn't tell. She waited, her eyes searching for the first sliver of an opening. It threatened but never came. And everything went black as the car jolted over a pot hole, and she woke.

She blinked and sat up, massaging a crick in her neck. "How much farther?" she asked.

"About five minutes," her father said.

His hands were clamped on the wheel, and his jaw was

rigid. Maria glanced into the back. Betty was lying on the seat, gentle snores coming from her open mouth.

"I think all the excitement got to her," Maria's father said.

"Yeah," Maria acknowledged. "How are you holding up?"

"Me? Oh, I'll be fine. You know, when I said we could do something together, I didn't mean run from something called a Demon," he laughed, but it was short-lived humor.

"I know," she said. "I'm sorry. I didn't think..." she trailed off.

"Didn't think what?" he pressed.

"Didn't think my past would come back to haunt me like this," she told him. "I tried so hard to pretend it was just a way for me to escape, like the stories I used to read." A question that had been bugging her for the last few hours bubbled up on her lips, and she couldn't keep it from coming out. "Why did you stop calling me Ria?"

He started and glanced at her before looking away. "Well, after you came back, you asked me not to," he answered with a sad smile. "You changed, you know."

"I suppose I did," Maria said. *I don't remember asking him not to call me that.*

He drove past the dull neon sign that said "Pins and Pool" and pulled into the parking lot of the motel. Betty woke when the engine turned off. She pulled out a mirror and in four seconds flat fixed her hair and put on some bright lipstick.

"I'll go organize rooms," she said and let herself out of the car.

The silence was oppressive until Betty came back a few moments later and tapped on the window. Richard rolled it down, and Betty bent down so she could peer inside.

"Should I give fake names?" she asked. "And I'd pay

with cash, but I only have a twenty."

"I think you can use our real names," Maria told her. "And here's some money."

Betty took the bills Richard and Maria handed out to her, counted them, and stuck them in her ample bosom.

"I'll make up names for us," she declared. "You can't be too careful in times like these."

Maria nodded and watched the woman hurry into the front office.

"Are you going to tell me what happened?" Richard asked.

She looked at him from the corner of her eyes. "You're not going to believe me."

"Try me," he encouraged.

She sighed. "I found a Door, a magic one. I heard music from behind it, and I opened it. I met a man named Cedar Jal. He's a Guardian of the Path - the Path is the magyc in his world. That magyc was dying, and he needed to get back so he could fix it, and he needed me to help him, so I did." She left out the bit about how Cedar had cut her throat, in order to free her blood, so he could use the First Magyc in it to help him escape his prison and traverse worlds, though her fingers went to her neck in a forgotten gesture. "I got stuck there for a bit, running away from sorcerers and Men in White. And then I met a Witch who sent me home, using another Door like the first one. She said it was the Way of Things."

Her father was silent for a long time, digesting what she had said. Maria knew how hard it must be for someone like him, who had only ever known the hard, cold world they were in now, to think with something like that. He finally released his pent up breath in a huge sigh.

"Okay," he said.

"Okay?" Maria repeated, surprised that he could come

The Other World

up with such a simple, calm response to her story.

"Okay," he repeated.

"Okay." Maria waited for him to say more.

"I take it you didn't tell anyone that?" he asked.

She laughed. "They would have locked me up in a room with padded walls." She paused. "Why didn't you send me back to the counselors?"

"I thought that was why you ran away in the first place," he said. "That and the fighting. I didn't want to push you away any further." He made a noncommittal noise. "I guess it worked. You stuck around. For a while at least."

Maria swallowed, unwilling to acknowledge what he was insinuating but feeling it had to be done. "When I got home, I didn't think I would ever go back to that magycal place. I didn't want to lose anything more, so I pretended I had just imagined it; that way I could keep it forever. The kids in school thought it was so cool I had run away. I tried to be more normal and fit in better than I had before. It helped that I was a bit of a celebrity."

"I remember that," he said. "On your thirteenth birthday, you wanted to throw a party and invite half a hundred people from school. You had never wanted that before, not since your mother died."

"That was *so* awkward," she groaned. "Do you remember the cake?"

The cake, which was in fact an *ice-cream* cake unbeknownst to them, had melted into a puddle of gloop on the table before they had realized what happened. Mr. Martelli from apartment 182 had come to the rescue with some Italian pastries made with nuts and sweet cream as a substitute.

Her father chuckled, then sniffed. "What am I going to do if you leave me?"

Something went hard and cold in Maria's chest. She didn't want to think about that eventuality. "I don't know what's going to happen, dad; I really don't."

Her father pulled himself together, using that odd core of strength he drew on when things got rough and nodded. At that moment, Betty returned, holding three key cards. Maria took one and let herself into the room with the corresponding number.

The motel was pleasant enough, plain yet comfortable. She looked around, examined the tiny bathroom, turned on the shower to see how hot the water was, and opened the mini-refrigerator. It was empty, and the coffee machine sitting on the tiny counter had seen shinier days. Then she lay on the bed and tried to read the ancient magazine, but she couldn't concentrate. She was left staring at the ceiling, hoping for sleep that didn't come.

She decided to text Matt and Josh and let them know where she was, but when she tried to turn on her cell phone, a blinking red light told her she had no battery power left. *Just my luck,* she sighed. An old, clunky T.V. sat on the dresser, but Maria had no wish to turn it on, scared of what it might tell her.

So she sat in silence until a knock sounded at the door.

A number of options flashed through her head. It was her dad, coming to talk or something. It was the policeman coming with news, good or bad, and her heart leaped to her throat and started pattering wildly. Then she realized that she had not told the police where she was going to be. Maria got off the bed and went to peer through the peephole. Her heart rate increased three times.

Recognizing him immediately from the slouch of his shoulders and the careless way he tilted his head, she opened the door without thought. Matt stood in the doorway, his features hidden in the shadow. A wave of relief washed over Maria, but then anger at his childish reaction of going ahead alone, not answering his phone, and scaring everyone half to death replaced it.

"Hi," she said, her tone abrupt. "I thought the band had decided to stay in Brooks."

She waited for him to say something, but he just stood there, as if he had forgotten what he came for in the first place.

"Matt?"

Matt stirred a little. "Yes. I went ahead."

"We didn't know where you were," she told him, hoping the accusation in her voice was kept to a minimum, but she was too upset to care much. "You didn't answer your phone."

"I know," he replied.

"Did you hear about...about what happened to Adam?" The thought brought tears to her eyes.

That half-shadow figure that was Matt nodded.

She felt her chest constrict a little. "Matt, I'm sorry..." she began, but stopped when a soft laugh began to dribble from his lips, sending a shiver down her spine.

"It's not what you think," he said, and that's when she noticed his voice sounded strange, too high, like he'd taken a gulp of helium, yet rough at the same time.

Be careful. In a sudden strangled desire for self-preservation, Maria tried to close the door, but Matt moved faster than was humanly possible, putting his foot in the way then shoving his shoulder through the gap. Trying to force the door closed proved to be of no avail, and Matt slowly slid inside the apartment.

Maria tried to breathe in deep, even breaths, but the movement in her chest was limited by the boulder in her stomach. She held Matt's eye as he came closer. His face was wooden; his eyes too bright.

"What do you want, Matt?" she asked.

He chuckled and took a step closer. When he touched her skin, his hand felt cold and brittle. "You don't know?"

"No. No, I don't," she said.

"Think, Ria. Ria, Ria, Little Ria."

The name resonated with her, reminding her of the comfort and protection of a happy childhood with her mother and father together, but used in such a menacing way now made that warmth wither and die. Then she frowned. He couldn't know that name. "What did you call me?"

He took a step back and cocked his head at her. "Ria, you really don't understand what is happening here."

"Who have you been talking to?" she whispered.

"I haven't been talking to anyone," Matt shrugged. "You're special, you know that? Which is why I have to take you to him."

She shook her head mutely. *He's right. I don't understand.* "Why are you doing this?"

"The sands under your feet are a-shifting. Worlds hang in the Balance," Matt said with his oddly ringing voice. "You are the one that can tip them one way or the other, Ria."

He stopped suddenly. His left eye was twitching, and he peered at her almost curiously. "Maria?"

"Yes?"

"What…" he looked around. "What am I doing here?"

"You…came…" she stammered in confusion, completely unsure of what was going on.

"The band was going on tour…" he said slowly, putting a hand on his head, probing with a finger as if he could dig the words out. "We were going to leave tomorrow…we made a last…there was a last-minute rehearsal to work out, a bug Adam had with the set list...he was always so particular..."

Maria grasped onto that like a drowning man grasps at driftwood. "Did you fix it?"

"Yes." He stopped and frowned. His head snapped awkwardly forward like a puppet being controlled by an impatient child.

"Did...did you..." the question faltered on her lips as the gleam crept back into Matt's fevered eyes.

"I was sent to find you," he told her, his head tilted at an odd angle. "It took a while. You hide yourself quite well, *Aethsiths*."

His perfect pronunciation of the alien word was unnerving.

"I wasn't trying to hide," Maria protested, backing up a step, and trying to think of something to use as a weapon.

"The others were touched by your Mark, but they were unable to tell me where you were."

Ria closed her eyes, and a tear slid down her cheek. *Adam*, she thought, the keyboardist's warm laugh ringing through her head. *Finn*.

Something warm burned inside her jacket, and she remembered the paper. With a surge of wild hope, she dug into her pocket and pulled out the paper, thrusting it in front of her like a sword or a shield. Matt gave a small smile and did not stop his slow, sure march forward, his legs dragging a little as though he were too tired to move.

The wall suddenly at her back, Maria's only option was to scoot to the left, and Matt leapt forward, his hands frozen in uneven claws that clutched at her neck, digging into her flesh as he pressed down, keeping the air from her now burning lungs, his eyes gleaming brightly.

"The sands are a-shifting," he whispered in a harsh voice. "Don't struggle, Ria. It's going to be alright. Just come with me, and everything will be as it should."

Maria's vision dimmed as she tried to push him away, tried to bring her knee up, but the left side of his body held her motionless as she lost her hold on reality. Her eyes burned with tears and bright white sparkles that popped into blackness as her consciousness slipped away.

When the door exploded inward with enough force to send both of them tumbling sideways, Matt lost his grip on her throat for a moment, but then he was on top of her, his forearm now finishing the job his hands had begun, and Maria fell into a soft grey-gold light…

AETHSITHS PART I

In this world that looked familiar but felt so different, Cedar Jal was forever going over the time in Demona with the girl, trying to see if there was something that he had missed, some clue to her true identity that he had not seen.

The hope ignited by the appearance of Ria, invisible though she was, was spluttering and fading. She was somewhere here, in this world, but Cedar was not confident of their ability to find her. The air here smelled bitter and the sun wasn't warm enough, neither of which was helping reconcile the idea of this world and *Aethsiths*. Even more disheartening was once she left, his guitar had reverted to its previous unmagycal state, and his bow would not come no matter how he tried. It left him with a vulnerable spot swimming in his innards.

"You spent four years in this place?" Luca Lorisson said, a similar look of distaste on his face as they rested, sitting on a patch of the stuff that passed for grass in this place, which didn't quite cover the dirt.

Cedar sighed. "I wasn't in this world; it was a Void of sorts, and I told you, it wasn't four years. At least it didn't feel like four years."

"That's lucky for you," Luca commented. "This place is horrible."

Jæyd Elvenborn peered about with her sharp eyes. "I can almost see," she murmured. "Almost."

Cedar's eyes were hard when he looked at her. "I thought you said you could see her now."

"I can," Jæyd said, her finger pointing straight and true as it had every time one of the other Guardians had asked for direction. "And I can see you and Luca and Timo. I am speaking about other things. I can almost see them."

"Right," Cedar said, standing up, his tired legs protesting every movement. "Well, I don't care about other things. I just care about Ria and getting her out of harm's way. And then getting out of this place."

He pulled his guitar onto his back. He could not remember it feeling this heavy or unwieldy. It dragged his shoulders down without mercy, and for the first time in his existence, Cedar found himself envying Jæyd and her little flute. "Let's get a move on."

The other Guardians pulled themselves to their feet as enthusiastically as Cedar had and the four began the slow trudge down the dirt road along a sagging fence. The cows in the paddocks ignored them as they walked. In the distance, a white house sat beside a brown barn, but otherwise their eyes found no sign of human life.

"Are you sure we're in the right place?" Luca asked. "The longer I stay here, the more I think we can't be."

"I believe the Man of Tongues to have sent us true," Timo said, his deep voice tired.

"How do you know?" Luca demanded. "For all you

know, we could be wandering around the Wastelands...or someplace worse."

"This is someplace worse," Cedar muttered.

"Even if that were so, will complaining do anything to solve it?" Timo asked rhetorically. "Jæyd said she can see the girl."

"*Aethsiths,*" Luca said with a pointed glance at Cedar.

"Alright, I'm sorry," Cedar said. "We should have kept her with us! Are you happy now?"

"I won't be happy until we're back in Demona and away from this...*place.*"

Cedar sighed and stumbled as his feet found a different surface. Smelly black stuff, running straight as an arrow down the greenness of the fields with a broken line painted down the middle, it was something that he had not seen before, but even so Cedar could recognize it for what it was.

"I think this is the road the farmer was talking about," Timo said, standing where the dirt road went over a deep ditch and opened into the unusual road in a wide 'V'. "The Eye-sixty-seven."

"There is something very wrong with this world," Luca said darkly, kicking his feet along the strange road, his scowl deepening.

Cedar ignored him and stepped to the middle of the road. "Which way, Jæyd?"

The elf looked off in the distance at an oblique angle towards a dense tangle of trees across the fields lining the side of the road. "That way, though there is no road, but perhaps there is another one that joins this?"

"I think we should take the farmer's word," Cedar said. "It is his world, after all."

"Something's coming," Luca said, looking over his shoulder. He turned, putting his hands up to his eyes, squinting behind them. "It looks large."

The Guardians hurried to the side of the road and stood there, all peering down at the thing barreling towards them with a growing rumble.

"Maybe we should step away," Timo suggested as it came closer.

"No, it looks like it's keeping to the road," Cedar said, his gold eyes fixed on it. "I want to see what it is."

Cedar caught a glimpse of a face through a glass window and on reflex his hand lifted in a salute. The thing went by like a huge arrow riding on thunder. It had wheels, but it was many times the size of a wagon. It trumpeted at them twice as it passed and buffeted them with hot wind and black smoke.

"What in Demonfire was that?" Luca coughed out, waving his hand in front of his nose and grimacing at the offensive smell.

"I am not sure, but we should keep watch for them if we are going to be using the same road," Jæyd said stepping back onto the flat black path.

Beating down on them, a slave master with a burning whip, the sun gleamed as bright as the one in Demona but was a pale bleached color which failed to inspire. Cedar tried to staunch the flow of sweat from his brow, but it continued to trickle down the sides of his face, soaking his collar and making his shirt stick to his back.

"I have to sit down," Luca groaned. "If I don't, I might just fall down and never get up."

He veered off the road onto the grass and weeds and flopped down. Timo said nothing as he staggered past Cedar and sat with his back to Luca's, his head bowed and his wide shoulders moving with each breath. Cedar was most distressed to see the line of fatigue between Jæyd's brows and the way her feet dragged as she went to sit with her companions. After a moment, she looked up at Cedar.

"It is not good for us to be here," she said softly. "This world is sapping our strength. We have to hurry."

Cedar could only nod in tired agreement. "If only we knew how much farther it is."

"72 miles, however long that may be," Luca said, his voice muffled by the arm he rested his face on.

Before Cedar could say anything, Luca pointed his other arm at a large green sign at the side of the road. The sign said Shoredon 156 miles, West Temple 102 miles, Brooks 72 miles.

"How do you know it is the town called Brooks?" Timo asked, his head tilted and he squinted at the sign.

"It has to be," Luca said and mimicked the accent of the farmer. *"Ain't too fah from 'ere. Y'kin be there afore lunch."* Returning to his easy Isosian lilt, Luca mustered the energy to grin at them. "He must have meant the closest city with that optimistic estimate on the time."

"Look," the elf said, an attentive expression on her tired face. "Another one of those wagons."

The weary group stood and gathered at the side of the road, watching the only other wagon to come along this road move towards them at great speed, expecting it to pass, yet this one did not. It slowed and pulled off next to them, the large black wheels crunching on the grass and gravel. It was much smaller and sleeker than the first and looked like some kind of carriage. A part of the shiny black covering was lowered and a man peered out.

Aside from the farmer whose barn they had borrowed for the night and asked directions of after Ria's visit, this was the only other person they had seen in this world. Cedar was oddly comforted by his normal looks, though his clothes were odd. *Like Ria's when she first came to Demona with me*, Cedar thought.

This new person was young, about twenty and five, perhaps more but not yet thirty. He had brown hair, spiked with some kind of shiny film which smelled like nothing Cedar had ever smelled before. His brown eyes were direct, but a film hid an edge of panic that showed in the way his jaw clenched.

"Yup, you've gotta be the ones she was talking about," the young man muttered, more to himself than them, staring at the musical instruments and their persons. He gestured for them to come closer. Cedar stepped up to the other-world carriage, ducking his head to peer inside.

"Greetings," he said.

"Greetings," the man inside repeated, his eyes widening, and he began to gesture in a theatrical way, pointing and miming as though he thought Cedar was a little on the not-quite-bright-side. "I am, uh, called *Josh. Peters.* And you are…?"

"My name is Cedar Jal," Cedar said.

"Are you a friend of Maria Westerfield?" Josh asked.

Cedar frowned, and then he remembered. *Ria, short for Maria.* A surge of excitement swept through him. "Yes! Do you know her?"

"I used to think so, but at the moment, I'm not so sure of that. She sent me out here to collect you guys."

Cedar sat in the front seat of the vehicle beside Josh Peters, his guitar between his knees. Cedar hadn't thought it was possible, but the car smelled even less appealing on the inside, made worse by the sunlight flashing off the hard black surface in front of Cedar, blinding him.

He was startled and pleased when Josh reached over and flipped down a visor that blocked the sunlight, and he could see again. Cedar was aware the man driving the strange carriage was looking at him surreptitiously, his eyes flicking back to the road every so often, but always returning to Cedar.

"So...how is it that you know Maria?" Josh finally asked.

"It's a long story," Cedar said, and Josh barked a short laugh.

"She said exactly the same thing when I asked her that," he said.

Cedar glanced into the back seat, where Jæyd, Timo and Luca sat huddled together, Luca with a miserable look as he squeezed his shoulders together and tried to lean into the door, Timo sitting between the others with his customary serene expression and Jæyd's eyes vacant as she gazed out the window, her eyes occasionally flickering as things flew by the window at blurring speeds.

"She stayed with us for a little while," Cedar said. "How is she?"

"Maria? Oh, she's fine, I think. Better than the rest of us, really. A little shaken, but fine."

"Shaken?" Cedar queried.

"Adam...one of our friends was...uh...murdered today," Josh said, his hands tightening on the wheel in front of him. "She started acting strangely after the Inspector showed us the paper." He looked at Cedar. "What's this about *Aeth...Ace...Aceth...Aythsythe*?" Cedar cringed at the mangled pronunciation of the magyc word. "What is the prophecy that Maria keeps talking about?"

Cedar was silent. "There is a Prophecy that says a woman with silver eyes, named by the Path as *Aethsiths,* or the Songstress, will come and aid the Guardians when their need is greatest." Cedar drummed his fingers gently against the hard, unyielding guitar case. *When their need is greatest.*

"And you're these Guardians?" Josh asked, glancing

first at Cedar, then at the three in the back seat via the small mirror hanging from the middle of the ceiling.

Cedar nodded.

"And she's going to save you?"

After a pause, Cedar nodded again, feeling as though he was sealing his fate with the gesture.

"I was afraid you were going to say that," Josh said. "Then we'd better get you there on the double."

Without Josh seeming to do anything, the car sped up and Cedar increased his hold on the handle of the door, sucking his breath in with a hiss. Josh looked at him. "Maria said you weren't from around here."

"You could say that," Cedar said through clenched teeth. He was used to Doors, and skirting Death's Realm, and magycal currents, but this carriage was something he didn't like at all. It gave him a vague nausea that threatened to crawl up this throat and come spewing out his mouth.

Josh glanced in the mirror again, looking between Jæyd, Timo, and Luca. His eyes lingered on the elf whose foreign features made her stand out even more than the others. "So, where exactly are you from?"

"Demona," Luca said. "A different world than this."

"I see," Josh said with admirable aplomb. "And how did you get here?"

"Riding a wave of magycal energy pulled from a rainbow, directed by a Demonhärt on advice from a crazy pseudo-Daleman-sorcerer," Luca explained, relish evident on his pointed face as he watched shock and disbelief war in Josh's expression.

"Luca," Jæyd admonished. "Try not to confuse him too much, please. He is trying to help us."

"Let's get one thing straight," Josh said. "I am *not* trying to help you. I am trying to help Maria."

"Thank you anyway," Jæyd said with a decorous nod.

"We appreciate it. Truly."

"You're welcome," Josh replied, grudgingly. "I think." He paused and adjusted his grip on the wheel. "She's a special girl, you know," Josh continued. "Don't let her do anything stupid, okay?"

Cedar looked at Josh. "You know her well?"

Josh smiled. "Yeah, I would say so."

"For how long?"

"Almost ten years," Josh told her. "She went to my school, and when she came back, she was famous. The girl who ran away, and the girl who came back." He shook his head and chuckled darkly but did not share what he found amusing.

Cedar stared at him in shock. *Ten years?* "How old is this Maria?"

"She turned twenty-one a couple days ago," Josh said. "Why?"

"The last time I saw the girl called Ria she was only twelve years old," Cedar said in a wondering tone.

"Well, yeah," Josh shrugged. "When she ran away as a kid."

"In my mind, I saw her less than a month ago," Cedar said, his mind trying to comprehend how that could possibly be. *It's like the time in the Void,* he reasoned. *To me it felt like a few days at most, to Demona it was four years.*

"Oh."

At that moment, the carriage jerked and swerved to the side of a road, a rhythmic banging from the rear accompanying the bouncing of the carriage and Josh swore.

"What is it?" Cedar asked.

"Flat tire," Josh said.

Cedar was nonplussed and waited for Josh to explain further. He waited in vain. Josh threw open the door and stepped out of the carriage. The door slamming shut left the Guardians in a stuffy silence.

"What do you think he's doing?" Luca peered out the window, trying to get a look at where Josh had disappeared to.

"No idea," Cedar said. "But we don't have time to waste."

"Do you think we should help him?" Timo asked.

"We have no idea how anything works here," Luca said. "We would only make things worse. I vote we stay put."

Cedar rolled his eyes and after a few attempts, figured out how to open the door, and then he stepped out of the carriage, his body heavier than usual and infused with vertigo from the ride. He kept a hand on the metal body to guide and steady himself as he made his way back. Josh was kneeling at the back end of the carriage, his hand over his eyes. He looked up when Cedar's shadow fell over him.

"What is the problem?" Cedar asked. "Can I help?"

Josh grimaced. "Maria really wasn't kidding when she said you weren't from around here. Yeah, you can help. Get everyone out of the car."

Cedar nodded. He tapped on the window and gestured for them to join him outside. The other three piled out, Luca with an exaggerated moan of relief. Josh was pulling out a shiny black case and a small twin of the wheel from a built-in storage compartment at the rear.

"This will go faster if I don't have to jack up the car," Josh said. "So two of you are going to have to hold it up while I change the tire."

"You'll want someone big and strong. Here's your man," Luca volunteered, pushing Timo forward.

Timo and Cedar gripped the underside of the strange vehicle and held it up while Josh took off the wheel and put the new one on. Cedar's muscles burned and sweat ran into his face, but he held on with grim determination.

"Okie-dokie, we're all good," Josh said.

"Does that mean we can put this down?" Timo asked, his voice strained.

"Yes," Josh said. "Let's go."

They arrived in the alien town with square buildings and dead streets when the sun was beginning its descent from its zenith. The greyness of the buildings crowded into the sky and the colors were flat. They stopped at a corner, Josh tapping the wheel, peering about but not looking at anything in particular.

"What are we waiting for?" Cedar asked, restless impatience infusing his limbs with motion as he tried to get them moving again with nothing but sheer will.

"For the light to go green," Josh said, and gestured at a single red light shining above them, suspended on a black rope.

"This is where Ria lives?" Luca asked, peering out of the window.

Josh nodded.

"Why would she possibly want to return to this?" Luca made a disgusted face.

Josh turned a glare on the dark Guardian. "Because it's home."

"Do you know where she is now?" Cedar said, quickly diverting the conversation before it turned into a confrontation.

"I told her to go get Matt and bring him back to her apartment."

"Then we go there."

Josh gave him a strange look. "Yeah, sure." He pulled out a small thing, touched it, and it lit up. He touched it a few more times, and frowned.

"She's texted me an hour ago," he said, then paled. "There was a fire at the hotel. Matt is missing."

"Who is this Matt?" Cedar wondered.

"Her boyfriend," Josh told him, still looking at the bright little thing in his hand.

"Oh." Cedar fell silent, and like the slow creeping sunrise, he realized Ria had made a life for herself here, had spent years building that life. He thought he had missed only a month, but now he saw he could be going to find a complete stranger that he knew nothing about. An anxious queasy feeling joined the sickness from traveling in the other-world-carriage in his stomach.

"She's at the Motel 4 on Channel Drive," Josh said, looking up, oblivious to anything going through Cedar's head.

"Then we go there," Cedar said, and put the gnawing doubt away, where it could eat holes in him in the darkness.

"First I have to get gas," Josh told him.

Cedar nodded, trusting this man to do right by Ria. They went to a brightly lit place that looked like a meeting place for carriages and wagons, and Josh got out to do something around the back. Then he got in and pulled away. They moving fast again, heading out on long, wide roads with trees on either side, and few cars.

Josh didn't say anything, driving as though he were willing the motel and Ria to appear before them. Cedar was left alone with his reminiscing and uncertainties. What were they going to find with this new Ria? What if the girl they knew had gone, and left *something* - he couldn't think of the right word - in her place?

"She's not answering her phone," Josh's quiet voice broke into his thoughts, and he turned to see Josh put the small lighted object in a hollow between the seats.

"Is that a bad thing?" Cedar asked.

"I hope not," Josh answered grimly. "I hope she's okay and hasn't left the motel because I have no idea how to find her."

"The Path will lead us to her," Cedar said, trying to sound confident.

"What is this Path thing?" Josh said. "Is it like a GPS?"

Cedar blinked. "I don't know what a Gee-pee-ess is. The Path is the force of life, the source of magyc where I come from."

"Right," Josh said with a long measured looked at Cedar before he looked back at the road. "Is that something that Maria does?"

The name still threw Cedar off, and it took him a while to formulate an acceptable answer. "I believe this world doesn't have magyc, that is correct?"

Josh chuckled. "You could say that."

Cedar shook his head. "Well, that is as strange to me as the concept of magyc is to you. In my home, magyc is common; everyone knows what it is. Well," he amended, thinking of the Justice of D'Ohera, Trem Descal, and his warped sense of magyc. "Most people do. When I knew Ri…Maria, she could do some magyc."

"Is she going back with you?" Josh asked abruptly.

"I hope so," Cedar said.

"Why?"

How to describe ten thousand years of history in a few words? Cedar didn't know, but he tried. "Magyc is fading from Demona, and *Aethsiths is* the one who will restore it."

"And you think Maria is this woman, this *Aythsythe?*" Josh asked, his face a mask of confusion. "Why?"

Cedar shrugged. "Because of things that have happened - signs, or omens, if you like."

Josh frowned. "What if she doesn't want to come back

with you?"

Something in his voice made Cedar stare hard at him, and hope shone a little brighter. "You don't think that's going to happen, do you?" he said, a light feeling lifting a weight from his shoulders. "You think she's going to leave."

Josh's throat worked, and he took a deep breath before speaking. "I don't know. Everything just went to hell. I don't know what's happening any more, what's real and what's make-believe." He paused, and continued in a subdued voice. "But yes, I think Maria is going to leave."

They said nothing more after that. A short time later, they pulled into a flat black expanse marked out with white lines and concrete logs. The Other-world carriage stopped, and Josh pointed.

"There's the motel."

The Guardians peered out the windows, then exited the carriage for a better look. It was flat and uninteresting, a white square with doors and windows. Someone had thought it was a good idea to paint them orange. The trim was green and made it look like a badly decorated cake.

"Ria's inside there?" Cedar asked, looking at Jæyd for an answer.

The elf peered into the distance, her eyes narrowed, and then glanced around. "I can no longer see her," she whispered.

Cedar started. "When did you lose sight of her?" he demanded. "Why didn't you say something?"

"I cannot be certain," Jæyd replied, looking drawn and uncertain. This world was taxing the elf as much if not more than the others. "In the carriage, it was too fast. I lost sight of her. She is here, but now I cannot see her, and it was only a moment ago."

"Well, we'll have to find out, even if we have to beat

down every door," Cedar said grimly.

"Let's try something a little more normal first," Josh told him. "Come with me."

They went into the building, into a small room marked "Front Office – Vacancy," following behind Josh. A young man with orange-brown hair and a sprinkling of acne sat behind the front desk. He looked up when Josh walked up. Josh smiled, and inquired if someone by the name of Maria Westerfield had checked in. The clerk stared at him with a suspicious look.

"She's a friend," Josh explained.

"There's no one here by that name," the clerk said.

"What about Ria?" Cedar pushed forward and gave the clerk a hard stare, daring the boy to cross him.

The boy gave him a wide-eyed look, taking in Cedar's clothes and the guitar on his back.

"It's her birthday," Josh jumped in, pushing Cedar behind him and giving the clerk a disarming smile. "And I hired this band to play her 'Happy Birthday.'"

The boy looked uncertain, in a way that suggested he was uncertain of Josh's sanity, not of the truthfulness of the story. He checked the large box on the desk and shook his head. "No one named Ria either. Sorry." He brightened up. "Hey, can you do 'Into the Future' by Heroes in Hiding?"

Cedar shook his head. Josh gave the boy a strange look and hurried the Guardians outside again. He took up the strange object he had tried to contact Ria on before and started doing the same thing again.

"She's still not answering," Josh said, frustration mounting in his voice. "I think her battery died."

"What?" the Guardians looked up as one, concern flashing across their faces.

"Her battery - it doesn't work anymore," Josh explained.

"Is this battery important?" Timo asked.

"Well, it powers her cell phone, so if I want her to answer, then yes," Josh replied, with incredulous glances between the Guardians. "She could be fine."

The Guardians relaxed at this answer, but Cedar was still ill at ease, well aware Josh did not think them capable of doing anything for Ria. While everything looked to support this sentiment, the Guardian refused to give in to pessimism. Cedar took charge, a habit this new world was not going to undo.

"We need to find her as quickly as possible. We should split up." He looked down the street. "Jæyd and Timo, go down that way. Luca and I will go the other way and-"

"Hang on a moment," Josh interrupted. "I've gone to a lot of effort to get you here for Maria. You are *all* going to stay put until *I* figure something out. No one is going to listen to you because you guys look like the crazy circus came to town."

Luca frowned and looked down at himself. "I have no idea what you're talking about, but I think I should be offended."

"You be whatever you want to be," Josh said. "Just be quiet and let me think."

The young man stood there, tapping his chin and glancing around with a pained expression, and the Guardians became increasingly antsy. Cedar itched to pace, his feet assuring him he would feel better if he were moving, but Cedar felt this would only annoy Josh Peters. Then Luca gave a strangled moan, clutching his head. His fiddle dropped from his shoulder and hit the ground with a terrible discord. Josh started.

"Is he okay?"

"No," Cedar said grimly. "He's about as far from okay as you could get."

They were all afraid this would happen, so much so that they didn't voice it for fear of tempting fate. With the magyc - albeit fading magyc - of Demona, Cedar felt *something* was aiding Luca with his dark burden. Here, no such relief offered itself. The dark Guardian had held up admirably, but Cedar was not surprised that he had worn down.

"I'm fine!" Luca spluttered. "Just give…give me a moment."

He fell to his knees, breathing in noisy gasps through his mouth. His condition did not alleviate, and he pressed his forehead to the ground.

"We should get him to a hospital," Josh said.

The other Guardians were already shaking their head.

"It would do him no good," Jæyd told the Other-world man.

She chewed her bottom lip, partly in worry, partly in thought, and offered Josh his first look at her sharp teeth. Cedar watched as Josh averted his eyes with an uncomfortable look, and the young man's gaze flitted around, as if he were now unsure what it was safe for him to look at. It made Cedar feel very much like the circus act Josh said they were.

"Maybe we should put him back in the carriage?" Timo asked, kneeling beside Luca.

"It's called a car, and what is that going to do?" Josh was losing what little equilibrium he had managed to scrape together. "Is he…is he dying?"

Luca rolled over, lying spread eagle on the hard ground, face screwed up in pain. "Not dying. Dying would be more pleasant than this. My head's just going to explode, so you might want to stand back. I have a lot of brains."

"How on earth can he be joking right now?" Josh gaped. "Never mind."

"Just help me stand up before you hurt yourself with all that thinking," Luca growled and coughed, then threw a shaking hand in the air.

Cedar leaped forward and pulled the other Guardian to his feet, grunting with the effort. He didn't know how it was possible for the emaciated man to weigh so much. Luca leaned against Cedar, took a deep breath, then stood on his own.

"I don't know where Ria is, but I can tell you there's Demon around here somewhere." He tried an insouciant grin. "Where there's smoke, and all that."

Electric tension ran through Cedar, his muscles taut as he readied himself for action.

"Where?" he asked in an even voice.

"What do you mean, a Demon?" Josh asked, his voice strangled with slight panic. "What is that?"

"Something you don't want to have to deal with," Cedar replied grimly.

"Something *we* don't want to have to deal with, seeing as we don't have any magyc," Luca said, sagging against Cedar again.

"We need *Aethsiths*," Jæyd added quietly.

"And what are the chances she's where the Demon is? Pretty high, right?" Luca tried to grin. "If you want my advice, we should be going that way."

He nodded down the street.

"Get in the carriage," Cedar ordered.

"Wait a moment…" Josh said.

The Guardian rounded on him. "She is in danger here, and that danger is growing the longer we wait around-"

"You just said you can't do anything!" Josh cried, running his hand through his hair in a gesture similar to the one Cedar made when he was distraught. "We should call the police!"

"I do not know who these police are, but unless they have magyc, they will be able to do less," Jæyd explained gently, taking the man's arm and leading him back to his carriage. "We have to find this Demon before it finds her."

Something in the elf's calm voice quieted Josh, and he opened the door and got into his carriage without a word. Then he started and got out again. Cedar was about to have a stern word with him, which might have turned into physical violence given Cedar's current mood, but Josh pointed with an excited expression.

"I think that's her dad's car!" Josh cried,

He was pointing at a larger, cream vehicle that looked nothing like his. Luca stumbled towards the car, then jerked, spun in a full circle, and then turned slowly until he faced the motel. He waved his hand, trying to point but his arm was too heavy to hold up.

"That way," he gasped.

The line of doors all looked the same. Cedar ran ahead, then ran back and grabbed Luca. The dark Guardian staggered along, one hand on Cedar's shoulder, the other grabbing the wall for support. He stopped outside one door with "19" in black letters under the peephole.

"She's in here?" Cedar clarified, making ready to break the door down.

Luca shook his head, gasping and shaking. His skin was now green, tinged with blue, though his cheeks were spots of red and his lips stood out in stark white lines. He waved his hand, indicating Cedar should go on. Luca collapsed in front of the door two down, curled up in a ball, and grunted in suppressed pain. Cedar didn't have to ask this time.

The flimsy lock gave way on the first try, though something solid on the other side impeded the door's motion. Muffled thuds and growls came from the dim room, and movement of shadows, then a body rammed into Cedar like a charging horse, sending him falling against something soft with hard edges, but the creature was not going for him at all.

A figure - a woman - lay on the ground, trying to squirm away. The creature fell upon her, and her attempts became more frantic. Cedar rolled off the bed, gaining his feet and leaping over to the struggling pair.

He received a jolt that numbed his arm to the shoulder when he laid a hand on the attacker's shoulder. At Cedar's touch, the person turned, and the Guardian gazed into the warped and savage gaze of a Thrall.

Sour bile twisted in Cedar's stomach and threatened to come up. Human in form, but twisted beyond recognition, the creature shoved at him with preternatural strength. Cedar grabbed onto it, praying the others would arrive soon.

More shadows came, the bulk of the Daleman, and the sweet woodland scent of the elf. Together they restrained the Thrall, and when they held it immobile between them, Timo gazed at it with an expression of pity and disgust. The elf was stoic, her entire body rigid as she held it.

"What do we do with it?" Timo asked. "We cannot hope to free it, not here in-"

He stopped, suddenly preoccupied as the Thrall bit him. The Daleman put his forearm against its throat, forcing its head back, though its teeth still snapped feverishly.

"Don't hurt him!" a rough, strangled voice called out. "Dear god, don't hurt him!"

The victim of the assault was struggling to get up and failing, oxygen-deprived limbs too weak to hold her up. Another shadow fell over them. Luca stood in the doorway, looking as though he were going to throw up or faint, or perhaps simply keel over and die, holding onto the frame for support.

Whatever had made this Thrall was battling inside Luca. From the looks of things, it was winning, but the dark Guardian was putting all of his will into fighting. Cedar didn't want him to do anything, certainly not to use the Demonhärt, but Cedar could do little as he watched Luca stumble across the room.

Luca grabbed the Thrall around the throat with one hand, a red gleam in his eye. Cedar thought he was going to crush the life from the thing, but then the Thrall went limp and unresisting, and something black pulsed in the man's throat, and like a poison, Luca was drawing it out. The effort threatened to topple the Guardian, yet he hung on with grim determination.

Thick, black ropes of solid mist dissipated, slipping from under Luca's fingers, twining around his wrist. He grappled with it as it moved slowly but surely up his arm, until a second hand gripped his arm, this one pale and tipped by feminine nails.

The blackness hissed and spluttered, jerking back as if stung. Then it began to disappear, silently screeching in agonized torment.

The body went limp in Cedar's grasp, was still for a moment, then the young man began to stir. Cedar tensed, wondering if he was going to fight.

"What...where am I?" the former Thrall asked in a frightened voice.

The Guardians relaxed as it became apparent the young man was not going to cause any trouble. Luca's hand dropped from his throat, and the Guardian gave the ghost of a carefree smirk.

"Well, nice to meet you, it's been fun, but I'm going to go now," he said, slurring the last three words, and he toppled, his eyes rolling back in his head.

Cedar caught him by one arm, and the owner of the feminine hand caught him by the other. Luca's head fell back, but he did not hit the ground.

"Luca!" Cedar demanded and gave the man a gentle slap on the jaw to revive him.

It didn't work, and Cedar pressed his fingers against the hollow under the other man's ear, trying to find the thud which indicated life. It was not there. He pressed harder, willing Luca's heart to beat. Then Luca was gasping and squirming, pushing him away with an annoyed look. When his eyes fell on his other caretaker, he went slack, his mouth falling open.

"I think I've died and gone…somewhere," Luca commented in a wondering tone. "Greetings, *Aethsiths*."

One by one, the Guardians turned their gaze to what Luca was staring at. Jæyd was the picture of shock, eyes wide, mouth ajar. Luca was at a loss for more words, and Timo looked like a small boy on his first day of school, confronted with a kindly-meaning teacher's request to tell his name. Cedar was finding it difficult to breathe, and all his thoughts were dim against one observation that was too much to fit inside his head.

The woman before them, crouched beside Luca, was slim, her cheeks the only roundness her face possessed. Her skin was pale and her hair was dark, an unusual black that was red and burgundy and purple disguised as midnight, but it was her eyes that held the Guardians transfixed. They were pale grey-blue which could only be described as silver. She looked like she stepped off the walls of the Guardians' Hall in the Crescent Temple.

She stared at the Guardians, as though uncertain they were real. The silence stretched on and Cedar wondered what she was going to say, then if she was going to say anything at all.

Luca spoke first, as he got up with all the grace of an arthritic old man. He waved away their assistance, but Cedar held onto him and helped pull him to his feet anyway.

"It would have been much more helpful if you'd looked like this when we first met you, you know," Luca complained, and straightened his back. "Then we wouldn't have to go running all over Demona, finding Makers of Marks and arguing about Prophecies and all that, you being the spitting image of *Aethsiths.*"

Ria stared at him, then started to smile. The smile turned into a laugh. "I'm sorry. I was only twelve."

"Oh, I'm not blaming you. I'm blaming Cedar, who has the excellent timing of a drunk former lover," Luca smirked. "At a wedding."

At 5'6", Maria was a thumb taller than Luca. "You're short," she said.

He sniffed at her. "I didn't make fun of your stunted growth when you were this high…" he held his hand out at knee height. "Kindly return the courtesy."

"How long ago was that?" she asked, her voice dreamy. "Ten years?"

"Actually it was more like a fortnight ago," Luca shrugged. "You grow like a weed."

The girl stared at him. "You're serious?"

"Deadly," Luca answered with a bland expression.

She looked at the other Guardians for confirmation. They nodded.

"How is that possible?"

The all shrugged.

"How did you get here?"

"That is a long story," Timo interjected. "A more pressing concern is how we get back. And what we do with him."

The young man who had been a Thrall stared at Ria with emotions sprinting over his face, too fast to be recognized as any distinct one, just a sort of miserable and hunted desperation.

"He has a name," Ria said softly. "This is Matt."

At that moment, Josh came into the room. Two men in uniform were behind him. Jæyd and Timo promptly let go of Matt.

"Is everything okay here?" one of the policemen asked, his hand hovering suspiciously near his hip.

"Everything is fine," Ria stepped forward.

"Would you care to tell us what happened here?" the policeman continued, with a wary glance at the disarray.

"I thought I saw a mouse," Ria answered smoothly, and put her hands to her face as though hiding a blush. "Matt tried to get it, and they heard the crashing. I'm sorry if I alarmed everyone." She gave a nervous giggle.

Josh nodded, and after casting long glances at the group gathered in the messy room, the policemen left.

"Thank you for getting them," Ria told Josh.

"Um, you're welcome, though I think your friends sorted it out," Josh replied.

"No, I meant thank you for getting the Guardians," Ria corrected.

"You didn't actually see a mouse, did you?" Josh asked.

"No," Ria shook her head.

"You getting too good at the lying thing," Josh said with an unhappy expression. "It's kinda starting to scare me."

"I'm sorry," Ria replied, putting a hand on his arm.

"Are you going to fill me in?" Josh prompted.

Ria looked at Matt, then at Luca, then at Cedar. "I don't think that's necessary."

"Fine," Josh said in a tone that meant it wasn't fine at all. "What's going to happen now?"

Ria looked at the Guardians for answers.

"The Nine have returned to Demona," Cedar told her quietly. "We saw it with our own eyes. The pieces of the Torch the princess recovered did not make the Torch whole."

Josh and Matt looked nonplussed, but Ria looked as though she understood the significance of Cedar's words.

"But why did you come for me?" she asked. "You don't think I'm really *Aethsiths?*"

Cedar looked her up and down from head to toe. With his whole heart he wished it were different, that he could still undo what he had done to this woman when she was a little girl, but his gut, and his eyes, were telling him it was truly *Aethsiths* who stood in front of him.

"Yes," he told her. "I do."

"Nothing has happened to me," she said. "Nothing has changed. I don't feel any different."

"Perhaps when you return to Demona you will," Timo suggested. "There is no magyc here to rekindle."

The veiled joy on her face made Cedar's spirits lift and banished some of his insecurity and doubt. *She is coming with us!*

"How are we going to do that?" Luca spoke up. "Unless you have a Man of Tongues hiding in your pocket."

"We are going to find a way," Cedar said firmly.

"Wait, Maria," Josh interrupted. "Is this really what you

want?"

Without hesitation, Ria replied. "Yes."

"Why?" Josh was struggling to understand. "You don't have to do this-"

"But I do, Josh," Ria explained in a soft voice. "I can't make you understand why, but I have to. I've always had to, ever since I heard the music. You *know* that too, I think."

Josh shrugged helplessly, then held something out. It was a notebook with a black cover, and a name - Maria Evelyn - was scripted in silver.

"This was going to be for Christmas, or whenever you filled up the other one," Josh told her. "I grabbed it on a hunch. For you to remember us by."

"I'm not going to forget you. I might even see you again, sometime." She threw her arms around his neck and gave him a tight hug. Cedar's chest compressed, and though she spoke softly, he heard her. "I'm the girl who came back, remember?"

"I remember," Josh told her, squeezing her tightly. "Take care of yourself, okay?"

"I will," she promised. "You too."

"What about Matt?" Josh wondered. "He looks…" He gave his friend a concerned look which said everything that needed saying.

"He'll be alright," Ria said with a glance at Cedar. "Right?"

Cedar looked to Jæyd, who gave a little shrug. Cedar turned back to Josh and nodded. Josh didn't look convinced.

"Anything I should know?" he pressed. "Anything that might come up?"

"Nothing we could tell you," Jæyd answered. "He is either strong enough to overcome it, or he will succumb to it. I do not think anything exists in this world that will help him."

"Well, that's comforting," Josh sighed and ran his hand through his hair in an anxious jerk. "I'll take care of him," he promised Ria.

"Thank you," she said.

"Let's go," Cedar said.

"Wait," Ria said, and for the first time, real doubt clouded her face. "I have to say goodbye to my father."

Cedar followed Ria as she hurried to the next room and knocked on the door.

"Ria, we don't have time for this," Cedar tried to say, but he was cut off by her glare and the door as someone on the other side opened it.

An older man with thinning blond hair and glasses opened the door. Blue eyes took in her mussed hair and the red marks on her neck and widened in alarm.

"Maria!" he cried. "Is everything alright?"

"Yes, yes, I'm fine," Ria answered, stepping closer to him.

Reassured, the man moved his eyes to the people standing behind her.

"Maria, who are they?"

"Dad, these are my friends. Cedar Jal, Luca Lorisson, Jæyd Elvenborn, and Timo of the Dale. Guys, this is my father, Richard Westerfield."

"Pleased to meet you," Richard said, holding out his hand.

Cedar shook it, as did the others in turn. Somehow, Cedar knew this was the last hurdle. If anyone could make Ria stay, it was this man. And with a sinking feeling, Cedar knew that if he tried to intervene, his actions would backfire.

He could do nothing but watch and hope.

A FAVOR

S'Aris O'Pac of Lii walked briskly across the northern flatlands of Demona, her dress now mostly dry. Only the hem was still damp on her legs. The Man of Tongues' spell had spit her out on flat land in the shadow of the Dalemounts but without their protection and unfortunately dripping wet. The odd flower he'd given her was still in her tightly clenched fist. She did not recognize the variety of flower, and its place of origin made her feel that it could be useful later. After she had put it into her dress for safekeeping, she'd tossed a coin to decide where to search first for the Ghoris princess. Elba and Samnara had won over the Sisters, and so she made her way east.

Despite the bath she endured to get here, the Witch's knee-length dress was more grey than white with all the residue of Demona clinging to her, reminding her of the leagues and days and nights which she had spent traveling the foreign land. As she walked, her thoughts turned often to Nyica and Lii, so far away and getting farther with every step.

I was so close to being able to return to the Coven, and then it was all snatched away, S'Aris thought.

She replayed the events at the Crescent Temple, the reforming of the Amber Torch, and the music the Guardians had played. Even the mere memory of it made her heart race and gooseflesh rise on her bare arms. V'Ronica of Lii, friend and aid to the First Guardian, and namesake of S'Aris's faction, had been there in spirit, S'Aris was sure of it.

She was pulled from her musing by a sharp pain in her side, as though a wasp the size of a cat had stung her. The pain did not abate, continuing to burn as the Witch fumbled within the pockets and compartments in her dress. It was hard to concentrate, distracted by the pain, but eventually she found and opened the right one. She pulled the scrying mirror she had made for communicating with the assassin and the princess of Ghor. The pain in her side diminished, but her hand tingled and burned.

An odd red light surrounded the shard. In S'Aris's shaking hand, the glass reflected the light in a scattered pattern as the Witch stared at it to see what was the matter. A trickle of blood seeped out of the glass and into her palm, then the red light faded. S'Aris swallowed and knelt down, wiping the redness away on the grass. She waited for more from the scrying glass, but it remained clear. S'Aris stayed crouched close to the ground for a long moment, a frown on her face as she thought.

The princess had not contacted the Witch via the mirror. This was not as disturbing as the fact that the princess had also failed to answer S'Aris's calls. A scrying mirror weeping blood was not something the Witch had encountered before. She didn't know what it meant, but she didn't like it at all. *If only I could research the matter in the Library, but those books were too far in the opposite direction.*

She thought about calling Berria, but after what just happened, she didn't know what was going to happen on the other side. Putting the mirror away, the Witch turned north towards the trees which sheltered the city of Elba and doubled her pace. That night she camped under the first of the trees, the slender bows failing to offer much protection against the brisk wind which sprang up, but it was better than nothing.

A small Witch-fire burned blue and purple. S'Aris was wary of other travelers and potential visitors seeing it and seeking her out, but no one came to bother her. She set wards at the four corners of her camp and curled up, her arm under her head as a pillow.

When the sun rose, she awoke and set off immediately, pausing only to grab small handfuls of berries just starting to ripen. They did little to sate her hunger, but the distraction took her all the way to Elba.

The walls of Elba were solid oak trunks, cemented with resin and tied with rope. The gates stood open, the sigil of the city carved and painted in the wood: the tree with seven boughs surrounded by sun, moon, and north star.

Unlike most of the Cities of Demona, the Gates of Elba remained unguarded and un-surveilled, and the Witch passed through the shadow of the gates and then into the First Square without incident. *I must find a tavern. Mouths are always prone to moving after a free drink or two.*

S'Aris made for the widest street, where she assumed the most people would be and so would be the highest chance of finding information. Several blocks down, she found what she was looking for. Nestled between two trees standing like sentinels was a respectable-looking tavern, called *Lady on the Wall*, and cheerful music spilled out even at this time of the morning.

The Witch stepped lightly up the stairs formed of tree roots and went through the yellow doors, which stood wide open. Many paintings hung on the walls, all of a lady with raven hair in different poses and places: a garden, brushing her hair, even one in the tavern which had been named for her.

The tavern was not full, nor was it empty. One in three tables was occupied, some by those finishing a late breakfast or starting on an early lunch, others by more permanent sort of guests, staring with glassy eyes at half-full steins of beer or overturned liquor glasses.

Walking up to the bar, S'Aris prepared a story for the keep. She knocked politely on the bench, waiting for him to put a plate of eggs and bacon in front of a red-headed man before he turned to S'Aris.

"Hello," the Witch smiled. "I've just arrived, and I am looking for tidings of a friend of mine, Carolyn Betters." This was one of the pseudonyms Her Majesty Berria In'Orain used, and the name S'Aris had first known her by.

The keep looked at S'Aris as though she were mad. When he spoke, he did so very slowly, to give her the best chance of understanding his words. "This is a big city, miss. I've never heard of this person. I'd try the Papers and Records."

"Thank you," S'Aris said with a sweet smile.

She left the *Lady on the Wall* and continued into Elba, the unarticulated hope that she would somehow run into the princess guiding her feet and her eyes. S'Aris saw many people, but she did not see Carolyn Betters or Berria In'Orain.

The Witch stopped several people on a whim and asked after her friend, but all she received were strange glances. One old man patted her shoulder sympathetically and pressed a silver Katon into her hand. S'Aris watched him walk away with a bemused expression. She thought about running after him, returning the money, and explaining that she was neither feeble-minded or homeless, and had no need of his charity, then she shrugged. He would not miss the coin at all. It disappeared into one of the many magycal folds of her dress, and she continued on her way.

By sundown, she had reached the opposite wall of Elba. She used the Katon the man had given her to take a room at the closest inn, a little place with green eaves and blue walls. After a dinner of hearty stew and potatoes, which merited a second helping, S'Aris arranged a hot bath for a few extra Melbori and two scullion girls carted up buckets of steaming water to fill the tub.

Untying the belt of beads and laying it across the table, S'Aris slipped out of her dress and into the bath, soaking and scrubbing her skin until it stung, then lathered up her hair, enjoying the sensation of dirt and grime leaving her body.

Wrapped in a thin towel, she took everything out of her dress and laid them on the small table beside the bed, finding a few things in the deepest pockets that she had forgotten were there, including one last roll of bandages and some extra coin.

Piled together on the inadequate surface, her effects were an impressive array. S'Aris gazed at them, and a fresh wave of homesickness washed over her. Picking up a vial of moonlight gathered at midnight from a blue moon, she turned it over in her hand, watching the silvery grains fall from one end to the other.

When the Darkrobe who also bore the Mark of V'Ronica told S'Aris she would be leaving to help the Guardians, S'Aris had packed everything she could fit in her white robe in an hour, including three of the four gifts the Darkrobes of her faction had thought to present her with: a life-preserving elixir of everbræth and other ingredients long since gone from this world, a Master Key which would open almost any lock, including those protected by magyc, and a spiral slice of unicorn horn as large as her palm. The fourth hung from her belt in the form of a large, dark bead circled by a pale green stripe.

Her foresight had prevailed; in all her journeying, she had wanted for nothing so far, despite the troubles her companions oft became embroiled in, much to their dismay and general mystery. *Except perhaps more bandages,* she thought as she examined the frayed hem.

She took her soiled and torn dress and washed it in the now luke-warm and grey water. Wringing it out, she hung it in the window to dry. She toweled her hair, set new wards in the four corners of the room and slipped into bed wearing only her skin. The sheets were worn but soft, and the Witch was asleep in moments.

In the morning, she sat upon the bed with a threaded needle held in her teeth, folding up the frayed bits of the dress where she had torn off cloth to make bandages for the Guardians and Ria and sewed the dress up with neat stitches. Then she put on the clean and mended garment and packed all her vials and objects back into their places. The final thing was to tie the beaded belt at her waist, and she felt like a respectable Witch again, clean and presentable, an ambassador the Coven could be proud of.

Breakfast was a thick porridge of barley, oats, and buckwheat sweetened with honey. The innkeeper, a motherly woman with meaty hands and a round face, gave S'Aris a generous splash of cream and a kind smile and whispered, "On the house, my dear." S'Aris nodded her thanks and ate with quick bites, trying to decide whether to stay longer in hopes Berria turned up, or to leave for Samnara.

Some intuition urged her to make for the City of Iniquity. If she reached Samnara, it would be the farthest she would have been from home. *Next I'll find myself in Gulmira with the dwarfs or in the Wild Islands chasing down some mystical creature in a fire mountain or something,* she thought with mixed feelings of pride and bitterness.

The Witch slipped the scrying mirror from her robe, and whispered Berria's name, her breath misting on it. She watched the fog fade, hoping the princess's face would resolve, but her hope was unrewarded. For the first time, she tried reaching the assassin, but achieved similar results. The Witch had not tried before because she wanted to give Liæna space and time to do what she needed to do. Now S'Aris wished she had braved the assassin's displeasure at what she would surely see as a clingy attempt to draw her back into the fold.

Putting away the mirror, S'Aris's disquiet grew, though she knew the mirror worked - she had spoken with Berria shortly after the Eight Demons had returned to this land, and the princess's voice and face were as clear to her in the mirror as if she was standing right in front of her.

The Witch set out for Samnara within the hour. The Carriage would be faster, but she only had a small purse from the Coven, and Samnara was not that far. She made her way through the packed streets and markets of the City of Trees, towards the northern Gates of Elba and the peninsula beyond.

The Gates were in sight when S'Aris began to suspect she was being followed. Slowing her pace, she moved to the nearest table in the market and picked up a jar glazed in green and blue stripes, holding it up the light. Under the pretense of examining it, her eyes darted from side to side, but she couldn't see anyone who stood out.

A tugging on her dress made the Witch drop the jar. She caught it in a fumble and looked down. A young elf looked up at her, white blonde hair falling into quiet, observant brown eyes.

"Hello," S'Aris said. "Do you need something?"

The elf held something out without a word. It was a shard of glass. S'Aris took it. She didn't have to give it a second look to know what it was.

"Where did you get this?" she asked.

"A woman came to our house. She said she couldn't carry this because the Men of the Rose would be able to find her," the elf said in an old voice.

Men of the Rose would be the Men in White, S'Aris thought, a cold clenching of her heart accompanying the connection. "Thank you," she remembered to say belatedly.

The child gave a small smile and turned to go.

"Wait!" S'Aris called. "Do you know where she went?"

"She went to Samnara to become the sun," the elf called back and disappeared.

S'Aris blinked. *Very well then*. On a second thought, the Witch decided she would take the Carriage. S'Aris went to the station, which smelled strongly of horses and leather oil, and purchased a ticket. She paced the small platform, her arms wrapped around herself, until the battered carriage pulled up. She swung up and into the carriage and waited with her hands flat in her lap and her feet jiggling under her. The carriage was filled slowly, taunting her with the lack of speed, and when it finally set off, it went at half the pace she wished. Still, they reached Samnara in much less time than it would have taken her to walk.

Unlike Elba, the Gates of Samnara were watched, the bureaucracy making a long line. Getting in turned out to be simpler than she could have hoped. A poultry farmer with a noisy, smelly wagon was fourth in line to pass through the Gates. After a glance around to make sure she wasn't being watched - everyone was looking nervously at the Streetwardens or had their heads down - S'Aris crouched under the large wheels. Within a few moments, her bath was for naught, but she made it into the City.

When she judged she was far enough in to be safe, she slipped out from the wagon and found a quiet place partially concealed between two potted plants. She pulled out the mirror the elf had given her, turning it over in her hands. From of her dress, she pulled a few choice vials and pouches. She poured and mixed drops and pinches of these things and rubbed them into the surface of the mirror.

When she made the scrying glass, the Witch had taken an eyelash from the princess. With the magyc of the glass, S'Aris could jury-rig a compass which would use the princess as its "north," and now that she was closer, hopefully glean enough information to find the princess.

The Witch watched the surface of the mirror. The edges began to frost over, and her breath clouded the glass. *She is nowhere close.* S'Aris stood and clutched the scrying glass. Her palm started to tingle then go numb. Using her new tracking glass, the Witch wandered up and back the streets of Samnara, going forward and back when the mirror warmed and cooled.

It took her to the Shipwreck Districts. In other Cities it would be called the Skids. When the mirror was hot enough to sear her skin, S'Aris was standing in front of a large square building with one door high above her, and no stairs. Orange stone showed under the crumbling plaster, and though a sign hung by one corner above the door, the name had long since been rubbed away.

S'Aris stared up at the building, her head tilted as she figured out how she was going to get up there. She walked around the block and came to the back of the building where a drainpipe offered a way up to the roof. She crossed the flat expanse of the roof and peered over the other side.

Two Men in White stood in the alley and the Witch shrank back, the knowledge of the terrible omen thudding in the tight warmth of her chest, then poked her head out so just her eyes showed. After a moment, the ground opened up and the Men went down a stair into the darkness. The ground closed up after them, the faint grind of gears and the rumble of runners moving the door to conceal the secret entrance.

S'Aris peered over the edge and found the top lip of the door frame with her eyes, which looked to be just in reach of her foot. Her hands trembled as she thought about what she was going to do, then she thought of Berria, and they clenched into fists of resolve. The Witch pushed her short blond hair behind her ears and swung her legs over the edge of the roof.

She turned and slid down, bracing herself with her elbows, her feet dangling in empty space until she was hanging by her fingers. Still her feet didn't find the top of the door frame. She lowered herself as far as she could, squeezing her eyes shut, toes searching for the ledge as her fingers began to lose hold. The tips of her fingers burning, her arms rubbery as they struggled to hold her up, and then her feet found the small lip and she slid down, hugging the wall.

Breathing slowly and evenly, she tried not to over-think what she had to do next, in case she talked herself out of it. With a wiggle and a jerk, she dropped straight down. For a brief moment she was falling, then her hands closed on the frame where her feet had been, and she slammed into the door hard enough to knock the breath from her. Her fingertips slipped, but she managed to keep her hold until she got her feet under her on the small ledge under the door.

With one hand, she reached down and turned the handle, but it wouldn't move. *Locked.* Using the same hand, she reached into the easiest pocket of her dress and pulled out a Master Key, hoping this door was not one of the few it would not unlock. It opened the door, and she kicked it farther open and fell inside.

She lay on the floor, hugging it, as tears of relief wet her cheeks and the stone. *That was crazy,* she thought. *I am crazy. I'm an Ayr-blessed Witch, not a mountain goat.*

She picked herself up and lit a wishwood twig. She felt a twinge of guilt at having withheld the last few she had from the Guardians when they went into the maze of starless night or whatever the Man of Tongues called it. S'Aris shuddered. Falling through that darkness would haunt her nightmares for a long time. She would have passed them up if the need had become most dire, but she had learned it was best to have a few things in reserve, a few cards up her sleeve, in crude parlance.

In cautious, measured steps, she started into the building, pausing to look around corners before moving on, turning her head, attempting to see in all directions at once. She thought the tunnel had taken the Men somewhere else, and the building was deserted, until she found the person in the far back room, limp and tied to a chair.

The only clues to the identity of the person were the curtain of rich mahogany hair over her face, and the satin trousers, or what was left of them. For a moment, the Witch feared she had lost Berria to Death. But then the princess's head rolled back and she drew in shallow, gasping breath.

S'Aris knew over a thousand different combinations of herbs, tinctures, and poultices. She could set broken bones, sew torn flesh back together, and clean the blood up without flinching. But the sight of the princess tested all the Witch's equanimity to the limit.

Berria could not see S'Aris, for her eyes were crusted shut with blood. Her satin clothes had been reduced to rags, the skin under it bruised and lumpy. Her face looked as though it were made of clay that a child had tried to re-sculpt, her fingers were swollen and her wrists hung at an angle that made bile rise in the Witch's mouth.

She pushed away the sickening sensation, crossed the room with silent steps, and knelt beside the chair. The princess stirred and struggled faintly when S'Aris began to untie the ropes which held the princess upright.

"Wh...who is it?" Berria rasped.

S'Aris had to figure out how to speak past the lump in her throat before the words would come. "S'Aris."

Tears tinted pink with blood leaked down the princess's face, and she shook with silent sobs of relief. S'Aris's own vision blurred, and she could no longer see her fingers or the twists of the knots she was undoing clearly.

"How...did you find me?"

"Never mind that now," S'Aris said, her voice low and soothing. She brushed her tears away and pulled the intricate knots loose.

"They'll come back," the princess warned, the words grating from her harrowed throat, her arms and fingers twitching with reflexive motion, unused to fee motion.

"We'll be long gone by then," S'Aris promised.

A scraping sound came from the passage, followed by

muffled voices. Berria seized up in terror.

"You must leave now," she told S'Aris, her voice broken and urgent.

"I'm not leaving you. Now be quiet and let me concentrate," S'Aris said.

Her hands shook, and she tried to ignore the voices coming closer. Someone grabbed her arm far in advance of the voices. S'Aris looked up at a middle-aged Man in White. His green-brown eyes were flat and promised no mercy.

"How did you get in here?" he asked.

His voice froze the air in S'Aris's lungs and spikes of terror through her, but she pressed her lips together, determined not to show she was intimidated. He squeezed her arm, hard enough to bring tears stinging to her eyes.

"You are a Witch," he said, looking her up and down, and his lips pursed in thought. "We have no need of your particular talents at the moment, but you may come in handy at some time in the future. Come with me please."

Instead of following, S'Aris twisted away from him, the motion straining the joints in her arm, reaching for the knife in her boot, but he pulled her up, jerking her arm behind her.

"Or if that's how you prefer," he said with bland disinterest.

He swung her into the wall with as little effort as removing a coat. The impact shifted everything in her body slightly off and S'Aris fell to the floor, surprised to find that it accepted her with the gentle kiss of a feather bed. Warm, salty blood filled her mouth and some part of her realized that she was not perceiving everything exactly as it was.

She tried to lift herself off the ground, but her arms wouldn't move. One was pinned under her, the other lay stretched out above her. Her hand spasmed and clenched into a weak fist with her effort. The Man in White came over, the heel of his boot landing square on her hand.

The Witch felt all twenty-seven bones in her fingers and hand grind against each other, cells being crushed, flesh protesting against a force it could not withstand. She heard someone cry out in pain, a disembodied sound, and she could swear it was someone else, though it sounded like her. The pressure increased in cruel increments. Her gaze began to turn black, but she fought against it, blocking out the pain and moving her other arm achingly towards the beads around her waist. Her fingers brushed the cool, smooth spheres...

...then everything was white and free of the awareness of pain.

S'Aris opened her eyes and neither the princess nor the Man in White was anywhere in evidence. She looked down and found her body was whole again, but she thought perhaps the apparition she was looking at wasn't really her body. She looked around, seeing nothing but empty whiteness.

"Hello?" she called out, her voice swallowed in the vastness that pressed close at the same time.

"Greetings," a warm voice answered.

She turned, though perhaps she didn't move at all, and saw a person sitting there in the cloudy white haze who had definitely not been there before. His knee was clasped in His hands, and His leg was draped over the other. Brown hair was swept to the side, and a widow's peak accentuated the pointed features of His face. He wore worn clothes with an old-fashioned aura to them, as if He had stepped out of the pages of an ancient tale. His eyes were pale blue and as warm as His smile.

"Who are you?" the Witch demanded.

"You can't guess?" He asked, a teasing lilt in His voice.

She didn't need to guess; she already knew. S'Aris swallowed, and spoke the words wishing they weren't true. "You're Death."

"Some people call Me that," He acknowledged. He leaned forward. "But My name is Northirion Fynstaer."

S'Aris had never imagined Death would have any other name but Death. She didn't think she could call Him Northirion, or whatever He'd said. *I don't think I can call Him anything really.*

"What do You want with me?" she said, smoothing down her dress nervously, a habit she had picked up at the Coven when waiting for one of the more formidable Darkrobes to admit her for a critique or lesson.

"Most people find that somewhat obvious when I appear," He said in a mild voice.

He stood and walked over to her. He was tall, and looking up at Him made S'Aris feel like a child gazing up at an eccentric grandfather - strange enough to inspire awe and a little trepidation, but underlying this was a trust that He would do everything in His considerable power not to let her come to harm - and she wondered what He must think when looking down at her.

"I've died," she said, her voice small. "I'm to be taken to Your Realm now."

Death regarded her. "Come. Sit by Me."

She did as He bid because she could think of nothing else to do. "Is this Your Realm then? Have I arrived already?"

He waved His hand. "No. A little piece of the space between worlds and the Voide, or what you call the Nexus."

"It doesn't look anything like what I imagined," she told Him. "I thought it would be darker."

"I can make it so, if that would make you more comfortable," He offered.

"No, I'm fine," S'Aris said, smoothing out her dress again. "This is not how this usually goes, is it?"

"That depends on what you mean by *this*," He returned.

"Being taken to Your Realm," the Witch clarified. "When someone dies."

Death was silent for a while. "This may come as a surprise to you, but I don't believe there is a usual when it comes to dying. People react differently. Some people accept it in a sort of bland way, like porridge for breakfast after forty years of porridge for breakfast. Some people resist, but I sit with them, talk for a bit, then they come willingly."

"And what if someone doesn't want to come willingly?" S'Aris asked, a twisting of apprehension in her stomach.

Death leaned forward, His light blue eyes intent. "In every person, there is an innate sense of right and wrong, a sense of what should be and what should not be. Your Coven has a term for what I am referring to."

"The Way of Things," the Witch whispered.

"Precisely." Death looked pleased. "And every person who lives in any world of the Path knows, somewhere in themselves, that the right thing to do when one dies is to allow Me to take them to My Realm."

S'Aris knew exactly what He was talking about, a warmth in her throat and her fingers resonating with His words. "And what happens to them once they get there?"

"That, my dear, is entirely, and I mean, *entirely* up to them." Death folded His hands. "Many choose to stay; some for a while, some for longer."

"And what of those who don't want to go at all?"

S'Aris said. "There are stories of people who start the journey, but come back, some in a miraculous faction."

Death rolled His eyes. "You'd be surprised how much hubris some people have." He gave her a significant glance.

"You mean Ria?"

"I mean your friend Cedar Jal. Ria is quite delightful."

"You've met the Guardian?"

"On a few occasions. He delights in abusing the phrase *to cheat Death*."

S'Aris frowned. "But you've allowed him to remain of this world each time?"

"There is no *allowing* as you know it," Death explained. "It is a contract, an ancient contract, made at the birth of Time. It was not fulfilled, and so he remained."

"That is a very big idea," S'Aris said.

"Then perhaps it is best not to dwell on it," Death said. "I try not to."

"You can't mean You don't understand it," S'Aris accused. "It's what You do."

"And so you fully understand all facets of the Way of Things, as that is what you do?" Death returned.

S'Aris could only gape at Him.

"I thought not," He answered His own question with a chuckle. "No. I may seem omniscient to some, but unfortunately I am not."

"It's time to go then," the Witch said, her heart fluttering though she tried to appear calm.

Death turned to look at her. Something about His face made S'Aris think if He were to turn His head, she would see a vast space filled with the answers to all the things one wondered about as children while staring up at the night sky and counting shooting stars.

He gave her a sad smile. "I know the time of leaving is not easy. I don't think it will ever be easy. But it is the Way of Things."

"I'm ready," S'Aris said.

"My dear, it is not *your* time."

S'Aris gaped at Him, unsure what He meant by this. Her body, intense pain making it throb in hot, angry jolts, floated somewhere near the edges of her consciousness. It was broken, battered, and she had thought that the Man in White had seen to it that she would never use that body again. The Witch swallowed, uneasiness pressing on her tighter and tighter.

"I don't understand what You mean," she said.

"I think you do." He spoke kindly, and gave her shoulder a gentle squeeze.

A different emotion began to clog the empty spaces in her chest. Now it was hard to breathe. All the Witch could think of was getting away, getting away from here, and not having to think *that* thought. Despite herself, tears burned her eyes. She blinked hard, refusing to acknowledge them.

"When one dies, one loses everything. When one loses a friend, it is so much worse."

The way He said it was like running a hand up velvet the wrong way, gentle, yet thrilling in its wrongness. A rushing in the Witch's ears reduced her willpower to a ruin. She shook her head, back and forth slowly, knowing it was futile but unable to stop.

"Are you trying to tell Me something?" Death asked, smiling kindly.

S'Aris shook her head more forcefully and started crying. Death enfolded her in His arms and patted her back until she stopped shaking.

"Better?" He inquired.

She shook her head again.

"I thought not," He said. "Are you ready?"

"No," S'Aris wiped her cheeks.

Death smiled patiently. "We have time."

S'Aris stared up at Him. He looked down at her. She was struck by how safe it felt standing here in His space.

"Have we met before?" she asked.

He smiled at her, and that was His only answer.

"Never mind," she said, turning away and straightening her dress.

"My dear, sometimes life can seem very complicated. Death is simpler, but even it has its subtleties."

His words were sensitive, but bland and unhelpful. She frowned. Why was He taking all this time to talk to her, if she wasn't the one who was to die? S'Aris began to suspect that Death had another reason for this visit, and though it was not a happy thought, it could be happier than the alternatives.

"Why have You brought me here?" she asked Death.

The Witch waited, impatient and yet terrified of the answer.

"At last, a pertinent question," Death smiled. "Do you know why the Witches' Coven is called the Coven of White and Black?"

S'Aris had never given it any thought. "No."

Death gave her an exasperated look. She shifted, uncomfortable, but merely shook her head.

"Do you know why it was so easy for the First Guardian to assume and accuse the Coven of practicing Demon magyc?"

S'Aris paused, stumbled over several possible answers, then shook her head. "Our histories say it was because he was biased - arrogant and biased."

Death shook His head. "It is because the Witches come as close to Demon magyc as anyone can come to it without actually doing so."

The Other World

The sensation of intense affront made S'Aris inarticulate for a long moment, as she battled with the desire to argue, but how can one argue with Death?

"I mean no offense. I am simply stating what is," Death continued. "The Way of Things, the manipulation of it, space and time, is the closest thing the Path can reach before it becomes the Voide."

"I don't understand."

"It's a circle. One feeds into the other, and back again, in an endless loop. Black into white."

He lifted His hand and drew a Mark in the air: a single circle with a diagonal slash marking it exactly in half. One half was black. The other was white. S'Aris stared at Death's Mark hanging in the space above her, solid and translucent at the same time. Despite the dividing line, the black seemed to fade into the white, and the white into the black, in contrast to the crisp and definite edges of the circle.

"Black and white," S'Aris stated, pointing like a child to the two colors which had ruled her life for as long as she could remember.

"Black and white," Death repeated with a smile. "The Witches' Way of Things is, in addition to being the closest thing to Demon magyc this world has to offer, the closest thing to My own magyc."

S'Aris felt as if her thoughts were likened to a stream with a massive buildup of logs damming it up.

"How?" was all she could manage to get out.

Death laughed. "I couldn't tell you. The Builders made me the way I am, and the Builders taught the Witches the Way of Things. Why or how - that is for them to say. All I can tell you is that what you can do, and what I can do are different orders of the same thing."

"The Way...of Things," S'Aris gestured as if her words

were things floating in the air and if she moved them into the right place, they would somehow make sense. "And Death...*You*...are similar...?"

Death smiled. "It is not important, and it is a story that goes back to the Beginning, before Time, really. You don't need to understand all of it."

S'Aris looked at Him, her eyes squinting as she tried to piece it together. "Why are You telling me this?"

"Because I need a favor, S'Aris O'Pac of Lii."

The Witch wasn't sure she had heard correctly. "Pardon?"

"I need a favor."

More confused by the minute, S'Aris tried to reason out what He was talking about so she didn't sound completely stupid, but she could not. "Why? What?"

Death sighed. "The *why* requires a rather delicate explanation. The *what* is only slightly easier." He regarded her for a long time. "I need your help to bring the Guardians or-" He paused and chose His next words with care, "-perhaps *Aethsiths* Herself, to My Realm when the time comes."

S'Aris frowned. "That makes no sense. If it is time to bring them to Your Realm, why don't You simply take them Yourself?"

"It will not be that sort of time," Death said. "It will be somewhat premature, and therefore out of My hands."

"I don't understand," the Witch shook her head.

Death rubbed His chin. "People think Me all-powerful. That is an untruth."

S'Aris blinked, struggling to follow His words.

"I cannot do anything I want," Death told her, spreading His hands, a slight, mocking twist to His lips. "Would it be that I could, but alas, I was not granted omnipotence."

He looked at her, willing her to understand, searching her eyes to find some spark of recognition. He saw nothing and was disappointed, but not angry. He tried again.

"There is a simple reason for My existence. My purpose, My sole Mandate, is to keep the Balance between the Path and the Voide, in order to keep Chaos at bay. If I were to abuse the considerable power vested in Me to do so, I would only undo Myself, inviting Chaos into existence by My action."

"So You want to do something that You feel is outside Your Mandate, and You think by having me do this, You use a loophole in this law?" S'Aris said, the absurd logic difficult to think with.

"Exactly!" Death exclaimed, a smile growing on His face and lighting up His eyes.

"I do not see how it's any different," S'Aris said.

"Perhaps in essence it's not, but semantics and technicalities can be useful at times."

"And why are you relying on semantics and technicalities *now*?"

A shadow of memory darkened Death's eyes, something so black and terrible the mere suggestion of it would make strong men quake. It was regret, so vast it could drench the whole world in a flood if allowed to be unleashed and felt fully.

"Because I will not have another world brought to ruin on My conscience, if not on My hands."

The words were stark and empty of anything volatile, but they were weighted, dragging the speaker down even as He fought to rise up. S'Aris considered all He had said, wondering at the wisdom of opposing His wish after seeing that look in His eyes and decided she was not the one to do so at this time.

"You said You need me to bring them to Your Realm?" the Witch asked. "When?"

"When the time is right. You will know when this is," Death said. "Can you do this for Me?"

"Traversing the Nexus is something only Darkrobes can do," S'Aris indicated her white dress.

Death held out His hand. In His palm were three Witch's beads and a pebble, flat, smooth, and a pale orange color. S'Aris ignored the familiar beads and picked up the strange rock, cupping it so her fingers just brushed the surface. It was soft, and the weight was so slight it was like holding a feather. "What is this?"

"In My Realm, where the Great Waters meet the land, there is a city called Lore. The beaches there are beautiful, a rainbow of every color imaginable, and in My Realm, imagination is so much broader than here." He nodded at the stone in her hand. "This will be your Grounding."

She understood the concept of a Grounding though she was not a Darkrobe. A Grounding was a tie to a world, the rope a Witch could use to tether herself when traversing the dangerous shifting maze of the Nexus.

The stone became much heavier when she realized the implications of Death giving this to her.

"I'm not a Darkrobe," she told Him. "I have never been into the Nexus or gone to another world."

"There's a first time for everything, my dear," Death replied and pressed her fingers closed over the Grounding. Then He put the beads in her hand. Though she had not spelled them, as a Witch, S'Aris could sense what they did, and the amount of power in the small objects gave her a head rush, like taking a deep breath of frigid air or a deep gulp of strong wine.

"Where did You get these?" she asked through the icy throbbing in her chest and blood.

"A mutual friend gave them to Me," Death smiled. "I believe you're acquainted with M'Rella?"

The name brought a rush of grief, but the glad warmth at the touch of the beads dispelled it. The two Witches had only known each other very briefly, but M'Rella was the first Witch S'Aris had spent any time with since leaving the coven four years ago. S'Aris nodded in answer to Death's question.

"I thought so. Now, I have to be going. And you need to be returning to the world."

"Wait," S'Aris said, in the vain hope of putting off the inevitable pain - both physical and emotional. "What's going to happen?"

Death was silent for a long time. "You are going to be fine. You will figure something out."

"How do You know?"

"Because you don't have a candle calling Me," Death told her. "You are not on your way to My Realm."

The feeling of hard beads - her own beads which she had spelled herself - in her fingers made her look down. That hand was empty, and she held M'Rella's beads in her other hand. The sensation was weird, like a shadow pain in a lost limb, and the faint vestiges of a thought - unleashing the spells stored within the most dangerous bead she kept at her waist, the one she would not use until she was sure she was at the last moment of her life - tickled her mind, reminding her that somewhere, she was in grave danger. The Witch frowned and shook her head, then looked back up at Death.

"No," she said.

Death raised an eyebrow, but something in His face said He was not surprised by this, had expected it even. "That is a very powerful word spoken in a very interesting tone. Would you care to elaborate?"

S'Aris was flustered, a tight pressure of nervous energy settling in her stomach when she thought about standing up to Death Himself. She steeled herself and continued.

"No, I am not going to figure something out," S'Aris repeated. "I already figured out what's going to happen."

"And what is that?"

S'Aris laid out her terms. Death listened, His arms crossed, and inscrutable expression on His face.

"That is quite something to ask," Death said. "You understand that her body is broken beyond even the ability of a Witch to heal? She is only alive because of sorcery keeping her so."

"You have magyc," she told Him. "You could undo this. I know it."

"My magyc involves dying, death, and traveling to My realm," Death countered. "I am not sure what you are proposing I do."

"You don't have to take her," S'Aris pleaded. "If you don't take her, she will be forced to stay here. I can heal her, if I have time."

Death regarded her with compassion overflowing in His gaze. "You are a smart young woman, S'Aris of Lii, but in this moment you are being foolish. Partly because you cannot know all that I know, and partly because of your love for your friend."

"But You could, couldn't You? If You wanted to?" S'Aris tried one last time.

"That is true, in a sense. I have the power to undo death, just as I have the power to inflict it. Just because I can does not mean I should," Death countered. "There is a point and purpose to Death. If I choose to allow her to escape this contract, then what of every other person?"

"This is one person," she argued.

"It is *always* one person," He explained gently, and

sighed. "I cannot do what you are asking of Me."

S'Aris blinked, tears stinging her eyes. "Then can you give me time? Don't take her now."

He looked at her for a long time. "You understand what I told you about the Balance of the worlds and My duty to keep it?"

S'Aris nodded. "I did. And if the world is so precariously balanced that that tips it over the edge into Chaos because of this, then so be it. All I ask is time."

Death gave a wry chuckle, then raised His eyes to the sky or whatever was above them in this pristine white pocket.

"It's like herding cats with you lot," He mumbled to Himself. He glanced at her with a sardonic twinkle. "I would never have signed up for this job had I know that you would be what I would have to deal with."

"Thank you," S'Aris bowed her head and accepted the compliment. "Do we have a deal?"

Death held out His hand. The Witch shook it, and her palm burned as though Fyr had breathed upon it. She gasped and pulled away, for a moment afraid her hand had been reduced to ashes, but when she looked down, it was still there. Shining in her white skin was Death's Mark, though it was slightly wrong: the upper segment, which was usually black, was white, and the half that was usually white was black.

The longer she looked at it, the more wrong S'Aris felt in her own skin. Her hand was weighed down, as though an invisible boulder were bearing down on it. Worse, it felt as if her hand were sitting on a bed of spikes, pushed down by the boulder. At the moment, she wasn't certain she would have the strength to hold the Mark for long. She looked up at Him with wide eyes.

"Just this *one* time, I give you permission to use it," He

told her. "It will give you the time you requested for Berria."

S'Aris stared at her hand, afraid to touch it, and she nodded. Death made a shooing motion with His hand, looking as though He was sending a petulant child to bed.

"Now go. I will be waiting."

S'Aris returned to her body with a scream. The heel of the Man in White's boot came off her broken hand, and somehow this caused even more pain. The Witch had never imagined such excruciating sensation could exist, never thought her body could withstand such anguish without shattering.

She felt the string of beads in her hand and the single bead, larger than the rest. She saw it in her mind's eye, a circle of black with a pale green stripe painted across the middle. Special sand was mixed into the clay, and this gave it a grainy look and texture, like an orange peel.

The Man in White kicked the Witch in the small of her back. Her kidneys were bruised and protested loudly. The thought of more pain, as yet uninflicted, made S'Aris shudder and gasp. Somewhere, near enough to feel but not to touch, Death was waiting with infinite patience.

It reminded her of the other beads, the ones M'Rella had spelled and were now in S'Aris's hand. Instinct made S'Aris change her course of action, and she gripped the large silver bead Death had gifted her with between her fingers. Despite knowing that it would hurt, probably enough to kill her, she rolled her body around. The leg of the chair pressed into her shoulder, and her hand fell on the princess's leg. The Mark Death had placed on her hand warmed, and Berria cried out. Knowing the time was right, S'Aris concentrated on the magyc in the small sphere, crushing the bead with her fingernails, and it burst like a

The Other World

ripe grape.

Waves of black light and sound rolled out from where she lay, twisting and spinning in dark eddies that enveloped everything. S'Aris squeezed her eyes shut and felt Death move closer. Then the world fell still and a hand was on her shoulder as a familiar voice spoke in her ear warmly, urging her to get up.

Somehow, S'Aris complied, the pain no longer chaining her, but propelling her. The Man in White was frozen, and the princess was hanging over the arm of the chair, her chest rising and falling rapidly. Her face was twisted in pain, and S'Aris couldn't keep the words from revisiting her. *You understand that her body is broken beyond even the ability of a Witch to heal? She is only alive because of sorcery keeping her so.*

The Witch clutched her broken hand against her chest and pulled the ropes away from the princess. Somehow she pulled Berria up, and the two stumbled out of the room. As S'Aris supported Berria's weight, a shadow with a kind smile guided them. S'Aris didn't see or hear or feel beyond impressions and dull, thudding awareness of things moving past.

They emerged into the streets of Samnara. The light made the princess sob in pain. S'Aris helped her to a doorway, lowered her to the ground as gently as she could, then collapsed beside her. *I have to get things, something to help,* her muddled mind thought.

Going through the pockets of space cleverly sewn by the Way of Things in the simple piece of fabric the Witch wore had never taken so much effort. The dress felt heavier, everything it carried pressing on her tender body. With sporadic exertions, the Witch clumsily assembled what she needed in the hollow of her lap with her one good hand, her mutilated one cradled against the hollow between her breasts, which rose and fell after each painful breath.

The first thing she did was give the princess a generous gulp of the magycal painkiller the Witches simply called *lethe*, then took one herself and allowed the thin metallic taste to numb her mouth and travel to the rest of her body. Without pain to distract or deter her, she stood and hauled the princess up again, and they were moving towards the gates of the city. S'Aris did not know what she was going to do when she got there; she just knew that she had to get out of the city.

Everything - people, animals, carts, even the air - remained still around them thanks to M'Rella's spell, but as they continued along the road, farther and farther from the lair of the Men in White, the people began to twitch and move in short bursts, and leaves frozen in the air began to drop almost imperceptibly towards the ground. Then the spell broke, and Time crashed around them. People stared at the battered pair as they staggered past, their eyes burning into the Witch.

S'Aris rubbed the fading Mark on her palm with her thumb. "I need a little help right now."

And Death was there. Between the two of them, they carried the princess out of Samnara to the scrubby woods at the edge of the peninsula. The cliffs were breathtaking, a stiff wind whipping the grass into a fervent dance and giving the grey water white caps.

The Witch laid the princess on the ground and clasped her hands with her own good hand, the one with the Mark, and for a moment, Berria relaxed, the sheen of pain leaving her face. Though her eyes were still swollen shut, she turned to face S'Aris.

"I can feel Him nearby," she murmured. "Though why He hasn't come for me, I don't know."

"How does she know?" S'Aris turned her face slightly to ask the shadow at her shoulder.

"When a person's time comes, Walls become thin, veils are lifted, which allows them to see what they could not before," Death told her. "I will give you a few moments alone now."

S'Aris nodded and looked down, brushing a curl of dirty hair from the princess's forehead. In the light, each bruise and cut stood out on her skin. Though S'Aris tried not to look, she couldn't help but see them, and tears stung her eyes.

"I should have come sooner," she murmured, the words catching in the lump in her throat.

The ghost of a smile lit Berria's face for an instant. "You came. That is all that matters."

S'Aris wanted to speak, wanted to say words that would heal the princess and make everything right, but she didn't know what she should say. She wanted to comfort the princess, but now it was not the princess who needed comforting, just as He had said.

"Is there...anything I can do for you?" the Witch asked, her voice thick.

"Find my family." Berria said, her fingers and feet twitching. "Go to Nitefolk. Find Haman. Tell him...tell him I'm sorry."

S'Aris nodded and the dam behind the Witch's eyes broke, the trickle becoming a silent flood. She shook, wrapping her arms around the princess, not even feeling the protest of her crushed hand. Berria tried to smile again and failed.

"It's alright, my friend. We will see each other again; I am sure of it." She sighed, a long, slow, peaceful farewell.

S'Aris looked down, and though her eyes saw the spark of life had faded, her heart refused to believe it. She shook the princess, but Berria gave no response. S'Aris clenched her teeth, her shoulders shaking with the strain of her grief. She didn't know how long she cried, but the tears eventually abated, and S'Aris became aware of the shadow solidifying at her shoulder.

"Now I will take care of her, and I promise she will be looked after well," a familiar voice said. "But first, I believe you have something which belongs to Me?"

S'Aris looked down at her hand, blinking away the last of the tears which burned and blurred her vision. The Mark was dark against her white skin, and though it looked as if a hole had been cut through her flesh, her hand was heavy and frozen. She offered it to Death, and He took back His temporary gift. She gasped and winced when it left with the kiss of fire.

"Farewell for now, S'Aris of Lii," Death said softly, and then He was gone without waiting for a reply.

The Witch knew without looking that Berria was gone with Him, leaving only the shell of her body. In slow, shaking movements, S'Aris bandaged her hand and her bruised ribs as best as she could, then gathered what scant wood she could find and built a pyre. Lighting it with purple Witch fire, she reduced the princess's body to a thimbleful of ashes, cold and numb despite the heat of the flames.

The princess would not have her body placed with ceremony within the vaults of the royal families, nor would her likeness be carved on the door to the mausoleum. Her urn was a small glass vial, entombed in S'Aris's robes. *I will return this to Ghor, where it belongs. It is the least I can do.*

The Witch stood for a long time watching the fire burn itself out in fits of pink sparks, and then stared at the scorched bit of earth the fire left, thinking morbid thoughts about the last of the princess's legacy.

The Other World

No, it is so much more than that, the Witch thought. *She could well be the reason this world has a chance at all.*

It was the princess who had made the connection between the Guardians and other events, the princess who had taken it upon herself to seek them out, the princess who had the Path-dreams and who had gathered the pieces of the Torch. S'Aris realized it would now be her duty to chronicle what the princess had done so the story could be placed on the shelves of the *Tyomewaerr,* the elves' magycal library which held the stories of the world. *I'll just add that to my list of things to do. But first things first.*

She clutched the strange orange stone from Death's Realm, and it warmed her cold hands. Then the stone disappeared into her robes, along with M'Rella's beads, and the young Witch turned, her face set, to find the Nitefolk, and the last of the line of Orain.

AETHSITHS PART II

Ria looked up at her father and realized that this was it, the moment of decision, the point of no return. And she wasn't ready. Just as she had been certain, so many years ago, that the right thing for her to do was to go home, she was certain she had to leave now. She knew too, with her high chance of death and the low chance of finding a Witch to call a Door to send her back to this world, she would never see her father again.

"Did you get news about Matt?" Richard asked, misinterpreting her distress.

Ria nodded, fighting to keep the tears from coming to her eyes. "He's fine. He's with Josh." Her vision burned and swam, and when she blinked, she felt hot tears slide down her cheeks. "Dad, I have to go."

Richard was silent for a long time. "Right now?"

Ria nodded again, her expression guarded and dejected. He tried to say something, but his mouth couldn't form the words.

"Your mother..." he began and then stopped. "You're all I have left of her."

And suddenly Ria put her finger on it. It wasn't just her leaving. She was reopening old wounds, wounds which had scarred over but underneath were as raw as the day they were made. The ghost of her mother hung over them, torturing her father but giving them both strength. A voice in a forgotten dream whispered in her ear. *Remember Maria, no one can make you do what you do not want to do - anything you do must come from within you first.*

She didn't want to hurt her father. She wanted to stay and care for and protect him. But she couldn't leave the Guardians, not when her instinct told her that if she didn't, her time here, or in any world for that matter, would be very short. Everyone's time would be short. Ria stepped forward and put her hands on his shoulders.

"Dad, you have to let us go. She doesn't belong in this world anymore. Neither do I."

Two tears rolled down his cheeks, and he brushed them away. "I know. It's just hard."

"I know. I know," she murmured, and crushed him with a fierce hug. "But you're strong. I know you're strong. You'll be fine."

She straightened suddenly, a horrible thought occurring to her. "The Demons will come for them." She looked at the Guardians for the confirmation she didn't need. "Somehow they can't find me, but they can find me through the people close to me. Adam, Matt..." she looked at her father. "I don't know how, but if I leave, they'll still be in danger."

"Fantastic," Luca muttered. "What are we going to do about that?"

Ria glanced around, trying to find the question to the

answer she didn't remember getting. Something to hide them from evil eyes. Something to repel the Demons. *Something to do both.* Fleeting snatches of memory came back to her. *Demonbane.*

"Have you ever heard of something called Demonbane?" she asked, rounding on the Guardians.

"Of course," Jæyd replied, looking a little taken aback. "Dragons are oft called that, in olde stories."

"Well, I don't have a dragon," Ria laughed hopelessly. "It can't be that."

"A dragon's scale, or dragonbone, would be called Demonbane," Jæyd explained further. "Why are you asking now?"

"Something…I remembered, sort of," Ria said slowly, rubbing her hands together. "Someone gave me Demonbane, to hide me from the Nine, before I left…"

She looked down at her palm, as if the answer was there.

"Was it the Witch M'Rella?" Cedar asked, a slight frown on her face.

"Yes!" Ria looked up, her face bright. "M'Rella! She said something…something about…I don't know…damn! Why can't I remember?!"

"Knowing Witches, and as we're talking about a very witchy Witch, that probably has something to do with Midnight," Luca commented.

"What?" Ria asked, trying to pay attention through the echoes of the words *bathed in midnight* bouncing from ear to ear.

"Midnight hides things, keeps them from sight. It also makes people forget." Luca winked. "My mother *was* a Witch, you know. I was young, but I remember a few things."

Maria began to rub at her palm, then scratch. Cedar

grabbed her wrist before she hurt herself.

"What are you doing?"

"It itches!" Ria exclaimed.

Cedar looked down, and they saw something move beneath her skin. Ria blanched. She clenched her teeth, and pinched the skin. A drop of blood welled up, then fell away, revealing a tiny white chip. Ria gasped, as the memories came flooding back. *Leaving the Guardians in Catmar and running to Balmar, the City of Fire, with Juff; the Witch M'Rella was going to give her something that would help her, but the Maker Adar Kerstel had gone back on his word; the Witch gave her something else, then sent her back here.*

"I remember! She gave me this to hide me." She looked at her father, and a calculating look came over her face.

She held out her hand, and he gave her his. She pressed the chip of Demonbane into his palm with a frown of concentration. It disappeared. The Guardians looked at her strangely, and then shared a significant glance.

"There," Ria said with a satisfied smile. "That will keep you safe. You have to stay with Betty and the boys until I'm far enough away that the Demons won't hurt you."

Richard nodded, staring at his palm with a faraway look in his eyes. "Okay, Maria. I love you-"

A horrible sound, like a rock-slide and a hundred wounded cats yowling, cut him off.

"I think we have company," Luca said, sweat beginning to appear on his forehead.

The echoes of the dreadful roar made Ria's ears ache, and she twisted her head, trying to dislodge the sensation.

"I'm not fluent in Demon," Cedar told her grimly, "but I'm pretty sure that was not a friendly greeting."

"I thought this was supposed to hide people," Ria cried, looking down at the small sore on her palm where the Demonbane had been.

"It does," Jæyd said. "It *was* hiding *you*. Now it is hiding your father. And the Demons are looking for *you*."

"How did they get here fast?" she complained. "I just got rid of it."

"They're looking for you," Cedar told her. "And like M'Rella said, you shine like a beacon on a moonless night."

Seeing the man with the face and golden eyes of her dreams in front her was doing funny things to Ria. Everything inside her felt like it was crawling over everything else. He too looked shorter than she remembered, though she still had to look up at him to meet his gaze.

"Then we have to get far away from here," she told him.

Ria looked at her father and could tell by the way he pressed his lips together, he was trying to hold back tears. Suddenly, she wished she had more time, more time to sit, and talk, and ask all the questions that she had never thought to ask before. But the Demon screamed and reminded her why it was a good idea for her to go now. She threw her arms around her dad one last time.

"I'll come back for that birthday thing," she said, hoping she would be able to keep that promise. "I love you."

"I love you, too." He released her, stepped back, and gently pushed her away. "Go. If that's what you have to do."

It is. Ria turned and ran with the Guardians.

"Where do we go?" she asked.

"We have no idea," Luca said and made a sound which could have been a chuckle, but it sounded more like choking.

Ria looked him over more thoroughly and saw the dark

Guardian was in bad shape. He was short of breath and drenched in sweat. When he raised his arm to wipe it out of his eyes, he noticed her worried look.

"I wish everyone would stop looking at me like that," he glared at her. "I swear I'm not about to drop and die."

"If that's true, I'd hate to see what you'll look like when you are dying," Ria said and was gratified to see the Guardian's mouth twitch up, even if it was forced and short-lived mirth.

"So what's the plan?" Ria tried again.

"We have no plan," Cedar said, eyes fierce as they ran down the street. "We just had to get here before the Demons did, find you, and after that, I haven't the faintest clue. You don't happen to have any ideas, do you?"

Ria laughed, gasped, and focused on breathing deep steady breaths. *I'd forgotten how much these people like to run*, she grimaced. *And walk, for days on end.*

"No, I don't have any ideas," she managed to get out. She dragged to a stop. "Okay, stop. We have no idea where we're going, so running is pointless." She took a gulp of air. "And, I haven't exactly been keeping up with the whole magyc thing, you know, so I don't know how to call a Door to another world."

"You did last time," Cedar said.

"No, your music did," Ria corrected him. "I just opened it."

"You are mistaken," Jæyd told her, her auburn plait swinging as she shifted her weight from foot to foot. "The Guardians' magyc is not the magyc of Doors and walking between worlds. No matter how hard Cedar played, he would not be able to do that." The elf gave her a hard look. "It is like putting a side of beef in the oven and taking out a cake. It is impossible."

"Fine, but I still don't know how I did it," Ria said. "It

had something to do with the music."

"Well, that's not going to help," Luca informed her, hanging onto the silent Daleman's arm to keep himself upright. "We have no magyc here. Zip. Zero. None."

Ria stared. "What do you mean?"

"We have no magyc," Luca repeated slowly. "We can't even call our weapons, and this might as well be a whale for all I can make music with it." He indicated the violin over his shoulder with a betrayed expression.

"What about the dream?" Ria demanded. "There's magyc here!"

"We think there's magyc where you are," Timo said, looking down at her, his pale blue eyes calm yet alert. "We could call our weapons to hand when you came in the dream."

"I don't have magyc!" Ria asserted, throwing her hands up in the air, unsure how to make them understand that she really, truly, had *no* idea how to help them or how to *rekindle* anything, as Timo put it.

"Well, you'd better figure out how to get magyc otherwise, we're in a world of hurt," Luca said. "Because if I'm not mistaken, that's a Demon."

Ria whirled around. Standing on the corner, beside the crossing sign, was one of the Nine. Just like when she was a child, they terrified her with their angles and their shadows and the red glow to their eyes, like a cat's in the dark, but creepier.

Then she didn't have any more time to think, for the Demon turned and gazed at her. It did not move or blink, and Ria got the idea of a snake hypnotizing its meal. It was not the same one as before, and it was joined by another. They did not come towards her, they waited, and their stillness was more unnerving than if they gave chase.

"I think we might have solved the problem of the Nine

being in Demona," Ria said, keeping both eyes on the Demons, though they remained where they were.

"How so?" Cedar asked, his head jerking towards her.

"Because they're all here now."

"What are they doing?" Timo asked, as nervous as she had ever seen him.

"It looks like they're keeping watch," Cedar said.

"For what?" Luca blinked.

"I have no idea." Cedar turned to Ria, who shrugged.

"I suggest getting away while we still have legs to run," Luca said in a sagacious voice.

Ria agreed and turned to run, the Guardians surrounding her and keeping pace. The grim thought that their actions were futile dogged her steps: it wouldn't be long before the Demons caught them.

And they only mentioned to me now *that they can't do magyc,* Ria thought.

"So we need a plan right now," Cedar stated.

His golden eyes burned, and Ria recalled how terrifying his power could become when he was motivated. *Or angry.* But in this world, he was powerless. His guitar pulled his shoulder down with a weight that was not real, at least in the world of its origin.

A roar behind them made the Guardians flinch, but Ria knew it was just the sound of a car. Josh's black sedan pulled up alongside them and skidded to a halt. Without waiting for an invitation, Ria pulled open the door and shoved Cedar in, then sat in his lap when she saw how little room was left when the other Guardians piled in the back.

"What are you doing?" Ria demanded, bracing herself on the dashboard and glaring at Josh.

"Making sure you make it out alive," Josh said with a grim smile. "And getting that Demon far away from Matt, your dad, and Betty. Now, where to?"

The answer came to her with the sound of bells and far off voices singing a chorus of hope and answered prayers. "The store."

"Giovanni's?" Josh said, surprise flashing across his face. "Okay. But why?"

"I don't know," Ria admitted. "It's just where I need to be."

Josh lost the Demon in his break-neck race through the streets, and Ria was thankful a policeman didn't ticket them for speeding. She felt naked and exposed now that she had lost the protection the goblin Witch M'Rella had bestowed on her, though before the Guardians had showed up, she hadn't remembered it was there.

She felt as though the Demons would find her at any moment, and she was unable to do anything to escape their attention. The day was fading when Josh pulled up outside the little luthier's shop. The sign on the door was welcoming, promising shelter, and Ria couldn't wait to get inside. She jumped out of the car and went for the door, pulling her keys out of her jacket pocket.

"Now what?" Cedar asked, catching up to her.

"One step at a time," Ria said as she led them to the dim front room. "I'm kind of making this up as I go along."

"Very well." Cedar did not look happy, but he had no choice but to follow her.

This was her world, and even if she didn't know what she was doing, she had a better chance of getting them out of this mess than he did. The ghost of Ria's party remained, the faint scent of candle smoke, and the bright table cloth draped over the front desk. Something moved in the corner and gave Ria a heart attack, until she saw it was only balloons stirring in a draft.

The Guardians relaxed in this place. Though they understood little of this world, strings and frets and soundboards they understood better than most. Luca seemed the most at ease as he jumped up and settled himself on the workbench.

"This is nice," he said. "You make these?"

Ria shook her head. "No, Giovanni makes them. I help him at the store."

"You know, you promised to show me your music if I ever came here," Luca reminded her. "You remember?"

Ria did. On the plains of Demona on the way to the Sister Cities, the dark Guardian and she had talked of the Prophecy of *Aethsiths,* and dying, and family, and music. She dug into her pocket and pulled out her iPod. He stared as if it were something dead, and she laughed.

"No, you have to put these things in your ears…" Ria showed him how to wear the earphones and chose a song, one of *those* ones, called "Unloved" by Sword in the Stone. The music startled Luca when it started, but then he relaxed and got into it. His eyes brightened and his color improved. When the song ended, he untangled himself from the wire and handed it back.

"Not bad," he said. "Pretty handy little gadget. Did your Scholars make that?"

Scholars were like Demona's scientists, if she remembered correctly. They didn't get on with Thaumaturgists, but if they worked together, they could make some pretty cool things, like M'Rella's cold box, otherwise known as a refrigerator.

"Yes, I think so." Ria laughed, taking a childlike delight in his foreignness.

The shop offered peace, a quiet solitude and a magyc bubble which protected it from the goings on of the outside world, even when that outside world consisted of Demons. It was easy to forget her problems here, bathed in the stillness and the scent of wood shavings. A light turned on in the back, drawing all their heads.

"Who's that?" Cedar whispered, leaning closer to Ria.

"I think that might be Giovanni," Ria replied. "He likes to work odd hours."

"I don't like it," Cedar said. Ria wasn't sure if he was referring to the guitar maker himself, or that Giovanni was here with them. "We should leave now."

"And where are we going to go?" Ria said. "We have no plan. The Nine are out there, looking for me. I have no idea what to do to give you guys magyc here, and none of us know how to call a Door."

"Have you tried?" Jæyd asked.

"No!" Ria snapped, feeling accused and useless. "I don't even have the first idea of where to begin!"

A sound came, a faint click, and a heavy sliding of metal on metal. Ria froze, recognizing it immediately.

"What was that?" Cedar said.

"Don't move!" Ria ordered.

"Maria? Is that you?" a voice called out of the dark.

"Yes, Giovanni," Ria answered. "I'm sorry if we startled you."

The old luthier came into the light, still holding the shotgun warily. "Who are all these people?"

"Friends of mine," Ria said. "You can put the gun down."

Giovanni did so, then looked closer at the Guardians. His eyes took in their instruments, and a fond glow softened the hard edge of his gaze. "What are they doing here?"

"Hiding," Ria said.

"From what? I hope not the law?"

"No, just from what's out there," Ria answered with a vague wave at the outside world.

"Your mother used to do the same thing," Giovanni

said.

"She loved it here," Ria said, looked around at the workshop, the wooden shelves. "She said it reminded her of home."

Sometimes her mother would bring her along, and they would sit here for hours while her mother told her stories and the old luthier, who had more brown in his grey hair at the time and fewer lines on his face, would strum on guitars, tuning them by ear and setting them back on their stands. Giovanni chuckled, and something in his expression caught Ria's attention.

"What?" she asked.

"I always wondered what she meant by that," he said, and shook his head. "She has been gone for how many years now Maria?"

"Almost fifteen," she answered.

"Then I think it will be alright if I tell you her secret," Giovanni continued. "You mother was not of the same country as I."

Ria stared at him. "I don't understand."

"It must have been difficult for her, pretending for all those years." Giovanni shook his head again, this time a sorrowful gesture. "She would come here and ask so many questions. I was younger than you when I left to come here, and sometimes I did not even know the answers."

"If that's true, then where was she from?" Ria asked with a confused frown.

"She never told me," Giovanni said. "If she had, I would tell you now."

"What does that mean?" Ria asked.

"Perhaps nothing, perhaps everything," the old man shrugged. "Sometimes, people want to leave their past in the past, and it only causes hurt to bring it into the present."

The box her father had given Ria warmed in her jacket, and an idea sprung to mind.

"Do you know of any other place my mother liked to go?" Ria asked.

Giovanni didn't have to think long at all. "She used to visit the old school on North Bay. You know the one?"

Ria nodded. The building had been condemned years ago because of asbestos in the wall, and it stood lonely and abandoned over its kingdom of weeds, caught between demolition and red tape. She turned to Cedar.

"That's where we have to go," she said firmly.

Cedar accepted this without question or comment. Ria was glad because she wouldn't have been able to explain it anyway.

It was a cool Monday evening. People were out, walking dogs, jogging, and several groups of kids on skateboards passed the cars crawling along the road.

"There it is," Josh said.

The school was pretty. Big trees stood over the playground and sports field, the white chalk lines faded, and cracks in the basketball court snatched by hungry weeds. Signs warning of the penalties of trespassing hung on the sagging chain link fence.

The red-brick took on a brighter hue in the orange and pink of the setting sun. Wide stairs led up to double-doors, and a round stained glass window with the forgotten crest of the school looked out like an eye. Auxiliary buildings flanked the main structure, sheltering a courtyard with a fountain in the rear.

Ria knew this because of a dare several schoolmates had imposed on her in the seventh grade. She had been dared to stay overnight in the empty school. She had been so scared until Josh showed up with snacks and a portable radio.

She looked at Josh, wondering if he remembered that time. He caught her eye and smiled, the same memory reflected in his eyes. Ria noticed the Guardians' increased interest in the school, and the hushed wonderment growing in the car.

"It reminds me of the Crescent Temple," Timo was first to give voice to the feeling.

Luca looked doubtful. "It doesn't look much like it, but something…it's like a child's doll version of a real person. The eyes are buttons and the hair yarn and it doesn't have fingers, but it's definitely recognizable as the same thing."

"Yes," Cedar agreed.

He looked at Ria, and she smiled at him briefly, eyebrows raising in question. He shook his head and got out of the car. The Guardians clustered around the fence.

"Should I wait for you?" Josh asked.

Ria hesitated. It was comforting having Josh at her back, but she couldn't justify keeping him here. She shook her head. He reached over and gave her a hug.

"Until next time," he whispered in a throaty voice.

Ria smiled, not trusting herself to speak, and got out of the car. Cedar turned to her when she walked up behind him and glanced over her shoulder at where Josh was standing, but didn't say anything, though she sensed he wanted to.

"How do we get in there?"

"There's a gap in the fence around the back," Ria told them.

They walked along the sidewalk and Ria nodded at the people passing by. All of them gave the Guardians strange looks or double-takes. Timo got most of these with his fur lined breeches and the drums on his back. Cedar, in his smart shoes, grey trousers and a white shirt with small wooden buttons, could have stepped from a bizarre business meeting and forgotten his blazer and tie. Luca looked like he was in an indie punk-folk band or maybe a renegade pirate captain. Jæyd, her lips pressed tightly shut and her hair over her ears, her white clothes still somehow pristine, looked like a model for a conservative vintage hippie magazine.

Across the lawn, Ria saw the rip in the fence. She turned to the Guardians to show them, then froze. Standing across the street was another Demon, ruby red eyes shining. It stood, still as a statue, and Ria froze.

Somehow, no one noticed the creature standing right in their midst. It was not invisible, but something about it just shifted the eyes to the left or to the right. People found reasons to alter their paths so they edged around it.

Ria thought it was something it was doing, some subtle influence it was exerting. Its glowing eyes sought hers out, and in the cold gaze, she saw the passionless patience of the hunter.

"Run," she said grimly and took off.

They pelted down the street, Ria in the lead. She skidded to a halt and pulled the fence back for the Guardians. Luca's coat got caught in the twisted wire, and Jæyd had to rescue him from its clutches before Timo could duck into the schoolyard. Cedar took the flap of braided metal from Ria and gently pushed her through before following her.

Ria expected screams and crashes as the Demon pursued, but the normal evening small-town sounds frightened her more. *They were only after her, and she was the single thought on their dark, alien minds.* The Demon calmly stalked after them and walked straight through the fence, tearing it in two as if it were gauze.

The Guardians ran for the doors, which were locked.

Before Ria could despair, Luca whipped out a metal file and had the doors open. They ran inside, spread out, looking frantically for the next turn. Ria's heart pounded, and like a bleeding stag chased by bloodhounds, she grew more desperate and wary as she went, expecting teeth and claws to jump out at her at every turn.

The air was stuffy, unused to human presence. A yellow plastic sign warned of a wet floor, though the floor hadn't been wet for quite some time. Ria's eyes moved up the stairway, and the black box warmed against her chest.

"This way."

Running through the corridors, Ria prayed for the same guidance that had led her to Giovanni's store. Whatever it was answered and took her to an open room which had probably been used for assemblies and Christmas shows.

Stacks of plastic chairs were shoved against the side wall, but one had been taken down and set in the middle of the room, near the stage. A faint beam of light from the high, square windows lit the chair like a spotlight. *That was where my mother went to be alone when this world got too much for her.*

Ria sat on the chair, and the ghost of her mother became more solid, almost as if Ria could reach out and touch her. To her surprise, tears threatened, for the first time in years.

Through the blur of her vision, Ria saw the stairs that led onto the stage. Leaping up, she ran onto the stage, and saw the curtains closing off the right wing were mussed, while the left curtains were closed tight. She pulled the curtains further open and looked into the gloom, eyes narrowed as she attempted to discern shape and color despite the lack of light. On a chest of forgotten props and an old mixing console with half the faders missing, were things that could never be part of this world.

If this was where my mother went, then these must be my mother's things. Ria swallowed, her hand trembling as she reached out to touch a string of beads sitting on a folded white cloth with the soft brush of one finger. A long time ago, Ria had seen a similar string at the waist of a young woman who called herself Witch. This new view of her mother brought further tears, this time of disbelief, to her eyes, and a tight pressure in her chest. *How could this be possible?* she wondered, as she brushed the wetness away.

"Guys!" Ria cried over her shoulder, her voice cracking. "Guys! Over here!"

The Guardians came together from the four corners of the hall they'd scattered to, Cedar and Timo taking the stair on one side of the stage, Luca taking the other, and Jæyd vaulting onto the center with gymnastic grace. They crowded around her and surveyed what she had found.

Loosely organized in piles were vials of different colored substances, some liquid, some grainy, and some that looked like pure light. Gems of varying sizes and colors, pouches of pungent herbs, spools of thread and string, lumps of gold and silver, and a dozen other sundries, enough to fill a good-sized suitcase, were covered in a film of dust.

Ria picked up what looked like a bone whistle, turning it over in her hand. On the side was a single symbol, an old rune she couldn't read, a circle enclosing a spiral of dots. The Guardians moved their shocked eyes from the cache to her.

"How did this get here?" Cedar whispered.

"I'm not sure," Ria said, though several ideas occurred to her, each more fantastic than the last.

Luca voiced them for her. "If this was where your mother went, and your mother put these here, your mother was a Witch."

"Or she knew one," Ria remarked softly, replacing the whistle in its space.

"Right," Luca nodded agreeably, and rolled his eyes. "Because that takes *less* imagination to made sense."

The sound of a door crashing open swung them around to face the back of the auditorium.

"So, what now?" Luca asked. "You going to whip us up a spell or a potion with that stuff?"

Ria gave him a look. "No. Wait," she said as the Guardians began to move away. "I want to bring this." A forgotten backpack sat on the floor against the mixing board. Ria opened all the zippers and dumped the notebook with doodles over the cover and two empty CD cases out, then scooped all the materials into the bag. It was heavy when she put it over her shoulder. *How do they carry all this stuff?*

"Let's go."

Ria started towards the backstage area. Stairs took her down into a corridor, where door after door with numbers and letters mirrored each other down the sides, between banks of dented lockers, graffiti love notes, obscenities, and the existential truths of school children scratched into the paint.

The door at the other end opened to the quad at the rear. Benches sat along the walkway, probably intended for studying on nice days, but most likely used for other things. The fountain in the middle was nonfunctional, but an inch of green water from the last rain sat in the bottom. High walls enclosed the area.

Three Demons appeared from the other side of the quad and stood there waiting. *For the others*, Ria knew.

"So what do we do now?" Luca asked in a whisper. "Because - and I hate to say this - it looks like we're trapped."

Ria agreed, and her heart sank as she tried to find the nonexistent way out. Two more Demons appeared, coming out from the door in the other building. Another climbed over the wall in the back in way that sent chills running down her arms and legs from the frozen lump in her stomach. A seventh came over the roof, almost insect like. And still they waited, red eyes glowing, standing like stone statues.

They must have some sort of telepathy, Ria thought with growing despair. Then her chin came up and her eyes grew bright. *Wait, if they have their magyc here…*

Ria turned to explain her revelation to the Guardians, but she didn't get a chance. As one, the Demons opened their mouths and howled, raising the hair on the back of her neck as the unearthly screech undulated across the open space between them. In the air, directly in front of her, a Rift opened into this world.

Ria was caught in the gale of icy wind that blasted through from the other side of the Rift. The Guardians disappeared from view as she was stuck in the event horizon of the phenomenon, space warping around her. She held up her hand to protect her face and tried to see past the stinging force battering her. The Rift grew wider, a black tear in the fabric of the world to whatever lay behind it.

Grey mist swirled, pouring out like dry-ice fog at a concert. Through the mist, fuzzy and obscured, was a vast space. Ria thought she saw walls and columns and high windows which allowed swords of sunlight to cut through the grey.

The scene clarified, becoming a grainy old photo. People moved in the monochrome, and sounds reached her ears, muffled and distorted. Ria leaned closer, pulled in by the vortex of the Rift.

With a burst of bright gold light, everything went sharp enough to cut through her; her eyes flew open wide, and she was frozen there. Reminded of her dream in the car, pressed close against a window and made a spectator, Ria watched.

Through the Rift, three people battled a Demon with ice blue eyes. It knocked one of its assailants away, a man, and the other two set on it with a fury, streaks of gold battering it like so many falling stars. The man lay on the floor. A magnificent sword lay out of his reach, wavering between the weapon and the shadow-guitar outlined in golden light.

His hair was jet black and golden eyes were wide as he stared directly at Ria. His clothes were Demonan, but with subtle differences that were hard to pinpoint and could only be described as old-fashioned. Ria *knew* she was looking at the First Guardian.

She reached out, curious whether he was solid or a phantom of light and imagination. "What are you doing here?" she asked, though he was too far away to hear her.

Then she saw the Demon beside him. It was moving, shrinking and growing in the undulating space within the rift. She was about to do something, then realized she couldn't, the invisible window to the world prevented her from coming into contact with the past. Then she forgot what she wanted to do. Her mind was blank of everything that had happened, everything that was happening. All that she had room for inside was the music.

Whatever she had experienced during her first time in Demona was a mere shadow compared to this. That had been the Path, of that she was sure, but only the sliver which touched that time and place. This was so much more.

It enveloped her in a shroud of sound and light and magyc. The music built in layers and tiers, weaving together in an intricate pattern of sound and silence. She made out a bond, or connection with the man on the floor, growing stronger as the music swelled. She shared what he saw and felt; she knew his awe and echoed his exhilaration.

The Path spoke to her, giving her Truth and Wisdom in inexplicable ways. It did not use words, or images, or anything else Ria was familiar with. Yet she understood. She knew the history of the world, saw Nothing for the first time, and then Chaos snuffed it out. She lived the beautiful maelstrom of Chaos as One of Two, vast and virtually unlimited, then sped forward towards the present time, through the stages of existence. It was too fast, and in slow-motion at the same time. And then she surpassed the present and went into the future.

Something of her mother's talent in her saved her from being overwhelmed by the many threads of the Way of Things. The strains of music carried her higher on the crying notes of a violin and the thrum of a guitar. Her eyes flew open, and infinite possibilities were within her grasp. Surrounded by golden light, her fingers caressed the strands, molded them and reformed them again.

And she understood.

She understood that whether Destiny had brought her here, or if Cedar had intervened and brought her to a new Destiny, the questions and their answers no longer mattered. All that mattered was here and now, this moment, this decision and its consequences, the path it would take her down. She closed her eyes, took a deep breath, and fell into the golden light.

Her place, her duty, her function, was hers only if *she* chose. No one could choose for her, dictate her options, or force her to decide. No such thing as Fate or Destiny ruled her life. The strands of Time flowed in infinite directions. Any one of them was open to her; she only had to grasp it.

The Prophecy was not Truth; it was one of a thousand Truths, a million Truths, and it was she, at this moment in time, who would make it Truth or Untruth. Tomorrow it would be another, but right now, in this moment that was all moments, she cradled the worlds in her hands.

In less than an instant, she knew who she was. All the insecurities and shadows disappeared, leaving only gold light and powerful certainty. It was all within her reach, if only she chose to reach out and grasp it.

Bolstered by the magyc of the Path, Ria stood transfixed, aware of herself as a vast point of potential, a point of emanation from which everything flowed - the Path, now and then and forever - and everything around her as a solid and vivid presence. In this state, everything was clear, including her conscience and her purpose.

Taking a deep breath of the Path which filled her lungs and her heart, she chose.

AETHSITHS PART III

When the Demons appeared, Luca Lorisson thought he was going to die. Sooner than the others, if the Demonhärt he carried had anything to say about it. It squeezed his lungs and made his blood too thick. His heart stuttered, and red mist clouded his vision as he fought to breathe. Not for the first time he missed the pouch the Witch S'Aris had made for him. It was lost at some point when he was closing the Rift, though he didn't remember taking it off.

More of the Demons came, and Luca started to go faint. That sick twisting feeling of losing himself pressed on him, and he couldn't tell where he stopped and the blackness began.

Seven, he thought. *Only one more to go before the Nine-that-were-now-Eight were all present.* Fear gripped his mind, and paralyzed his thoughts. A cool breeze banished the fever on his brow, and Luca closed his eyes, relaxing. Part of him was repulsed by the sweet coldness playing over his skin, and he looked to see the huge Rift towering over them.

Feelings, sensations, and emotions twisted inside him. He felt he was being eaten from the inside by the hot and cold ropes writhing, consuming first his body, then his mind, and finally his very being, until there was nothing left but emptiness.

He struggled against this fate, choking back the taste of blood in his throat. Where the golden light fell, it made his agony at once worse and better. Then his eyes fell on the shapes inside the light, and suddenly everything else became insignificant.

One shape was small and light, a woman standing with her arms outstretched. He couldn't see her face, but he imagined she must have an expression of ecstasy. The other figure was far away and blurry, but Luca could make out a man, lying on the ground, gazing up in wonder. The light fell on the man's features, dark hair and gold eyes, his mouth hanging open in awe.

Then a third shape came into view. This one was darker than the other, sucking in the light and nullifying it. It was also coming nearer, and something close to Luca resonated with every step it took through swirling silver and grey, getting more solid the more it gained a hold on this world.

Only Luca could see it. Jæyd stood to his left, face beatific as she beheld the miracle in front of her. Timo had braced himself against the wall, leaning into the golden cyclone. Cedar was on his knees, the wind stirring hair, mouth hung open just like the man inside the - *what was it?* Luca wondered. *It wasn't truly a Door precisely; it was more like a Window - not something you could step though, but something you could look through and see a piece of what lay on the other side.*

Through the Window, a claw appeared, reaching for

Ria. Luca shot forward, propelled by some ancient instinct, and swept her out of the way. The pair of them crashed to the floor in an ungraceful landing, Luca's weight expelling the breath from Ria's lungs when he fell on top of her.

The Window and the glow from the other side faded, the Rift closed with a snap, taking that long ago place with it, and Luca came back to himself, like a boxer recovering from the reeling disorientation after a right hook. A remnant of the light remained in Ria's face, burning in Her eyes. It seared through him, carrying it with one thought: *Now* Aethsiths *has come.*

The Demonhärt warmed, an odd icy warmth which was not unpleasant, just unexpected, and it told Luca his thought was Truth.

A detached exhilaration took hold of Luca. *Finally, finally, after all this time, She had appeared, just as the Prophecy said.* He looked down at Her, their faces as close as lovers. Her expression held no recognition, and for a moment, Luca was afraid Ria was lost in the vastness that was *Aethsiths*.

"Ria?" he asked hesitantly.

She stared at him wordlessly, something that was *more* trying to break out of the shell of flesh which encased it, then She gripped his arm with such strength he gave a muffled squeak of surprise.

"Luca," She said with her teeth clamped together. "You're hurting me."

"Oh, sorry." he scrambled off Her, and helped Her up.

She massaged Her side and winced. "You have the world's sharpest elbows."

"I hone them every day," he replied, and She gave a breathy laugh, then winced again. "I don't mean to put a damper on things, but we have more company."

The eighth, and now final, Demon stood before them.

The Rift was gone, but the world still remembered its existence, like a bruise after a blow. The God of Stone stood impassively, gazing at them with icy blue eyes. It was disconcerting, and Luca wished it would stop, but it got worse when the Demon bowed, deference and respect irreconcilable with the concept of the Nine.

"*Aethsiths,*" it growled. "Your presence is requested."

Ria stood and walked forward until She was in front of the Demon, arm's length from it. It didn't move and the girl stood still, serene, looking up at the beast. A golden glow surrounded Her, pulsing with Her heartbeat and the ache in Luca's head. A similar field enveloped the Demon, dark where the other was light.

The world spun, and his vision made copies of the Demon and the girl, fading and multiplying, hurting his eyes. The same endless vastness he'd thought he'd seen beneath Her skin a moment before was becoming more visible now, and that wasn't helping. The girl said something, and Luca was sure he misheard.

"I have a message for your master."

What in the nine hells is happening right now? Luca looked around, wondering if he were hallucinating.

Ria continued. "He has overstepped his bounds. The Balance of the worlds has been threatened."

"This he knows," Stone replied.

Ria - or *Aethsiths?* - shook Her head. "He doesn't know of what he speaks. I cannot help him."

The Demon regarded Her and bowed again. Then it reached out and grabbed Ria. A crack sounded, then a white light, and the smell of something burning. Luca blinked against a fierce gust of choking wind, and when he could see clearly again, Ria was no longer held by the God of Stone. The creature was angry, and it howled, a mouth full of razor fangs wide and black. Its companions echoed the cry.

"I think we're really in trouble now," Luca said.

Ria was backing away as the Demons continued their unearthly opera. The Guardians came together and stood at Her side. The glow had faded from Her face, and a boulder settled in Luca's stomach when he saw Her expression.

"They have their magyc," Ria told them, and Her expression suggested something abominable. *If we can harness it, we can use it.*

"That doesn't do us any good," Cedar growled, his hand tight on the neck of his guitar, as if he meant to use it as a club.

"Now is not the time to be scrupulous," Ria countered hotly, Her eyes blazing with fire to match Cedar's. "If that magyc gets us out of here, we're going to use it!"

Cedar looked at Her as if She were insane, and Luca's hope wilted a little. *Aethsiths would never say something like that,* he thought, *so we're all going to die.*

"Would you rather end up dead?" Ria demanded when none of the Guardians said anything.

Everything was moving in slow-motion. The Demons had started towards them, but their movements were imperceptible. It was a sort of a blessing, giving Luca time to think. His first thought was not very helpful.

Her mother is a Witch. That makes Her half a Witch.

Why that was important, he couldn't say. A grumble came from all around, and the ground shifted under Luca. The sky grew dark, and purple lightning jumped between the dark patches and the darker patches. *Sorcerer,* the wind whispered.

Cedar and Ria were still arguing about the merits of using Demon magyc to get back to Demona. Luca's mouth was thick, and his lips felt like they had been glued together. He needed to do something, and it came to him slowly, a firefly that blinked in and out of his consciousness. If *Aethsiths* thought She needed music, She would have music.

He did something crazy, something which was never going to work in a million years, but he had to try. Struggling to remember what it felt like to call music forth with the effortlessness of breath, he put his lifeless fiddle under his chin and drew the bow across the strings, the motion forced and awkward. Surprised to hear a clear, pure note ring out, he put his fingers on the strings, and played three more notes, each time the bow moving in smoother, surer draws.

Ria looked dazed as the notes danced to Her, then intense concentration made Her face go hard. A glow grew in Her eyes, and She mouthed words, no sound, just a motion of Her lips, but the world responded with a startled jolt as magyc flowed from Her body, draining into the world, and for a moment, this small patch looked like Demona.

Cedar stood there, and a shining longbow grew from his guitar, responding to his need of defense. The golden-eyed Guardian gaped at it, then at Ria, who was still weaving the magyc light with Her fingers. Timo held the halberd in place of his drums. Luca felt the dirks stir underneath the black wood of his fiddle and he smiled.

"*Aethsiths,*" Jæyd whispered, holding her rapier above her head.

Luca's elation swelled, then abated as inertia bucked him, and he stopped playing, the effort to draw the bow and bend the strings too hard against the decay of this world. Ria fell still as well, but the golden light stayed a moment longer, growing fainter.

"We still need a Witch to open a Door," Jæyd said. "We cannot take on all of them, and we must get to the Crescent Temple to relight the Torch." *Even if we have to leave the Demons here and sacrifice this world to them*, the unspoken words sparkled in her eyes, her vision encompassing more than the needs of here and now, but also their future and the future of all.

"We have half a Witch," Timo said, looking at Ria.

"Actually, we have a whole Witch," Ria replied, with a nervous look at the stormy sky. "Luca's mother was a Witch, and half and half makes one."

A far-off roar sounded.

"What was that?" Ria whispered.

"Sounded like a dragon," Cedar grimaced. "A big one."

The sky cracked open. The Guardians raised their weapons, unsure what to do with them. They pointed them at the Demons, black shapes in the eerie light, but they did not move.

"What are they waiting for?" Timo asked through gritted teeth.

Above, the sky broiled and writhed, casting shifting shadows and odd patterns over the courtyard. A stiff wind, smelling of cold stone and smoke, tugged at their balance, making the overgrown trees and shrubs dance in agitation. The Nine seemed not to notice. They stood silent watch, like prison wardens.

"The Sorcerer," Ria and Luca answered together, their knowledge coming from different places but the same certainty.

Luca felt it in his bones, and that foreign part of him that he knew so intimately now. The Demons had delved into whatever magyc allowed them to traverse worlds and called the Sorcerer, the Placer of Pieces, to this world.

The Other World

The Nine pulled the proportions of the world out of alignment, as if it were fighting their presence here. A tornado descended from above them and the fearsome roar sounded again, raising the hair on Luca's neck.

"If anyone has any ideas, now would be a good time to voice them," Cedar said.

Luca looked at Ria, and She gazed back at him. The silver in Her eyes ringed the pure gold light of Her pupil. Luca was reminded of Timo's eyes when the Man of Tongues had sent him the riddle, though his whole eye had been golden, as if a sun sat inside his head and shone out.

The Demonhärt knew Her somehow, knew the woman as *Aethsiths*. Luca suddenly realized that the Demons had been right since the first day in the forest and the golden dream that had called all the Guardians to Cedar's aid, when the girl had sung and banished one of the Nine back to the Void. It had known Her then, called Her *Aethsiths*.

Something about their lack of familiarity with time was responsible for that, Luca knew. They could see past what the girl was now, to what she would become in Her future.

Luca, tied to a world of the Path, governed by Time and the Cycle, was having a hard time integrating this fact into his way of thinking. The subtle nuances of the Demonhärt helped him to comprehend it, a little. At least it pushed his horizons farther out, so he could catch a glimpse of something beyond what his experience told him was the end of all things, with nothing existing outside of these bounds.

He shook his head to clear it. *Between us there is a full Witch, and in that odd bag She carries, there's everything a Witch would carry,* he knew. *But that Witch was untrained. Could She Call a Door?*

"So, what are we going to do?" Ria asked quietly.

"I don't know why You're asking me," Luca replied. "You're the one who looks like You have an idea You don't want to say."

Ria gripped his hand tightly. Luca's eyes flew open, a warmth filled him, mingling with the power of the Demonhärt. Suddenly the reaches of the Nexus and the fabric of the world, built by ancient, powerful hands didn't seem so daunting.

A voice from a shared memory danced between them, the faraway voice of the elf warm and reassuring. *Listen, just like you did before. Let the Path use you...*Ria looked at him again, and they stepped forward as one. Ria turned to Cedar. "I need you to play."

Cedar looked at the longbow, and with great effort pulled the guitar back to him. It was pale in this world, more real than it had been when the Guardians first arrived, but without a solid foundation of magyc, its identity and strength wavered.

With an expression of grim do-or-die, Cedar settled the instrument against his body and started to strum. In the next instant, Jæyd joined in with her flute, and Timo braced them with a simple drum line, one hard thud for each heartbeat, a tattoo with his fingers for every breath.

Ria closed Her eyes and swayed to the music. Then She started to sing, and an electric tingle jolted through Luca. The words were ancient, the words that gave birth to the watyr and eyrth and ayr of the world.

The storm over them sensed the change, and the clouds and lightning began to thrash more frantically. The sky split open in a gaping green mouth, growing wider to devour them. The Guardians began to move around *Aethsiths,* their footsteps adding to the song.

The golden light spread, bringing everything it touched to a new state. The trees *knew* where they came from, why they existed, and the stone was reunited with the essence of itself.

The Demonhärt pulsed in time to the song. It too was reminded of where and when and why, and it tried to break through the walls of this world into its home. Luca knew how they were going to call a Door.

He thought of his mother, M'Lia of Lii. She had been a Darkrobe, but she had given up the blacks for brown when she left the Coven to wed Thad Lorisson and become Amalia Lorisson. *If she could see me now,* Luca thought with a sardonic smile. *Of course, she would probably lose it if she knew I was going to do this with a Demonhärt, but it's not like I have a choice right now.*

Then he thought of Liæna and how he had been afraid that she would draw away in revulsion if she knew he carried a Demonhärt, something she had sensed but not fully known about. Instead, she had helped him to feel strong enough to share his burden with the others and gain further strength from their support and friendship, with her explanation of the assassins' Theory of Three, and *Solu* - the word that had no accurate translation, but could be said to mean *acceptance* or *peace*.

Ria's voice brought him back, and he took a deep breath, knowing he could not turn back once he started on this path. He touched Her arm to gain Her attention.

"We need a Grounding," he told Ria. "Otherwise, we'll be lost."

You are the Grounding. The words came out of Her mouth, but Luca heard them in his head. His fingers closed around the Demonhärt, the rough hard surface stinging and burning his flesh. He gripped *Aethsiths'* hand and allowed the Demonhärt to work through him.

Suppressing a shudder, he let the magyc flow. It was a strange sensation, like having something slimy slither through his veins and ooze out his pores, but it was better than the first times, when he had saved the Man in White, or closed the Rift in Demona after the Nine came through, or when the Man of Tongues sent them hurdling along the rainbow. *Aethsiths made it easier; She takes the black and makes it light.*

Luca more sensed than saw the tear in the world. The Demonhärt pulled it apart, giving access to the Void or the Nexus. The greyness frightened him - it would be so easy to get lost in there, floating on pale smoke until you drifted out of sight. He clenched *Aethsiths'* hand, and was reassured when She squeezed back. The Rift was cloaked in a facade, and Luca knew he could only see it because of the expanded vision given to him by the Demonhärt.

If he squinted, he saw the form given to the Door by human perspective. It was a huge stone arch, which held a roughly formed wooden door, reinforced with iron bands. Light shone through the uneven edges, and the cracks between the hinges. Symbols made of light raced along the grain of the wood, and in the pattern of the stones, giving it the appearance of sparkling.

Aethsiths was still singing with Her eyes closed, one hand extended, the other gripping Luca's so tight it was cutting off the blood flow. She opened Her eyes, and they widened as She gazed up at the Door towering over them.

The storm tried to crush the song with thunder, and the song battled back, dancing out of reach, taking the thunder and incorporating it into the melody. The wind howled, and a voice called something in words almost as old as *Aethsiths'* song. The Door began to shrink and fade.

"You have to open it!" Luca called to *Aethsiths* over the thunder and the music.

The hand She held out to the Door shook as She pushed against the force that held the Door closed. She could not grab the handle, and the Door remained elusive though it sat right in front of Her.

The Guardians' song faltered when Cedar changed his tune. *Aethsiths* turned Her head slightly, listening. A smile played over Her lips. Jæyd and Timo picked up the shift, matching Cedar, the flute taking the song higher, Timo urging it onward.

The song spoke of calling and memories of a home lost; of refusing to give up hope even when the world is darkest; it told of the differences between a world of magyc, everything limned in gold, and the Voide, where everything is cold; the song pleaded for aid, and gave as a reason not fact but desire; it was the song Cedar had played to Ria that first day when he was trapped in the space between worlds. The Door stopped diminishing, and ever so slightly, began to fight against the Sorcerer's words.

Aethsiths reached forward again, and with a shove of Her hand, opened the Door.

The Door stood wide, into a world of nothing and everything that strained the eyes, like trying to look left and right at the same time. Luca saw a city one moment, a huge boat upon silver waters in the next, and then a thousand thousand points of bright white light which couldn't be stars because there weren't that many stars in the sky.

"We have to form a line," *Aethsiths* told him in Ria's voice. "So we don't get lost or separated."

"You go first," Luca replied. "I'll hold it open."

He saw *Aethsiths*' shining eyes take him in, the doubt dimming Her brightness. He squeezed Her shoulder.

"I'll be okay," he promised. "Now go."

She nodded and took Cedar's hand and gestured for him to take Jæyd's. The elf took Timo's and the big Daleman held onto Luca's one hand. Luca's other hand held the Door open.

It was heavy and tugged at him, wanting to close, the world recognizing it was unsafe to have this gaping wound, and if it remained, the world would die a slow bleeding death as whatever Balance the Walls between worlds protected was undone.

Aethsiths stepped through and was swallowed by the mist. Cedar followed, then Jæyd, then Timo. Luca was straining not to let go of the Daleman's hand and hold the Door open. He wedged it open with his shoulder and watched Timo duck inside.

Luca stepped forward, ready to face the Nexus, when a hand fell on his shoulder. He turned his head and stared into pale green eyes. Luca had the idea that he had seen those eyes before, but he didn't know where. The man said something in the olde language, but Luca couldn't understand it.

He thinks I'm Aethsiths, *because I'm holding the damned Door,* Luca realized. If it were any other time, in any other circumstance, Luca would have cracked a joke and laughed.

Behind the man, a great bulk moved. Luca's eyes moved to it, and his face froze in a mask of something between terror and wonder. A dragon, the size of a small mountain, reared its head up and bellowed. Its eyes shone red like a Demon's, sending uneasy chills through Luca.

The man studied him, understanding dawning in the strange eyes.

"You are not the one they call *Aethsiths*," he said, in a smooth, pleasant voice with an ancient inflection on the words.

"No," Luca said. "Who are you?"

"I am called the Sorcerer."

A tug from Timo's invisible arm pulled the dark Guardian closer to the Door. The Sorcerer's grip on Luca tightened, and pain began to numb that arm. Luca broke out in a cold sweat. Then Timo's hand was wrenched from his, and the Sorcerer pulled Luca away from the Door. It inched closed, and the aching embrace of despair overcame Luca.

Two golden eyes preceded the appearance of Ria's face appearing out of the gloom, and She shoved the Door open again with little effort. She still clenched Cedar's hand in Hers. From a great distance, She called something to Luca, but the words were lost in the intervening space. Luca felt as though he were in a bubble, separate from the world.

Aethsiths came forward, let go of the Door, and punched through Luca's bubble, Her hand closing on his wrist. The despair was banished, and a hot boil in his blood borne of rekindled hope and desperation aided Luca in pulling free from the Sorcerer's hold.

Spitting, angry howls followed him, the slamming of the Door a thunderous and reverberating clang which made his head feel like it was inside a bell. Somehow, *Aethsiths* maneuvered along the murky passages of the Nexus as Luca was lost in a fog. He kept crashing into things, things with cruel edges that bruised to the bone. He couldn't see anything, and only the pressure of Ria's hand kept him from seizing up from the terror that he was floating away.

Then it began to change. Behind his lids - he hadn't realized he had closed his eyes - the colors solidified, and light made the grey turn to white smoke. Luca shot out and hit solid ground.

This world did not greet Luca with a soft welcome; it slammed a stony salutation at him. It was a world without magyc, that Luca could tell in an instant, but it was a different kind of magyclessness than the other world, the world of *Aethsiths*.

That world was a channel in cracked, hard earth where water once flowed, but that was so long ago that over the millennia, the wind had blown away not only the dry riverbed, but the three layers of dirt and stone under the bed, leaving no trace or memory of the river.

This place was just as devoid of magyc, but instead of a slow draining, it was as if it were flash frozen in shock, the magyc stripped away so suddenly it scarred the memory into the world itself while the world was left reeling and confused. It had not recovered and wandered around like a vagrant, searching for something that it didn't know; it only knew it had to look.

Luca didn't like either one. A second blow hit him, this time from inside him. The Demonhärt thudded against him, hitting tender flesh with cruel blows of dark power. Perhaps the Sorcerer was using it to hurt him, perhaps it had awakened in the journey through the Void and was now inflicting pain to get what it wanted, or perhaps Luca's will had finally broken and he was no longer strong enough to keep the terrible, black waves of night at bay.

He writhed and squirmed, wanting nothing more than to be rid of this thing, but he held on, feeling that only his connection to it was keeping it from hurting the others. *And now I'm going to die,* the dark Guardian thought and watched the thought float away.

The others were standing close to him. He could feel them as intense, hot, pillars of fire that warmed the coldness inside him and burned everything else. They stood around, their voices washing over him.

"Where are we?" Timo asked.

"I don't know," Cedar said. "It feels wrong, but different than the Other World."

"This is the Wasteland," Jæyd's cool voice uttered, strains of despair growing with every word.

The absence of magyc wore on Luca, no walls or barriers left to hold back the power of the thudding black Demonhärt. As a last resort, he conjured Liæna's face to hold on to reality a moment longer, but even that could not withstand the insistent battering from the dark nothing.

Path keep me, Luca pleaded to anything that could hear him, and then the nothing won, taking him into a whiteness that was more black than anything and filled with the presence of a man with starlight hair and pale green eyes.

EPILOGUE

High up in a tired blue sky, an eagle soared with serene majesty, sharp eyes taking in every detail of the land below. The land was as drained as the sky above it, the greens greyer than something more vibrant which signaled life. Small creatures scurried about, but the eagle was not inclined to hunt just yet.

Soon, his flight took him over a small river. The currents of air were cooler here, pushing the hot air up, creating a delightful thermal for him to ride. The eagle did so, swooping in lazy spirals, higher and higher, until the river was an almost invisible line across the plains.

The eagle dipped one wing slightly as a breath of air tipped him to the left. A shadow passed over him, but he was not concerned. He was king of these skies. Nothing hunted him. The shadow moved off, and the eagle wheeled around, angling down, his mind now turning to his next meal.

Distorted by the hills and cracks of the land, the shadow continued to more or less follow along the river. It was long and lean and deceptively small. The shadow belonged to an airborne creature large enough to carry a full-grown cow in her talons and a wingspan equal to six horses nose to tail. Shades of blue in the tough, metallic hide blended to create a color which defied comparison. The color faded around the underside, effectively camouflaging her against the sky. Her kind called themselves Drakaesthai. The rest of the world called them dragons. Her name was Fainethiar.

The air was thin this high up, but the dragon used more than just her wings and aerodynamic form to fly. She felt the breath of life in the air, the heartbeat of the sky, the magyc of elemental ayr. The magyc flowed around her and through her, guiding her with wordless music, the melodies of flutes and pipes and the rush of the wind in trees.

Few Drakaesthai came this far south. They made their home beyond the Gorge, on the other side of the Barrier Bridge, farther than any other creature with legs could walk and any other creature with wings could fly. Fainethiar had been trapped here for some time, not by chains or other physical barriers, but a tugging in her heart which would not allow her to leave.

Right now, she was not thinking of home but just enjoying the sun and the drift of wind on her body, eyes sweeping the ground in great, lazy arcs. Today the whim to fly had taken her, and she just kept going, looking for nothing and something at the same time.

Premonition and hope kept her onward, though as time dragged on and the pale sun began to descend in its erratic pattern towards the horizon, in the general direction of the Silver Sea today, her spirit flagged.

After one last glance in a full arc, her serpentine neck

curving under her for a brief look behind her, Fainethiar made to wheel about and return to the small mountain niche which was her shelter in this land.

The dragon was unprepared for the jet of ice-cold air that appeared in front of her. It was like running into a brick wall. The stream of air buffeted her from side to side, sending her into an ungraceful plummet. All of her bones protested, and her wings burned and strained as she attempted to right herself.

When accompanied by head-over-tail tumbling, free-fall was a most unpleasant sensation. Her last meal, a scrawny buck of the variety the scattered people of the Wasteland called two-tailed deer, threatened to come spewing out.

The dragon righted herself at last, too close to the ground. Her eyes widened as she saw the flat expanse of dirt and stone coming at her. Her shoulders felt like they were being ripped out of her spine when her wings flared on reflex.

Her fore claws plowed into the earth, compressing her joints and bones, but slowing her little. Her head jerked forward into the ground. She tumbled over and slammed through something which felt like trees. Crashing and crackling accompanied her bouncing roll until at last she landed and lay still.

Her side shuddering with shallow hyperventilation as her mind whirled, the dragon pieced together broken fragments of awareness of what had just happened. No other explanation made sense. *It* had *been magyc,* she realized in shock. *But magyc does not exist in this place any longer.*

Groaning, Fainethiar picked herself out of the heap she had landed in with ginger movements. Branches and leaves that her scales had grabbed fell away as she rolled and lifted her body into a sitting position. Her head pounded with whiplash. Everything hurt, but didn't appear to be broken. She took several deep, slow breaths, dreading the sharp spike of pain which would accompany a broken rib. A little tenderness made her wince, but no great pain.

She stretched, arching her back and flicking her tail. Around her, a line of destruction had been carved with ungraceful slashes through the group of trees too small to be called a forest. Stumps with tops of jagged splinters lined the path, and downed trees like fallen soldiers littered the ground.

She made her way to the openness beyond the trees. It did not look like anything was amiss, but Fainethiar's dragon-eyes saw more than just the physical forms of the sky and air; they saw turbulent cyclones of colored light ripping into each other. The air bowed inward, as if supporting a great weight, then it broke and rushed outwards. The dragon pressed the sensitive ribbed fins which lined each side of her head back and ducked close to the earth when the magycal storm blew past her.

It was like wind and not at the same time. She braced against it, straining to keep her feet. The trees around her bowed and swayed, uncoordinated dancers running into each other in their confusion. After the first wave passed, a moment of stillness descended, then a second and a third wave came, each stronger than the last. Fainethiar shielded her eyes with one paw and leaned forward, fighting the stinging air.

In the middle of the plains a Door appeared. The land remembered such things as a dying man remembers the first of his days, without much belief or hope, or even awareness that they were real. But the Door grew with each passing moment, becoming more and more solid, until it lit on the ground. The shadow it cast was stronger than the ground it fell upon.

A great cacophony came from behind the Door. Some of the noise was a music whose beauty and power was enough to bring color to this dead world. For a few short moments, the leaves were green, and the trees stood in browns and golds. The sun was gold in the achingly blue field it traversed each day.

The Door opened, and the sound swelled and spilled out into the Wasteland with a gold light. People followed the noise. A woman came first, black hair flying in the gusting wind that pushed the brittle grass flat, her hand held out as if she had thrown open the Door. Behind her were four others - three men and a woman.

The second woman was an elf, and she landed the most gracefully. Her feet touched down and she rolled, coming up in a wary crouch. The two largest of the men landed somewhat less gracefully. The third fell spinning out of the Door as if he had been thrown and fell face first onto the ground. He shuddered three times but did not move to get up. When they noticed him, the others ran to him, their bodies hiding him from view for a long time.

Then a flash and a tingle Fainethiar felt in her bones washed over her, the trumpet of something Dark and something Light. The last vestiges of magyc faded in a rainbow shimmer. The small group surveyed their surroundings as the Door grew faint and disappeared, and the land returned to its grey half-life, no longer interested in the newcomers.

Fainethiar watched from the cover of the trees, her large golden-green eyes wide in shock. The newcomers looked around and debated amongst themselves. One walked to a rise to see what that vantage offered - *the elf*, the dragon noted, *and so far from her people* - then rejoined the others. The dragon shrank back into the thicker part of the trees to avoid discovery. The people stood around for a while, then began to move towards the mountains.

Fainethiar waited until they were small black dots before she emerged into the open. Her blood was hot, her smile fierce. Magyc ripples and currents coursed along her scales. The dragon had never felt quite as alive as she did now.

She leaped into the sky, climbing higher and higher into the air, until her breath froze in front of her and icicles hung from her wings. She roared, a fierce cry of delight, and then dove, sweeping down to follow the small band trekking across the Wasteland of Olde VarHayne.

Now I know the reason I have waited for so long.

*****

PRONUNCIATIONS

Aethsiths [Ay'th-siths]

Akorgia [Ak-or-ja']

Balmar [Bal-mahr']

Berria In'Orain [Be'-ree-ah Een-or-rain]

Camore [Ca-mor']

Carallión [Car-ra'-lyee-on']

Catmar [Cat-mahr']

Cedar Jal [See'-der Jahl']

The Other World

Cedar Rün [See'-der Rune']

D'Ohera [Doh'-hare-ah]

Demona [Dem-mah'-na]

Eohl'Dia-Stin [Yee-ole'-Dee'-ah'-stinn]

Ghor [Gore]

Gulmira [Gul-meer'-ah]

Hahlvetia [Hahl'-vee-sha]

Isos [Ee'-sos]

J'Erd [Jeh-er'd]

Jæyd [Jay'-edd]

Lan Holdun [Lan' Hole-dun']

Lii [L-yee] (If you speak Italian, it is pronounced the same as the word "gli")

Llaem Bli [Lay'-em Bly]

Lleana Nati of Spyne [L-yee-ai'-na Na-tee' of Spine]

Luca Lorisson [Loo'-ca Lore-is'-son]

Merailwyr [Meh-rai'l-were]

Morha [More-ah']

Nyica [N-yee'-ka]

Ria [Ree'-ah]

S'Aris O'Pac of Lii [S'Ar-is' Oh'-pack of L-yee]

Samnara [Sam-nah'-ra]

Sinora [Sinn-or'-ah]

Timo [Tee-moh']

Torin [Tore-in']

Trem Descal [Trem Desh-al']

Tyomewaerr [Tie-ohm'-way-er']

V'Ronica [V'ron-eeca]

X'Kpögh [As this is a goblin word, there's not really a good way to describe the way this word is said; approximately pronounced Kss-pogh, with emphasis on the hissing 's' and the guttural growl of the 'g']

If you enjoyed this book, please take a few moments to leave a review. It really does make a difference.

Nicole would love to hear from you! Please feel free to contact her online:

http://www.NicoleDragonBeck.com
https://www.facebook.com/nicolebeckauthor
https://twitter.com/dragonbeck
https://www.instagram.com/authordragonbeck/

Books in the Guardians of the Path series:

Book I: First Magyc

Book II: Ria's Mark

Book III: Omens

Book IV: The Other World

Coming in Summer of 2018: Book V: Death's Realm

ABOUT THE AUTHOR

Nicole DragonBeck was born in California one snowy summer long ago, the illegitimate offspring of an elf and a troll. At a young age her powers exploded and she was banished to the wilderness of South Africa because her spells kept going inexplicably awry. There she was raised by a tribe of pygmy Dragons and had tremendous adventures, including defeating a terrible Fire-Demon that had been tormenting a sect of Dwarf priests. In gratitude, they taught her the arcane magic of writing, and the rest is horribly misinterpreted history. She reads as much as she writes, is obsessed with dragons and Italians, enjoys cooking, listening to music, and can often be heard fiddling on a keyboard or guitar. She currently lives in Clearwater, Florida, is a member of The Ink Slingers' Guild, and is working on several novels, all of which have at least one mention of a dragon. She lists friends, music, and life among her greatest influences.

Made in the USA
Columbia, SC
17 April 2018